THE FATE OF ASTARAN SERIES: BOOK 1

CHASM OF DREAMS

Dakoda Mazzii

Copyright © 2025, 2026 by Dakoda Mazzii

All rights reserved. No part of this book may be reproduced, stored, or transmitted in any form or by any means, electronic, mechanical, photocopying, recording, scanning, or otherwise, without written permission from the publisher. It is illegal to copy this book, post it to a website, or distribute it by any other means without permission.

The characters and events portrayed in this book are fictitious or are used fictitiously. Any similarity to real persons, living or dead, is purely coincidental and not intended by the author.

This is a work of fiction that includes sexually explicit language and situations. All characters portrayed in sexual situations are 18 and older.

Dakoda Mazzii asserts the moral right to be identified as the author of this work.

Without in any way limiting the author's exclusive rights under copyright, any use of this publication to "train" generative artificial intelligence (AI) technologies to generate text is expressly prohibited. The author reserves all rights to license use of this work for generative AI training and development of machine learning language models.

This book was created without any use of generative AI including, but not limited to, artwork and cover design.

Editor: Lunar Rose Editing Services

Editor: Bernard's Editorial Services

Cover Design: Disturbed Valkyrie Designs

Interior Formatting: Disturbed Valkyrie Designs

ISBN: 979-8-9943136-0-2

ISBN: 979-8-9943136-1-9

ISBN: 979-8-9943136-3-3

Library of Congress Control Number: 2025927904

SEA OF STARLIGHT

THE FRELSE FJORD

OVERLEVENDE

THE GUDSTARER POOLS

THE ALDRIMER WALL

THE RUINS OF SVA...

ASTARAN

SCHOLAR'S NOTE: SOUTHERN REGIONS REDACTED BY DECREE OF THE SOVEREIGN

KETH RANGE
THE KALBOROS MINE

OPETH CITY
THE OFFERING FIELD

WOOD

THE SOLUMINE RIVER

PORT CITY OF MAKAAR
(ABANDONED)

LIFFS OF HOD

PROLOGUE

Centuries ago, the human kingdoms of Astaran joined together to defend themselves against the wrath of Hel's armies and their leader: the Archangel, *Chemosh*.

After realizing that she had betrayed them to destroy one of their most beloved worlds, the Gods of Lyrath severed her black wings, stripped away her power, and cast her down to Astaran as an exile.

With the help of her ruthless acolytes, the *Anakaii*, she regained her strength and systematically butchered all those who had once stood against her.

When her enemies had been defeated or driven into hiding, she proclaimed herself ruler of Astaran.

For over a thousand years, generations of humans have survived her cruel and oppressive reign. To her followers and underlings, she is known as **The Sovereign**...

CONTENT WARNING

Chasm of Dreams takes place in a primitive world where only brute strength, cunning, and cruelty have enabled its people to survive. Please be aware that there are graphic depictions of violence, death, death of a family member, imprisonment, slavery, child abuse, drugging, kidnapping, consensual sex directly on the page, unplanned pregnancy, suicidal ideation, and threats of sexual assault.

There is also **love, courage, kindness,** and **compassion**; all the makings for one *Hel* of a revolution...

"Why do the wicked keep on living, grow old, become mighty in power? Their progeny is secure in their sight; their offspring are before their eyes. Their homes are safe, without fear, and the rod of God is not upon them."

— *(BOOK OF JOB: 21:7-9).*

Dear Reader,
May the Gods bless you with the power to change your circumstances, the courage to challenge what you fear, and orgasms that can transcend space and time.

<u>*Pronunciations:*</u>
Astaran – (Aster-ahn)
Aida – (Ay-duh)
Tyran - (Tear-un)
Chemosh – (Kem-osh)
Anakaii - (Ana-k-eye)
Lyrath – (Lee-rath)
Overlevende - (Over-lev-end)
Vilje – (Vil-yeh)

CHAPTER 1
AIDA

I suspected most people experienced their dreams in some intangible way.

They could not consciously move through the infinite, suspended oblivion of their dreams like I could.

For me, the dreamscape was a physical space where I could travel freely. Night after night, since I was a twelve-year-old savage living among the other wild orphans in the forest, I jumped from my dreamscape to those of others, like a rock skipping over a pond. In the eight years since my ability had developed, I still had no clue how or why it happened. The dreams of the people I knew, however briefly, were laid bare for me.

Their nightmares, ambitions, and deepest desires—I had access and control over them all.

If I wished, I could bend them to my will with only a simple command into their dormant consciousness. It was a terrifying talent, and one I honestly had no desire to use. Only once had I wielded my power over an unsuspecting soul. The memory of the consequences that followed still threatened to crush me with shame. Since I had no wish to manipulate anyone and seemed to have no choice about where my consciousness wandered off to at night, I did my best to be a benign presence in their dreams. A silent observer.

Tonight, however, my dream had been borne on the wings of a happy memory. One of mine.

A crackling fire in the hearth before me, nestled in the lap of my mother, her dark, bronze hair flowing over her shoulders and tickling my neck. Her scent of fresh herbs and baked bread made my chest ache with longing. She was singing a song, the words barely a whisper as the dream distorted and vanished.

I noticed him there, too.

That calm and unyielding presence, which lingered in the back of my mind like a warm haze, had been a mystery to me since I was small.

Since the first time, my mind had turned inward to protect itself from crippling loss and fear.

A child with no one and nowhere to go.

Even though my dream-walking power had yet to fully develop, I could sense the tethers of other minds as a young girl. But somehow only one, like a buttery ray of afternoon sun, had always been connected to mine. Even without a face or voice, the presence had brought me peace throughout a life of loneliness and pain—a light in the dark.

When his vibration had intensified within my dreamscape nearly four years ago, it initially unnerved me. Gentle pulses of awareness evolved into nearly tangible visions of a golden mist with piercing gray eyes that would search wildly before hitting their mark on mine, becoming stoic, and seemingly... content. While I knew next to nothing about his physical appearance, I somehow knew that this presence was the soul of a male. One who did not wish to harm or pry but was unable to keep his mind disconnected from my own. Not that I minded. Over time, I came to appreciate his company.

And as the years passed, I stopped trying to figure out what all this meant or why he was there. In truth, I was beyond pontificating why my life had led me to where I was, to who I was. The agony and burn of wondering *"why me?"* and *"why them?"* had left me long ago. Life now was only a game of survival. One I was losing at a rapid pace.

Since all temples to the Gods had been turned to ash generations ago, it was a waste of time to try to understand my gift anyway, not to mention dangerous to mention it to anyone at all. As if sensing my internal disquiet, those gray eyes narrowed, asking questions I did not know how to answer. Maybe he was just as lost as I was...

A violent coughing fit near my head abruptly pulled me back to the waking world. Bleary-eyed and disoriented, my head throbbed with that all too familiar question, *"Where the fuck am I?"*

Crunchy, stale hay was plastered to my face and threadbare clothes. The stench of excrement hung in the air like a damp cloth wrapped around my head—ah, that's right, I was still in the tiny, crumbling cell of the village stockade. I grimaced at the thought; it truly was a sorry excuse for a prison. A short distance away, an elderly and very filthy man sat against the far wall. His raucous, wheezing cough suggested his poor lungs may indeed splatter onto the stone merely inches from my face at any moment. Finding this thought unpleasant, I began to rise from the stone floor, wrist shackles dragging, and braced my back against the wall. The man in this cell with me was likely here for the same reason I was... hunger. It was common in these villages to be arrested and executed for something as desperate as stealing an apple or a loaf of bread. If you were young and relatively healthy you could get lucky and work off your debt for an unfair number of months in some Gods forsaken mine. But if you were old and infirm, your chances of living to see the outside of the stockade were not good.

Even though I knew the answer, I asked him anyway. "Are you all right?" He only pinned me with a stony expression as if to say, *'What does it look like?'* but responded with a blunt "mind your own business, girl." Swallowing my bite of pity, I turned away to gaze at the sun just beginning to rise, its faint glow visible through the small rectangle window at the top of the cell. We both knew the truth; he would never leave this stockade alive. On the other hand, I was biding my time for the right moment to escape. I had escaped many situations like this before, and this time would be no different. Pretending to be a frail, helpless female had its uses.

A loud, jarring screech sounded from the cell door as the lock was pulled away. Nearly filling the doorway with his girth, stood a hulking Astaran Guard, who also appeared to be freshly dragged from his dreamscape. "Get up, girl," he grumbled. Wincing at the thought of being exposed to the twisted dreams of this vile beast, I took one last look at the elderly man who shared my cell. He did not so much as glance in my direction as I rose to my feet, which I noted upon a cursory glance, were in horrendous condition. I could barely make out my toes through the grime coating them. No thanks to the Guard who confiscated my recently stolen boots upon arriving here. At that moment, the only thing I was more desperate for, aside from a scrap of food, was a cleansing dip in the frigid embrace of the Solumine river.

The haggard-looking Guard shut the door and pushed me into the hallway, which led to the center courtyard of the stockade. I knew my chances of escape were better than the last time I had been in this position, thanks to the discovery of the nearly rusted-through manacles around my wrists. A quick inspection from the night before revealed they were just a jerking-twisting snap away from coming undone entirely. "Wait here, and don't say a fucking word," the Guard barked as he stalked off to a tent across the courtyard. Breakfast was being served; the smells of oat gruel and hot broth wafted across the courtyard from steaming pots. Other Guards, still rubbing sleep from their eyes, were beginning to jockey into position for a hot meal. My mouth watered and stomach clenched as my head swam with crippling hunger. It took all my strength not to run straight for the table and devour anything I could get my hands on, even if it meant a swift execution would find me soon after. I shook off the heavy haze of yearning and began to take stock of my surroundings, snapping back into escape mode within a heartbeat. The courtyard was a typical square with one side occupied by the breakfast station and Guards settling in to eat. I had been positioned against a stone wall on the other side, the door to the cell I just came from to my right, and to my left...was the swinging door to the stables. A foggy thought struck me then, making my scalp tingle with warning. *Why had I been pulled from the cell so early?*

I knew that trials for petty thievery rarely took place at first light. My spine stiffened as realization took hold. The Guard who took me from my cell had different plans for me. Plans I had no intention of discovering. The Guards were notorious for unwarranted beatings and other forms of assault...and for someone like me—a vagrant and a wanderer—there would be no one to plead my case or protect me from abuse. Of course, the real horror, and distinct possibility, was to be chosen as a *maiden*. A gut-wrenching normality in this world, all thanks to our depraved monster of a bitch queen. Known throughout Astaran as *The Sovereign*. Any of these Guards could fetch a decent pay bump in liquor or illicit drugs with knowledge of my virginity. To The Sovereign, young virgin females were only good for one thing: sacrifice to our ancient Gods—the same ones who deserted us to suffer beneath her heel.

The same ones who, at the time, had been erased from our stories and temples.

The same ones, rumor had it, who had cast her out of Lyrath. The Gods realm.

The thought twisted my empty stomach into a sickly knot as the pace of my breath began to stagger. I took one more glance at the sleepy soldiers and noted, with no little satisfaction, that none of them had yet to become aware of my presence, their attention focused on their meal. For now.

Without considering my fate if I were caught, I silently slipped into the stables. The sun had barely risen enough to fill the outside courtyard with light, making the stables almost completely dark. The horses still slumbered peacefully with rumps facing the door to their stalls. Not daring to breathe, I crept past each stall to the window on the far side of the room. Before climbing onto the haystack to access the window, however, I needed to first remove the manacles. Stumbling blind, my hands reached for anything hard I could use as leverage, before slamming a toe into the iron anvil near the wall. Biting back my curse of rage, I lowered my wrists to the protruding shard of iron that occupied one side of the anvil and pulled the chain in between my wrists taut against it. Bracing my foot on the iron, I yanked back with all my strength. After several teeth-clenching heartbeats, the chain snapped. Before I could marvel at my sheer luck, I leapt onto the haystack and thrust my palm into one side of the transom, which lifted just enough to squeeze my atrociously thin body through. Upon landing abruptly in the dirt on the other side, I noted that early dawn granted me the anonymity of only a few early risers who went about their business without looking in my direction. The forest to my immediate right loomed over the village, its strength and safety like a siren song in my blood. This forest, this wilderness, it was my home: the Furian Wood. A vast expanse of wild that stretched from both horizons of Astaran, only stopping at the feet of the sky-piercing behemoth of the Vazaketh mountain range to the Northwest. Rumor was, the Furian Wood continued onto the other side of the range and was so deep and uncharted, no living person had ever seen where it ended. Its mysteries and vastness are never to be fully understood. In the moment it took to draw breath into my lungs, preparing for my flight into the woods, I spotted a barrel of mostly decent apples, for the horses, no doubt. Next to the barrel, lay several sacks of grain. Swiftly, I began to empty the grain sacks onto the ground and stuff them with as many apples as I could carry. Saliva pooled in my mouth as the cloying, sweet scent of the apple drifted up into my face. For just a moment, I hesitated to glance over my shoulder at the small rectangular window above the cell I had just been brought from. A tender ache gripped my heart at the thought of the old man still inside.

It only took a second to decide.

Quickly and carefully, I hoisted myself onto the shifty crate tucked against the wall, rose onto my tiptoes, and dropped the freshest apple I could find through the small window. Another swift inhale later, I swung the apple sack over my shoulder and sprinted in the direction of the forest, my heart thundering with triumph.

Chapter 2
Aida

My breath sawed in and out of my lungs in ragged pants. I was much too weak for this type of exertion. In the months since winter had tightened its grip on Astaran, food has been scarce enough to drive me from the cloaking protection of the Furian Wood and into the many villages surrounding our capital city, Opeth. It was risky and I had never felt more vulnerable, but starvation didn't seem like a good way to go either. At first, I attempted to barter goods I had made in the forest: a comb made from elk bone, a necklace of raven's feathers, squirrel hide mittens…but it only lasted so long. I began to steal only when, even in my dreams, I was chased by the relentless squeeze of hunger.

Of course, I had another option.

I knew I could force someone to give me food.

All it would take was a handshake and a quick conversation, and later that night, I could creep into their dreamscape and command them to provide me with...whatever I wanted, really. It was heady and tempting to the point of pain, but I resisted. I never wanted to will or compel someone into doing anything ever again. If I starved from stubbornness... I suppose it was what I deserved. As I continued to scramble and leap through the woods, my mind began to drift toward Luke. The thought made my throat tighten as my vision blurred. He was the only person who had shown me any kindness and warmth in the many years since my parents had vanished... and I had failed him. Maybe I did deserve to starve, or be beaten, or get strung up like prey. Maybe running from my fate was futile. I shook my head, rubbing my eyes clear while dodging a fallen tree. I could hear Luke's warm, timbre voice bouncing around my skull as if he ran beside me, *"Now isn't the time for doubt, Aida. It will only get you killed."*

And he was right, of course.

Momentary grief at the thought of him would only hinder my escape. I needed to focus and put as much distance between me and what I knew was heading in my direction—hounds on the hunt for an escaped prisoner. Slamming up an iron wall around my heart, I shut out any thoughts of Luke and redirected my focus to the muscles in my legs, now whining in atrophied agony. Doing my best to ignore my feet, burning with fresh cuts and blisters, I ran like my life depended on it.

I had made it about a mile before I heard the distant baying of the hounds hot on my trail. I knew that I would have to change directions and confuse my scent. Before I even had the chance to think the decision through, I was pulling down the only pants I owned and tossing them into the steep ravine that hugged the Solumine river to my left. The hounds would surely follow the descending track down the ravine, giving my pursuers a difficult scramble back to the trail. This would grant me precious minutes to flee upstream, walking through the shallower parts of the river and, Gods willing, hiding my scent. As soon as I had thrown the pants, I was hurtling down to the riverbank before landing in the water with a splash. The ice-cold water was a welcome relief to my abused feet, but only for so long. My too-thin legs were pebbled in gooseflesh as I waded in the knee-deep river, trying my best to avoid smashing my toes on the river stones. I moved with a steadiness only found from digging deep and pushing aside my fear. One of the many things that Luke had instilled in me since the day he found me as a youth, crippled by a poacher's snare, soon to be carrion for the scavengers circling above. *"Never stop moving, Aida. Keep moving and stay alive,"* he had said to me.

But now... he was gone. *They...* were all gone.

And there were many days that I wondered what the point was in staying alive at all. But for their memory, if I could, I would keep moving—if only so they would not be disappointed as they watched me from their perch in Lyrath, the realm of the Gods. Only the most deserving souls and all-powerful Gods were given the chance to rest there. Luke, my mother, my father—that's where they rested now. There was no alternative I could ever consider.

The river began to widen, a swifter current joining it as I waded upstream. The sound of baying was still distant, but closer than it was before. I spotted a rocky outcrop a short distance ahead and planned to heave myself onto the ledge before sprinting up the ravine to the other side. Approaching the outcrop, I freed my hands of the apples by tossing the bag onto the ledge above me and began to climb. Tree roots and exposed stones provided enough grip to brace my feet and throw my leg over the ledge. Without taking a second to catch my breath, I grabbed the bag of apples and began to scramble to the top of the ravine, using any trees in my path to propel me upward. Once I had crested the hill, breath coming in and out in searing gasps, I was struck stupid by the sight of what lay before me...

The vast abyss of forest below went on for countless miles until it abruptly ended with a gigantic wall of mountains on the distant horizon—the Vazaketh. The towering, snowcapped peaks were the insurmountable barrier to whatever mysteries existed on the other side. The range wrapped around the vanishing point of the continent like a gigantic bowl, its end stretching far beyond my vision to the West and North. Uneasiness made my knees tremble as I realized that in order to evade my pursuers I would have to tread into parts of the forest I had only heard nomads whisper about around campfires. I found myself hoping that those dangers would prefer the company of the Astaran Guards chasing me, instead of wasting time with the skin and bones that I was. But at this juncture, there was truly no other choice. As I began my descent down the steep slope, clinging to branches and rocks jutting through the soil, my head began to swim. I knew my body was being pushed to its limits. The desperate flight from the prison had adrenaline and cortisol pumping through me enough to keep me alert, but the brief rest I had just taken was costing me. As I reached out for the next branch to hold my weight, I could feel my hand grab nothing but air as the tree limb wobbled into two. Vision blurring and panic seizing my chest, I floundered and lost footing—

In less than a second, I became a tangle of limbs, dirt, and pain as my body plummeted down the side of the hill like a rag doll.

Hips, arms, knees, and head rolling and breaking. My hands gouged the earth to slow my fall but found no purchase.

The sudden stop had crimson fireworks blasting around my vision as a burning heat bloomed across the back of my skull.

Luke spoke to me from a distant place... *"Keep moving, Aida. Keep moving."*

Darkness rushed in like a soft rain.

Chapter 3
Tyran

This dream felt different.

The same bright, crystal blue eyes stared back at me. The same eyes I had seen in my dreams since I was a boy. Through my early years as a slave, when the beatings and starvation would chase away any chance for peace, the mist-veiled shadow had brought me comfort when my darkest desires only sought blood. A flash of clenched hands crushing around a windpipe, dark eyes rolling back under my weight. An old man clutching at his throat for breath, face slack with horror as he locked me in his gaze, knowing I was the one who had sealed his fate. Anyone who dared lift a hand to me, or to an innocent, would eventually die in mysterious ways...

Born into a world of brutality with no kin to claim me, violence had become an instinctive and necessary skill for survival.

But I had never sensed any judgment for the visions and memories that this shadow had seen inside my head. She only observed, only witnessed. Those pale eyes—ever calculating and withdrawn. Countless times, I had wondered if she was an angel. Or one of the Gods sent to witness my crimes in this life, no doubt to document all my misdeeds and lay them before my feet on the day I entered Lyrath. If I made it that far.

Maybe she was my mother, watching over me from the afterlife.

But no. Even as a boy, I understood that her presence meant something more. Something not from my past, but my future.

Perhaps she did not wish to be known. Or know me. But our connection with each other persisted regardless. As if... *calling* to each other. In recent years, my pull to her had increased inexplicably. What had once been a star-flecked breath of knowing darkness in my dreams, had now become a visceral embodiment of an unmistakably female interest. And maybe I was imagining it, but sometimes she seemed just as curious about me as I was about her. While I knew nothing of her age, or what she looked like, or where she lived, her soul I had come to recognize. Like a line in a song, something about her sang to me. As a boy, when the nights were cold and empty, I had yearned for sleep if only to share space in my dreams with the mysterious presence that watched me from afar.

My little shadow.

Alarm sparked through my insides as I noticed her eyes had squeezed shut tightly. Wherever she was, she was in agony. My instinct roared to smooth away any discomfort from this being as I lifted my hand to her brow and willed calm into her body.

For the first time ever, she responded to my spectral touch as if it were somehow real. As if we weren't locked in the same subconscious illusion...

After a brief flinch of surprise, her eyes glazed and lids fluttered open, responding to my presence. *Gods... could she feel this?*

Hope began to flicker inside me at this shocking development. *Maybe we would have a chance to understand this phenomenon after all,* I thought. It had puzzled me as a child, but like anything, it became a part of my unconscious life that I came to accept. Even anticipate.

Without warning, the familiar shift to wakefulness began to fragment our connection as my outstretched hand slowly disintegrated into a shapeless glow. I could sense that this moment was passing, but clung on fiercely, afraid those eyes would look at me and that I would find fear there. The glittering darkness began to push us apart as her eyes moved further into the gloom, but not as alert and curious as we usually left each other. As I fought the sensation of being tugged backward, I reached out to touch them one last time before blinking into candlelight moments later.

Rising from my bedroll, I gripped the sides of my head, beads of sweat coating my bare chest. Something akin to panic was making my heart race. Recently, the dreams I shared with those eyes had been so pleasant. Consuming. While no definite communication had happened between us, it seemed to be understood that our mutual presence was all that was needed. As if this person also yearned for something—someone to just... be there.

I had often awoken with the tug of a smile on my lips and the indescribable desire for an embrace. But this...no, something was wrong with her, whoever she was. As my eyes slowly adjusted to the light, I could barely make out the sleeping figures next to me. The sound of their heavy male breathing was the only true sign that I was still in the same place I remembered falling asleep in—the tent within the encampment on the outskirts of Opeth City.

The Offering Field.

Through the small sliver of the tent flap, I could make out the faint gray of morning beginning to glow on the horizon. Slowly, I tugged a woolen shirt over my head, followed by a thick elk skin coat, boots, and the dagger I never allowed out of my sight. Careful not to disturb the soldiers all around me, I slipped from the tent.

The camp was near silent at this hour but would soon become a maelstrom of whining, grunting men. None of us enjoyed being pulled away from our stations or families, especially in the winter, all for the sake of The Offering. Yet every month, we were summoned here to this lifeless field in the shadow of the Furian Wood and commanded to provide extra security for our Sovereign, Chemosh. Our ruler was a horrifying force of wrath and frequently executed soldiers and court members who thought it wise to question her authority. No one had in many years. At the center of the camp, atop a pyre of freshly chopped timber, lay the altar where The Offering would soon take place. In a matter of minutes, in the light of the rising sun, we would all be forced to witness yet another sickening act of public execution. It was always a young woman, a maiden who had never known the touch of a man.. Offered up by her own family or imprisoned as a child, to ensure she remained pure. It sent my gut roiling with disgust. Feet leaden with dread, I dragged myself to the nearest kitchen tent, soon to be swarming with soldiers, and ladled hot broth into my steel mug. I grimaced at the steaming liquid, jaw clenching with disdain. It felt wrong to enjoy simple warmth through my fingers when a young woman, somewhere in this camp, would be mutilated and burned within the hour.

When I joined the Astaran Guard four years ago, it seemed to be my only real option to do something important. To be a force for good. Now, I wondered if I would've been happier living in squalor than being forced to participate in this gross abuse of power. The Sovereign spoke flowery things about how the sacrifice of a maiden to the Gods would promote growth and vitality into the soil, leading to more bountiful harvests and greater prosperity for us all. Some of the Guards, including me, believed this was a well-decorated lie to hide the monstrous truth. The Offering was her way to achieve forgiveness from the Gods who banished her from Lyrath more than a millennium ago. If the lore passed down from our ancestors was true, that meant that this "Sacred Offering" was only a twisted, narcissistic attempt to win back the favor of the Gods, using her own people like chattel. A cold, steely rage began to crawl through my veins as my hands shook with the urge to strangle this foreign beast, who believed herself the *God* of Astaran. As the sun began to break over the tree line, I stood there in complete stillness, contemplating not only my place in this world, but whether those blue eyes that haunted my dreams would ever be any part of it. Sorrow rested on my shoulders like a black stone; there was no hope for this nameless woman who would die today. There was nothing I could do...

"You're up early, Tyran," said a strong, familiar voice. The captain of my unit, Cordyn Mavers, was groggily emerging from his tent and striding over to my location by the breakfast table.

"Couldn't sleep," I answered, honestly.

He nodded in a grave way as if to indicate he understood

my meaning, knowing full well that most of the camp was restless with despair on the eve of The Offering. Only a select and savage few could sleep peacefully knowing they would rise the next day to see such a bloody spectacle, and I was not one of them.

Captain Mavers was considered young for his position, no older than his mid-forties, but what he lacked in age and experience, he made up for with fairness and compassion. He was a rare man indeed and one of the very few people I had ever admired. He dragged a hand down his face, absent-mindedly scraping his dark, overgrown stubble, which I noted was now flecked with silver.

Heaving a weary sigh, he then said, "I received word last night from a falcon emissary that there was an escaped prisoner from a village south of here, on the other side of the Solumine river. I was asked to employ a Guard to track down this person and bring them back to the camp for... questioning."

I knew what that meant.

This prisoner would be used as an example and publicly crucified for slipping the leash. The one bloodbath already planned for today would grow into two. The captain knew I was the best tracker in his unit and was one of the only people he could trust to skillfully navigate The Furian Wood and return in one piece. I nodded in acceptance, noting the twinge of pity that crinkled around his dark eyes; he wanted to give me an excuse to avoid the bloodshed taking place there that day. A rare man. Many Astaran Guards found joy in the senseless death and were even rewarded for their brutality.

The sun had risen high enough to bathe the camp in glowing gold, as more Guards began to flow from the tents. As the men moved around to tend to their various needs and duties, I noticed more than a few females who quietly slipped out after them, walking in the opposite direction—prostitutes.

Even though taking lovers, no matter how casual, was not a crime, it was encouraged even; the sight of it always filled me with sorrow. Did these women need to use their bodies solely to pay for food to fill their bellies or those of their children? I knew the answer, and it seemed tragic to me that they felt as if they had no other option. My throat tightened as an errant worry gripped me in a familiar way. *Had my mother been one of them?* Had she been impregnated by some handsy bastard who only cared for her long enough to wet his prick before shoving her away? Had she died at the hands of a... *customer*? Before bile could fill my mouth entirely, I shook my head, shoving those thoughts back into their pit.

Many of the females in the camp were keen to send lazy and inviting looks in my direction, but I never accepted their offers for company. The truth was... I had never taken a lover. I knew the mechanics of it, of course—observing creatures in the wild, or on the many farms I had worked in my youth. It was also impossible to be ignorant when subjected to the lack of privacy within the camp. When men were so desperate for affection and release, they did not even mind the proximity of their fellow Guards. No...my first lover would not be a prostitute. I knew that with certainty. Marriage, however, seemed like a faraway dream for a grunt soldier with little to offer except my bare hands, proclivity for violence, and skill with a knife. But I preferred it to the brief company of a woman likely riddled with diseases who could offer nothing more than her body. No. I wanted something different. Needed something... *more*. A love I had only known to be possible after it had been described to me once, by a great man and trusted friend.

The General.

My reverie was shattered by a deep, booming drum that carried on the morning mist from the other side of the camp. Both Captain Mavers and I instantly froze, sucking in a breath.

In fact, all the Guards near us stopped in their tracks, like deer catching the scent of a hunter. The drumbeats grew louder as my eyes caught sight of the torches pumping black, billowing smoke. We all knew who approached: The Sovereign. The Guards bearing the torches who preceded her arrival, wore head-to-toe black garbs, their faces masked save for their eyes. Each of them had a vicious thirteen-inch blade, which curved into a serrated point; a knife designed to gut and flay. Adorned across their chests was a depiction of a golden serpent devouring its tail, which glimmered under the torchlight. They were her personal squad of ruthless killers: The Anakaii. Delivered to her palace as children, all were raised in isolation and groomed into fierce, stone-cold warriors. The Anakaii were not small men by any means, but they appeared to be dwarfs in comparison to the looming figure who stalked in the center of the group...

The Sovereign, as always, was clad in blindingly brilliant gold. She stood almost eight feet tall, her broad chest and arms gleaming with pure-gold armor that ended with menacing gauntlets over her hands and a long, flowing skirt that fell to her bare feet. While her body was that of a powerful man, her face was lush with cat-like feminine grace. Her warm, tawny skin stretched tight over high cheekbones, and her eyes, wreathed in black kohl, burned like a blazing orange and crimson fire. The black curls of her hair hung loose to her shoulders, gently grazing the clasps of the ten-foot gold train that flowed behind her like a sparkling river of dawn. If she weren't the most ruthless being in the world, she might be considered majestic or even beautiful. Her full lips curved into a wicked grin as her eyes roved around the timid prey surrounding her. The massive sword sheathed across her back was the size of a man, with diamond and blood-red rubies glistening on the hilt. As she glided around the corner, approaching the altar and soon-to-be funeral pyre, that's when I noticed the maiden. The small, cloaked figure, wrapped in heavy, white velvet and was being dragged toward the altar. Guilt and rage squeezed my chest in a vice; this girl was probably no older than twenty, her future now ripped away. She was chained at her wrists and ankles, but all life had since left her form. She did not put forth an effort to walk toward her doom, leaving the Guards to bear her weight as her toes grazed over the grass.

I was going to be fucking sick.

The cold sweat of despair was dripping down my temple as I fidgeted with barely restrained hatred. Captain Mavers turned to me, his dark eyes full of understanding, and nodded once in dismissal. My instincts screamed to throw my dagger into the chest of this foul, ancient monster and haul this innocent girl into the safety of the forest. But before I could make a very foolish decision, which would almost guarantee a slow death for both me and the girl, I turned heel and ran to the edge of the camp toward the horses.

Chest heaving, I spotted my perfect, white mare, Cressida, drinking deeply from the water trough. I had been prepared for a quick exit once The Offering was finished. My travel bag with spare clothes, food, and blankets was already packed and tied to her saddle. Not wanting to waste another breath in this camp, I briefly patted her cheek, untied her reins from the post and swiftly swung myself into the stirrups before kicking her into a hard gallop.

Upon reaching the edge of the forest, I glanced over my shoulder to see the thick, black smoke of the pyre staining the sky with a dark cloud of pain.

CHAPTER 4
RAVN

None of it made any sense.

This day. This feeling. This... fear.

All of it was unfamiliar and frankly unwelcome.

I paced in my chambers, wringing my hands with fret, wholly bewildered by what was happening to me.

What did you do, Ravn?

I asked myself over and over. Each time more pleading than the last.

What the fuck did you do? Clenching my fists, I wedged one against the wall before bracing my forehead against it. Eyes squeezed shut, I recalled the events of the day that had led me to this twisted ruin of doubt and confusion.

The day had been just like any other. Like the thousands of days before this one, for as long as I could remember.

We trained.

We fought.

We studied.

And we bore witness to The Sovereign's judgment on those who broke her laws.

Sometimes it was a foolish priest who held secret discussions about the Gods in his hidden basement, betrayed by his own neighbors.

Sometimes it was a father pleading for the life of his daughter in a pointless attempt to save her from the fate of becoming a maiden. A most high honor in our society. And a precious gift to The Sovereign. Unwise.

Court members accused of stealing from The Sovereign or those who had broken the strictly enforced rules of propriety would all beg and plead. But any deemed unworthy of her mercy would face The Sovereign's eternal condemnation; the sentence typically carried out by one of the Anakaii cadets.

Another method she employed to cleanse us of our humanity.

This had been my life since my earliest memories. There was nothing more prestigious outside of the life of an Anakaii cadet and no greater honor to one's forefathers.

My path had been crystal clear.

Iron-clad.

Until this day...

Pushing from the wall to resume my pacing, I silently pleaded with fate to allow me this one transgression. This one show of weakness. While I was no coward and certainly no stranger to brutal punishment, I just couldn't fathom why I had done it and how I would ever explain myself if found out. Everything about the small act defied every savage lesson I had ever received. As cadets, soon to be warriors upon our 19th revolution, we had known only pain and discipline since leaving our mother's breast.

Compassion, love, empathy—all were seen as failings. A fixable error in our programming.

And those who could not be molded were cast out or had met their end in training.

And I was one of the best.

"The most cunning and skilled fighter in a generation," I'd heard them whisper.

So, what did this act of...*kindness*... say about me now?

It had been just like any other day...

Our training was finished; the mess hall cleared of any remaining food, and the cadets all summoned and filed into neat rows against the wall of the main hall. A dim ode to dark stone and flickering firelight, I knew that The Sovereign carried out her "trials" here instead of the throne room because she did not believe that these criminals deserved to look upon her gilded nest.

Joined with us in stoic silence were the members of her court and their wives. Village leaders, businessmen who dealt in slaves and precious stones, smugglers from distant parts of Astaran, and a few retired members of the Anakaii. And at their sides, trembling females cloaked in black garbs that covered every inch of their bodies and faces, eyes cast to the floor. Only once had I borne witness to the face of one of the court wives since entering this life, an ill-timed slip of propriety that The Sovereign rewarded with lifetime banishment from the palace.

The woman had been incredibly lucky that my master had not claimed her head.

Men she seemed able to tolerate, but the very sight of a young woman was a needle to the eye of The Sovereign.

"Filthy wretches and whores, they have no use other than

breeding." She would seethe, sometimes to herself. So well-renowned was her hatred for women that only very rarely would a brave one demand an audience with The Sovereign. Not all of them were murdered or banished for simply existing, though; you had to be useful to Chemosh if you wanted to live.

The doors had swung open briefly, allowing the soft glow of the afternoon sun to illuminate our motionless forms as we waited to be dismissed for our evening duties.

She had been so silent as she entered, I had craned my neck to see if anyone had walked in at all, when I saw a tiny, old woman hobbling down the aisle. I remember wondering if she knew how quickly she was inching toward death. The Sovereign watched her with scathing impatience, nostrils flaring as the frail woman made her way to the dais. Barely more than bones wrapped in cloth, the woman's papery hands trembled as she pushed back the hood over her snowy hair and looked up into the face of The Sovereign. My breath stilled when the woman smiled brightly, her skin crinkling around her features. The whole room waited for the inevitable, the silence louder than a roar.

"Greetings, my Sovereign," the old woman wheezed as she briefly tilted her head. Chemosh only stared down at her from the dais, her face perched atop a golden fist, the portrait of unruffled indifference. The woman tried to stand straighter, squaring her shoulders.

"My village has been struck by a plague, Sovereign. We have a desperate need for food and medicine." Gasps and murmurs hissed through the hall for only a moment before receding back into stillness, all eyes on the fearsome giantess whose lip curled into a smirk.

"Pray, where is this village of yours?" she asked the woman, her voice like the scales of a slithering serpent. Soft, yet pregnant with danger.

The woman, bracing herself on a dark wooden cane, hung her head. "Two days' ride south of here, we are one of the last villages before the wall, Sovereign."

The wall.

More murmurs echoed through the hall, mostly in disbelief. According to the lore of this land, that village should not exist, considering its proximity to the ancient boundary on the southern half of Astaran. Erected eons before even The Sovereign had laid claim to this world, it was said that Hel existed on the other side. Or a void of impenetrable darkness. No one really knew. And if anyone had ever returned from the other side, they had certainly kept their observations a secret till the grave. It was forbidden to cross over the southern boundary of Astaran by penalty of death. Chemosh's eyes, glinting like a smoldering fire, narrowed as she rose from her seat and loomed to her full height. A terrifying, golden behemoth. The room fell silent once more as if shrinking into the shape of the trembling woman who held her stare with The Sovereign as if it were her final act.

It likely was.

"Ravn!" she boomed, making my bowels leap into my throat. Shoving ahead through the throng of my fellow comrades, all of them stock-still and silent, I made my way to the dais before kneeling beside the old woman. Slowly, The Sovereign stepped toward her with calculated coldness until her looming presence was within inches of us both. Face painted with smug hatred, she whispered, "Listen well. Your village has been cursed by the creatures that exist beyond the wall. Your people were too weak to resist that power and deserve to die for their pathetic uselessness. Be gone from my sight—your time has expired in my kingdom." The woman trembled, mouth quivering into a tight line as she gripped her cane.

Though too old to act on it, I knew that rage was still potent in her heart.

The Sovereign only smirked before addressing me, still kneeling on the floor, awaiting my instructions. "See to it that you dispose of this hag before she infects us all with the plague."

With a final glance of disgust toward the old woman, she turned from the dais and stalked from the room, servants trailing in her wake. The exit of The Sovereign was the unspoken dismissal everyone had been waiting for, and within a few shuffling heartbeats, the room had cleared of every soul except for the two of us.

When quiet had returned to the hall, the old woman released a deep sigh and slowly turned in my direction. While expectant and wary, her face was unmistakably calm as she looked me over. I noted how her eyes softened as she beheld me with a twitch of her lips, as if she was remembering something pleasant.

I could only stare. *How was I going to kill this old woman?*

Snapping her neck would only take a second.

It would be over before it started.

Quick and painless.

"Do not kill me, warrior," she said, her filmy eyes locking onto mine.

"I have loved ones to protect. Children and the infirm who need to be moved. I never expected help from that beast. But I owed it to them to try. I owe them for all the happiness and joy in my life, don't you see?"

I should do it now—before she spoke more ill words about my master.

I flinched when she reached out a trembling hand, gently cupping my face, her skin like ice wrapped in leather. "You remind me of my son," she breathed, tears welling.

And something about the way she smiled into my face.

Like I was someone she loved and admired. Someone she missed desperately.

A mother looking into the eyes of her child.

A tiny fissure cracked within me.

Stunned, I remained on my knees, eyes wide.

Softer than the flutter of wings, she spoke words in a strange tongue before letting her hand fall from my face to grip her cane again.

"Come, warrior. Help me return to my people. I know there is goodness in you."

Shock and disbelief roiled through me like a storm. She knew nothing about who I was, who I had been trained to become. I had killed without qualms, disquiet, or regret.

As if her words had opened a subterranean pit of fire, burning began to crawl across my scalp as a flood of...

of...

feeling...

gripped my insides and squeezed.

All at once. I yearned, raged, mourned, and screamed.

I wanted friendship.

I wanted... *happiness*.

I wanted my mother.

I wanted to *fucking kill* my father.

All these thoughts and feelings had been stripped from me long ago—stolen from me.

Like a bundle of raw nerves set aflame, the long-suppressed emotions threatened to burn me alive. I did not realize I had collapsed to the floor, face pressed to the cold stone with my arms wrapped around my middle, until I opened my eyes to see the old woman's shoes near my face.

Gasping and grunting, I rose back to a kneeling position and saw nothing but patient amusement in her eyes. "What have you done?" I demanded, my hard-earned emotional control unraveling with every breath. After a few somber heartbeats, her face shadowed. "I only removed the cold cage around your very warm heart, warrior. You will find true strength when you listen to it."

The unfamiliar sting of tears made me gasp in disbelief.

What was happening to me?

Suddenly, she was gripping my shoulder with surprising strength, her face turning stern. "I need you to carry me, warrior. Help me get beyond the palace walls. You are not her slave. You have a choice now. Be the man who protects the innocent, not harms them."

But I did not have a choice. This woman had been commanded to die at my hand. That command was law. It was my religion. It was everything I had ever cared to know. *How could I defy it?*

Like a bloom unfurling... I realized I already was.

It felt like a splinter under the skin, something invasive that my body was desperately trying to shove out. In an instant, my entire world shifted on its axis as defiance sank deep, its roots spreading through my veins before entwining around my soul. Like sight being restored to a blind man, I saw my life for what it really was...

A tragedy.

A child ripped from his mother and subjected to abuse, torture, and manipulation.

Forced to live in isolation and bear witness to cruelty, death, and pain.

I was the well-conditioned product of generations of deceit, neglect, and slavery.

...And it pissed me the fuck off.

The sound of her labored breathing as she studied me warily broke me from my trance.

With a slow nod, I accepted her plea for help. I watched as relief made her sag, her body struggling to stay upright on her cane. At this point, I knew that only her bravery was keeping her standing.

"You'll have to pretend to be dead for this to work," I whispered. She only nodded before giving me a brief smile and stepping into my arms. "Do you worst, warrior." *Gods*, the woman was on death's door and more courageous than an untamed lion. Gently, I lifted her against my chest, one arm under her thin, knobby knees, and turned to exit the room. She tried to go slack and lifeless as I followed the corridor to the southern wing of the palace. The sun was nearly below the horizon as we left the inner palace and approached the enormous quarry pit. Nearly choking on the smoke of burning waste in the pit, I pivoted toward the southern elevation and the secret crack in the wall that I had discovered while roaming around the palace after curfew as a boy. While I had no doubt that most of the cadets knew of its existence, too, no one spoke of it, as if having such a secret was a treasure too good to spoil. Once in the dark shadow of the thirty-foot-high stone wall, I stood motionless, scanning the night for any signs of life. When I was certain I had not been followed, I gently set the woman on her feet and began to move the conveniently placed rocks that hid the hole from prying eyes. She would be forced to crawl on her hands and knees for a few yards, but would eventually find freedom in a dim alley on the outskirts of Opeth. Telling her as much in just as many words, she simply nodded before gripping my wrist and speaking in that same foreign tongue she had before. *Fuck*... I didn't know if I could handle another sudden burst of emotional violence. Ignoring the tremble in my voice, I asked her what she had said. She only smiled weakly and replied, "Thank you, warrior. May the Gods protect you." Like a parent reassuring a child, she patted my forearm once more before hobbling to the wall and disappearing through the void.

After several breathless moments, I dragged a hand over my face before quickening my steps in the direction of my chambers, eager to be alone...

With my head in my hands and knees bent to my chest, I sat against the cold stone wall and repeatedly replayed these moments.

I had awoken this morning as a hardened and cold-blooded servant of The Sovereign.

I would close my eyes tonight as a changed and lost individual, suddenly desperate for a life I had no chance of knowing.

There was only one thing I truly knew for certain: I was in imminent danger.

CHAPTER 5
AIDA

*J*ab, *duck, thrust, slice.*
   Luke's blade flashed like orange and yellow lightning as we sparred around our campfire.
   "Faster, Aida! Never expose your ribs and chest; keep your defensive stance no matter what. Arms up! Again!" Lungs burning with effort, I lunged for a low blow, which he expertly parried before striking me over the head with the hilt of his sword.
   "A real enemy will show no restraint, Aida. Focus!" he commanded, hardly out of breath.
   Scrambling away from the next assault, I rolled to my feet and readied my dagger for a gut-piercing throw. In the next breath, he charged, slamming me to the ground before I could

launch my blade. Pinned beneath his weight, I struggled to free my hands from his grip, rage pooling behind my eyes as panic set in. His face was serious as he studied me.

"If ever a man gets you into this position, you need to know how to get out of it," he murmured, as my weak attempts to dislodge him proved just how helpless I would've been if he were a genuine foe. Slowly, he released my hands and shifted away from my body to a kneeling position. Head pounding with anger, I waited for my heartbeat to slow.

"Show me," I demanded.

His lips twitched into a smile, the silver scruff on his face a glowing contrast against his dark green eyes. Raising his hand to his face, he pointed to his nose before redirecting his hand southward and pointing to his groin, a look of knowing savageness playing across his features. "While my hands were busy pinning yours, these two very vulnerable areas remained exposed. Do you understand?" he asked, calmly. Still seething from the bite of vulnerability, I only nodded tersely. I understood it just fine. Rising to his feet from the forest floor, he held out a giant, calloused hand. I studied it for a breath as a rush of gratefulness flowed through me at the empowering lesson he had given. Clasping his warm hand in mine, I rose to my feet...

But this wasn't happening right now.

No, it was just a dream, another *God's damned* memory. My heart stuttered with ache at the sight of him. Strong. And alive.

As if being chased by visceral pain, the vision muddied and shifted like ink in water...

I stood over a steep cliffside, looking down upon the Solumine River snaking below, eyes stinging with fear, my lungs locked into stillness. Snow was falling in thick, heavy clumps as I watched a flailing hand break through the violent rapids only once before being swallowed and shoved under again... to never resurface. Though I had faced this moment hundreds of times, reliving it over and over, the grief held within it punched a hole through my chest all over again. *I'm sorry... I'm so sorry...*

Suddenly, I felt a warm caress brush against my brow, as if trying to smooth away my pain. In less than a heartbeat, I knew it was him. The stranger who somehow wandered into the orbit of my own dreams. I pressed into the gentle embrace and breathed deeply to steady myself with his enticing scent—like summer rain and green things... like the Furian Wood. He smelled like home.

I only knew he was a man because his presence had always given the impression of masculinity. Unyielding. Confident. Violent. Traits that were rare for females in this world. But I had detected loneliness there too, and compassion. Even though I had never seen his face or heard his voice. While I had sensed the connection since childhood, in the four years since Luke had passed, the strange connection to this warm, glowing presence had only intensified. As if something was pulling us toward each other. In truth, he had become the only comfort I had come to expect, while barely surviving alone in the forest...

Something cold and wet gently pressed into my thigh, dragging me away from the subconscious.

My eyes struggled to open, as if my body was not prepared to deal with reality quite yet. Hesitantly, I began to flex my toes, still bare and pulsating with fresh lacerations. The abrupt skitter of hooves, startled by my sudden movement, crashed into the bushes nearby. There was dirt caked in my eyes and a film of something plastered to my neck and shoulders, which began to crack apart with every movement. Its metallic scent told me it was dried blood. Lots of it. Slowly, I began to right myself onto my forearms and lifted a hand to my face to scrub the dirt from my lashes. A white-hot lance of agony pounded through my head like a drum. The pain was so intense, my breath caught as I tried to stifle my cry. It was so dark. Had it just been early morning when I ran into the forest? Genuine fear settled in my gut.

Had I gone blind?

Was the brain trauma too great?

Squeezing my eyes shut to hide from this gut-wrenching panic, my thoughts drifted to my mentor and friend, Luke.

What would he tell me?

"Deep breaths, Aida. Listen to your surroundings. Assess your situation and make a plan. Deep breaths..."

So, I breathed.

In and out.

In and out.

Calm began to settle into my senses once again as I sent awareness through my body like a sentinel. My feet were raw and aching, but nothing felt broken. My legs were burning and covered in stinging scrapes. My hips were stiff, but breathing deep did not shoot pain into my spine, so there appeared to be no major injury to my back, Gods willing. I was very cold, and shivering sent painful spasms through my body like lightning. The only considerable damage appeared to be to the back of my head. Slowly, arms trembling with effort, I pushed myself into a sitting position against a stone. No doubt the same rock that had nearly cracked my head open like an egg. Squinting my eyes open again as much as I was able, I released a sigh of relief. The darkness was no longer total. The soft gray of morning was beginning to bloom above the trees, crinkling my brow in confusion.

A whole day? I had been unconscious for a whole day.

My trembling hand drifted up to delicately assess the back of my head, but even the feather-light press of my fingers was enough to make my stomach turn inside out, pulling a hiss through my teeth.

I was alive, but in bad shape.

I had no doubt the Astaran Guards had stopped their search for the night, hopefully in the wrong direction, but would resume at first light. Those cruel bastards loved the chase. My nostrils flared at the stink of a nearly rotten apple nearby. Savage hunger fisted my belly as I laid eyes on the bag of apples now scattered around the forest floor. This must have been what the deer had come to investigate. I muttered a brief prayer of gratitude to the Gods that nothing carnivorous had come to investigate my vulnerable, unconscious body, too.

Moving with deliberate caution, I gripped an apple between my fingers, brought it to my mouth, and sank my teeth into its flesh.

It was ecstasy.

My bites turned feral, juice and pulp dripping down my skin and onto my chest. It was the first thing I had eaten in three days. Chucking the core, I scrambled for another... and another.

Hunger now temporarily leashed, I knew my next goal would be water. Going back up the steep, near-fatal cliff face to reach the Solumine was not an option. I prayed for strength as I placed weight onto my haunches and slowly rose, back braced against the stone. The pulsing in my head felt like a stampede of wild horses, so I remained motionless until I felt confident my vision was in no danger of blacking out again. A quick glance at the sun rising to my right gave me my heading: North. Away from Opeth and the grip of the Astaran Guard. The further I ventured into the wilderness, the safer I would be —from capture and imprisonment, at least. Cold anger settled over my bones as I contemplated my very grave situation: no supplies, no weapons, no water, no shoes, and no fucking pants. The only garment acting as a barrier to my privates was a pair of filthy, once white, and now brown, under trousers, which only came to my mid-thigh. Thankfully, I had enough sense to not discard my long-sleeve tunic and deer skin vest. But if I did not find shelter soon, exposure would claim me before the Astaran Guard had their chance. Before I allowed myself to become hysterical over these facts, I forced myself to breathe deep and focus on Luke's words, which were on constant replay in my mind.

"Keep moving, Aida."

Steeling my resolve that I was *NOT* going to die today... I began to stumble northward.

CHAPTER 6
AIDA

By the arc of the sun in the sky, I had walked almost four hours before stumbling upon a calm riverbank. It lay at the bottom of a steep gorge, sheer stone walls on either side. As desperate as I was for water, it was imperative that I tread with caution to avoid another nasty fall. I studied the path leading down to the bank, chose my safest route, and slowly made my descent. Each rock I braced myself on was carefully assessed to ensure it would not give out under my weight. Once at the bottom, I cocked an ear to listen to the sounds of the forest: a jay swooped and screeched as it flew overhead, the gentle breeze rubbed through the branches, and the calm portion of the river before me gurgled in invitation. All seemed peaceful and empty. I could deny my thirst no longer. Stiff, sore, and muttering muffled curses the entire time, I slowly stripped off my clothes, leaving them on the dry river stones before plunging into the knee-deep water. In between gulps of near-freezing water, I scrubbed away the dirt and blood from my body, face, hair, and feet. Sadly, I hurried my bath and kept to the basics; Gods knew I smelled like a barn animal. But I knew if I lingered, I risked turning blue from hypothermia. Retreating from the river, I pulled on my soiled and tattered clothes, grimacing at the dirt that marred my mostly clean skin. My heartbeat was shallow and fast, head swimming with exhaustion. If I was going to continue my journey and hope to stay alive, rest would be required. From the corner of my vision, a dark shadow appeared to be scooped from the bottom of the sheer cliff face. It was a spot of soft rock that erosion had gnawed away over many decades, now exposed due to the reduced flow of water during the colder months.

The sudden relief of finding a hiding place nearly took me out at the knees. Quickly, I walked over to the small cave and crawled under the ledge on my hands and knees. It was just enough room for a smaller person like me. Curling up on the soft, silty floor with my back facing the cave wall only a few inches away, I watched the near-silent stream of the gorge until my eyelids fell shut like heavy, velvet curtains.

Chapter 7
Tyran

The steady drumbeat of Cressida's hooves against the spongy forest soil was a welcome distraction from the tragedy I had left behind. I could not help but wonder then, if it would ever end in my lifetime... the black horror of The Offering. Our ancient history had been purged when Chemosh arrived on this world, more than a thousand years ago. Great archives and treasure troves of knowledge in once towering, teeming cities; all had been destroyed by The Sovereign and her acolytes. Legends said that there were once many great cities and vast Kingdoms all over Astaran before she came. Chemosh, in league with the minions of Hel and her brutal cult of sycophants, the first Anakaii, had brought genocide and Armageddon upon each Kingdom that did not swear fealty. Within two hundred years, all the once prosperous Kingdoms of Astaran had been annihilated, until only Opeth remained.

I shuddered as I recollected that I had just been in the presence of this near deity and conqueror, with her black garbed cadre of psychopaths who served their queen with unwavering loyalty. Everyone in Astaran knew that Chemosh had bred her Anakaii warriors with the sole purpose of brutality, keeping only the most savage bloodlines to train behind the palace walls. In the years of "peace" that followed her conquest of Astaran and its people, the Astaran Guard had taken the place of what used to be governors, politicians, the justice system, and the banks. Gold was still the favored currency, but only the wealthiest and most loyal members of her court could access it. The villages and people throughout Astaran were provided with a highly regulated and taxed monthly stipend, which for most people was only enough to buy the most basic items to survive. The only ways to achieve wealth in Astaran anymore were to inform on or hand over suspected "traitors" to The Sovereign, join the Astaran Guard... or offer up your young daughter to be "worthy" of The Offering. I had witnessed the fallout and devastation of it firsthand. The practice was so damaging that it had torn entire villages apart.

The cool, misted breeze of the forest had long since numbed the skin of my face as I coaxed Cressida into a slower walk. Whoever this prisoner was, I was in no hurry to speed along their intended doom. Being the best tracker in my unit, I was often given these tasks, to my chagrin. Some of these prisoners or "defectors" were no more than starved and desperate villagers who stole or even killed their way into obtaining food or medicine. I never understood why I felt burdened with such shame when other Astaran Guards had no qualms about the suffering of their people. It wasn't as if my hands were clean.

I, too, was guilty of committing unforgivable crimes...

But I knew who was to blame for my internal conflict with morality: The General.

The memory of his bright eyes and warm smile flashed before my vision, tearing my chest apart with longing—and guilt.

Where had he gone after being banished that day?

Was he even still alive?

The ache deepened as I remembered tiny moments from my boyhood.

The weight of a blanket lay over me as I slept in the barn.

His face aglow with pride when I struck a target true with a dagger or arrow.

The soft thud of his heartbeat beneath his chest.

The General was the only soul who had ever shown me any kindness, until the Gods had blessed me again by being assigned to Captain Mavers' unit. A tingling itch around my right elbow was a constant reminder of what The General had saved me from, and all he had given after. Each day living under Chemosh's reign, being her complicit tool in the Astaran Guard, all of it was worth it, if only it brought me closer to finding The General again.

The shift in the breeze told me of river plants, fungus and visiting elk. The Solumine River was nearby. It was the great, serpentine life-giving force of Astaran. Its frigid, pure water sourced directly from the glacial plains deep within the Vazaketh mountain range. Crossing the river was indeed a physical marker of your place in the wild abyss of the Furian Wood. Once on the other side and continuing northwest, it could take many weeks of travel through uncharted wilderness to reach the base of the mountains. Knowing this information was vital to apprehending this prisoner. I knew that anyone who genuinely wanted to escape capture would continue North, with the hope that their pursuers would give up the chase. If they could survive...

Without proper training and supplies however, there was little that could not find you out here: wolves, great mountain cats, deep gorges and crevasse's, poisonous plants, and if the whispers were true, The *Mørkebringer*...

Ancient lore told of a race of people rumored to have great spiritual power, capable of directly communicating with the Gods, and bending a soul to their whim... with only a whisper into their dreams...

A shiver ran across my skin, ears cocked for any sound as we approached the river.

Could she be one of them? That presence that seemed to hover over my every thought?

Since The Sovereign had banned all sharing of recorded history long ago, after the great archives had been burned, our histories were passed down to each generation in secret. Being an orphan, I did not learn of these stories until The General shared them with me as an adolescent, when he was certain I was mature enough to keep them to myself. Many centuries ago, the *Mørkebringer* people had existed in their own great, mountain Kingdom before Chemosh's fall to Astaran. But after suffering devastating losses against the fallen angel's rebuilt armies, they had been wiped out and forced into exile. There had been no whisper or sign of their existence since.

My head began to throb with exhaustion. Gently, I tugged Cressida's reins to a stop. Her nostrils flared in anticipation of the river nearby, which we could hear gurgling on the other side of a small grouping of trees. Glancing up toward the sky, I happily noticed a decent gap in the tree canopy that would provide a perfect place to see the stars. We would camp here tonight. After dismounting from Cressida, feet once again on the loamy, forest soil, I took stock of my supplies strapped to her saddle. In addition to the Elk skin coat I wore over my thick wool tunic, my pack was fortified with a few apples, carrots, a handful of potatoes, some bread, cheese, a bow and quiver, a water canteen, a fish bone needle and thread, a wool blanket, a small hatchet for wood splitting, a brass compass...and a pair of iron manacles. For my prisoner. Shoving the manacles to the bottom of the pack, I released a sigh of discontent and led Cressida to the river for a drink. Silently, I hoped that this prisoner, whoever they were, would use this time to their advantage.

CHAPTER 8
AIDA

This place was ordinary.

And it appeared to be inside someone's kitchen.

The smell of yeast and herbs wafted over from the table where dough had been laid in great clouds, ready for the oven. I watched as a short, elderly woman waddled back and forth, her worn slippers scraping with each step over the stone floor. She was steady and organized, like she had done this process thousands of times in her life. I noticed her face as she crossed the room and began lifting the pillows of dough into their pans. Ah, yes. The baker from the village from which I had most recently escaped. Before my arrest, we had a brief conversation. Pity had shone in her eyes after she told me that she could not afford to give away her bread. I only nodded in understanding, the scent of the bread making my stomach ache with hunger. But before I could turn away from her small, rickety food stall, she told me that some discarded bread could always be found in the crates near the stockade. The burnt or stale loaves were recycled for the prisoners or used as filler in stews fed to the Astaran Guard. She gave me a knowing smile before turning away to greet a new customer...

A part of me marveled at how a woman who bakes every day of her life also dreamed about baking. I scoffed a laugh, as I continued to watch her. As she readied the dough for the oven, I peered over her shoulder, enjoying the mundane comfort of this age-old craft. A small pang of wistfulness stirred in my chest at the thought of my own mother baking bread long ago.

The feeling disappeared the moment I noticed a shadow fall over the old woman's face. Suddenly, her shoulders tensed as she hesitated, something like shock crossing over her features. I could see nothing out of the ordinary until she reached a trembling hand toward the dough and began to dig, tearing away stringy clumps with her fingers.

Her fingers... which came away bright red with blood.

I inched closer and gazed in disbelief at what this woman now saw buried inside the dough...

A human face. A young girl. Skin pale in death and eyes squirming with maggots.

Screaming in terror and sobbing with grief, the baker dropped the pan to the ground with a loud clang before running from the room. I could only stare, frozen. Suddenly desperate to be separated from her nightmare. She knew this girl. It was someone who had been important to her. A daughter perhaps? Backing against the wall of the kitchen, her screams ringing through my head, I clamped a hand over my mouth to muffle my cries. The anguish of her grief threatened to break me apart. I had to get out. Get away from this---

"There you are!" boomed a deep voice.

Fear gripped my heart with an icy fist.

A bruising hand had clamped on my ankle and dragged me from my resting place, ripping my hair over the stone and sending lightning bolts through the gash on my head. More hands pulled me into a standing position before I felt the cold iron shackles snap shut around my wrists now behind my back. Panic and blazing rage assaulted my every thought as I beheld the four Astaran Guards before me, their hounds baying loudly in anticipation of their reward. Maybe it was my flesh they craved.

Fuck.

I was so fucked.

One of them I knew. It was the Guard who had freed me from my cell the morning of my escape and then had let me slip away while finding his breakfast. I had little doubt that my disappearing act had humiliated him, and he had been personally tasked with retrieving me or risk severe punishment from his superiors. He stood over six feet tall, his face grizzly and scarred with deep gouges peppering his cheeks, likely from some horrendous childhood disease. His ochre eyes glistened with savage triumph, bloodshot and glassy as he inspected his prize. Me.

His wide nose scrunched as his lips curled into a sneer, a tongue darting out over his gross yellow teeth. I could almost see the sick machinations writhing inside that bald head.

"We're supposed to escort you to the Sovereign's camp..." He drawled, sending a knowing look in the direction of his companions.

"As I'm sure you already know... she enjoys torturing escaped prisoners," he said, now pointedly staring me down.

Numbing terror began to pool in my core.

"But... I suppose that can all wait till morning. We wish to have a little fun with you first."

An amused chuckle rose from the others, who were leering at me with predatory intent. Something ancient and deep began to yawn awake inside me. I may die tonight, but I would never be brought to heel by these animals. Wrath began to bubble under my tongue as I pulled shuddering breaths through my teeth, lifting my chin and squaring my shoulders. A brief flicker of surprise crossed over the grizzly Guard's features.

No, it was apparent that he wasn't accustomed to preying on those who intended to fight back.

"If you even think about touching me..." My gaze hardened as I leveled them with a glare. "I will find you in your dreams and bring your fucking nightmares into the light of day," I promised in a low voice, cold malice ringing through every word.

The group stilled, giving me a double-take. Satisfaction at their pause had me grinning wickedly as I scented the slow drip of fear spreading amongst them. They glanced at each other warily, shifting on their feet.

I looked each of them in the eyes and marked them with a curse...

"None of you will leave this forest. I will break the doors of your mind wide open and find joy in tearing apart your soul. Your bones belong to *ME* now!"

A moment of stunned silence hummed in the air before a raging fist, like a hammer, cracked across the side of my face. The blow threw me to the ground, making the horizon and the surrounding river spin like a top.

A voice thick with blistering hatred said into my ear, "You will never see another sunrise, *witch.*"

Yeah. Maybe...
The dark cloak of oblivion was thrown over me once more.

Chapter 9
Tyran

The fire, now more embers than flame, provided little warmth against the biting chill of this night. While glad I had brought a wool blanket, it only provided so much protection. Lying face up on my bedroll, head propped up on one arm, I thanked the Gods for giving me another night under the stars. Apart from riding in the woods with Cressida, gazing into the magnificent glow of the night sky was my favorite thing about being alive. In the clear gap of the tree canopy, I could discern several constellations. Draco, with its bright North Star, Theban. The small bear, Ursa minor, Polaris seen glittering brightly at its tail. Streaks of green and pink undulated across the sky like the breeze in a grassy field. The beauty of this world always took my breath away.

Some of my most treasured memories consisted of stargazing with The General, often on our trips together into the Furian Wood. With the permission of the noble family we both served, he would take me into the wild and spend days teaching me everything he knew about fighting, hunting, tracking, and survival. Every time I returned from those excursions, I was a stronger and braver boy than when I went in.

With one last prayer to the Gods, for The General's safety, wherever he was... I closed my eyes and drifted to sleep.

BOOM.

BOOM. BOOM. BOOM.

"Help me... please!" an exhausted voice cried from the gloom.

Those eyes. The same pair I always held here in my dreams pleaded with me. Directly to me. For the first time. *She*, I realized. Yes, it was a woman. Her face and body were cloaked in shadows that swirled like glittering night. Faintly, I could make out the curve of her lips and long strands of hair that shrouded her head; she was the physical embodiment of infinite space. But those eyes were as clear as they had ever been, blazing like the brightest aquamarine, with desperation and *fear*.

BOOM. BOOM. BOOM.

She again slammed her hands against the glass wall of my consciousness, seeking me out. Fierce determination settled over my body as the calm of impending wrath sharpened the blade of my senses. She was scared and in danger.

I needed to find her.

"Where are you?" I demanded.

She shook her head in silent panic. She didn't know. She then squeezed her eyes shut as if in deep concentration. Suddenly, images began to drift across the glass-walled space we were standing in. I could see a river gorge. Campfire light throwing shadows across the steep walls on either side. Four men, Astaran Guards, sat around a fire drinking a light amber liquid from glass bottles—Akvavit. One of them was a foul, lumbering giant with a dimpled, bald head and deep pox scars on his face. His eyes glazed with hunger, licking his lips in anticipation as he reached into his coat pocket and retrieved a small vial of opalescent powder that shimmered in the firelight. Unstopping the cork and dipping an elongated pinky nail into the powder, he brought it to his nose and inhaled deeply, eyes rolling back as he shuddered with ecstasy.

Fuck. It was lupinum. Or what the drug-addled soldiers referred to as *"moondust."*

Dread struck alarm bells as adrenaline began to course through me.

She had no idea how much danger she was in.

I had seen moondust in action and had fervently refused it whenever it had been offered to me. Many Astaran Guards used it, and it made them into lethal predators. The high it provided removed any shame or inhibitions a normal person would have, effectively turning you into a murderous monster. Too many times, I had witnessed females who spent the night with the wrong man being carried away from the camp, beaten and bloodied. Or had seen a fight break out among the Guards that always went too far, someone typically dead once the dust had settled. Out of the haze of panic, a small thought snagged on the logical part of my brain...

How was she showing this to me? Her eyes looked into mine then, like she heard me speak. But her dismay was palpable; she had no clue either.

And it didn't matter. She was running out of time.

Like a disintegrating bubble, the glass wall between us suddenly disappeared. Tentatively, I reached out to grip her small, mist-veiled shoulders, locking into her gaze.

"Hold on as long as you can. Buy yourself time. Find a weapon. Do *whatever* you can to survive. I'm coming for you. I'm coming."

Her eyes, lined with silver, hardened with resolve as she nodded. Reluctantly, I removed my hands from her and willed myself awake.

Launching from sleep, I frantically searched my surroundings, mind reeling with anguish as I realized two things at once:

What I had seen was in a dream.

It was also reality.

Wasting no time, I jumped up and gathered my belongings before shoving them back into my pack. Within the next moment, I strapped the bag onto Cressida and sheathed my hatchet next to the dagger at my waist before slinging the quiver of arrows onto my back. Two heartbeats later I was untying a startled Cressida, climbing into her saddle, and kicking her into a heart-pounding gallop. We raced alongside the river going upstream, heading north, Tears slid from my eyes, assaulted by the frosty night air as I began to pray.

I prayed to the Gods for speed and cunning.

I prayed that she would still be alive when I got there.

And I prayed I would be granted the bloodshed I craved.

CHAPTER 10
AIDA

I forced myself to remain motionless and only concentrated on slowing the heart now hammering in my chest. I had to remain calm and focus on my breathing.

My survival weighed heavily on them believing I was still unconscious for as long as possible. With my face and hair still plastered to the frigid river stone, I cracked open an eye, thankful to be facing away from the campfire—and the Guards sitting around it. Shadows cast by the firelight flickered and jumped like the dancing demons of Hel. Maybe they were coming for me now. Maybe I deserved this fate. Blood was indeed on my hands. Maybe this was Hel's sign that my debt was now due, for the soul I had unwittingly sent to the after world... whichever one had decided to claim him.

"I've never fucked anyone who was unconscious before," one of the Guards muttered lazily in my direction.

My attention snapped back to the present.

Cold sweat began to bead across my palms, still shackled behind my back. My shoulders and chest groaned in protest as I lay prostrate on the hard stone. I squeezed my eyes shut and focused all my remaining energy on stillness. The itching, burning wound on the back of my head was now secondary to my current terror, but I didn't dare twitch or adjust myself in any way.

"Nah, don't bother. More fun when they wiggle and scream beneath you," chuckled another.

Blood-red fury roared between my ears.

These men were not just grunts... they were sadistic monsters.

"I've got something special planned for this one, though..." the pockmarked one said, voice low and devious.

Adrenaline flooded my veins like a burst dam as I heard him grunt with effort to stand before shuffling in my direction. The sounds of his steps indicated he was lazy with drunkenness. My brain began to fly through my options and lack thereof at breakneck speed. In the spring and summer, water rushing through this gorge would be powerful enough to sweep a grown man off his feet and carry him away, but in the wintertime...barely a gurgle could be heard from the shallow river to my right. Escaping to the water was not an option.

Shit.

I had never been with a man before, but I knew with iron-clad certainty that my first time wasn't going to be with this hulking fucker. I sucked in a whimper of panic that threatened to escape my lips. I knew it was foolish to hope that my plea to the lonely man behind the glass, whose presence was always pulsing with a soft, warm glow, would help me in time. Running would be nearly impossible without the use of my hands, considering the steep hillside I needed to scramble up to reach the forest above. Now, I was beginning to understand how animals felt when backed into a corner.

Only one option remained: fight for my life.

The scrape of boots near my head indicated that I had run out of time. It was now or never.

"Hey, gorgeous... What's a pretty thing like you doing out here all alone?"

Even without looking, I knew the beast was grinning down at me, his boot nudging my thigh.

"Wake up, girly. Boys and I want to spend some time with you."

I kept completely still, waiting for the perfect moment.

Nasty, calloused hands gripped me around the arms and flipped me onto my back. It took everything I had not to cry out from the pain lancing through my head. I let my head roll to the side, limp as a fish.

"I said... wake up!" he roared, before a stinging slap struck across my cheek, knocking my head to the other side. I could feel his disgusting mass settle over my body, his stale breath warming my neck.

Faster than a pit viper, I slammed my head into his face full force.

Bone crunched as warm blood sprang out like a geyser, coating my neck and chest. As his hands clutched his face in agony, I slammed my knee into his groin with savage delight. His bellow of pain seemed to shake the walls of the gorge. Within the next second, my feet found purchase on his gut, and I kicked with every ounce of power I could summon, sending him flying backwards into the freezing river. Springing to my feet and crouching low, I bared my teeth at the other three Guards, their jaws slack in disbelief.

But I was done being broken and fragile. I'd had enough of this shit.

If these were going to be my last moments, I'd go down fighting, tooth and claw.

"Come on!" I demanded.

They all rose as one and unsheathed their blades, which were as long as my forearm.

I didn't care.

"How pathetic! Three armed men against one starved, injured, and restrained *GIRL*! I pray Hel will welcome you all to *BURN* and *ROT* for *ETERNITY*!" I spat, chest heaving with adrenaline.

A cold blade pressed into my throat as my hair was gripped by a wrathful fist.

The grizzly Guard, his voice trembling with rage, shouted into my ear, "I'll see *YOU* in Hel, witch!"

... I waited for the final blow. The warm spurt of blood running down my neck...

But instead, I heard a whizzing sound followed by an abrupt *THUD*.

The beast behind me jerked in an unnatural way, releasing his grip on my hair inch by inch.

"Up there! In the trees!" The Guards began to shout as they scrambled for their weapons.

I whirled and raised my foot to land another blow, but there was no need. His features now slackened with instant death; an arrow had found him through the back of his head and out of his left eye. As if in slow motion, his body fell straight back into the river. Dead.

Face contorting with fury at the sight of his murdered companion, another Guard sprinted in my direction before he was brought down by another arrow through the throat. Falling to his knees, eyes bulging in shock, only a hoarse gurgle escaped his lips before he too fell dead to the floor. Another Guard had aimed his arrows into the dark tree line above the gorge and let loose a volley, aiming blindly. I charged. Angling my shoulders, I sent the full force of my body into the impact, sending his back into the cliff wall. It seemed to only piss him off further, however. Bellowing like a berserker, he swung his dagger, missing me by only an inch. I ducked the next swing, but he swept with his legs, knocking mine out from under me, and I watched the world tilt sideways as the impact pushed the breath from my lungs. He had me pinned on my back in a second, teeth bared as he hovered the blade over my chest. I bucked and thrashed, but his weight over my hips held firm, further crushing my hands shackled beneath me. Black eyes glinting with malice, he raised the blade and readied to impale me through the heart...

A sickening crunch echoed through the gorge.

The Guard went limp, slumping forward and pinning me under his weight. I roared with anger as I tried to drag myself from underneath his lifeless body. Then I saw the handle of a hatchet protruding from the back of his skull. In the next moment, the dead male was lifted away from my chest. Rolling to my side, I coughed and gasped for breath against the floor. I felt cool hands at my wrists, unlocking the manacles. Stifling my cry of ecstasy as my shoulders righted themselves forward again, I scrambled away toward the cliff wall. The dagger intended for my chest mere moments ago now lay discarded next to the dead Guard. Without another thought, it was gripped in my hand, angled outward as I crouched low. Panting and disoriented, the first thing I noticed was the bodies of all four Guards now grotesquely sprawled around the campsite. It truly was a massacre. One I felt no drop of guilt about.

But the next thing I noticed was the man before me.

He was also crouched low with his hands raised. The same way you approached a frightened animal. His face was grim as he stared, and I noted the way his eyes assessed me in a professional way, taking stock of my mental state and injuries.

He looked... young. A grown man, but still lean and firm with youth. His dark blond hair fell in soft waves that came to rest on his shoulders. His face, cast in relief by the firelight, indicated a square jaw, high cheekbones, and a straight, graceful nose. My body no longer responding to my brain, I began to slowly relax at the sight of him.

He too watched me.

As he looked directly into my eyes, something like... *wonder*... drifted over his face. Then, shock as he breathed, *"It's you."*

His words struck a chord inside me that echoed like a pealing bell, both haunting and intimate. I blinked into the flickering dark, blood smearing around the edges of the scene as I studied him... ignoring the way the cold metal inside my heart began to heat beneath his stare.

The second I noticed the Guard uniform underneath his coat, however, my body tensed again. "Who are you?" I demanded, gripping the dagger tighter.

His brow briefly furrowed with indecision, eyes glancing around the camp before returning to mine. Within a few heartbeats, he blew out a deep sigh and replied,

"My name is Tyran. I will not harm you. You are safe."

CHAPTER 11
TYRAN

What have I done?

The question seemed to grow louder as the minutes ticked by.

There was no hiding from the enormity of this complete disaster. Still crouched low, doing my best to appear non-threatening, I surveyed the carnage around us. Four Astaran Guards were dead at my hand. The scene was like that of a nightmare. Limp, lifeless bodies lay scattered with black pools of slowly drying blood oozing into the stone beneath them. Two, I had claimed with an arrow. In the second it took for the second arrow to find its mark, I had already started sprinting to the edge of the gorge, ducking behind trees and boulders to stay out of sight. A volley of arrows sailed overhead into the dark tree canopy. I could hear her fighting, her rage reverberating off the cliff walls of the gorge.

She was going to fight to the death.

The crunch of gravel punctuated with grunts of exertion sounded less than ten feet from me. Instantly, I knew one of them was trying to escape from the gorge, no doubt to bring back reinforcements. A second later, another arrow quickly knocked in my bow, I stood up and aimed down the slope, releasing the arrow into the retreating Guard's face without hesitation.

There was no time to contemplate the consequences of this ordeal.

All that would have to come later.

I sprinted down the hillside, leaping over the Guard's twitching form, and could see her legs kicking and flailing beneath another hulking giant, his blade hanging above her chest. My heart thrummed like a bird's wings as I flew down the hillside, scraping my hands on rocks and trees as I went. The Guard began to raise his shoulders, preparing to impale her. Sucking in a breath, I gripped my hatchet tight, and then it was flying end-over-end through the air, finding its mark on the back of his head. I ignored the burning in my lungs as I moved toward the young woman still pinned to the ground by the Guard's body, her shrieks of terror clawing at my insides.

Reaching the floor of the gorge and striding past the now cooling bodies without a second glance, I yanked the Guard's body off her and quickly rummaged through his pockets for the manacle keys. Finding them in his coat pocket, I unchained her wrist restraints and watched her scramble away like a terrified animal released from a snare.

The sight of it turned my stomach with pity... and relief.

My one focus in that moment was to establish her condition. I knew once that was determined, we had to clean up this mess and get the fuck out of here.

The way she had fought back indicated she was more woman than girl, but her thin body was stark with starvation. And... *Gods*, she was filthy. All bare skin visible on her face, legs, hands, and feet was marred with streaks of dirt and dried blood; her hair was a dark tangle of leaves and twigs.

But those eyes...

Even dilated with fear and shadowed by the firelight, I knew them well.

They had come to me in my dreams so many times. They felt as familiar to me as the cloaking comfort of the Furian Wood. Her face, currently hardened with distrust and wariness, was round in a pleasant way; her pert nose and full lips barely visible behind the curtain of grime. She was...

"Who are you?" she demanded.

Warring indecision clanged through my mind at her question. Was she technically *my* prisoner now? ...No. But we *were* both fugitives.

Was I officially a traitor to The Sovereign? That answer also seemed obvious.

The killing of four Astaran Guards in exchange for her life had put us both on the never-stop-hunting-them-down list. I knew this with certainty. But for now, I chose the shortest truth and told her my name. It was time to leave this bloodstained gorge behind us and begin our flight into the wilderness. The particulars could be sorted out later.

Slowly, I rose to stand and pinned her with a look of calm determination. The same look The General had given me hundreds of times when giving me a command, only to observe my reaction.

I tilted my head, gesturing toward the campsite, and said, "We need to keep moving."

Her head jerked up at that remark as she slowly rose to her feet, her back still pressed against the wall, but said nothing.

"The bodies must be burned with all their belongings and weapons departing with us... Gods willing, the snowpack will hide any evidence left behind."

After another quick glance at the carnage surrounding us, she only nodded in agreement and lowered her dagger. My chest deflated with relief at her acquiescence; it appeared shock had not consumed her entirely then. Yet...

We worked long into the night.

Both of us grunting with effort, we heaved the bodies by the arms and legs and laid them next to each other in a small alcove tucked under the cliff wall. Any useful food, clothes, and weapons lay stashed by the side of the fire. After a few trips to the top of the hillside to retrieve bundles of firewood, a half bottle of the remaining Akvavit was poured over the pyre and set ablaze. We both stood motionless as the fire roared to life, flames lapping up the side of the cliff like hands scrabbling to escape the burning maw of Hel. After a moment, she took her leave in the direction of the river. I noted that she had discarded her filthy clothes on the river rocks and waded in, scrubbing off the dried blood caked to her face and neck. Quickly turning back to the fire to give her some privacy, I prayed to the Gods that snow would begin falling and it would be heavy enough to blanket this gorge and hide the blood-spattered river stone from the light of day.

Chapter 12
Aida

With a quick glance over my shoulder to ensure the man, Tyran, was not looking, I stripped bare and waded into the river. The frigid water was almost warm in comparison to the numbness which had settled deep into my bones...

He saved me, I thought repeatedly, the matter-of-fact bouncing around my head like a chant that I was still struggling to believe, my mind reeling with the questions that erupted like fireworks. The strange connection between us had led me to him. And he had listened, and somehow... had found me. I had been just a heartbeat away from the most gruesome end I could ever have imagined... and he saved me.

He had also damned us both.

Chasing a young thief was one thing, could be dismissed even. But murdering four Astaran Guards was another situation entirely. We would never stop being hunted now. The only hope we had was to vanish into the wilderness. And go where? I had no clue.

In the years after Luke died, my survival instincts had become dulled, but maybe that was just my will to live. There had been days, weeks when the desire to hunt or trap food was almost non-existent. Only until I was almost mad with hunger would I make the effort to forage or set snares. The day I decided to leave the forest, to grovel and barter in the villages, I had felt so defeated... and *sick* with loneliness. The forest had been my home since the age of seven, after my parents had disappeared. As a child, you could find groups of nomadic orphans often flocked together. The more numbers you had, the safer you were. Our days had been filled with exploring the forest, foraging, catching game, and organizing raids on unsuspecting villages. We became known throughout Astaran as the *Villdyr*. The "wild ones." The camaraderie found there with the Villdyr was necessary for survival.

There was only one rule: upon the age of sixteen, you were banished.

It was a protective measure to defend the younger children from the needs of violent men and desperate women. And while I understood why the rule had been established, it made it no less painful to be forced to leave the safety of the group and wander the wilderness alone...

Luke found me soon after. He didn't have to stay with me, teach me, but he did. He was in my life for almost a year and had given me the hope and structure I never knew I needed... until he was killed in cold blood on a frigid Oktober morning.

Since that terrible day, the desperation for another human's presence had been almost crippling. It wasn't lost on me that the true reason for my departure from the wilderness was the heart-wrenching desire for human contact. Now, it seemed I had human contact in spades. The burning throb on the back of my head reminded me that this was not the time to strike it on my own, however.

As much as I hated to admit it, I needed this man's help. And I couldn't stifle my curiosity regarding the other part to this equation either...*How the Hel was I connected to this stranger's mind? And why?*

Once healed, we could go our separate ways. I had never felt responsible for anyone but myself and I certainly wasn't about to start now.

Sighing with resignation, I ended my ice bath and waded back to the riverbank. Arms wrapped around my chest and teeth chattering, I walked over to the campfire, now smoldering low, and began to rummage through the piles of supplies we had taken from the Guards' lifeless bodies. The smallest pants I could find were still two sizes too large, but they were clean. Pulling them to my waist and cinching the belt as far as it would go, I pulled on a long-sleeve tunic and vest before wrapping my hair in a loose braid. While I sat and laced up the boots that dwarfed my feet, Tyran approached me.

I rose to stand, and for a few tense moments, we only stared at each other. I gnawed on my bottom lip, uncertain how to break the ice that encompassed our bewildering circumstances.

"What's your name?" he asked, the gentleness in his voice catching me off guard.

But I couldn't help noticing that *he* was the one who appeared nervous as his hands idly tapped his thigh... *Didn't he just slaughter four people?* I thought, confused.

"Aida," I replied, a little tersely.

Something flickered behind his eyes that I couldn't place. I averted my gaze.

"Did they hurt you?" he asked, voice now taking a sharper edge.

Glancing at my feet and then back to his face, I responded, "No."

He nodded and exhaled deeply, as if he had been holding his breath to await the sordid details.

I continued, "I uh...fell...down a hillside two days ago. I have a wound on my head that needs stitches." No need to dance around it.

His eyes widened at that statement, but he only nodded, gesturing up the cliff side and the route leaving the gorge.

"Shall we?" he asked with a tight smile, a dimple barely pressing into his cheek before vanishing. I nodded in agreement as we began to make our way out of the gorge and back to the forest above.

CHAPTER 13
AIDA

Once at the top of the hillside, I did not look back at the gorge below. I did not wish to see the carnage left behind, as if turning my back on it would somehow make it disappear. He gestured for me to follow and walked into the dark curtain of the forest. The night was quiet aside from the crunching of the leaves beneath our feet, its stillness a stark contrast to the murderous event which had just occurred nearby. Though some pale shafts of moonlight broke through the gaps in the trees, Tyran's back in front of me was like a dark wall that I followed from a safe distance. Every few feet, he would glance at me over his shoulder to check that I was still there. I wasn't certain if he did so because he was concerned that I might have collapsed somewhere on the trail, or if he wanted to ensure I had not taken flight. I smirked at the thought. If I weren't in such a pathetic state, I would have definitely disappeared by now. Years of living and hiding in the Furian had taught me to become like a wraith if I needed to. And for some reason, it seemed like he knew that already...

Suddenly, I spotted a magnificent white horse tied to a small birch tree. She was easily sixteen hands tall, elegance and strength exuding from her every movement. Even in the dark of night, she was a bright beacon. I slowed as we approached, and I couldn't help my gape as I stared at her, which Tyran had noticed.

"This is Cressida," he said, affectionately, soft smugness alighting his features.

"She's beautiful," I replied, and I meant it. She was the most beautiful creature I'd ever seen.

He nodded in agreement before offering me his hand to assist me into her saddle. While it had been a long time since riding atop a horse, I was not a novice. Ponies were kept by the Villdyr, and we frequently trained with them as children. I stepped into his hand and swung my leg over, at once feeling lightheaded from the motion, but also because I was now very far from the ground.

Tyran, noticing my hesitation, asked, "Are you all right?"

I nodded and attempted to redirect my attention away from his hand that now rested on my calf. He noticed this too and quickly moved away to rummage through the pack of supplies on the ground, before asking again, "Do you need to eat?"

That one simple question triggered my body to nearly come apart with the ravenous hunger I'd indeed been suppressing for days. A gurgling growl erupted from my stomach two seconds later. Without another word, he reached into the pack and pulled out a large chunk of cheese, a few slices of ham, and a quarter loaf of bread, almost pushing them into my lap. Before my brain could muster the politeness to say, 'thank you,' I was stuffing my mouth with food. A few muffled moans escaped my lips, beyond my control at this point. Tyran pointedly ignored me, busying himself with tying supplies onto Cressida's saddle bags to give me a moment. A few minutes later, food thoroughly consumed, he grabbed the horn of the saddle at my front and swung his leg over to sit behind me. It was only then that I realized how tall he was, a few inches over six feet. It was apparent that getting into her saddle was not trouble for him at all. Our proximity, bodies flush in the saddle, my back to his front, did something inside me that I could not articulate. He must've felt it too because I could feel him tense at the contact. Wasting no more time than necessary, he gently kicked Cressida into a walk. As if there was some unspoken agreement between us, he proceeded northward. Further away from Opeth and those who would hunt us to the ends of the earth. I realized at that moment that he probably needed to vanish into the wilderness as much as I did, his life in just as much peril as mine.

THE SUN BEGAN ITS LAZY ENTRANCE INTO THE SKY A FEW HOURS LATER. In the faint light, I noted that we had now reached a denser, more ancient part of the forest. Brief panic mixed with mild curiosity tingled across my scalp... I was unfamiliar with this place. In every direction, giant, moss and lichen-encrusted trees bowed over the forest. Their gnarled and looping roots, shooting from the ground like the body of the great sea serpent from our legends, *Ægir*. Only by listening to the elder nomads who would babble incessantly after too much wine would you hear such stories. But I had always listened. The idea that such great beasts could exist had always fascinated me.

Suddenly, for the first time in hours, Tyran spoke.

"The air of this forest seems... knowing," he whispered softly.

I knew what he meant. We were being watched.

His comment made me wonder if he was the superstitious type. Many nomads in the Furian Wood had tales which spoke of dark things that lived deep in the woods, too. Most of them I had chalked up to folklore intended to scare young children. But I couldn't even deny my own experiences living in the wilderness: finding animal bodies turned inside out, seeing pawprints of creatures I did not recognize... or the sounds of blood-chilling baying from a distance...

A soft whistle from Tyran had Cressida increasing her pace.

All day we rode; only stopping briefly to stretch, relieve ourselves, and eat.

During one stop, while sitting cross-legged against a towering oak tree, I took a moment to simply bask in the joy of the forest again. Pulling apart my braid, I absent-mindedly picked twigs and burrs from my hair as the sun warmed my face. Just days ago, I had been held prisoner in a drab and filthy prison, then almost killed from falling off a cliff, before being brutalized and nearly murdered by four men.

The bright sun filtering through the swaying, green canopy glittered like a golden mosaic. The sound of the wind as it caressed the tree branches was like a heart-song. The breath of Astaran. I closed my eyes in sensuous gratitude for the peace it brought me and silently thanked the Gods for the gift of another day.

When I opened my eyes, Tyran was staring at me.

He too sat below a great monster of a tree, arms resting atop his knees. In the bright light of the sun, I studied him for the first time. While his face was indeed strong and angular, his expression was kind as he returned my gaze. My breath caught, as I beheld his bright, blue-gray eyes... like a storm over the mountains. His hair was the color of warm honey, strands of it slipping around his face in the breeze.

Gods... he was handsome. Extremely so.

And the way he was looking at me now...

I winced with shyness, fidgeting with my hair. Needing to break the silence in some way, I stated the obvious.

"It's lovely here... maybe spring will come early this season."

Still staring into my eyes with that calm intensity, he shook his head as if my words had pulled him from a trance before lightly clearing his throat.

"Yes, I hope you're right," he replied, giving me a small, dimpled grin.

The sight of it sent a pulse of warmth through my chest, alarm bells ringing. I squashed the pleasant thought quickly, averting my gaze.

We needed to separate. As soon as possible.

Just because he had saved my life didn't mean I owed him anything. And whatever this strange connection was—no, that didn't matter either.

I was better off on my own.

The tiny, nagging defiance that reared its head at that notion, I squashed that quickly, too.

"We should make camp here for the night and... tend to your wound," he said, tentatively.

My heart began to flutter with anxiety at the thought of what was to come. In the roughly ten hours since leaving the gorge, the wound on my head had reduced to a slow, pulsing throb, but each time I moved my hair or turned my head too sharply, searing pain would scorch me to the bone. Yes, the time had come to address this, and it would not be pleasant.

Sensing my dread, Tyran said, "It's going to hurt, but if it's any consolation, I know what I'm doing."

Of course, I knew what to do about it as well. Luke had taught me a wealth of knowledge regarding field dressings and medical aid. The only problem was that I could not see or access the back of my head. Steeling my nerve into hard acceptance, I sighed, "Okay. Let's get this shit over with."

Chapter 14
Tyran

I kept replaying it over and over in my head.

The sight of her sitting against that tree, the sun dappling the soft planes of her face, her eyes closed in serenity. Something in me ached as I watched her. Her chestnut hair, mostly clean of blood and debris, flowed down her shoulders almost to her waist. A few loose strands held aloft by the breeze glowed a deep bronze in the sunlight. My fingers itched to touch her hair and discover if it was as soft as it looked. Gripping my arms tighter to keep that odd sensation under control, her vivid, blue eyes opened... flooring me all over again. I had seen many women in my life, nobility and prostitutes alike, but no one had even a tenth of the beauty that Aida had. Her pale skin was clear and soft—like an eggshell, flawless. I noted the way pink began to bloom beneath her cheeks as she stared back at me, her hands running through her hair, as if to draw me in further. She had asked me something. Right. Spring. "Yes, I hope you're right." I grinned, trying to hide my embarrassment from being caught staring at her. The last thing I wanted to do was make her uncomfortable. Abruptly, I remembered her telling me about the injury to her head. My stomach dropped with guilt at my forgetfulness. I had been so focused on putting as many miles as possible between us and the killing field at the bottom of the gorge that I had forgotten about her wound. Thankfully, I knew how to treat varying injuries and illnesses, thanks to not only what The General had taught me as a boy, but to the Astaran Guard as well. It was going to be a nasty procedure, and I sent up a prayer to the Gods that she would not hate me at the end of it.

Our campsite for the night was in a small clearing of trees, not far from the Solumine, whose soft gurgle could still be heard dozens of yards away. While only a short hike to retrieve water, the location was nestled deep enough by the surrounding trees to hopefully hide our fire. Confident about the relative safety of our location, I dismounted from Cressida and offered my hand to Aida. Her face was worn with exhaustion, and the small winces that puckered her brow as she moved told me of the immense pain she was in. Hesitation briefly tightened her full, pink lips for only a moment before she accepted my help, placing her frighteningly cold hand in mine. Suddenly fearful she would collapse, I moved to grab her waist to assist her down, but withdrew quickly, finding her elbow to be a less intrusive alternative. For the second time today, I chastised myself. She was wounded, frightened, and we knew nothing about each other...

I needed to keep this bizarre urge to touch her under control.

Once settled and supplies unpacked, I set to work sharpening my hatchet in preparation for collecting firewood and building materials for a primitive shelter. Distracted by my task, a warm knicker from Cressida had my head snapping up to see Aida feeding her an apple while stroking her snout and smiling gently. My chest began to tremble, a long-forgotten emotion struggling to break free at the sight. Needing a distraction from this unfamiliar feeling, I told Aida that I would return shortly and left to retrieve what we needed for the night.

When I returned to the campsite, the sun now fading behind the darkened tree line, I found Aida staring into the flames of a small fire she had created, sadness shadowing her features. Startled by my sudden appearance, her head jerked up as awareness came back into her face. She spoke then and said, "I know how to build a shelter. I can help." Unaccustomed to being helped by a woman, I only nodded hesitantly, unwilling to admit that the faster we erected the shelter, the faster we could tend to her wound...

Now fully dark with the haphazard shelter complete, we sat in silence near the fire, snacking on whatever food was left. "I set some snares... that way," she pointed in the direction behind the fire, in the opposite direction of the river. I nodded in appreciation. Having a capable female around was... strange, but not entirely unwelcome. Watching her pick at her food, her gaze concentrated on the fire, I found myself wondering just how long she had lived in the woods, and if there was any place she called home. I certainly didn't have one. Not anymore.

But I knew she was stalling. While I understood why, I also knew that her injury needed to be addressed without further delay. I cleared my throat, unsure how best to approach it before saying, "You can trust me, you know. I've done this before. Many times." I said matter-of-factly. She looked at me then, eyes wary and glassy in the firelight. While I had hoped she knew I was referring to her injury, her doubtful gaze told me otherwise. Once again, I was internally chastising myself. Of course, I couldn't expect trust from her immediately; that would be a selfish mistake on my part. This world was cruel and unforgiving, especially to women. But I didn't cower beneath her stare because I had meant every fucking word.

As if sensing the direction of my thoughts, she exhaled deeply before nodding in defeat. My shoulders immediately relaxed with relief, happy I would not have to do this by force...

Accepting her wordless consent to begin, I reached for the supply pack and retrieved the fishbone needle and thread, several strips of linen, a small bottle of the Akvavit liquor, and a leather strip... for her to bite down on. I laid the wool blanket down as close to the fire as I could without it catching, then gestured for her to lie down. Her shoulders squared with resolve before doing as I instructed, wincing at the movement the whole way. Supplies ready and within reach, I gently began to move her matted hair away from the wound. A gasp escaped my lips without my permission as I beheld a huge gash, four inches in length, still slowly oozing blood.

I noted that she had placed the leather strap between her teeth when I heard her muffled voice say, "Do it!"

Gods, this was one of the most brutal head injuries I'd ever seen.

For a moment, I was in shock and totally bewildered that she had survived this without major trauma or blindness. It was truly a miracle, especially considering all the abuse she had suffered after as well.

"The wound is going to need close to ten stitches. Before

that happens... it will need to be sterilized." I stated, fully focused on keeping the tremble out of my voice.

I watched her hands curl and fist around the blanket beneath her, knuckles white.

I began.

Her voice broke with a scream as the liquor flowed over the wound. Moving quickly, needle in my right hand and my left hand braced on the other side of the gash. I pushed the skin together and made the first stitch. Her blood-curdling screams of agony threatened to shatter my eardrums, but she kept still, pressing her face into the blanket. She was panting and sobbing, my heart ripping apart at the sound.

"Halfway there, Aida. You're doing great..." I said, placating.

Her sobs turned into wheezing as her legs twitched absently. Alarm rang through me as I hurried through the final stitches.

She had stopped moving. Unconscious.

Laying the linen over the newly stitched gash, I began to wrap her head with a long piece of fabric before rolling her over onto her back. Bringing my fingers to her neck to check her pulse, I sighed with relief at the low, steady beat I found there. Gently grabbing her under the shoulders, I dragged her feather-light form to the cover of the shelter. I noted with alarm just how thin she was, clavicle bones and ribs jutting unnaturally underneath her pale skin. After laying the wool blanket on top of her, I nestled down beside her, checking her pulse every few minutes. Face slack and lips slightly parted, she looked so innocent.

But she was brave.

In fact, she was the most courageous female I had ever encountered.

As I lay there, fingers brushing the silky skin beneath her

jaw, something in me stirred awake as I began to acknowledge what this was...

This woman had *power* over me.

I had seen her in my dreams, and she had seen me in mine. *What did that mean?*

I had killed for her. Truly, there was no going back.

Something had made us destined to find each other. There had to be a reason. There had to be an explanation. Maybe the Gods had shown their hand in this. Maybe they had sent me to find her.

And my attraction to her? Another thing entirely. Magnetic.

But she was stubborn, feral, and distrusting. Winning over her affection would take time. Which I suddenly had plenty of now.

Satisfied with the pace of her pulse, I removed my hand from her sleeping form, ignoring the cold absence there, and settled down to sleep. The night grew colder as the fire began to dim, casting shadows on the moss ceiling of our shelter. Awake and at war with myself, I contemplated two paths set before me.

In one, Aida chose me as her friend, protector, and companion. Whatever she needed.

In the other, she chose to be alone, casting me aside. After all, she owed me nothing. Saving her life was a decision I would've made with or without knowing who she was, mysterious dream connection or not. For most of my life, I had endeavored to protect the innocent, no matter the consequences. What was life for otherwise? But I wasn't a self-righteous fool; my heart was stained black just like so many others in this wretched world. I knew my crimes couldn't be justified. Yes, I had killed to protect the innocent from further harm, but I had also killed out of vengeance. And pain.

Could someone like her... ever want someone like me?

I had nothing to offer: no family, no home, no money.

But I didn't dare ignore this feeling. Whatever this was, I wanted it badly. I would just have to prove to her that having me around was for her benefit, as much as for my own.

With one last look at her peaceful, sleeping face, I closed my eyes and sent a prayer to the Gods.

I prayed my little shadow would allow me to stay with her. To whatever end.

Chapter 15
Aida

Liberated from the discomfort of my body, my subconscious wandered into dark places.

Tyran's tether was closest, of course, considering we were sleeping next to each other somewhere deep in the wilderness. That fact alone was miraculous to me. It somehow didn't feel real to have him so close after all this time. I only stood there, in the space between, staring at the thread that would lead me to his dreamscape. And I was frustrated. Here he was, helping me, saving my life, and tending to my wounds —things I hadn't asked for but had no doubt needed. And why in *Hel* was he so fucking good looking too? How was it that I had never seen a man so handsome in my entire life? Somehow, it made me more perturbed. I knew more about him than

I had ever asked to know. I knew he was capable of rage and violence. And I assumed, like all men, he was capable of dark things. I just needed to confirm those details so I could move on with my life without feeling in his debt. Maybe he was a womanizer. Or a thief... or a morally black drone who obeyed every murderous command.

There was only one way to find out.

Carefully, I beckoned the golden chain into my hand and slipped into our shared mental pathway like smoke on the breeze...

Tyran's dream was bright and airy. I knew from the way the scent of jasmine floated on the breeze that it was a springtime day. The Furian was a vibrant green all around me, bright blue breaking through as the branches swayed in the wind. Suddenly, the tinkling sound of... *laughter*... sounded from behind me. I turned to see a modest cabin nestled between the trees, grayish smoke puffing from the brick chimney. Cautiously, I approached the home before pressing my body flat to the wall and peeking through the window.

Everything inside me went still at the sight I found within...

I noticed Tyran first. His lean, tall frame facing me from the other side of the wooden table he was seated at. His face was warm with adoration; his lips set in a genuinely happy smile. It was the kind of smile that knew no sorrow or pain. No loss or grief. Only joy. I blushed at the sight of it, grinning to myself at how contagious it was. But most shocking of all... was the small, dark-haired little girl that sat in his lap, her hands carving furiously with a knife as she shaped a lump of wood into something that appeared to be a bird. Suddenly, an adult woman crossed in front of the window, making me shrink back to the wall. After she had passed, I leaned forward again and watched her place another small baby into Tyran's open arms. This one was a blond little boy, his eyes a bright gray. Just like Tyran's. I swallowed as I watched the woman lean forward to press a kiss to Tyran's mouth. He opened for her, relishing in the kiss, his eyes lingering on her face as she withdrew. Maybe this was someone he had lost... Or someone he knew and was eager to get home to. As I watched the scene play out, I was struck by how familiar it all seemed. Once upon a time, I had watched my own father kiss my mother in such a way. A deep ache burned inside me as I contemplated just how buried those memories were to me now... and how unlikely it was that I would ever experience them myself.

So, he had someone then. Someone he wanted. Good...

We could move on. Go our separate ways.

Suddenly, the woman turned away from the table and approached the window where I lurked like a Peeping Tom. As her face turned into the light, I stumbled back a step, a curse slipping through my teeth...

Fuck. It was... *me.*

I didn't appear to be much older. But it was definitely me. Flush and pink with health, I looked...content. Happy. My head was thrown back in easy laughter in response to something Tyran was saying to the children.

The children...

They were mine.

And this... was Tyran's dream? His desire?

I took another step back, my foot stepping off the porch in retreat. I shook my head in disbelief as the cabin grew further into the distance. I had entered his dream tonight, intent on finding evidence of his cruelty and ill will. Anything to exercise this inexplicable pull I had for him. But instead... I found him only wanting *me*.

A person he knew nothing about...

Someone who had lost the ability to trust or depend on anyone.

A woman who had sworn never to allow her heart to open for another soul again.

CHAPTER 16
AIDA

The sharp bite of frost in the air stung my cheeks and nose as I awoke to see the icy cloud of my breath, flecked with gold by the rays of sunlight which filtered through the gaps in our shelter. The bedroll beside me lay empty. Worry skittered down my spine as I quickly rose onto my elbows and scanned around the campsite. Upon seeing Cressida, still tied nearby, I released my breath. Tyran must have left to check the snares then. Reaching for the water canteen lying next to my feet, I drank deeply and rose to a sitting position. Thirst sated, I gingerly prodded the bandage wrapped around my head, a soft tug of tenderness forcing me to bite my lip.

Damn. What the fuck was I going to do?

Wrapping the wool blanket around myself a little tighter, I took in the soft silence of the morning, my thoughts in a restless melee.

It didn't matter, I thought. His assistance, his compassion, his strange dream...none of it. The further away I was from him, the better off we both would be. He didn't understand just how broken and twisted I was, and I had no intention of him finding out. Whatever he desired from me was only an illusion. The same kind of distorted reality I had experienced in the dreams of countless others. A way for the mind to escape from the wretchedness of this world and all the evil that lies within.

Today. I will leave today. It was better this way.

Movement in the foreground told me of Tyran's approach. I rose to my feet and watched as the steam of his breath billowed away from his face. He was a lithe and graceful hunter, barely making a sound as he walked toward the campsite. As if alarmed to see me alive, his steps halted when he noticed me standing there.

"Good morning," he stated, with a brief tilt of his head, eyes roving over me in cautious assessment.

"Good morning," I replied, suddenly taking interest in a speck of moss on the ground. Taking that as permission to approach, he slowly moved closer until only the pit of ashes from our former fire was between us. "Thank you for my stitches... And for saving my life and all." I blurted, gratefulness temporarily winning the battle over my desire to flee. He only nodded, averting his gaze to the ground, lips tight, as if he understood my hidden desire as well. He seemed... disappointed. I wouldn't linger on how that made me feel. It didn't matter how I felt anyway...

A chilly breeze rushed through the campsite, further accentuating our awkward silence.

Out with it, you coward.

"I uhm... need to get going if I plan on making it to the base of the mountains before the spring melt." I gritted out. Tyran's eyes snapped up to meet mine, a flicker of shock crossing over them.

"You're leaving?" he asked in disbelief, his face stern as he took a single step toward me.

"Yes," I replied, replacing the urge to fidget my fingers by gripping them firmly into the wool blanket.

"But you're still injured. What's going to happen if you succumb to fever? Or if you fall into some *Gods forsaken* hole?" he asked with another step in my direction.

I scoffed, my temper flaring.

"I'll be fine. I've survived worse injuries." I retorted, ignoring the sudden ferocity in his demeanor. Part of me wanted to shrink in response to it...but the other part... wanted to push back with everything I had. He was close enough to touch now, his head bent forward as his gaze bore into mine. I stared back, pain tingling across the wound on my head as I craned my neck to look at him.

His chest heaved in suppressed anger as he said, "I can't let you leave. Not yet. It would be... *irresponsible*."

"Is that so?"

"Yes."

"Are you certain it's not because you want something else?" I spat, his proximity putting me on edge. His brow furrowed for the briefest moment before relaxing into cold detachment.

"Are you implying that I wish to take advantage of you?" he asked, his voice barely more than a whisper but simmering with rage. It wasn't what I was referring to, but it would work for this conversation.

"And how can I know for certain that you won't?" I shot back.

He retracted from my space by only a few inches, crossing his arms over his chest. His face was completely serious when he asked, "Why don't you just look inside my head, Aida?"

My vision went red in the same moment that something inside me fluttered obnoxiously in response to my name on his lips. Before I could respond, he spoke again, his deep voice descending to an intimidating octave...

"Admit it. You need help. And I refuse to let you leave until you have healed. Do we have a deal? Or do I need to find those iron manacles?"

"You wouldn't fucking dare." I hissed.

"Don't test me, *little shadow*."

Crimson flooded my cheeks, my eyes widening in surprise. *What the Hel did he mean by that?* He smirked in response to my gape, proud of himself for striking a nerve.

I couldn't put a finger on why I was so angry. All he wanted was to help me... But I didn't appreciate being so exposed. I'd spent my entire life hiding, and now this stupidly handsome blond man was going to act like he knew everything about me?

Well, he had another thing coming...

"Listen to me." I seethed, jabbing a finger toward his chest.

"I don't stay with anyone. I don't travel with anyone. And I certainly don't *need* anyone." The words had a bite that I didn't feel, a cold void left in their wake. His eyes softened with an indiscernible emotion. Something like...*pity*... before he nodded his head once and stalked away from the camp.

I stood there motionless, head pounding as I watched his back disappear into the surrounding woods. It could've been twenty minutes or maybe an hour before I finally released my frustrated sigh of resignation. The woods around me were quiet and peaceful, their inhabitants slow-moving in the cold of morning. But inside me… a combination of guilt and sadness squirmed together in a nauseating soup. With another swig of water, I made up my mind to lie back down under the shelter, clutching the wool blanket around me tightly. As I lay there and stared at the slivers of sunlight that came through the wooden slats, I desperately wished I had been more careful and had not injured myself trying to escape. *I wouldn't be in this position right now*, I told myself. But as my eyelids grew heavier, an unbidden image floated in from the peripheral—a stilled moment from Tyran's dream.

Tyran's lips and mine… pressed together in joyous contentment.

Chapter 17
Aida

When I awoke, I could tell that a significant amount of time had passed just by the way the sun was warming my legs, which stuck out from under the shelter. Groggily, I turned my body toward the opening and rubbed the sleep from my eyes. When my eyes adjusted, I noticed Tyran sitting beside my feet, his back turned to me. Upon hearing my movement, he glanced at me from over his shoulder.

"I'm glad you were able to get more rest. We will need to keep moving soon," he muttered before he turned his back to me again. Sitting cross-legged, I removed the wool blanket, surprised by how warm it had suddenly become. I stared at the back of his head for a few heartbeats before slowly scooting over to sit beside him. No longer under the cover of the shelter, I squinted up into the sky, the towering spruce trees around us swaying gently in the sunlit breeze. A moment later, Tyran cleared his throat before saying, "I'm sorry."

My eyes drifted to study his face, confused. But he kept his gaze trained directly ahead, refusing to meet mine.

"Sorry for what?" I asked, guilt roiling beneath my skin. He had done more for me than—well, since Luke had been in the picture. I was the one who should've been apologizing for being so ungrateful...

"For forcing you to stay. I just..." he paused, briefly glancing at me warily.

"I'm just... so curious about you." he breathed, his voice breaking in the smallest way. I feel like I know everything about you—and nothing at all. I want you to trust me, is what I'm trying to say," he finished, his face strained with conviction.

Trust.

Gods... I barely knew the meaning of the word myself.

I remained silent, weighing his offer. Was it so wrong to want an ally? Someone I could rely on again? But flashes from a tormented memory began to rise in the back of my mind, quelling that desire in less than a second. Trusting someone meant they could hurt you when they eventually succumbed to the God of death that shadowed our every step. Maybe Tyran was as noble as he claimed to be. And just as lonely as I was. But to keep him close would only weaken the defenses I had worked so hard to build these past four years. I exhaled deeply, pained by the odd hollowness that had found a place behind his eyes. As I deliberated my reply, I couldn't help but stare at his profile and marvel at just how much of a conundrum he really was.

An Astaran Guard... with a noble soul? I had never realized

that could exist. But the more I studied him, the more out of place he seemed. Most Astaran Guards were dark-haired and dark-eyed, their faces set in menacing scowls. But Tyran... well... he reminded me of the sun.

"Listen..." I whispered, fighting off the tremble in my voice. But he cut me off a second later.

"Let me escort you to the Vazaketh. That's all I want—and if you want to separate after that, then I'll let you go," he said firmly, his gray eyes guarded as he drifted his gaze to mine—where they remained for a long time. *Gods...* his stare was powerful. Dominant. Yet wholly... gentle. It did things to me I couldn't explain.

"Besides..." he continued, his lips lifting deviously.

"I honestly don't believe you're capable of staying alive out here," he finished, arrogantly popping a chunk of cheese into his mouth. My face heated at his audacity, my softened thoughts toward him vanishing into dust. But before I could decide if I wanted to shove him or erupt with a slew of curses, he wisely deflected my attention elsewhere.

"I stumbled across some tracks on the way to the snares, it looks like a few wagons, footprints, and this..." he said, holding up a pale crystal pinched between his fingers. I recognized it immediately as a trinket only found when a vagabond or shaman desired for someone to find it and follow to find more. In the deepest parts of the Furian wood, there was only one group of people who would be traveling in the wilderness together, leaving traces of their presence to be found by others who knew what to look for: Nomads. Their tracks indicated a possible gathering nearby, to trade. Now that the weather had warmed by a fraction, it told us all that spring was near. My spirit lifted. I could gather supplies and be ready to set out on my own shortly after. Tyran, noticing the shift, watched me carefully and lowered his hand, his expression tense.

Shit...

"Can I bring you to them?" he asked, softly.

I swallowed, fidgeting... and hating how apparently easy it was to read me.

And I couldn't stand seeing the look of disappointment on his face another second if I were being honest with myself.

Slowly, I rose to stand before turning around to extend my hand to him. He studied it for a moment before clasping his hand and mine and rising to his feet, his face instantly brighter. Excited. I pulled my hand away quickly, clearing my throat and dropping my gaze away from his shit-eating grin. It was only a sign of truce... for now.

Playfully, I plucked the faint, pinkish crystal from his outstretched hand. Satisfied with the relief he exuded, I gave him a sly grin in return, doing my best to ignore the way his eyes glazed when they looked into mine. With a deep breath, I pulled myself away from his almost chipper orbit and gestured ahead of us as I said, "Lead the way, sunshine."

Chapter 18
Aida

The tracks continued northwesterly, the elevation gradually climbing as we went. I inhaled deeply, appreciating the sharp scent of the sky-high balsam fir and pine trees that saturated the thinner air here. Apart from the steady plod of Cressida's hooves, the peace of the forest was only broken by the occasional startled squirrel or rabbit. The evening had brought a near-freezing temperature drop, and I found myself grateful again for the wool blanket Tyran had insisted I use.

For the hundredth time this hour, I caught myself staring at his profile as he walked Cressida beside me. Refusing to ride on our way to find the nomad encampment, he had stood motionless with arms crossed as I pointlessly argued that I was capable of walking just fine. A smirk of amusement had played across his features before he offered to either drag me into the saddle himself or use his hands to hoist myself up. The dull throb at the back of my head eventually won out, a reminder that I would need to save all the energy I could if I was to make my escape later. Pushing it down deep, I dismissed the hollow cry of sadness that thought sent ringing through me.

Abruptly, the echo of murmuring voices and clanging utensils cut through the forest, making our heads snap up as Cressida was brought to a quick halt. Tyran's focused gaze flicked up to me briefly as he signaled to remain where I was before walking up the hillside.

Yeah, that wasn't happening.

With as much stealth as I could muster, I dismounted from Cressida and tied her to the nearest tree before moving to follow him. Halfway up the slope, he turned back and noticed my presence, rolling his eyes, but otherwise unsurprised. Once to the top of the hill, we both crawled on hands and knees to find ourselves looking over the edge of a deep cave mouth, the stone concave just enough to provide a brief ceiling for the dozens of nomads milling about around their fires on the floor below. For a few moments, we simply watched them go about their business: chatting, trading goods and furs, haggling and bartering, stirring steaming pots of stew, and drinking from homemade casks of wine and mead. There were a few children, but no sign of any Villdyr, and to my even greater relief, no Astaran Guards.

"We'll have to go around the hillside to get down to them," Tyran murmured next to me before slowly crawling backwards down the slope. I followed, accepting his hand when he offered to help me to my feet. Out of nowhere, my foot snagged on a root hidden by the foliage, making me lose my balance for a split second. I stumbled forward, his grip catching me on either side of my ribs in an instant.

My breath caught as I fumbled for a lame excuse, our sudden proximity making my knees wobble. His hands only squeezed tighter, our noses near touching. *Shit...*

Mumbling a brief apology, I righted myself away from his hands and moved to step away from him. As I headed toward Cressida at the bottom of the hill, arms wrapped tightly around my middle, I didn't allow my thoughts to linger on the ghost of his hands on my body.

CHAPTER 19
TYRAN

I needed to focus. Or distract myself at the very least.

When I caught her mid-fall, her warmth had crashed over me like a wave, her small frame perfect between my palms. I didn't blink. Didn't breathe. Unsure of what to do and unable to let go of her at the same time. Longing climbed up my throat as her cheeks crimsoned, her teeth biting into her bottom lip from embarrassment. And they were so close to mine that I could feel her breath against my skin. Two heartbeats later, the moment was over as she pulled away and descended the hill. Leaving my hands empty and useless at my sides.

Right. I needed to focus. If we were going into the nomad camp, it would require a full removal of anything that could associate me with the Astaran Guard. Slowly, I made my way back down the hill, pointedly ignoring the beautiful, dark-haired woman who was gently stroking my horse with her back turned. Ignoring me.

With a quick change into my hunting attire, I had successfully abandoned any evidence of my former life. Although my relatively clean-shaven appearance could be a giveaway to some, my size and stature were typically a good enough repellent from any would-be challengers. It was a necessary improvement, too, considering the immense animosity toward the Guard, which was undoubtedly held by nearly every inhabitant of Astaran.

And I didn't blame them.

The Astaran Guard had been the burning and brutalizing right hand of The Sovereign for centuries. If the Anakaii were her pure-bred attack dogs, the Astaran Guards were the horde of mutts that were only loyal in exchange for money, food, or drugs. Their presence only meant suffering and unfairness to these people, and especially to the nomadic groups that inhabited the most remote parts of the Furian wood. Most were refugees from villages abandoned or destroyed by The Sovereign, happier to live off the land than play the cruel game of life as her pawn or slave. And in truth, I envied them...

"Well, don't you look uncivilized," Aida smirked, her eyes bright and dancing with mischief as she took in my new clothes. I scoffed, averting my attention back to divvying up our loot, which we needed to barter. I didn't dare ask Aida what she intended to procure from the nomad encampment. If I were being honest, I was too afraid to learn of her intentions. She had yet to mention any family or anyone who might be looking for her. And she had been entirely willing to travel deeper into the wilderness, away from Opeth and the only civilization that existed in this world.

Deep in my bones, I knew that she intended to disappear.

I could only hope she would allow me the chance to disappear with her.

I had nothing and no one either, it seemed. And the thought of her wandering aimlessly all alone...

"Are you all right, Tyran?" her soft voice asked, cracking through the haze of anxiety I had wandered into. I noted the way her face tightened with a flicker of concern, making my throat tighten inexplicably as I shook my head. "Fine," I replied with a weak smile. For a moment, her gaze roved over my face, as if she contemplated pressing the issue before withdrawing back into cold indifference. I wondered then if the mask she wore was as hard-earned as mine was, crafted from a life of mistrust and abuse.

I wondered if she had ever let anyone on the other side of it.

With Cressida safely hidden behind a row of trees, nibbling at whatever greenery could be found beneath the frost, I hoisted the bag of goods brought to trade over my shoulder and glanced back toward Aida.

"C'mon, let's see what kind of trouble we can get into here."

CHAPTER 20
AIDA

Stepping into the nomad camp felt all too familiar. The soft squelch of the forest floor, recently disturbed by the newcomers. The billowing smoke from dozens of fires peppered the forest around the cave entrance. The bats screeched high above, annoyed by the sudden intrusion. The soft rustle of makeshift tents as folk came and went. In what felt like a lifetime ago, I was busying myself with the duties that came with a temporary encampment as a Villdyr. When I had been with them, the older children would direct the smaller ones to play scout along the trails to ensure our group had not been followed before setting up for the night. It was imperative to remain unseen, our movements untraceable, lest we draw the attention of slavers. And when the moon was bright and full, we would pause our wanderings to enjoy our spoils and dance around towering bonfires. A soft pang clenched around my heart at the memory.

As soon as Tyran and I cleared the forest's edge, the dull roar of their fraternizing diminished to only the crackle of their fires, as the nomads turned to take us in. They were wary of strangers, especially the near-giant man who stood beside me, his hands loosely hovering over his daggers.

I knew there was only one way to ease the tension.

"We come to trade!" I said loudly, my voice echoing against the cave ceiling as I held up one of the bags. After a beat of assessment, their collective murmuring and shuffling resumed once more. Tyran leaned down, his cocky smirk playing over his words even though I had not turned to look at him. "Don't stray too far, little shadow. I'll be doing some reconnaissance of my own here today. Cressida and I will be waiting for you in one hour. Got it?"

I tensed, unsure whether to lash out at his sudden pushiness or...

Demand that he call me that again with his hot breath against my ear.

"Aida?" he asked, jerking me away from that image.

I started, flicking away the pleasantness of that thought. *Gods, what was wrong with me?*

"Fine." I spat before stalking away in the direction of the camp, disquieted by the notion of his eyes following me the whole way.

I NEEDED TO FIND A WEAPON MORE SUITABLE FOR HUNTING, AS I STILL had every intention of leaving at the soonest opportunity. So, I began my search for a bow and quiver of arrows. At first, I silently took stock of what had been laid out across various carts and wagons, keeping my distance from curious eyes. I found plenty of animal pelts, herbs, roots, hand-made quilts and clothes, traps, and snares, but no signs of the weapon I was seeking. After I had inspected each cart at least twice and was considering giving up the search, a soft hum in the tent toward my left caught my ear. I paused to listen.

It was a song. One I had not heard... in a very, very long time.

My breath caught as the melody lifted the lid of my subconscious by a tiny degree.

My mother sang this song to me as a child. It was sweet and light and...

Before I even knew what I was doing, I was charging into the tent, slamming back the tent flap in my urgency. A haggard-looking woman yelped, startled by my sudden appearance.

Shit. "I... I'm sorry. I thought... never mind–" I turned to leave, my cheeks hot with humiliation and anger.

"Wait!" the woman yelled, nearly leaping in my direction with her hands outstretched. I stepped out of her grasp, hands reaching for my daggers on instinct.

"Wait, young one. I have something to show you. Please sit down," she pleaded, her thin, black hair bobbing as she ushered me toward the table in the center of the tent. It was only at that moment that I took stock of the virtual emptiness of her space. I saw no baubles, trinkets, clothes, or jars. Only the sole wooden table, fitted with two stools, and a solitary candle in the center.

Odd. To say the least.

"What do you want?" I demanded, in no mood to be hustled.

"Please. Please sit. I will tell you everything you want to know." Her dark eyes fluttered, a mostly toothless grin emerging in an attempt at friendliness. I knew better.

"Try anything unsavory and I will not hesitate to kill you..." I trailed off, prompting her to reveal her name.

"Call me Madisha, child. Or just Madi. Please, sit." She insisted again.

I only had another half hour before Tyran would no doubt come looking for me... this better be good. Sighing with resignation, I took a seat, hands resting across the dagger at my thigh.

Madi took the seat opposite me, rifling through a bag under the table that I had not noticed mere moments ago. "Ah, aha. Yes. Here it is. See?" she mumbled from under the table before yanking a great bow and quiver of arrows from the bag and laying them before me on the table.

I did not even attempt to hide the shock on my face.

I had told no one about what I was seeking... not even Tyran.

"H...How did you know I was looking for this?" I whispered, my fingers gently running across the black feathers on the arrows. Crow or vulture, I assumed. The woman stayed silent.

Head snapping up from the table, I leveled her with a glare. "How?" I demanded.

Her face had turned solemn, but one cheek lifted as she shrugged. "You are the one who came to me, child." I could only shake my head in disbelief. There were a million things in this life I may never comprehend, my own gift among them. But this felt different. It felt... intentional. Something or someone had led me here. Part of me wanted to balk at the idea that there was any divine purpose afoot, but another part went quiet as my blood began to chill in my veins. I *really* needed this fucking bow though... So, I decided to ignore the alarms that pealed and clanged inside me, intent on getting what I needed and leaving as soon as possible...

"Here, I have things to trade." I blurted, yanking my pack into my lap as I rifled through its contents. With haste, I pulled out some snare wire, a small knife taken off the body of one of the dead Astaran Guards, wild mushrooms I had chanced upon earlier this morning... and the pale crystal Tyran had found near the nomad tracks. The one that had brought us here.

The woman, Madi, gasped suddenly, nearly knocking over her stool as she backed away from the table. Her eyes were wide as she pointed at the crystal with a trembling hand.

"Where did you find that, girl?" she snapped.

Technically, I didn't. Tyran had brought it to me...

"On the trail that led us to the encampment, due east..." I replied, studying her. She didn't seem afraid. No, she was astounded, her head shaking back and forth as if she couldn't believe her eyes.

"What is it?" I asked, my gaze returning to the small and seemingly inconsequential rock cradled in my palm.

Quicker than a spark igniting, the woman launched toward the table and gripped my hand with hers. Finding my feet in the instant her hand met mine, I yanked back on instinct. A squeak of fright slipped through my teeth as I struggled against her iron grip.

"Let go of me!" I shouted angrily.

I investigated her face then... and my breath froze.

Only the whites of her eyes could be seen, rolled back into her skull, lids fluttering.

Gods...

I had to get the fuck out of here. My thoughts scrambled as I continued my attempt to pry my hand from her grip, her hold on me now reaching the point of pain.

She spoke, her voice suddenly taking on a darker edge, as if the words had crawled up through the earth to find their place on her lips.

> *"Fire in the sky...*
> *Black wings...*
> *Death is not final...*
> *The great deceiver must have you...*
> *War is coming, Dream Walker...*
> *You must wield it...*
> *You are the only one who can."*

SHE GASPED ONCE BEFORE BEGINNING TO CHOKE AND SHAKE violently. Releasing her grip on my arm, I watched her collapse into a convulsing heap.

And I could only stare at her. Frozen with terror.

"Aida, are you alri--" Tyran's voice trailed off as he entered the tent, his narrowed gaze darting between me and the woman on the floor, now beginning to pant and moan as she attempted to right herself. The look on my face must have been enough to indicate that I was in no condition to provide answers, because he asked no questions before filling my vision with his face. I was barely aware of him, my thoughts scattering like insects exposed to the light. Vaguely, I noticed others who had entered the tent to aid the woman, all of them throwing withering glares in my direction.

Tyran's face slowly came into focus, his deep, calm voice filtering into my awareness like a flame in the fog. I could sense his hands stroking the hair behind my ears, his smoky eyes wide with concern.

We needed to leave. Now.

In the next breath, my body barely communicating with my mind, I stood up. If Tyran was surprised by my sudden snap back to reality, he said nothing as he waited for my next move. I could sense his hand pressed to the small of my back, ready to pull me back from whatever abyss from which I had just emerged. And I was too shocked to brush him off anyway.

Slinging the bow over my shoulder and shoving the quiver of arrows into my pack, I slowly placed the small crystal in the center of the table with trembling fingers.

"I'm sorry… but you're mistaken." I breathed.

Upon hearing my words, the woman looked up into my eyes… and *smiled*.

I fled from the tent without a backward glance, Tyran at my heels.

CHAPTER 21
AIDA

How?

What?

And... *who* had been speaking through her?

I raced into the forest, feet barely touching the ground as I fled, my fear and adrenaline fueling my sprint. A soft snow had begun to fall, the wisps of ice melting against my cheeks as I collided into them.

Away. I had to get *away*.

From anyone who knew who and *what* I was.

From anything that sought to expose my darkest secrets.

From the dark recesses of my mind that I had vowed to keep buried.

"Aida! Stop!" Tyran shouted, a tinge of panic in his

demand. I whirled, startled that he had kept pace with me. The itch to continue my flight until my legs gave out was stronger than my desire to discuss this with him, but with effort, I planted my feet.

"Aida, what happened back there?" he pleaded, chest heaving and arms raised in surrender.

And what answer could I possibly give him?

His eyes zoned in on my throat as I swallowed.

"It was nothing. Just the ravings of a mad, old woman." I replied shortly, conscious of his discerning gaze, which sought to strip me bare. Which was not going to happen. Up ahead, I could see the bright, white contrast of Cressida's coat just beyond the trees in front of us. Eager to divorce myself from his assessing glare, I turned my back on him and moved toward her, desperate to be further away from the nomad camp. Like a sprung trap, he gripped my arm tightly, turning my body into his. I couldn't help the hiss that slipped through my teeth at the contact, but I managed to stop short of biting his arm when I noticed the somber look on his face.

Fuck...

The intense way his eyes bore into mine, his jaw clenching with frustration... I knew he had so many questions, but I truly had no answers to give. For a split second, I wanted to give him those answers. To share this welling hole of pain I kept inside. For a split second, I thought maybe he could take it, maybe he could bear that burden with me...and still want me in the end.

The sting of tears threatened to cloud my vision, my throat going tight.

I'm sorry, I wanted to say. But no words came out.

Tyran's face began to soften at the sight of my obvious distress, his brow tightening with concern as he seemed to count my every breath.

Gods, when he stared at me like that.

I didn't think it was delusional to assume that he wanted me. After all, I had seen the way he watched my lips when I spoke. The way he always withdrew his hands, as if fighting his desire to touch me. A warm pulse began to pull me closer to his chest, rising and falling as his breath began to steady.

His grip on my arm loosened as his hand drifted to squeeze mine, an effort to reassure me. I couldn't help being drawn to him like a magnet, his steady, warm heartbeat thundering inside his chest. His breath caught as I placed a hand there, enjoying the feeling of it beneath my fingers. I looked up at him and sucked in a breath at the heat I found in his gaze.

The want. The desire.

More than anything in this world or beyond, I *wished* I could be what he wanted. I wished I could be someone who was stronger than their darkness. But it was consuming me, and I knew it would eventually consume him too... if he got too close. He deserved more than what I could offer. Even if the idea of him being with someone else was enough to boil my blood...

I could almost feel the walls of my heart creaking shut as they moved to re-cage the bleeding mess inside me. A painful reminder that joy was not within my reach.

You will bring him nothing but death and ruin, a distant reminder sounded from within.

I stilled, swallowing around the burn in my throat. The aching hollow in my chest yawned open once more as I moved to step away from him. He let me go, his expression pained as he studied my retreat, as if he could see the wall rising between us. I couldn't grapple with the idea of him wanting anything from me. I was too broken. Too lost.

Maybe one day he would understand...

I took a step back, wrapping my arms across my chest as I

shuddered. Not from the fresh snow, but from the ice resolidifying over my heart.

"Are you all right?" he asked, remorse darkening his features.

Was I?

Was I all right?

Knowing I would have to leave *this* behind?

So, I decided to lie.

"Yes. I'm fine. Just a little freaked out." I smiled weakly, shaking my head with desperate hope that he would believe me.

He only stared, his jaw working. And whatever he was contemplating saying... I really didn't want to hear. Threading my hands through his, I gave him a slightly more reassuring grin.

"C'mon... let's get out of here."

Tonight. I would give myself one more night—to feel, to live, to enjoy the presence of another.

But, come morning, I would be gone.

CHAPTER 22
TYRAN

We continued west until Sundown, the soft snowfall transforming the forest into a silent world of white. That silence was further punctuated by the lack of conversation between Aida and me since leaving the nomad camp. In truth, I was at a loss for words entirely. Upon walking into that tent and seeing Aida's face blanched with shock, my instinct to fight off an enemy or kiss her until she smiled again had possessed me so wholly, I had barely noticed the writhing crone on the floor. Something had taken place that seemed to strike into Aida's very soul, and I yearned to be the one whom she trusted to talk about it with. But I wouldn't push it. I knew her trust would have to be earned, if she didn't disappear before that could happen...

And then she had fled into the woods like a frightened deer, terrified of what she had seen. When I managed to slow her down, I had been shocked by the way her mask had slipped, allowing her grief to shine through. I knew she had secrets and memories that haunted her, but watching her nearly collapse under that weight was almost more than I could bear. And then, when I had placed her small hand in mine, she slipped again, stepping close enough to touch me. Close enough to share my breath... and Gods, I had wanted to claim her trembling lips so badly. Had wanted to do anything that would distract her from her agony. But her defenses were made of solid iron, and she pulled away from me a minute later.

The worst part of watching it play out was the familiarity of it all.

The truth was, I knew exactly what it was like to reject anything that could weaken you—even if it could have brought you happiness. Before The General had entered my life, I was a cruel, feral, ruthless boy. Hurt had always come from every direction, so lashing out had become instinctual. For Aida, it was cold detachment.

In the hours we had spent together since that moment, her small back pressed to my center, I replayed that moment over and over.

I knew she wanted to run. I could see the nervous light in her eyes that preyed on her day and night. And I wasn't certain I could stop her.

But I wasn't sure I could let her go either...

Aida was hurting. And though I knew she would never admit it, I knew she was scared too. Just like me, her traumatic past had shaped her into someone who only knew fight or flight. And I hated that for her, even though I understood it completely. And if it hadn't been for the General who had shown me what else life could be... I likely would've never survived to adulthood.

But knowing this about her did nothing to quell my ever-growing feelings for her. In fact, the extreme opposite was happening... I wanted her to feel *everything*. With me.

Comfort. Pleasure. Safety. Happiness. I wanted to give it all to her.

As the last rays of the sun turned to twilight, we made camp against the side of a large outcrop of boulders, evidence of our climbing elevation in the direction of the Vazaketh. With the fire roaring, we wordlessly set about collecting snow to melt for drinking, setting up snares around the camp, and sharpening our weapons. After a brief trip into the surrounding wood to relieve myself, I returned to find Aida studiously carving into her new bow. Careful not to disturb her, I seated myself a few feet away to watch. With her lips set firmly and brow scrunched in concentration, she chipped, sawed, and sliced. I had become so engrossed in watching her work, I had almost forgotten to address our meal for the night. While Aida had been conversing with the strange nomad woman, I had procured some vegetables, herbs, and, to my shock, a hand-drawn map of the lesser-traversed, western sections of the Furian wood. While I was certain it was less than accurate in terms of scale, it provided a decent warning regarding deep crevasses, waterfalls, and known bear caves. Reluctantly, I stopped my staring and got to work on a hearty root vegetable stew.

"That smells divine," she said brightly an hour or so later, a warm smile on her lips. My breath caught at the sight of it.

"Who taught you how to cook so well?" she asked, before returning her focus to her carving.

"An old warrior and hunter. The man who raised me, mostly."

"Your parents?" she asked softly, eyes never looking up from her craft.

"Orphan. They died or sold me into slavery. I guess I'll never know." I shrugged, fixing my gaze on the steam rising from the pot. She went still, wincing as if troubled by my nonchalance.

"My parents are gone, too," she breathed, her grip on the bow tightening until her knuckles went white. Like dark clouds before a storm, something I thought I had forgotten began to well in the back of my mind...

Flashes of pain and heart-wrenching desperation. A small person.

Cold, shivering, and utterly alone...

Disturbed by my sudden vision and the faraway look in her eyes, I decided to change the subject.

"Who taught you how to carve like that?" I cleared my throat as I nodded in the direction of her skillful work of art. Her glazed eyes, blinking back to the now, tensed for a moment before she answered.

"I was raised with the Villdyr. It was a skill I learned from the other children," she replied, sullenly.

Ah. Well, that explained some things.

The Villdyr were the equivalent of folklore and myth; vagabond children who lived like feral wraiths, always a step ahead of any trap laid to find them. In my book, they were the bravest and most cunning souls on Astaran.

She leaned forward then, handing me her bow so I could take a closer look. I took it from her chilled fingers, gazing in fascination at the warm, honey colored wood she had adorned with intricate carvings of stars, moons, and planets. Each relief exposed the lighter wood beneath, making them stand out with stunning contrast. I gaped at her, impressed.

"This is incredible. You have a gift." I told her honestly. Her face fell, my words striking a chord, before she leaned over to take the bow from my hands.

"Thank you," she murmured, tucking her knees to her chest.

Shit.

Of course, she had a gift. The one I hadn't mustered the courage to ask about. As if it wasn't something incredibly profound. As if it weren't indeed a giant, soul-exposing beast that we were both happy to ignore in the corner of the room.

Her connection to my mind. And my connection to hers.

I could not deny that I wanted answers. But something about it didn't *feel* intrusive.

"Will you explain it to me? One day, I mean." I asked, gently. The pale blue of her eyes seemed to shrink in the firelight as her jaw set in defiance.

I swallowed. *Fuck...* too far.

"No, Tyran," she whispered, her gaze penetrating deep into the heart of the crackling fire.

"I don't even understand it myself," she admitted, her eyes meeting mine briefly. I stilled at the vulnerability I saw there and decided to take a leap...

"Did your parents know about it?" I asked, mentally preparing for her to shut me out. But surprisingly, she only shook her head, her gaze distant.

"I can't be sure. I have memories of sensing her—my mother. But they're dark and unclear..." she paused again, her eyes falling to the bow still clenched in her hands. I pushed on, intent on keeping her talking.

"And what about me? Do you remember when that started?"

Her eyes flicked up to mine, her brow lifting at my boldness. I considered shrinking beneath her stare, but I didn't. Even though I realized that she didn't owe me any answers, that didn't mean I wouldn't try to get them. She paused for a long time—long enough for me to wonder if she really didn't know, even though I certainly remembered.

"What I do know is that this connection—whatever it is—has gotten stronger over time," she said nervously. I nodded.

"And... Do you have this with anyone else?" I prodded, pressing my luck.

She bit her lip, glancing into the darkened forest around us, an indiscernible expression crossing over her features before she replied, "No" on a deep exhale.

My head went completely silent—except for the deep booming of my thunderous heart.

Only me?

I nodded as if completely unfazed at this news. But inside, I was reeling in astonishment. At this point, it became clear to me that anyone who argued that we were not somehow destined to meet... was in pure denial. Suddenly, Aida's body tensed as a distant howl ripped through the air. The hair on my neck stood straight at the sound. *Wolves.* From where she stood tied nearby, Cressida whinnied anxiously. Reaching for the dagger that The General had made for me, I searched the darkness for any hints of predators. After a long silence, I began to relax by a little. Returning my gaze to Aida's profile, I admired her from afar, pleased to find her cheekbones already less gaunt than they had been when I found her in the gorge. Noticing my stare, her eyes met mine as she breathed, "There's no point getting to know me, Tyran."

Too fucking bad, is what I wanted to say. But instead, I asked, "Why?"

Her face flushed crimson with anger. "Because...I'm... I'm..." she floundered for the words.

"What. Beautiful? Brave? Interesting?" I asked her point-blank.

Her cheeks blazed to a deeper hue. It had to be my new favorite color.

"No. I'm none of those things," she rasped in a thick voice.

Hard disagree. New mission accepted... make Aida feel as beautiful as I believed her to be.

"Yes. You are." I stated, my eyes never leaving hers.

"But you don't know me! Not really. I'm not... okay," she said, voice breaking. I clenched my hands together, fighting the urge to reach for her. Instead, I decided to pour more fuel on the fire...

"I can't help but be curious about you, Aida. If you want me to stop, then I'm afraid you'll have to adjust to the disappointment... because I want to know you better." I confessed.

She stared at me blankly as a single tear fell, her throat working. I only stared back, determined for her to see just how serious I was. I might have been raised as a feral orphan who had no allegiance to anything or anyone and liked to kill out of spite. But I was no liar. Aida's presence in my life had always been something that I had cherished. Now that I knew her in the flesh... I doubted that I could ever let her go. So what? She had some demons. Who in this *Gods-cursed* world didn't? That certainly wasn't enough to keep me from her now.

She bit her lip again, the sight doing strange things to me, before yanking her gaze from mine. As expected, I watched as she wrangled her emotions back into their icy cage, quickly swiping away any evidence of them from her cheek.

"I'm tired," was all she said before turning her back to me and lying down to sleep.

Chapter 23
Aida

Turning away from him, I pretended to sleep, ensuring he could not see the tears that streamed without end. After some time, he laid a blanket over me, making my heart ache even more. And now here we were again, in this place of the infinite, far removed from our bodies asleep by the fire on the cold forest floor. Weightless and untethered to my body in the dreamscape, yet somehow still connected to *him*.

Like stepping through a sunlit door, I crossed over the threshold of Tyran's mind.

Recoiling in horror, I stood transfixed as I watched his dream tonight. I could do nothing but stare as the slaver approached a young boy with straw colored hair, a whip gripped tightly in his meaty hand. The boy, sensing the approach, dropped his shovel and took off into a run before being caught by other men who sneered with malicious intent. The whip came down across the boy's back. Once. Twice. Three times...

I squeezed my eyes shut, nearly choking on my scream.

Stop. Please! Stop! I begged.

But no one could hear it. It had already happened. This was one of Tyran's memories.

The slavers dropped the boy into the dirt, threatening to do worse if he did not comply as they stalked off into the fields to prey on the other slaves.

A soft gasp escaped my lips as the boy struggled to right himself, blood streaming through the tattered clothes across his back. I stretched out my hand, as if I could help him somehow.

And then... I realized that I could.

Leaving him was the only way I could spare him from more pain.

I had to leave. Now. Or I may never find the strength to do it again, my own selfishness crying out to keep him.

With my mind made up, I turned my back on the boy in the dirt and climbed up his glittering, golden rope to return to my sleeping body.

Eyes snapping open, I slowly turned over to find Tyran fast asleep, his brows furrowing ever so slightly at the sickening childhood memory he was reliving deep within his subconscious. Releasing a shaky sigh, I silently collected my bow, dagger, and clothes. Careful not to make a sound, I stuffed my supplies into a pack and slowly stood over him. His hair, a few shades darker now than it had been as a boy, lay in soft waves over his brow. His full lips, the ones I often caught myself staring at, were parted slightly. If I did not possess the knowledge of the terrifying dream he was having, I would have assumed that he was dreaming of something benign. Maybe, after I was gone, we would still share dreams. As we always had.

A crack, deep and devastating, pierced me through the middle.

I must leave. I must go...

My hand flew to my mouth to stifle my sob of grief.

And with one last look at his handsome sleeping face, I slipped into the black of the night.

THE SUN WAS RISING AT MY BACK THREE HOURS LATER. AND FOR THAT entire time, I had not looked back once. Legs becoming leaden with my increasing despair, I shoved past the thoughts that threatened to cripple me. *What would he think when he awoke?*

The man who had saved my life. More than once. The only person who could potentially shoulder this weight, this curse with me. Someone who thought that *I* was beautiful.

And I left him.

I quickly rubbed away the tears that were attempting to spill over again. I had to keep moving and find peace with this, and, in time, he could too. So, I trudged on. Ears alert to the awakening sounds of the forest around me, I could hear bird song, squirrels chasing each other across the limbs high above, and the soft drip of melting snow that still clung to every tree branch.

It was just me and the forest now. It had to be...

My near suffocating intent to feel sorry for myself was cut short a moment later when a high-pitched scream shattered through the peace of the morning. No... not a scream. A cry.

Shifting my steps into a stealthier rhythm, I followed the

sound. As the cries grew louder, I became more confident of their source: a fawn. I quickened my steps, the distressing bleats triggering an unfamiliar instinct to come to its aid. Crouching low in the thicket, I pushed aside a tangle of leaves and spotted the fawn struggling to rise from the ground, its tiny leg caught in a snare wire. In the shadow of a great oak tree, it had somehow stumbled into the trap, its mother nowhere in sight. From my vantage point, I could see the fur of the leg soaked dark with blood as it thrashed and yanked hopelessly. I sighed, briefly at war with myself, I was a hunter after all. But I had personal experience with being caught like prey... and left to die.

And at this moment, I could not accept the suffering of this infant animal if I could help it.

As I moved to step away from my hiding place in the bushes, a flicker of movement in the trees caught my eye. Narrowing in on the dark canopy above the fawn, its wailing became more heart-shattering by the second. My eyes caught the movement again.

I froze instantly, my breath sucking into my chest as my body went rigid.

The tawny tail of the mountain lion, painted with a black tip, swished again. The giant cat sat directly above the fawn, its claws flexing into the bark as it waited patiently. Its yellow eyes blinked lazily as if savoring the ease of this kill. One that would not even require any energy to chase.

Fuck.

Helping the fawn had seemed simple enough, but getting between a giant predator and its meal was another thing entirely. Shaking my head as I pondered my own stupidity, I moved to nock an arrow into my bow, my eyes never leaving the big cat. With the arrow nocked and aimed skyward, I concentrated on my breath.

Inhale.

Exhale.

Inhale...

Suddenly, the cat's eyes snapped directly to mine as if I had made a sound, when I had not. Adrenaline set my heart into a gallop as I realized why: the cat had caught my scent. Slowly, it rose into a crouch, no longer idly enjoying the desperate sounds of the fawn. Now, it saw me as a challenger.

With my arrow aimed directly at its heart, my arm began to tremble as fear gripped me in a vice.

Just shoot.

Do it. Now. Don't be stupid...

But I was paralyzed.

The cat's eyes dilated as the pungent scent of my hesitation rang like a dinner bell.

Don't be weak. It's you or the cat... It's you or the...

Tears spilled as my teeth clenched, the arrow quivering as my resolve wavered. As the truth cleaved me open like an axe. I wanted the predator to live—not me.

But in the instant before my despair could turn into recklessness, the cat leaped to the ground just feet away from me and its prey. Cries now turning into panicked wails, the fawn yanked and writhed, its small body losing its balance and collapsing into the dirt over and over.

With its black tipped ears pressed back against its head, the cat flashed its razor-sharp canines at me before taking another step toward its prize.

Not again...

Black feathers stung my cheek as I released the arrow an instant before an ear-shattering roar ripped across the forest. It stumbled for a moment, teeth bared with pain, before collapsing into the brush a few feet away, the arrow protruding from the deep wound over its heart.

I stood then, knees shaking as I stepped toward the deer. Now frenzied with terror, the fawn lurched and leaped, its bleats near keening.

"Shhhh. Hey, it's okay. I'm here to help." I whispered reassuringly, tremors of adrenaline making my hands shake as I reached for its tiny leg. The wire had cinched so tightly, it had cut down to the bone. Certain I was only there to do harm, it bucked and struggled more at my approach.

"Please, hold still. I need to find a way to cut the wire." I pleaded.

The fawn's eyes widened at the sight of my dagger as I tried to wedge the blade between the wire to sever it. Suddenly, the deer went still, the white spots on its back shuddering as it fought against exhaustion. Thankful for the lack of movement, I sawed quicker, wondering how long it had been stuck here without any nourishment. But the snare was of a higher quality than I had anticipated, composed of multiple strands, and difficult to cut. It was clear that it had been intended for much larger prey. Panic started to close around my throat, my teeth grinding with frustration as my fingers sought to pull the wire wider, in the hope the leg could slip out. I ignored the bite of pain as the wire sliced into my hands. "Fuck!" I screamed, my tears of rage threatening to spill over.

I was useless. Had I almost let that cat attack me?

And now, I couldn't even save this helpless creature.

Releasing the fawn's battered leg, I rolled back onto my heels and hung my head in defeat.

I couldn't save it. I couldn't even save myself.

And maybe, I was tired of trying.

I was tired of running.

I was just... *so tired.*

Out of nowhere, a warm hand placed itself over mine and squeezed.

My head snapped up to see the storm cloud of Tyran's eyes gazing into mine, the concern and worry I saw there was enough to shatter my heart into a thousand pieces.

I gasped but could not find the will to flinch away from his touch.

He followed me. He found me... again.

And something settled deep within me nodded in acceptance, as if I already knew he would.

Inching closer, he reached up to cup my face with his other hand, stroking away a traitorous tear with his thumb.

"You can't run from me anymore, *little shadow.*" He breathed, a warm smirk playing across his lips. I gasped, the tears spilling freely against his hands.

Gods knew I didn't want to.

I cracked a small smile before throwing my arms around his neck, relishing the tight embrace around my waist as he held me.

"You can't understand the fears that plagued me when I woke to find you gone..." he murmured against my hair, breathing deep.

"I'm sorry, Tyran. I just... I didn't know how..."

"Shh. It's all right, let's discuss this later," he stated calmly, pulling away to look at my face, his fingers busy stroking back the hair around my ears. His presence lifted the burden on my heart in an instant, my despair floating away on the breeze. The exhausted bleat of the fawn sounded once more as I watched Tyran's eyes dart back and forth between it and the dead cat close by.

A heartbeat later, he was reaching into his pack to retrieve a pair of rusty medical scissors and the bottle of Akvavit, with only about two inches of the amber liquor left inside. He quickly splashed the liquid over the fawn's leg, which made her squeal even louder.

"Should give her a head start to stave off infection. I think she will be okay if she can find her mother," he said absent-mindedly, focused on the task at hand. With a snip, the wire released its coil from around the leg of the fawn. We watched with joyous relief as it bolted away. Heading south, it was out of sight a minute later. I closed my eyes briefly and smiled, welcoming the silence left in its wake.

Tyran and I enjoyed that silence together, his hand threaded through mine, intent on only looking at each other. With the sun now making its slow arc overhead, the day had turned flawless. The sky was on its way to becoming a bright, cloudless blue.

And today was the day.

The day I would allow myself to trust again.

To start anew.

CHAPTER 24
AIDA

The blood from the slain mountain lion was still warm when Tyran and I began to disassemble its body, piece by piece. The cat's fur was dense and soft, but without any way to tan the hide, it would only rot without proper treatment. Which was a damn shame. Fleetingly, the thought of staying here and building a more long-term smoking shed and cabin had occurred to me. But I couldn't deny my urge to continue west. To see what so many others would never have the chance to see or had died trying: the mysteries that lay beyond the towering Vazaketh...

"Here. This is yours." Tyran said, the mountain lion's bloody teeth cupped in his palm. I took the teeth, flashing him with a weak grin of thanks.

"I don't deserve them. Not really." I sighed, keeping my gaze averted as I rinsed the blood from my hands before stowing away the teeth in my pack.

"You shot it through the heart with an arrow," he scoffed, giving me a pointed look.

Ignoring the unfamiliar comfort of how easy it felt to tell him these things, I decided to be truthful.

"I... almost let it kill me. For a moment. I wanted it to live. Not me." I whispered, shame nearly making me choke on the words. I could sense the weight of his stare on my face, but couldn't look at him. Placing the knife on top of the cat, he paused his dismembering to come sit beside me. With the remaining water left in his canteen, he rinsed the blood off his fingers.

For a long moment, we only watched as Cressida idly nibbled at some low-hanging branches, the afternoon throwing a golden sheen over whatever snow had survived the brief warmth of the day.

Just when I was beginning to think he would let that admission slide, he spoke.

"I remember when it happened. The first time I sensed you here," he said as he gently tapped the side of his temple.

The statement struck me like a zap of lightning.

Breathe, Aida. In and out.

"What do you remember?" I asked, feeling somewhat out of body. I had never discussed the moment he was referring to with a soul. Ever. It had become a part of me that I longed to forget...

He exhaled deeply, running his hands through his long locks, obviously just as nervous to discuss the subject as I was.

"Bits and flashes for a long time. Sometimes awake... but almost always in sleep." His gray eyes warily met mine, reading my reaction. Remaining still, my breath shuddered as I waited for him to continue.

"Something shifted that night, though. Like a loose rope pulled taut. I could... *feel* you. Your pain. Your agony. I never knew anyone could ever feel as lonely as I was, until that moment."

A quaking canyon of grief threatened to swallow me whole all over again as the memory resurfaced. Like a wound being sliced open. Tyran studied me patiently, a soft frown of knowing on his face.

Gods, I knew I hadn't imagined it.

Tyran had been there.

The day I had awoken alone in a dark forest with only a small basket of food and a vague note written in my mother's script...

Be strong, my love. Your dreams will guide you.
Please stay hidden.

THERE WERE NO WORDS TO DESCRIBE MY PANIC AS I SPRINTED BACK toward our village. I had fallen, removing a chunk of flesh from my knee. But fear and desperation kept me in motion.

Tyran had been there.

When I stopped short at the edge of the forest, my eyes widened in horror as I watched my house succumb to the inferno. I waited for them—my parents. No one had even attempted to put out the fire. Not a soul. From the dark shadow of the wood, I watched until every post became a black and gray cinder. The rain had begun to pour, turning the ravaged heap into steaming ash. In my grief and rage, I had fled deep into the forest before collapsing in the hollow of a tree. Wet, cold, and sobbing. I had cried so hard I had made myself sick.

And Tyran had been there...

"I thought I had imagined it. I thought the sorrow had made me go insane." I muttered with disbelief.

I had lain there in the dark, praying I would wake up from this nightmare—and then I felt it: warm light.

Behind my eyelids, igniting my bones, cracking through the black cloud over my heart, and filling me with a golden peace. It had been... almost holy.

The feeling had rescued me at that moment. At the time, I had believed it was my mother's guidance from the afterworld. It gave me the strength I needed to rise from my hiding place the next day to search for the famed Villdyr. The ones my parents had told me stories about when they would put me to sleep...

"It was you, wasn't it?" I asked reverently, warm tears streaming as I searched Tyran's face. His jaw clenched, silver lining his eyes as he relived the memory with me. His hand reached for mine as he nodded. I took it. Grateful for his touch. Grateful for him in ways I couldn't properly express.

"Why did you run, Aida?" he asked, voice low but tight with emotion. *Damn.*

Out with it then. I was done running from him.

"I left because... because you don't know what I am. Not even *I* know what I am, or why I have this ability. Everything that comes near me withers and dies, and... I couldn't bear it if you became one of them." I confessed, averting my gaze to our joined hands that rested on my knee.

Out of the blue, Tyran's body began to shake with laughter. My head snapped up to see his head thrown back and his eyes squeezed shut, his straight teeth gleaming as he laughed. The sight of his handsome face, overcome with joy, may have distracted me if I hadn't been completely outraged at his mockery. Heat flooded my cheeks as I moved to wiggle from his grip and stalk away. He snatched me around the waist before I could rise from a sitting position; however, his face sobering a bit at the sight of my fury.

"How dare you mock me?" I spat, actively contemplating slapping him and biting his lip at the same time. He swallowed, his hands exploring my ribs as he pressed closer.

"I'm sorry. I don't mock you at all, Aida. Let me explain," he said warmly, his eyes lingering on my lips before releasing me. I waited as he cleared his throat, a brief laugh escaping through his easy grin. "I want to tell you a story, little shadow. If you'll let me."

Fuck.

That name...

I only nodded tersely, ignoring the heat that flooded between my legs at the ghost of his body around mine. Shaking my head to clear away the fog, I sat up straighter to listen. Tyran righted himself as he sighed sadly, his body strung tight.

"I was a slave my entire life. Sold from one farmer or tradesman to another. Hard labor, tending to horses, working the fields, you name it. I was a ruthless and ill-tempered boy because of it, too. Always starting fights. Always inviting punishment. Pushing too far. And finding ways to hurt people like they hurt me. Broken glass in their food. Nightshade berries in their wine..." I held my breath as his voice took on a harder edge. "The General was the only person who had ever shown me respect, care, and kindness. He taught me how to defend myself. How to be a man and not just a victim..." he paused, his eyes glancing at mine. I only waited, my heart growing softer toward this tortured soul with every movement of his lips.

"When he was ousted by the vile scab that ran the estate,

the one we both had lived and worked together on for many years, I just... couldn't stay. I wanted to do something important, like he had always told me I was capable of. I didn't know where to go, but figured the Astaran Guard would've been a good place to start." Reining in my urge to roll my eyes, I only nodded. He gave me a knowing grin. "Yes, I know. I was naïve. I had no clue what kind of despicable creatures existed within the Guard. And control it." He sighed deeply again, his face turning serious. "I left the estate the following day, making my way toward Opeth to enlist. On the road, I came across a slaver with a wagon of kids. All as young as I had once been, shackled and chained together like animals." Struck by a sickeningly familiar horror, I watched his eyes cloud over with that same rage I knew all too well. Slavery was common in this world. A detestable and dehumanizing practice that showed us all where we really belonged: crushed under the might of The Sovereign and her cruel enforcers.

"I pretended to offer gold for one of the girls..." he continued, his voice barely above a whisper.

"I watched that fat fuck lumber out of his seat, imagining the pleasure I would find in taking his life the whole time. When he realized I was not interested in buying any of the children, but only sought to liberate them, he got in a few good blows, but I won in the end. Without a single drop of remorse, I choked the life from him and set those children free. Grinning like a fool as I watched them disappear into the forest." He shifted suddenly before slowly placing both his hands on either side of my face with unbridled tenderness.

"*Don't you see?* I laughed because there is no way in *Hel* that you could ever scare me away. My entire life has been a violent race against suffering and death. And I had moments, too, where I believed I was better off... just ending it. I, too, asked myself, 'What was the fucking point of it all?' You fear losing me? No, Aida. I fear losing *you*. I have felt you here." He laid a hand across my heart, my chest heaving from his proximity. From the rawness of his words.

"And I won't let go now. There is nowhere you can go where I won't follow." He finished as his eyes lingered on my lips that were parted slightly in complete awe.

Laid bare. That's what we were to each other.

I closed the distance as his mouth crashed into mine like a battering ram, hot and insistent. His face, his scent, his tongue, his soft lips... I was consumed by it all. As if he had yearned to do it for days, his warm hands explored my neck, hair, and shoulders before making their slow descent toward my ribs. His tender kisses claimed every inch of my tattered soul.

So...this is what *desire* felt like. Incredible.

Like the breath of air that keeps you from drowning, I savored the taste of his mouth and every brush of his fingers as we kissed each other with a passion I never thought could exist. The lines of his hard body pressed into me as he wrapped me around the middle and pulled me into his lap. I yelped in surprise before melting into his touch, his shoulders rippling under the caress of my hands. I wrapped my arms around his neck and gasped when he stroked my backside. Heat and light. That's what he was. I chased it like a burning star sailing through the night, my body drawn into its orbit.

He kissed me back with all the compassion and rage he had just described. Needy. Wanting. Desperate. His mouth claimed me, his hands gently finding their way into my hair, careful of my still-healing head wound. I took his lip between my teeth and tugged, eliciting exciting groans from him. Gently, he lay me onto my back, his strong body hovering over mine on the forest floor, his hands cradling my head like a pillow. Giving him unlimited access to penetrate my mouth with his big, tender tongue, I couldn't stop myself from grinding against his hardness, my hips moving without my consent. Not that I gave a fuck.

Gods be damned, his cock had to be huge...

A second later, a gurgling growl erupted from my stomach.

Tyran brushed his lips over mine once before grinning against my mouth. "Hungry?" he asked, playfully. *Ravenous*, if I was telling the truth. In more ways than one.

I clung to him tightly, with no desire to break our contact. He chuckled before placing another soft kiss on my lips, a promise of continued revelry. "I don't want to stop either, but I also skipped breakfast to hunt you down this morning, so…" I pulled away to search his face, his grin going lazy as he looked at me with a potent mix of awe and want. Like I was something to be protected and cared for. Something warm and wet pulsed through me at the sight of it. But cold and emptiness assaulted me a moment later when he lifted himself off my body and pulled me upright. He brushed the leaves from my hair, lingering over the dark waves that fell over my collarbone.

"This. This is all I want. If you'll let me in," he said gently, his fingers lightly drifting across my neck, before laying his hand to rest over my heart. I inhaled deeply, stupefied by the joy that threatened to swallow me whole.

"It's always been yours, I think."

Even when I didn't know it.

Even when I couldn't fathom opening myself up to care about anyone else again.

With a grounding sense of conviction, I placed my hand over his.

CHAPTER 25
RAVN

I had been dreaming of green things again.

Flowers swaying in a bright clearing.

The wind rushing through a lofty canopy of trees.

A soft female hand reaching into the dirt to pull up plants in a garden...

Then lightning struck.

Launching awake, I gripped the sides of my skull to keep its contents from spilling onto the floor, the migraine chopping away like an axe. Throwing my body out of bed, I stumbled across the room to the water pitcher and chugged desperately. Dribbles of water streamed down my chin and bare chest. With painful slowness, the intensity of the throbbing assault began to lessen. Squeezing my eyes shut and biting my lip, I inhaled and exhaled deeply, biding my time until the storm had passed. These savage attacks had been happening for weeks now and recently had been ratcheting up in intensity. And they always happened at night, just after the dreams of peaceful, green things had begun. It was starting to feel as though some greater force was meant to punish me for even the faintest of thoughts—dreams, even—of a life outside the one I was destined to follow.

The path chosen for me. A path of bloodshed and servitude.

When the migraine had subsided to a low, aching pulse, I cracked open an eye. Then two. Hands gripping tight on either side of the small vanity table I used for shaving, I lifted my head and looked into the mirror. Long gone was the dark-haired boy who used to vomit in a broom closet before he was led away to train with the other Anakaii warriors. A man stared back at me now, his face bleak and haunted. Years of the fiercest training with the cruelest men in the world had indeed transformed me body and soul. While The Sovereign abhorred facial hair, she had allowed us to maintain longer tresses, if we wished. My thick hair was almost to my shoulders now, and black as a crow's feathers. The soft, boyish features had been replaced with sharp, straight angles that cast dark shadows over hazel eyes, more green than brown. My skin, now deep bronze, thanks to many years of training in the courtyard under the bright Astaran sun, was strung tight over my hard-earned muscular form. I had always been taller than the others I was raised with, too; we were the next generation of male warriors, destined to be hand-selected by The Sovereign herself.

To be chosen as an Anakaii warrior was not just an occupation; it was a birthright.

Like my father and his father before him, going back five generations.

Two months from now, on the morning of my nineteenth year around the sun, I would swear my undying fealty to our ruler and be sworn in as a new member of her ruthless, personal guard. I had trained my whole life for this moment. Every scar and wound had been for this. I had never known any life outside of this stronghold, buried deep in the center of Opeth city. Taken from my mother so young that I could not even recall her face. It was as if she had never existed.

The thought sent a numbing cold crawling down my spine before I shook my head and shoved it away. These thoughts would not serve me here. Only the most cruel and brutal men were selected to join the ranks of the Anakaii. Compassion was never tolerated, and The Sovereign had a special talent for sniffing it out. If anyone were deemed unfit to serve as an Anakaii, a swift execution would be the best thing that could happen to you.

Gods be thanked that no one had witnessed my critical lapse of judgment with the old woman I had been tasked to kill. A moment that I couldn't shake loose, like a shard of glass under the skin. Countless times, I had wondered if she had placed me under a spell with a form of old magic long since banned by The Sovereign. A kind of lost soul alchemy. Abilities only vaguely discussed in the rare book collections held here in the palace. The only surviving archives that told of the world that existed before The Sovereigns' arrival.

Yes, a spell. That's what it was. Only a brief dissolution of my hard-earned, pitch-black soul.

Sighing deeply, I turned toward the window on the far side of the room and walked over to sit on the stone sill. The sun was beginning its slow ascent over the eastern horizon behind the palace, casting its light over the city. Toward the green, rolling hills beyond. For a moment, I yearned for the vision of an eagle. I wished to see that dense wall of green that marked the start of the Furian Wood for myself. So many miles away from here.

Foolish.

I highly doubted any of the chosen warriors in this palace had such selfish desires. Upon swearing our oath to The Sovereign and drinking her blood, we would also swear to abandon any life outside of the Anakaii; to be celibate and marriage-less until our dying day. Unless we were selected to breed the next generation of warriors, of course. As our fathers had been. Our whole lives and futures would belong to The Sovereign once this sacred ritual took place.

It was... the highest honor.

The idea of women seemed abstract anyway. From an early age, we had been taught that women were only creatures for breeding and distraction. They held little significance compared to the might and cunning of men. The only women I had ever encountered beyond the criminal trials were the wives of the few men who held a place in the Sovereign's court, chosen by Chemosh to function as her governors, tax collectors, and regional commanders of the Astaran Guard. Under penalty of death or exile, the women were required to be covered in head-to-toe garbs of black. Their faces shrouded and veiled.

Only by overhearing the whispers of a few Guards did I even become aware that amorous affection even existed. Some of the men had spoken of beautiful women who charmed them into their beds as if under some spell. But I would never discover this for myself. My destiny was a life of obedience to only The Sovereign.

A quick rap on the door pulled me from my contemplation.

"Wake up, Ravn. The Sovereign has summoned you," said a

raspy male voice. The Captain of the Anakaii, Tylor. A gruff and blunt bastard, but decent enough.

Ignoring the nausea trying to rise into my throat, I quickly walked over to the door and opened it. Leaning against the frame stood the captain, a mid-sixties male with silver hair and dark eyes. His gaze was uninterested as he beheld me, clad in only pants.

"Get dressed," he demanded, folding his arms impatiently. Moving quickly, I tugged on our standard black leather training armor. Fitted with various plates, it covered my body like a second skin. With one last glance into the mirror, I sheathed my monstrous, double-bladed sword on my back and strode into the hall. Tylor, while a large man over six feet tall, was almost a head shorter than I was. He gave me a cursory once-over, seemed to determine that I was decent enough, and gestured for me to follow him to the throne room. The wide, arched halls were still mostly dark and quiet at this hour. The hiss of the fire in their sconces was the only sound as we passed. The palace was an enormous, sprawling labyrinth of stone that bore almost no decoration or adornment... save for the room which held the seat of Astaran's power. Before pushing open the gigantic, onyx doors that led to the throne room, Tylor briefly turned toward me, whispering low, "Mind what you say in there, boy. You are not a chosen Anakaii... *yet*."

I swallowed, took in a deep breath, and pushed open the doors.

There was no grander or more magnificent space in the whole of Astaran.

Heart hammering and footsteps light, I cautiously entered the glorious rotunda and stood in the center. The throne room was a mosaic of golden, glittering refraction. It was what I imagined it would be like to step into the heart of the God realm. The rising sun that streamed through the towering windows on the eastern side of the room lit up the space with golden fire. The walls encircling the room were adorned with gigantic, golden mirrors, each frame composed of gold-plated climbing vines which continued up until meeting at the ceiling, where they dropped into a diamond chandelier the size of a boulder. It looked like the crystalline core of a golden star.

And at the back of the room, glowing in the rays of warm sunlight, sat The Sovereign atop her white, opal throne. The opal dais was massive; its surface bright with flecks and streaks of green, orange, and blue that made the throne appear alive with prismatic energy. As always, she was adorned in her standard uniform of golden armor with its flowing, silken train and a sparkling crown of blood-red rubies resting atop her ink-black hair. She was the most fearsome and intimidating creature *anyone* had ever seen. Every movement exuded lethal grace as she spun her gigantic sword by the hilt, the tip twirling on the opal near her feet. I sketched into a bow and dropped to one knee. "Glory to The Sovereign." My eyes remained trained on the pale marble floor until she spoke.

"I have need of you, Ravn." Her voice was both an ancient wickedness and a sultry purr. The hair on the back of my neck rose, and my skin pebbled with gooseflesh at the power in it. I looked up then, fixing my face into a fearless expression before replying, "Your desire is mine, Sovereign." Her blazing, orange eyes roved over my form, assessing. With my chin up and shoulders straight, I did my best not to fidget under her stare.

"The time for your oath draws near. Have you any *wants* you wish to fulfill before swearing your allegiance? Time with a woman, perhaps?" she drawled, lips curling into a wicked smile.

This was a test.

"No, Sovereign. To serve you is my greatest desire." I said, firmly.

She lifted a large, graceful hand to errantly toy with a strand of her dark hair.

"What a pity. You are one of the finer males of your generation... A *'real catch'* as they say."

I kept my expression blank, even though my head was swimming with confusion.

Why was she telling me this?

"It's for the best, though..." she continued, "Outside this city, the commoners are rats compared to us. They are not worthy of your time, or your *seed*... and since no whore could ever fulfill your life as I have, you should consider yourself *blessed* to be in my service."

Though shocked at the direction of this conversation, I kept it hidden as I bowed again.

"Yes, Sovereign." I agreed. After a long moment of study, her expression grew bored. Dismissive.

"You are to tend to the maidens in the dungeons until it is time for their Offering Day. One of the other Guards has... fallen ill," she said with disgust, obviously annoyed by our mortal weakness.

No one had ever seen The Sovereign under any kind of affliction. She was centuries old or more and showed no signs of ailment or age. We all just assumed she had never been sick in her long life. And would seemingly live forever... Briefly distracted by that thought, I quickly returned my attention to the command she had given. "What is to be done for the maidens, Sovereign?" I asked.

I knew that the young females destined for the sacred Offering were kept in this palace, but had no clue about the lives they lived. Her head tilted by a fraction as she fixed me with a predatory gaze.

"They are to be given only one meal and one glass of water each day. They may use buckets of cold water to bathe and will not be given new clothes until their Offering Day," she replied, face cold and unyielding.

Icy horror wrapped around my stomach. Not even animals were treated this badly. Though I had experienced countless lessons in brutality in my years of training with the Anakaii, my tolerance for such abuse was to be expected. But for a young woman who did not possess that kind of learned fortitude, it was surely torture.

I only nodded and hardened my features obediently. She leaned toward me then, her teeth glinting with feral delight.

"And if anyone touches them... they will first lose their hands...

and then they will lose their cocks."

CHAPTER 26
RAVN

"Yes, Sovereign," I replied, bowing deeply and doing my best to appear unfazed. A bored wave of her fingers was my sign of dismissal. Once on the other side of the doors, I released a shuddering breath. The sun had crept up enough to glow through the eastern-facing windows in the hallway, which told me that our training routine would not begin for another hour. Moving with purpose, I found myself in the dining hall a few minutes later. Thankfully, only one other Guard was here, quietly drinking his ration of hot broth from a steaming mug. Oblivious to my presence. As quietly as possible, I plucked a various assortment of fruits and bread slices from the nearest table, wrapped them in a small towel, and slipped out. Though I knew the direction to the dungeons,

I had never been there myself. Even as a boy, I never had the desire to explore the dark underbelly of this keep, happy to remain in ignorance. Upon turning a corner, I slammed to a stop before almost colliding with the man who had just escorted me to meet with The Sovereign, Tylor.

"Where the fuck are you going in such a hurry?" he grumbled, pinning me with a glare.

Bringing myself to my full height, I replied, "The Sovereign has tasked me with tending to the maidens, captain."

His eyebrows shot to his hairline, a look of amusement lighting up his features.

"Did she now? Our empress is up to some games, I see," he implied impishly. Strangely, he looked me over a second time as if he noticed something new about me in the past thirty seconds. I remained silent, my face a hardened mask of calm.

"Well, I'll let you get to *that*, then," he said ominously, as if something about it was somehow taboo. "But don't forget that you and Akton are standing watch in the courtyard today," he said with a brief glance out the window, assessing the time by the light in the sky. "We have dignitaries from our northern region who were invited to the palace. The two of you will escort them to The Sovereign," he finished as he stepped around me and continued down the hall. Once his footsteps were out of range, I continued toward the end of the corridor, a headache threatening to ignite inside my brain...

Upon descending the ancient, stone stairwell on the south wing of the palace, however, a rancid stench blasted into my face like a battering ram. Instantly, I knew where it was coming from.

Teeth grinding with disdain, I continued my descent into a dim hallway that reeked of putrid rot. With no choice but to continue through this corridor, I held my breath as I crossed in front of the only door standing ajar. Creeping on silent feet, I was in the middle of sending up a prayer to the Gods that the vile creature who lived and worked in that room would not notice me...when the door swung open.

Shit.

The man who stood in the doorframe was more corpse than human. His dark blue robes swallowed his frail, scrawny frame, a necklace of bleached sparrow skulls crowning the saggy, sallow skin around his neck.

"Well, isn't this a pleasant surprise?" he smirked as he looked me up and down like dessert.

I could almost see the fork tongue that flitted through his teeth. Accepting my fate but not deigning to hide my displeasure, I replied, "Isn't it a bit early to be torturing young men, Raziel?" His black eyes glinted deviously as his lips pulled back over decaying teeth.

"You're wrong, boy. There is never a bad time for that," he sneered, his grin making my insides go sour. Swallowing my disgust, I glanced into the room behind him. The dim laboratory was filled to the brim with a plethora of bubbling pots, glass bottles filled with steaming liquid, and various plants that grew from pots and hung from lines across the ceiling. There was a cacophony of animals rattling and pacing in their cages, their yips and howls of terror adding to the cloud of wickedness that hung over the room. I grimaced, the smell coming from the room enough to sear the hair in your nose.

Raziel was bound to The Sovereign and had been her chief alchemist for many decades. He was responsible for the various drugs and tinctures the Astaran Guards used to "take the edge off" or, more often, increase their lethality. One of them was Moondust...

Over the years, I had witnessed many of the Anakaii ingest the white, glittering powder before training, enhancing their strength and ferocity. Warriors had been killed by their own comrades during such episodes. I had always thought it was detestable waste since many of the Guards would eventually succumb to the drug entirely, becoming dependent on it just to function. And The Sovereign never seemed to care about what we did to ourselves anyway, as long as enough of us remained to follow her orders. And *this* sickly serpent was to blame...

"I see you carry food for the maidens..." his beady eyes roved over the tightly bound parcel gripped tightly in my arms. A look of perverted mischief crossed over his features, making his lip curl over decaying teeth.

"Be sure not to linger. Their siren song may suck you into the trap between their legs," he cackled with fiendish glee, his stringy, black beard bouncing with the movement before slamming the door shut.

Gods, I hated that motherfucker.

Shoving aside my contempt, I blew out my breath and nearly ran toward the end of the hall. Dangling from a nail driven into the stone, I spied the large iron key that unlocked the door at the end of the corridor. Eager to be far away from Raziel's foulness, I quickly inserted the key and turned, heaving my weight against the door. Slowly, it groaned open into another dank stairwell. Grabbing the torch from the nearest sconce, I descended into pitch blackness. Despite the growing warmth of the coming spring outside, it was cold as ice down here. The stairwell had to be at least a hundred steps, and it seemed to corkscrew into the very heart of the world. No windows. No light of any kind. My heart raced with anguish at the thought of being kept prisoner in such a place. Once at the bottom of the stairwell, I lifted the torch to assess the layout. Rats scampered away from the light, disappearing through cracks in the walls. The room was not large and contained cells on either side, each wrapped with vertical iron bars that ran from floor to ceiling, save for a small gate. I began to cast the torch glow through each cell. In the cell closet to the stairs, a skeleton had been left on the floor, no one bothering to remove it.

Had she been a maiden, too?

Had she found a way to end her suffering before becoming a public spectacle?

And since when did I even care? Hel, just weeks ago I would've turned a blind eye to anyone's pain if only to please my master...

A light cough sounded from the other side of the room.

Upon reaching the cell at the end of the corridor, I extended the torchlight into the dark, cramped space...

And the breath froze in my lungs at what I saw.

Three girls.

Two of them, much younger than the other, both no older than thirteen, lay curled together on the bare stone floor. All three of them were awake and staring, eyes hollow and glazed. They stared at me as if they had little energy to do anything else. Like the very idea of moving or defending themselves was too exhausting to contemplate. Fixing the torch to the nearest sconce on the wall, I knelt and began to open the parcel of food. They only stared, shadows flickering across their gaunt faces. Afraid the rats would swarm if I laid the food on the ground, I merely kept my hand outstretched and wordlessly gestured for one of them to grab it.

None of them moved. Heaving an exasperated sigh, I changed tactics.

"My name is Ravn. I've been tasked with tending to you. Please eat." The older female started at that and slowly began to lift herself from the floor. Once upright, she swayed before catching herself against the wall. Gods, she was so weak and thin. As she shuffled toward the bars of the cell, the glow of the torchlight danced across her features. She was tall, statuesque even. She wore the standard white velvet for the maidens, but the hem was dirty and frayed. In fact, the whole thing was streaked with grime. Her head lifted by a fraction as she approached, and my thoughts went blank as I took in the details of her face.

Although drawn with near-starvation, her face was undeniably beautiful. Her eyes were a deep green, like clover, and red-rimmed with weariness. A spatter of freckles adorned the pale skin of her nose and cheeks. Her bright copper hair, stringy and unwashed, hung past her shoulders, a stark contrast against the white velvet robe.

"You don't speak like an Anakaii," she rasped, voice dripping with spite.

"Because I'm not. Yet." I replied.

Tentatively, she reached through the bars and took the food from my hand.

"Why would any man elect to participate in such cruelty?" she said, eyes burning with hatred.

The truth was easy enough...

"I have no choice in the matter. It's who I was born to be." I answered firmly, ignoring the itch of doubt I could feel worming its way through my skull. Her gaze penetrated me through the bars. With effort, I suppressed the urge to squirm under it. After a few heartbeats, something like...*pity* shadowed her features before she turned away to sit against the wall. Now further unsettled, I averted my gaze toward the younger girls who were raising themselves into a sitting position. Each of them sent cautious glances my way, but were otherwise silent. The older female began to divide the food into three parts before handing the portions to the girls. Silently, I cursed myself for not bringing more food. Spying a bucket in the corner, I quickly ladled water into three cups and placed them gently onto the floor on the other side of the bars. I watched in silence as they ate without savoring a single bite. Chewing and swallowing as if it were their duty. It occurred to me then just how hopeless they were. Not surprising, considering their fate was essentially sealed. What surprised me the most, however, was my visceral aversion to the guilt that twisted my stomach...

"What are your names?" I blurted, trying to distract myself from their despair. The copper-haired female, still young, was likely no older than her early twenties. Her gaze lifted to mine, confusion furrowing her brow, but after a moment, she gestured to the young girls beside her.

"This is Kalan... and her twin, Masha." Both girls were tawny-skinned and black haired, like me. Their eyes were dark pools of wariness and fear... they could've been my little sisters...

"My name is Helena," she finished.

Somewhere deep inside, the name plucked a chord, the sound ringing through me with soft vibration.

"It's uh...nice to meet you," I said, sheepishly, averting my gaze to the filth-coated floor.

Soon, I would need to return to the palace and be in formation as tardiness would demand lashings. Helena's eyes left mine to stare at the wall, hollowness returning to drain away any comfort the meal briefly provided.

I had never seen anyone this vulnerable and despairing. It was devastating.

Surely, the Gods preferred their "gifts" to be treated better than this?

And what if they didn't?

What if they were just as cruel and unfeeling as The Sovereign?

What did that make us to them? No more than an insect under foot...

Unable to stomach these thoughts any longer, I swiftly rose to stand and reached for the torch.

But then I hesitated... slowly pulling back my hand. With one last glance at the girls, I strode into the dark pit of the stairwell.

At least they would have some light for a little longer.

CHAPTER 27
RAVN

When I emerged from the dank gloom of the dungeon chambers, I pulled in a breath and placed my hand on the wall for balance. Something akin to panic was making my heart fly as I contemplated how surreal everything had suddenly become— the empathy I felt. The grief and the guilt. All these feelings I had never been allowed to experience were assaulting me. Changing me. It felt like being reborn. *I had to help them... somehow,* I thought. But how the *fuck* was I going to do that? The idea alone would've been enough to get me killed.

Jerking upright, I began to walk toward the direction of the courtyard. I couldn't risk anyone seeing me in this state.

I found Akton standing alone in the courtyard, which had

been cleared of any remaining Anakaii cadets. We stood here in formation every morning to learn of our lessons and duties for the day before dispersing to attend to them in various places throughout the palace. Squinting into the sunlight that was beaming into the exposed, rectangular courtyard, I moved to stand beside him in front of the iron gate that connected the palace to the sprawling city beyond. The morning was cold, but not intolerable, and the fact that I was standing watch with Akton made it even more pleasant. I cleared my throat as I approached him. He glanced at me from over his shoulder, smirking at my tardiness.

"Only you would get away with sleeping in for your watch," he grinned.

"I wish. I was summoned by The Sovereign before sunrise," I replied, my eyes forward as the iron gate began to creak open for the group of dignitaries whom we had been tasked to escort today. From what I could see from here, it only appeared to be a group of five men, all cloistered together and talking amongst themselves as they waited for the gate to rise.

"A special mission?" he asked quietly. I kept my face blank as I nodded.

Something like that, I thought.

The men, all similarly dressed in a set of black waist coats and trousers, entered the courtyard and walked in our direction. Akton, ever the socialite, waved and greeted them all with a firm handshake before asking them to follow him into the palace to find their quarters. I remained in place, ensuring the gate had shut all the way before following. But when I turned around to join them, I was startled to find one of the men still standing in the courtyard and staring at me.

He stood only a few inches shorter than I, his black eyes roving over me in quiet contemplation. And when his gaze met mine... visceral shock made my heart skip a beat.

He watched as the realization spread over my expression, erasing my stoic posture for a brief second as I fought to collect myself. The man grinned, enjoying the way he could instill fear in me.

"*Father.*" I breathed.

He nodded in appreciation as he took me in. I rose to my full height, a wall of adamant slamming down around my emotions as I squared my shoulders.

"You've grown," he said in a voice that set my teeth on edge. I wanted to scoff, but managed to rein it in. *No shit, you haven't seen me in nine years.* I thought, coldly. Not a single visit. Not a solitary letter. Nothing. But this, of course, was completely normal. When a retired Anakaii was chosen to breed the next generation of cadets, it was customary to be raised by that warrior until we were brought to the palace at the age of ten, and given to The Sovereign. Part of me wanted to accept that my father had no choice but to give me up—but another part knew differently. I knew his brutality. I knew his cunning. And I knew how glad he likely had been to be rid of me...

I remained silent, not allowing a single crack to show through my mask of indifference. The dark, russet skin of his face crinkled from behind his pitch-black beard as he grinned with pride. I hated the way it made my stomach turn inside out.

"So, she's managed to turn you into a fine-tuned machine after all. I wasn't certain you had it in you... considering how weak you were as a boy," he muttered, studying me for any break in my composure. I gave him nothing, my lips upturned with a smirk. A thrill shot through as I detected a tiny sliver of disappointment cross over his features. *It'll take more than that to bait me, motherfucker.* He stiffened in response to my steely gaze, averting his eyes skyward to the looming, stone spires on the roof of the palace whose shadows were beginning to creep further away from where we stood.

"So, we're going to play *this* game? Well, I—"

"State your purpose here, *Iderius*." I barked, cutting him off. I was sick of his presence taking up my space and was done with the small talk. His face settled into that hateful glare that I remembered so well as he replied, "It's classified, *cadet*."

"Then you best be about your business," I stated curtly, jerking my chin toward the steps that led into the palace. He scoffed at my boldness before nodding to himself. His eyes drifted to mine again as he stepped closer. I went still, my hands clenched into a fist at my side.

"I'll do that... but first, don't you want to know how your mother is faring?" he asked in mock sympathy. I blinked, taken aback as my insides coiled into a knot. A devious grin pulled his lips higher.

"Ah. I thought so. I knew you never changed. You might wear that costume, Ravn..." he whispered as his eyes roved over my frame. "But you'll never be as cold-blooded as The Sovereign demands. And one day... it'll come back around for you."

I wanted to split his skull open *right here* on the stone floor and watch his brains slide from his ears into a gory puddle. I stepped closer, my nose almost touching his.

"What did you do to her?" I seethed, my vision going red as the blurry memories of my mother began to pepper my mind. She had been fair in every way that my father was dark. With bright, hazel eyes and long, blonde hair, she was the kindest soul I'd ever known. Though my time with her had ended when I was only three, she had left a mark on me that could never fade.

Satisfied that he had finally found the right button to push, he smirked and shook his head, disappointed in me for an entirely different reason.

"We tried to have another son... but were *cursed* with a daughter. I had arranged for the sale of the child to take place soon after she had given birth... but found them both gone the next day," he replied with icy casualness as he stepped away from me toward the palace doors. I could only stare after him, frozen, as he glanced at me once more from over his shoulder and said, "It's for the best, I think. Your mother was a pathetic *witch* anyway."

CHAPTER 28
AIDA

As usual, I was aware that I was in the dreamscape. There was no other place where oblivion beckoned, and I followed willingly, like a layer pulled back from the world. One that only I had the ability to navigate.

And, like usual, I hated this dream.

Though I never had the choice of which dream I started with, over time, I had mastered the ability to move to another. Or someone else's.

But I never allowed myself to leave *this* dream.

It was part of my penance.

To look away was to forgive myself... and that I could not do.

So, I watched this same vision from the past, buried deep within, for the millionth time...

The young girl before me had fierce, wild eyes. Bright blue. The contrast between her dirty, pale skin and dark, untamed hair was striking. Her nose was bloody, her teeth bared in savage determination as she blocked blow after blow from the equally filthy boy who had her pinned to the ground.

August...

Another Villdyr child stepped into the fray then, breaking up the fight. Fighting amongst the Villdyr had always been the default way to resolve a grievance. When you combine young tempers and desperation, sparks are bound to fly. Whether it was a spat over food, clothes, or defending a friend or sibling, it was almost always settled with fists.

I kept watching, knowing full well what came next, my shoulders bowing with shame...

August was pulled off my twelve-year-old self, spitting and kicking as he went. He had been almost sixteen at the time and likely restless at his pending expulsion from the group. He had attacked me that day, accusing me of stealing his shoes. It had been a false accusation that time, but when he struck, I had held my ground. The fight was short but had left us both bloody and heaving. Others in the group had redirected us away from each other to cool our blood.

But I couldn't shake it. My rage and spite pooled in my mouth like venom.

I closed my eyes that night with intention. I wanted to *hurt* him.

Fueled by my desire for retribution, my ability had evolved that night. It was the first time that I forced myself to take a leap beyond my own subconscious and enter that of another...

Like throwing a hammer into a pane of glass, I broke

through the fog of the dreamscape to find a vast array of glimmering, strobing pulses that flashed brightly all around me, some more muted and distant than others. Even as a child, I knew what they were. And in that moment, I came to understand true power. And just like anyone who was too naïve and ignorant to carry such a burden, I abused it wholly...

Drunk on my newly discovered ability, I located the sleeping vibrations of the other Villdyr. As their young bodies slumbered next to mine, the darkened mist of my star-flecked form drifted into their minds one by one, until I had found my target. Giddy with power, I felt invincible.

August's deep, rust-colored tether was thick and spiny as I gathered it into my hand. Following the pull of his vibration, I let it drag me inside until I found myself standing in his dream. Somewhere on the shore of a misty lake, he had been skipping rocks next to an older man. His father, if I had to guess.

Please, Aida. Don't do this. I begged my younger self. But nothing could stop what had already taken place...

With his back turned to me, I crept toward him on silent feet until I stood directly behind him.

Vengeance and humiliation had been my only goal. But I was a child and a fool...

"August. Do you long to swim? Find me a rock at the bottom of the river. Don't return without it." I whispered into his ear, grinning like a cat. I left his dream as quickly as I came and returned to my body, in complete awe of how my power had developed and what new opportunities it could bring me...

I awoke to a deep, gray sky the next morning. It was cold to the point of pain, the chill deep enough to make your bones feel brittle. A chorus of shrieks coming from the direction of the river had thrown me into full alertness. I watched as the young girl in this story, me, ran toward the edge of the ravine. Horror had seized me by the throat at what I had beheld there.

Helpless, we all watched as he leapt into the raging rapids below.

"He can't swim!" The others had shouted, but it was too late. Stunned into silence, we watched a single hand break the surface of the water as it moved downstream. Only to be sucked under... and never resurface. Shock crept over my young face before I collapsed to my knees and vomited.

It was me. I had killed him.

But it was what I wanted. Wasn't it?...

His warm presence alerted me to his arrival before his voice did.

"Who is that?" Tyran murmured cautiously.

And for some reason, I was comfortable with him here. Witnessing this. After all, he had exposed his darkness to me.

Tyran's warm, glowing form stepped up beside me as he gazed at my most formative memory. "A Villdyr boy named August," I replied.

"And who's the girl...?" he asked again, voice tinged with sorrow.

"That's me. Age twelve... I killed him. I didn't mean to... but I did. I wanted him dead. But I didn't mean it, not really." I stammered over the lump in my throat.

Grief and self-hatred yawned into a dark hole beneath my feet. The vision vanished, and we stood once again in the glass room of Tyran's dreamscape, darkness on all sides. Suspended in space...

Tyran turned to face me then but stayed silent, allowing me to explain.

Heaving a sigh, I struggled to find the words. "At the time, I didn't know how any of it worked. And for the most part, I still don't. That night, I discovered I could inject myself into another's dream. All it took was a suggestion..." I breathed, ashamed of how easy it had been.

"I willed him to jump into the river. I only wanted to hurt him. I had no idea he couldn't swim."

Tyran's eyes widened in shock at my revelation, but he kept quiet. Contemplating.

"I've had the 'gift' for as long as I can remember, always in tune with the subconscious of others. Especially yours, for whatever reason..." I continued, my eyes fixed on the buttery light that exuded from his form.

"But that was the first time I realized I could access it. The first time I had bent another to my will. And the only time. Ever since, I've been running from it. Never daring to use it."

Pausing for a moment, I gave my aching heart the chance to slow.

"Every time I dream, for nearly ten years now, I enter the dreams of those I've met, even if I don't know them well. Sometimes, all it takes is a brief meeting of our eyes. In their dreams, I can see their innermost desires... and their darkest nightmares. And if I think hard enough, focusing all my intention on a command, the next day they will wake up and do it. Whatever I ask. It's horrible... it's..." I began to choke as sobs ripped through my throat.

Gods, I was a monster. I buried my face in my hands, expecting his revulsion and fear.

Tyran only watched me, eyes wide and brows furrowed in deep thought.

It felt like a lifetime had passed before he slowly reached out for me, taking my hand in his. With a gentle touch, he stroked his thumb lightly across the back of my hand. I stared at our joined hands in disbelief before raising my face to look at him. Stunning, blue-gray eyes stared back at me. His face was serious but kind as his other hand made the slow ascent upwards. I fought to keep my eyes from fluttering closed at his touch as his glowing fingers tenderly grazed my jaw. He cupped my cheek in his hand, his warmth seeping into my bones and turning my insides liquid. He spoke into my raw, vulnerable soul then. And with one sentence, gave me all that I had ever yearned to hear...

"You don't frighten me, Aida. I don't care about your Gods-given gift... I just want *you*."

CHAPTER 29
AIDA

He now knew my darkest secret.

It was the one piece of my soul that I had never expected to share with anyone. And he didn't seem to care. It was... *freedom*. And somewhere deep in my chest, awe, and something else like...*hope*...dared to grip me. It was an unfamiliar feeling, and I didn't quite understand how to deal with it.

The snap of a twig underfoot sounded his arrival from the direction of the snares we had laid the day before. After killing the mountain lion and saving the fawn, we had made camp underneath the sprawling arms of an ancient oak, its thick canopy acting as a roof to keep out the light drifts of snow. As he came into view, I noticed that the snares had been successful. Two skinned rabbits and a squirrel dangled from one hand, with a small, cloth sack carried from the other. His eyes met mine as a shy smile bloomed over his features, dimpling his cheek.

"We have breakfast," he said cheerily.

I couldn't help my blush as he strode into the campsite and seated himself between me and the fire. I watched him make quick work of the fresh game, slicing apart the meat to cook on a hot stone nestled close to the flames. We both waited, in somewhat awkward silence, for breakfast to cook thoroughly. I assumed that sitting near the fire must've been too hot as he began to remove his shirt, but he cleared the air a moment later.

"This shirt now reeks of rabbit entrails... Did you sleep well?" he asked as he rose from his spot near the fire and walked over to his supply pack still hanging from Cressida, for a new shirt, no doubt. The question sailed over my head like a kite as I stared, dumbstruck by the sight of his body. Though pale from being hidden during the winter, his olive skin told the story of countless days working in the hot sun. Stripes of pale-white scars zig-zagged across his back and lean torso. His shoulders bulged and rippled with every movement as he pulled the new shirt over his head.

Damn me to Hel... he was beautiful.

Blinking quickly to clear my thoughts, something else caught my eye. In the quick moment before he could pull the shirt over his head, I spied a deep scar over his right arm that formed an almost perfect band around his elbow. The dark, purple hue indicated it had been severe enough to nearly sever his arm completely. Hearing my sharp inhale, he turned to face me, confusion muddying his expression.

"Your scar...it must've been very serious," I said, nervously.

The question in that statement hung over the air like a mist.

He glanced down at his feet once before nodding gravely and walking over to sit beside me. I gave him space to choose whether he wished to explain, and waited in silence, as he had done for me. After a few moments, he spoke, his voice grave and haunted.

"I experienced nearly all forms of abuse during my time as a slave, Aida."

Deep sorrow crept over me as I listened, my stomach going leaden.

He paused to glance at his feet, the trauma of the story seemingly more graphic than he wanted to reveal. As if it were beyond my ability to control, my hand reached to curl around his. A light shudder ran through him at the touch as he looked back at me, his stormy eyes churning with emotion. I only nodded with a tight smile, offering my support. He entwined his fingers through mine and continued.

"I was only ten years old. I had stolen food from the kitchen that morning, not only for myself but to give to the horses. I guess I thought they looked too thin... But I was caught by the foreman of the estate. He was a skinny, serpent of a man, who frequently took advantage of the servants and slaves who answered to him. He told me that he would remove my arm at the elbow to teach me a lesson so I would never steal from the nobleman's house again."

I inhaled deeply through my nose as my stomach flipped inside out with rage. Just another hungry boy... to be mutilated like chattel.

"Before the blade could sever my arm completely... A man rushed over and barreled into the foreman, knocking him to the ground. I had seen the man around the estate in the days prior and was vaguely aware that he was the new farrier, hired to tend to the hoof needs of the horses. I watched him take a red-hot brand and hover it just inches from the foreman's face. He told him that in exchange for his mercy, he would be granted responsibility for me and demanded that no further harm come to me. So... the foreman left without another word, and the farrier stitched up my arm and kept me hidden in the stables while I healed. I came to know him only as "The General." His eyes lit up in the memory, and I couldn't keep back the tears now lining my eyes as gratitude for that man's actions struck me like a thunderclap.

I had no doubt that Tyran was feeling the same way as he said, voice thick, "He was very important to me. For many years, he was not just a friend... but a father. He taught me everything I know about how to stay alive, about how to fight. He was good when so many others were cruel. He taught me the importance of bravery and resilience, being a force of good in the world, no matter how sinister it became."

Tears streamed down my cheeks, my chest squeezing with recognition of the feeling. Noting my silent sobs, Tyran turned to look at me and did a double take, his eyes widening. He raised his hand, stroking away a tear with his thumb, his warm fingers gently curling into my hair.

"Please don't cry, Aida. Not for me. I'm all right now. Better than all right..."

I needed to know. So, I asked, "What happened to him? Where is he now?"

Pain darkened his features as he slowly let his hand fall away from my face and turned back toward the fire.

"I don't know. The year I turned twenty, the nobleman of the estate had banished him from the grounds one day. I never knew why. I wanted to follow him... but the bastard would only let me out of my contract if I made the choice to join the Astaran Guard. So, the next day, I did just that. I refused to live there without him anyway. But in the four years since, I've never found a trace of him, not a whisper. It was like he just vanished." His head dropped to hang between his knees, the picture of despair. His sadness was detestable to me to the point of discomfort. Scooting closer to his side, I gently wrapped my arm through his and laid my hand to rest over that wretched scar beneath his shirt as I leaned my head against his shoulder. I felt him release a sigh before feeling the weight of his head against mine.

I had never felt such a sense of belonging in my life.

A pulsing pressure was building within my heart, barely containing a feeling I was too afraid to name just yet.

"I lost someone important to me, too. He was my dearest friend... like family. Before him, my life had been nothing but chaos and fear. He guided me into the light. And I miss him every single day," I whispered, a warm tear slipping down my cheek.

Hesitantly, Tyran reached his arm around me to rest on my shoulder, tucking me into his side. I felt his warm breath against my temple as he inhaled deeply.

"I am grateful you knew him," he murmured against my hair. "...as I am grateful to know you."

THE RABBIT AND SQUIRREL, WHILE TOUGH AND A BIT CHEWY, WERE blissful. As we ate in companionable silence, my thoughts began to drift to less important matters. He had told me about his life as a slave and as a soldier... but had any women ever been a part of that life? Maybe I didn't want to know. Not really...

"What's on your mind?" he asked. I pretended to appear

aloof, my focus on nothing other than properly masticating the gamey meat.

"C'mon, your face is pinched as if you taste something unpleasant."

"Maybe I do." I teased. An outright lie. This was the best thing I'd eaten in weeks.

Tyran pointedly looked away, doubt dancing across his handsome grin. *Fine.*

"Well, since you asked..." I cleared my throat, suddenly not so certain I wanted to have this conversation.

"Spit it out, Aida," he said with a light chuckle before his teeth ripped off another steaming chunk. I sighed deeply through my nose, scrambling to find my resolve. After all, he was a few years older than I was. It wouldn't be the worst thing to know if he had taken former lovers...would it?

"I wanted to know... if you had ever been with a woman?" The last part came out half-strangled as I shifted nervously, keeping my eyes focused anywhere but on his reaction.

For several moments, only the twitter of birds and the rush of the breeze could be heard. Until he finally broke the silence, his voice quiet.

"No, I haven't," he replied. I met his gaze then, a well of relief oozing across my skin at his response. His nervous half-smile dimpled his cheek as a lock of his hair came loose across his brow. Tucking it quickly behind an ear, he asked, "And you? Have you ever...been with someone?"

"No. And if you hadn't rescued me from those monsters at the bottom of the gorge...my first time would not have been very pleasant." I replied as lightly as I could, not allowing the horror of that reality to settle any deeper than it needed to. It was over. They were dead now...

Tyran's expression hardened, his jaw going tight as he jabbed a stick into the fire.

"Aida... there's something about me you need to know."

My head went quiet at the graveness in his tone.

"I have a tendency to... well..." he released an exasperated sigh before throwing the stick into the flames. He turned toward me, his features twisted with frustration. I only waited, too afraid to hear what could possibly be so difficult to explain...

"Sometimes, my rage controls me. I've been bent to its will for as long as I can remember. The General helped me loads. He taught me how to control my urges. But when I saw you down there. When I heard your screams of terror..." he shook his head, his eyes pleading.

"I will never lay a hand on you. I will *never* hurt you. Ever. Please know that. But if anyone tries to harm you. Us. My instinct may be to kill first and ask questions later," he finished, eyes wary and brimming with shame.

That's what had been so hard to say? That he longed to protect me with the fierceness of a rabid animal? Did he believe me to be some delicate creature, incapable of savagery?

It would not do.

"Listen," I said, beckoning his eyes back to mine. "I don't know why the Gods saw fit to rip us from our homes, kill our parents, and subject us to a life of fear and desperation. What I *do* know is that this life has made us strong and capable. It also brought us together." I paused, rallying my boldness. With his wide eyes fixed on me, I placed a hand over his chest and gently shoved him onto his back. His warm breath left in a whoosh, his hands trailing across my waist as I aligned my body on top of his. I shivered. His touch made me come alive.

With delicate slowness, I ghosted across his neck with the whisper of a kiss, watching his throat bob as he swallowed. The grip of his hands tightened as he palmed me from behind, making me squirm against him. A soft moan escaped his lips.

My boldness and desire seized me in a vice grip as I continued my taunting, my mouth hovering over his with excruciating closeness.

"What I do know...is that *rage* has saved lives. It saved mine, and I will be grateful for it always." I finished, ending our conversation with a searing kiss. All tongue. Slow and sweet.

"Gods..." he moaned against my mouth, his hands squeezing my backside in earnest as he returned the kiss with his whole body. When he left my mouth to graze his teeth against the tender spot beneath my ear, I sighed deeply at the perfection of it. Giving him access to suck on my neck, I rubbed my body over his length over and over, a tight throb ratcheting up between my legs.

"Touch me, Tyran." I breathed. The words had come from me, but I couldn't register saying them, my head clouded with this insatiable hunger for his hands on me. He stilled, separating his mouth from my neck to look directly into my eyes.

"Say it again," he demanded, almost groaning. I didn't hesitate. Not when I needed him more than I needed air.

"I want you to touch me." I sighed, grinding my hips against him in emphasis. He licked his lips once before gently rolling me over onto my back. With one arm behind my head and his tongue gently thrusting into my mouth, he trailed his hands up the hem of my shirt. I writhed and groaned, his touch waking up parts of my body I never knew had been asleep. Warm fingers squeezed and caressed each breast as I arched into his palm, consumed with sensation. He shuddered, his kisses stuttering.

"More. Please." I begged, lifting my hips greedily. He grunted, his kisses growing more desperate as his hand drifted south. It struck me then just how special this moment was.

Our first time...

Panting in earnest now, I grabbed onto his arm, eager to be

part of this with him. And when his hands found that slick, pulsing space between my thighs... I couldn't breathe. I couldn't think. Distantly, I heard him moan my name against my neck as he nipped at me there, his hands rubbing all my thoughts into oblivion. Tenderly, he rubbed and caressed me, my legs splaying wide. I surrendered. Hips grinding against his fingers, I focused all thought left into crossing the horizon of this mind-bending feeling. As the sensation began to stretch my consciousness into near paralysis, eyes rolling back, his mouth angled over mine once more. I couldn't stop the pathetic whimpering he was wringing from me, swallowing the sound with each mind-numbing kiss. I was close, my body beginning to quake. He stroked me softly, sweetly, his hands reaching deep across my slit as I cried out.

"*Push me. Bite me. Break me.* I'm yours till death and far beyond it." he growled, his teeth nipping and biting his way down my jaw.

The dam broke. Exploded. As a wave of fireworks broke across my body. The coil within me was snapping and fraying. His strokes intensified as he swallowed my screams. I convulsed under his touch, the throes of ecstasy too much to tolerate. Gasping and panting, my rigid body went limp. I allowed it, too overcome with the mind-blowing reality of what he had done to me. As the haze began to lift, I met his heavy-lidded gaze, marveling at the awe I found there. Slowly, he retracted his hand from me and pulled down my shirt to cover my stomach. There were no words, and he didn't seem to need any. He only smiled, giving me another brief, soft kiss. As he pulled away, his flushed cheeks dimpled with a heart-shattering grin.

"I could listen to you make those sounds forever."

I only smiled back, my soul feeling lighter than air for the first time in so, so long.

As the sun made its descent toward the western horizon, the sky shifted to a bruising gray, and the heavy silence of impending snowfall settled over the forest. Expertly noticing this as well, Tyran began to fortify our shelter to withstand the snow's weight. After finishing the rest of the meat for dinner and briefly leaving to reset the snares again, Tyran returned to the campsite, casting shy smiles in my direction. Already under the shelter and wrapped in as many layers of clothes as I could find, I gave him a small smirk and gestured to the empty place on the bedroll next to me. Eyes briefly widening, he chewed on his lip for a moment before placing a spare wool blanket over Cressida and walking toward me. Turning onto my side to face him, I watched his tall frame crouch down and ease beside me. With one arm tucked behind his head as he lay down, I saw his brow furrow with frustration.

"What's wrong?" I asked, trying to keep the nervousness out of my voice.

Taking notice of my tone, he turned to me and offered a small smile to put me at ease.

"I just wish we had a view of the stars..." he replied.

I smiled brightly in return, chuckling in agreement.

His face froze, the smirk leaving his features as he stared at me, making my heart flutter like a bird in a cage.

"I love your smile," he said, softly. I bit my lip, a crimson heat blooming across my skin. I reached over to toy with a lock of his hair, his eyes closing contentedly at my touch.

Suddenly curious, I decided to ask, "What do you love most about the stars?"

He sighed deeply before turning his head to look at me.

"Is it such a mystery?" he murmured, bringing my hand to his lips.

Oh...

Sensing my quiet dismay, he continued, "They've always reminded me of you... Well, how you appear when I see you here." He tapped the side of his temple.

"You're not frightened of it?" I breathed.

His lips warmed my knuckles as he continued to kiss them, shaking his head.

"Never."

CHAPTER 30
AIDA

We awoke to a world of white. The snow had fallen all night and now lay in deep mounds, six inches thick, covering every surface from ground to trees. As I extricated myself from Tyran's warmth, he rose next to me, rubbing the sleep away from his eyes. Our shared dream had been euphoric. The glass room of his mind was where I now chose to remain, maybe forever. Or... for however long he wished me to stay. But we said nothing and only held each other in timeless comfort, until the rising sun reminded us to wake. With no real destination to speak of, I assumed our goal was to get as far away from the bleak wasteland of everything east of the Solumine. We both had had enough of the brutality and despair of the society that existed around Opeth and wanted no part of it any longer. I knew we would both be happier living in the wilderness anyway, despite the danger.

And for just a moment, I could envision our future.

Maybe we would cross over the Vazaketh and make an entirely new life on the other side. Together, we could build a cabin and live off the bounty of the wild.

Maybe we could even have a family, giving each other what we had both lost...

The thought filled me with such devastating hope that it brought tears to my eyes. I turned to see him looking at me, his eyes stirring with some wordless emotion.

Maybe he was thinking the same thing as I was.

He leaned in and pressed a light kiss onto the tip of my nose before pulling back to search my face. Before he could get too far away, I tilted up my head and parted my lips in silent response. He kissed me firmly then, his hands rising to cradle my face.

"Good morning, my beautiful little shadow," he said softly against my lips, his thumbs stroking my cheeks. Warmth unfurled in my core.

Yes, I was his. And he was *mine*.

He pulled away from the kiss and gave me a playful smirk, like he knew I would never deny his claim. He was right, of course... But I was in a playful mood this morning.

"Are you mine for the taking as well then?" I asked breathily, smiling against his mouth.

He pulled back again, giving me a firm nod. "If you'll have me..."

"I'll think about it," I replied with an impish grin.

Aware of my jest, he gave me a light poke to the rib cage, which sent me squirming away, giggling. His apparent gift for self-possession returned a few moments later as he turned from me to assess the surrounding wood.

"Where do you want to go, Aida?" He spoke the words softly, as if wary of my answer.

Just days ago, my response would've been simple enough.

To be far away from Opeth.

To be alone.

Reaching for his hand, I entwined my fingers through his. He looked at me, cautious hope hardening his features. Though different, my response now was just as simple.

"With you? Anywhere."

He only nodded, his relief palpable as he squeezed my hand.

Onward we would go, past the Vazaketh, to the world beyond.

THE SNOW, FORTUNATELY, DID NOT LAST; SMALL SPROUTS OF GREEN were now taking hold in pockets along the forest floor. As we rode, we discussed many things. I told him stories about my life living with the Villdyr children. He told me of his fondest memories with The General and showed me the beautiful dagger he had made for him on his eighteenth birthday. Expertly crafted, its hilt was wreathed in climbing roses painted with gold leaf; there was none of its equal I had ever seen.

Each night we stopped to make camp, the Gods would bless us with clear skies, blazing green and pink auroras, and brilliant stars. Bundled close together under wool blankets, we would identify every star and constellation we could see, our breath hanging over us like clouds. I had never had anyone like him in my life. Someone I not only trusted with my heart and secrets, but with my body as well. With only the gentle breeze and crackling fire for an audience, we would kiss each other breathless, hands exploring each other and heads swimming with need. Somehow, we always managed to find a way to stop ourselves before getting too carried away. And considering that my cycle had decided to come earlier than I anticipated, it was probably for the best that we kept things... modest. Being out in the wilderness was difficult for women for a multitude of reasons, dealing with our menstrual cycle being one of the hardest. But I was no novice. I knew how to keep clean, if enough cotton was available... Tyran surely had noticed the way I had cut additional strips from our loot of clothes and used them in unseen places, but he politely mentioned nothing. Nestled against his warm chest with his arm wrapped around my shoulder, his fingers would stroke through my hair. The calming, meditative gesture now becoming a prerequisite for sleep. And he always seemed happy to oblige me.

It had been a month since he had saved my life in the gorge. We had been lucky when it came to food; often catching rabbits, squirrels, and the errant chipmunk in our snares, in addition to a few edible mushrooms, and freshly sprouted wild herbs. While we crossed no great rivers, fresh water could always be found from tiny streams that trickled through the springs that were fed from high up in the mountains.

As we continued northwest, the barely audible clop of Cressida's hooves on the soft forest floor had been replaced by scraping rock and crunching gravel. As we ascended to higher elevations at the base of the Vazaketh, the trees began to thin, replaced by large boulders and piles of debris as tall as the walls of Opeth. Evidence of damaging spring floods and mountain slides.

The eerie quiet and barrenness of the mountains provoked me into asking a question I hadn't dared to utter until this moment. With his strong body behind me in the saddle, arms wrapped protectively around my waist, I found the courage.

"Can I ask you something?" I asked warily.

Noting my hesitation, I felt him lean down to press a warm kiss against the skin under my ear as he whispered back, "Anything."

Ignoring my shiver of pleasure and sudden peaking of my breasts beneath my shirt, I steeled my nerve.

"Did you ever meet The Sovereign... Chemosh... during your time in the Astaran Guard?"

His reaction was visceral, his arms going tighter around me as his breathing shallowed. Recovering a moment later, he slowed Cressida into a walk.

"No...but I've seen her," he replied, voice tense.

I stayed silent, hoping he would elaborate. His voice hardened into cold steel as he continued. "She is just as evil as you can imagine. Giant, powerful, and terrifying. She is a cold-blooded demon, and no one can do anything about it. Somehow our ancestors failed to defeat that monster, and we all now must live in the shadow of their great failure," he finished, hands clenching tight on the reins.

Though I had never seen the Sovereign myself, everyone in Astaran knew the legend of how she came to power.

She had once been an angel.

A mighty archangel of Lyrath.

The legends said that she somehow had angered the Gods, and they punished her by exiling her to Astaran. But even with some power removed, she had laid claim over this land. Great battles had been waged trying to take back our world... all had failed.

"Do you think it's true then? What the stories say? That she is a fallen angel..."

It took him so long to respond, I almost turned back to look at his face before he finally replied. "She is not human. And does not give a damn about human life. That is certain."

Before the ominous tone of that statement could take hold, however, Cressida's ears pricked up as she let out a whine of unease and slowed to a stop. A heartbeat later, Tyran had unsheathed his dagger, swung down from Cressida, and landed silently beside me. Eyes darting around us to the various rocky boulders strewn around the hillside, he grabbed another dagger from the pack and wordlessly placed it in my hand. Heart pounding, I gripped the blade and strained to listen for any sound that could spell danger. Cressida's nostrils flared, her eyes widening before she started to back away down the slope. Toward the cover of the forest. Tyran gripped her reins and silently stroked to calm her, but she was beyond it, only struggling harder to back away. Looking down quickly into Tyran's eyes, I could see a flicker of fear as he whispered, "We are not alone."

As if summoned, a hulking, black shadow crept into my peripheral vision. Head snapping back toward the direction of the steep hillside, my heart and breath froze over with horror at what stood before us.

Perched on its haunches atop a huge boulder sat the most enormous black wolf I had ever seen. The canid was the size of Cressida, but longer somehow. Eyes of blazing gold alighted us with predatory delight, tongue flicking over its gigantic, glistening fangs. Claws the length of my hand glinted in the sunlight underneath its massive paws. The creature was a vision of Hel and the hounds who obeyed its beckoning call.

There was no way we could run from it.

We would die here, right now.

Tyran readied his bow, nocking an arrow—the wolf snarled, the explosive sound ripping through my head, loosening my bowels with fear.

"When I tell you to run, you kick her into a gallop and get the fuck out of here, do you understand?"

I was vaguely aware that Tyran was speaking to me, eyes not daring to leave the nightmare which began to slowly rise into a crouch. Something deeper than terror began to torch my veins like fire. I would not flee and abandon Tyran to be shredded by this... whatever this was. It had to be more than an animal.

No. Tyran needed all the help he could get. I was staying. And we would die together.

With every ounce of reckless courage I could summon, I replied, "Fuck no."

The wolf's muzzle sneered, releasing a chuff of amusement before launching off the boulder.

CHAPTER 31
AIDA

Everything happened within the blink of an eye.

As the great mass of black fur sailed skyward in a ferocious arc of fangs and claws, Cressida reared back, flailing her front hooves in panic and throwing me to the ground with violence enough to rip the wind from my lungs.

Tyran released an arrow, his aim striking true and piercing the beast's shoulder.

The wolf's enraged bellow echoed through the surrounding valley.

In the next moment, Tyran released Cressida's reins, allowing her to bolt in the direction of the forest. I swallowed my shout as I realized my own bow was still attached to her saddle, but she was too far gone before I could reach for her, her survival instincts at full power. At least she would survive this. Now standing side-by-side, my small blade gripped tightly in my trembling hand, I noticed Tyran had nocked another arrow, bowstring groaning as he aimed to shoot. The wolf pounced with supernatural speed, swiping at Tyran with razor-sharp claws, the released arrow missing its snarling mouth by a hair's breadth. Tyran emitted a cry of pain before falling to the ground.

Frozen with shock, time seemed to slow as I watched the bright red stain bloom across his chest, spurting from the deep gashes that had slashed him from collarbone to ribs. His face, ashen and contorted with agony, looked up at me then, silver lining his eyes...

I knew what he was thinking... He believed these were to be our last moments.

The hope and joy we had found with each other were not to last.

There would be no bright, happy future for us.

It would end right here, on the rocky slopes of the Vazaketh.

The wolf paced as he watched us with sentient intensity, like he found pleasure in studying his prey come to grips with their despair. Tyran's hands gripped his chest, red rivulets cascading through his fingers, his eyes pleading as he shouted, "Run, Aida!"

Run where? I had no intention of escaping into the wilderness alone, leaving him here to die, even for my life.

My resolve was iron-clad. I would stay right here and die with him if that's what the Gods intended. Stepping over Tyran's body, dagger angled to make my last stand, I bared my teeth at the wolf in defiance. Something like surprise briefly crossed the wolf's features, giving me a quick blink. But the shadow of impending death returned an instant later as he reared back, readying to strike. White-hot rage began to wobble the edges of my vision.

I was *fucking sick* of people being taken from me.

Liquid flames of wrath pumped through my veins, the pressure building beneath my skin.

I wasn't going to be prey to this monster. Not today.

Power, cold and sharp, erupted like a geyser.

Slowly, as if time were holding its breath, the wolf's golden eyes began to dilate, his brows lifting in shock by just a fraction.

Physical sensation seemed to be receding away, like a wave being sucked out to sea, as I became less aware of my body.

No... I was *leaving* my body.

A quick glance behind me confirmed my assumption. Finding my physical form, face twisted with fury, my formerly blue eyes now dark, depthless voids... but otherwise motionless. Frozen in time.

Glancing down at my hands, shock turned to awe at the vision of the universe inside my skin.

As if the fabric of this world had been ripped away to reveal the infinite, star-flecked vastness of the night sky, in the shape of my arms, hands, legs...

This is how I appeared to Tyran in the dreamscape.

My astral form.

But I wasn't asleep and at the mercy of my own consciousness.

I *was* consciousness, given form.

Ancient, thrumming power radiated from my hands and feet in a diaphanous mist that cascaded down my legs into billowing clouds, like the swirling gas of a nebula.

Instantly, I was aware of two things: First, the dream

walking ability had evolved into something more powerful than I could fathom. As if a dark cloak had finally been pulled away, I was able to look *beyond* this physical realm. I stilled with awe as I beheld the billions of glowing vibrations strung between the walls of a vast canyon, like strings on a harp that stretched skyward into the infinite blackness.

Carved into the landscape of reality itself, the deep chasm appeared to hold the collective consciousness of all life.

And all of it was now accessible to me.

The second thing I knew... was that the wolf's consciousness was here too.

The glittering onyx rope of his mind lay pulsing amongst the throng before me.

I reached out to grasp it between my fingers and yanked.

Fast as a shooting star, my body was hurled into an enormous crystal palace. I rose from the floor, squinting into the brightness and gasping like a fish. When my eyes adjusted, I stilled. Every surface appeared to be composed of diamonds. Great, shimmering obelisks encircled the room I was standing in the center of. I looked up, my heart hammering like a drum as I beheld a giant domed ceiling painted with various depictions of gruesome battles. Great legions of beasts, *hounds*, ripping apart all manner of creatures... including people. Towering cities, engulfed by flames, their inhabitants running in terror. The images told the story of untold destruction, over many eons... on many different worlds.

"You are she," boomed a voice that rumbled like thunder.

My gaze fell from the ceiling and rested upon the giant black wolf, sitting atop a throne of petrified bones. His eyes, like golden flame, pinned me with a questioning look, but I said nothing.

"You are she. The last Dream Walker," he stated confidently.

What?

Trying to hide my confusion at that remark, I asked, "Who are you?"

His midnight black fur bristled at the question, annoyed.

"I am Sköll. Commander of Hel's legions," he replied with a huff, as if this was common knowledge.

Black, oily dread crashed into me like a wave.

The depictions on the ceiling were not just art—they were history.

This being was responsible for the damning of countless souls. This was the monster who legend said had helped Chemosh destroy the mighty kingdoms of Astaran and steal its throne. Thoughts began to race through my mind too fast to grasp. Taking deep, steadying breaths, I tried to recall how I had gotten here. We had been attacked. On the mountain... *Gods, Tyran...* he was injured. Rallying all the bravery I could muster and imbuing my voice with authority, I said to the beast,

"Do as I command, foul minion of Hel, and I will not boil your brain inside your head."

There was a heartbeat of tense silence before an ear-shattering roar echoed through the room.

No... a laugh.

Eyes squeezed shut and tongue dangling, the wolf laughed until breathless. I bit my tongue in anticipation, internally cursing my rashness. My mouth had always been a step behind my pragmatism. Maybe provoking an ancient demigod was a bad idea. When he finally recovered, he said, "It has been an age since someone has challenged me. And a young, human female no less. No. No, I will not destroy you today, dream walker. You may indeed prove useful to me in the end."

What the fuck did that mean?

Irritated and concerned this was taking too much time, I

spat, "And why would I help a hound of Hel who helped *that bitch* with the slaughter of my ancestors and destruction of their kingdoms?"

Faster than a striking snake, Sköll leapt from the throne of bones and stood over me with fangs bared. I held my breath with fists clenched, forcing myself not to cower.

"Do not speak of what you do not know, human! The *Morning Star* deceived us all. She is the reason I am damned to wander Astaran, powerless, until all the stars burn through their light. She commanded us to wage holy war on this world in the name of the Gods, but she betrayed them and damned us *all*," he snarled.

His face, just inches from mine, slowly began to relax. I noticed a deep weariness cross over his features before he turned back to his perch on the throne. Confusion must've been clear on my face because he sighed a deep chuff of exasperation before saying, "There is much you do not know, Dream Walker. Find the Begavet people. They can give you the answers you seek."

His voice turned to cold steel as he continued, "And remember this... when the time comes for the Morning Star to meet her end, I wish to be there. Now, be gone... I have tolerated your presence in my inner sanctum for long enough."

I stood speechless for just a moment longer before inclining my head into a small bow. He may have been a blood thirsty force of darkness, but that didn't mean I shouldn't show some respect. Upon finding the pitch-dark rope dangling at the back of his consciousness, I pulled myself out. With the ferociousness of a whizzing arrow, I was sucked back through the glowing void before being slammed back into my body. I winced, my head pounding as I refocused on the physical reality I had returned to. Chuffing with irritation, the black wolf stood staring for only a moment longer before turning and stalking away, the arrow still protruding from his shoulder.

Holy shit.

A breathy grunt sounded near my feet, where I instantly found Tyran... his face pale with blood loss, eyes wide with disbelief as he said, "What in *Hel* just happened?"

CHAPTER 32
AIDA

Tyran was weak, his heartbeat too thready, but the wound needed to be assessed, and remaining here exposed on this rocky slope was not an option. Fighting the urge to tremble from shock, I gripped him under the arms, preparing to flee toward the cover of the wood.

"Do you think you can walk?" I asked. Air hissing through his teeth, he nodded briefly, sweat beginning to bead across his brow. Using my weight to steady his balance, I lifted him up by the shoulder and wrapped my arm around his middle. With cautious steps, we descended back toward the forest. Cressida, Gods bless her, had not run far. Her nostrils flared at the sight of Tyran, but dutifully followed behind us. I bore most of his weight as we made slow progress to a safer place, where I could dress the wound. With the coppery warmth of his blood soaking into my shirt, I cursed internally, struggling to subdue my panic.

Please. Not him. I begged whoever wished to listen.

After what seemed like hours, I gasped with relief upon hearing the small gurgle of an icy mountain stream, tucked safely betwixt a cluster of dense trees. I commanded him to lie down. He obeyed, teeth chattering as his whole body shivered. Gently, I began to remove his coat and shirt. Pale and wincing through every movement, Tyran did not inspect the damage himself, his eyes remaining on my face. I released a shuddering breath at the carnage now exposed to the light. At the flesh torn apart by three gruesome gashes that slashed across his broad, beautiful chest. Swallowing around the lump in my throat, I didn't allow the uneasiness it brought me to show on my face. Just as Luke had instructed, I remained calm and stated the facts.

"The wound appears superficial..." I muttered, blinking away my tears of rage.

I should've flayed that wolf and left him to rot...

"It shouldn't need too many stitches. The muscle is mostly intact." I finished.

He only nodded, face grim, his soft blond locks turning dark as they lay plastered across his neck and brow. Quickly, I laid a wool blanket over him and got to work. After tying Cressida close to the stream to drink, I began to make camp. With the sun beginning its descent toward the peaks of Vazaketh, I only had about two hours before we were enveloped in its shadow. With speed and focus, I chopped enough firewood to last the night, collected multiple canteens of water from the spring, set snares nearby, and foraged for any herbs I could find. To my surprise, I discovered some recently sprouted wild garlic. From Luke's teachings, it was a highly beneficial herb for wound care. Just before the sun left us in total darkness, I had the fire roaring. Finding an extra shirt in the pack, I tore it into strips before crushing the wild garlic into a poultice. Tyran was silent as he watched me, but I knew he was in a great deal of pain. Though it was brisk with the evening's chill, sweat ran down his forehead in steady streams. Stepping into those sturdy boots of calm authority once again, I turned to him and said, "I'm going to start now. We don't want it getting infected." His eyes, while pained, hardened to steel as he gave me a terse nod and moved to lay down on his back. He kept his eyes on the fire as I pressed close and first washed the wound with near-boiling water. The only indication of his discomfort was the tight breaths sucked through his teeth, his hand white knuckling the hilt of his dagger at his waist. The stitching was the hardest part, but Luke had made me practice on the deer and wild pigs we hunted. I knew he was watching me from his seat in the God realm, steadying my hands and imbuing me with the confidence I needed now. After applying a final layer of poultice, I began to wrap the wounds. Grunting with effort, he rose to a sitting position, allowing me to wrap around his back.

"That should do it. We will need to rest here for several days until you've recovered." I said, gently, my body sagging from relief and exhaustion. Before I could pull away to clean up the supplies, he grabbed my hand, locking me into his hooded gaze.

"Thank you. You saved my life back there... are you going to explain how?" he asked, voice low and hesitant. I stilled.

Did I even know?

With a sigh of resignation, I gave him a subtle nod and sat beside him. For a long moment, I only massaged my aching fingers and stared into the fire.

How in the Hel would I explain this without sounding insane?

"It all happened so fast..." I whispered. "I saw you bleeding. I couldn't take it. I wasn't going to let him hurt you." I paused, my head scrambling for the words to describe it all.

"It felt like a cold fire blazing through me. One second, I was here, feet planted, and the next... I was leaving my body and diving headfirst into his mind." Chancing a glance over my shoulder, Tyran sat straighter, his face tight with an expression I could not decipher.

"My gift... somehow, a new door was opened. God's... I can't describe it. I could see them all. Every life. Stretching into infinity..." I paused to rub a hand down my face.

What if this was the final straw? The thing that made him want to leave *me* this time.

I looked at him nervously.

"What did he tell you?" he asked, only concern shining behind his eyes. I breathed deep, the memory of Sköll's dark omen still lingering over me like a cloud...

You are she...
The last Dream Walker...
You will prove useful to me in the end...
Find the Begavet people...

"He told me that Chemosh had deceived him. He said I was the last of my kind. And that I needed to find the "Begavet" people." I finished, wrapping my arms around my middle to quell the growing anxiety building within. With my back to him, I held my breath until he responded a minute later.

"Aida," he said, calm but strained. I turned to face him fully then, my fingers going to his pulse on instinct. Through his labored breaths and drooping lids, he managed a small grin.

"Yes?" I breathed, heart nearly seizing with relief.

"You are *truly* magnificent... Do you know that?" he stated, eyes lifting just a fraction to lock with mine. And though I could not conceive it, I knew he meant every word.

"I've never heard of the *Begavet*, people... but I'll do everything I can to help you find them."

I shuddered. The sincerity of his words and the consequences that could follow were too grave to consider. I returned my gaze to the fire, my stomach twisting with angst.

"What if... what if I don't want to know," I murmured. "Maybe we should just pretend like nothing happened and make a new life out there somewhere." I gestured to the surrounding wilderness.

I turned around again to find him smirking at me knowingly.

"The Gods did not plan for us to die today, Aida. Whatever their agenda...it will find us anywhere we go," he finished with a slur, before succumbing to soft snores a moment later.

Like a burst faucet now dripping with emptiness, my last scrap of energy left me. Releasing a deep sigh, I laid myself back onto the wool blanket beside Tyran.

And silently prayed he was wrong.

Chapter 33
Aida

We remained at the camp for another five days, allowing Tyran to heal. Spring had indeed arrived. I sent up a thankful prayer to the Gods for the warmer air, and for each discovery of new life growing in the surrounding wood. With Tyran on the mend, I took charge of collecting firewood, water, and food. Due to the emergence of many forest creatures looking to leave their burrows, my snares had been largely successful. We were well stocked with rabbits, squirrels, and edible mushrooms. Tyran was in the middle of exercising with his dagger, trying to test out the movement he was capable of, when I left camp to check the snares one evening. I had placed this one further away than the rest and walked almost a mile before finding it. The snare lay empty. Ignoring my frustration, I tried to remind myself of our recent success when a loud, droning buzz caught my attention. Looking up, I saw a swarming hive of bees that had established itself in the crook of a tree branch, only about fifteen feet off the ground. My mouth began to salivate at the prospect of fresh honey. Before I could really think about it, I was scaling the tree. Collecting honey, no matter the risk, was a specialty for all Villdyr children. Not only was it delicious, but its healing and anti-bacterial properties were unmatched. Eager and excited, I had to remind myself to stay focused or else risk breaking my neck. Upon reaching the branch and throwing my legs over, I sat motionless and allowed the bees to do their own investigation. After a short while, they must've determined that I wasn't any major threat and began to disperse. With steady hands, I reached into the hive and slowly retreated with a large comb between my fingers. Not daring to linger, I dropped the comb into the pack over my shoulder and began my descent toward the ground. Licking my fingers clean was nothing short of ecstasy as I sprinted back toward the campsite, golden treasure in tow.

When I arrived at camp, struggling for breath and grinning like a fool, Tyran marched over to where I stood and gave me a questioning look. Holding up the pack, I said through ragged breaths, "Honey!" His handsome smile and light chuckle only helped to further improve my mood.. "Sit down and remove the bandages," I ordered, giving him a grin. He obeyed and propped himself up against a tree. Kneeling beside him, I lifted the waxy comb out of the pack and placed it on a piece of cloth. For a moment, I marveled at my handiwork. The gashes were healing remarkably well, the tight scabs already looking less puckered. Throwing all my focus into keeping my fingers steady and light, I brushed the honey over the gashes. Tyran winced almost imperceptibly, but kept still as I finished, watching me. The skin of my cheeks warmed from my uninvited blush. His chest, though injured, was still magnificent. I noted with no small amount of relief that both nipples had been left intact as well. As I dipped my fingers into the comb once more, he grabbed my wrist before I could touch him again. Afraid I had hurt him somehow, I froze. Tyran's heavy-lidded gaze never left mine as he raised my fingers to his lips and sucked.

As he sucked, he watched me from under his lashes.

Something molten gushed between my thighs at the sight, my head becoming a fuzzy roar of need. Cautiously, I straddled him, before taking his face in my hands and laying claim to his mouth. The kiss was liquid heat, our tongues lashing... and the taste, *Gods*... the taste of honey on his tongue was enough to drive me wild. His fingers launched into my hair, grabbing onto my neck and holding me to him. Careful of his wound, I lightly grazed my fingers across the soft, blonde hair below his navel. He squirmed, releasing a breathy moan as he pushed me firmly onto the hard length between his legs.

I gasped at the contact. This man was hard and eager... for me.

The power in this knowledge had me surrendering to his mouth as he began to graze his teeth down my jaw, to the lobe of my ear, and down to my neck, sucking gently. His hands were roving down my back, over my hips, and began a slow trail up my stomach to my breasts. Strong fingers traced slow circles over each nipple, which pebbled through my shirt. A soft whimper rushed from my lips at the touch.

I wanted him. More than anything I had ever wanted in my life.

I wanted to be his first and his only.

Returning to my mouth, his kisses began to turn lazy, cherishing. The hand gripped in my hair slowly began to loosen, as if it took all his strength to do so. Pulling away from my lips, now swollen and wet from him, he said through breathy pants, "I *need* you, Aida. I want you badly… but I want it to be the right time." My body began to slowly cool from disappointment, and I only nodded. He was right, of course; he was still injured, and I didn't want to risk hurting him further if I got too…carried away. Sensing my displeasure, he gripped my chin between his fingers and pressed one last kiss to my lips, inhaling deep.

"We will have our time together soon, Aida. I promise." Meeting his eyes then, I gave him a simpering smile and replied, "I can't wait."

Chapter 34
Tyran

We continued west, exploring parts of Astaran I had only read about in books and seen on maps. The vast majesty of the Vazaketh mountains, looming on the western horizon, was a constant reminder of its insurmountable danger. Aida and I had spent many hours studying the towering peaks and would often debate the risks of trying to pass over, long into the night. We had found no safe route. The risk of catastrophic falls, mountain slides, and high elevation frostbite was too great. After agreeing that the route we had been discussing was futile and that we should continue our journey the next day, we would settle in for the night to gaze at the stars. Holding each other close under warm blankets, we would tell each other stories about our lives. Profound joy found me in those moments. I already knew that I was falling so deeply in love with Aida that it threatened to swallow me whole. Her body aligned with mine, hands roving delicately, mouths fused in soft passion; it was the happiest time of my life. Every time she touched me or moaned into my mouth, it took every ounce of concentration to not strip off her clothes and bury myself in her. I often found myself silently begging the Gods to give me patience so we could go at her pace.

Gods, she was so beautiful and her scent... like the mist that clung over a mountain stream, utterly free. Every morning when we woke next to each other, I couldn't stop myself from delicately toying with the soft, chestnut waves of her hair or drifting my fingers over her full, pink lips. And when she awoke and smiled at me, cheeks crinkling around those blazing, glacial blue eyes, my heart would stutter to a stop every time.

I would do anything for her.

In the weeks since the attack from that giant, black wolf, our dreams together often reflected her choice to remain in my dreamscape. I had the feeling that it had become her safe place, where she could hide from the horrors inside the minds of the billions of souls accessible to her through her terrifying power. We did not discuss her ability very often, as she seemed to have no wish to understand it. I knew it frightened her, but I couldn't help silently pondering what it all meant: *Why her? Why now? What was its purpose?*

Of course, it didn't really matter.

My soul was bound to her.

Wherever the Gods destined her to go, I would be there by her side. In my mind, there was no greater honor than to be the foundation for the person you loved.

The General had told me once of a great love he had lost many years ago...

The memory of his face instantly squeezed my chest with warmth as I recalled the conversation. We were sitting in the loft above the barn one night, the horses dozing below us as we prepared to sleep. His green eyes had been pained and shadowed with grief, no doubt remembering the woman who had once brought him such fierce joy.

"I have pity on men who do not see women for what they really are. Those men who only view them as property or for child rearing. They have swallowed a disgusting lie," he muttered, eyes blank and staring at the night sky through the window.

Since I fervently admired him in every way, I had hung on to every word as he continued.

"A good woman is as precious as a rare gem. More so. They are our complement in every way. Truly, a man is not whole if he has never experienced true love and passion. Lust will come and go... but finding a true mate for life is rare and special indeed." He turned his head to smile at me, then, before saying, "I pray the Gods will bring you and your mate together one day... and I pray you have the divine experience of knowing true love, Tyran."

Tears welling at the memory, I gripped the small frame of the precious soul riding in the saddle beside me a little tighter. I noted, with a tinge of relief, that her body had begun to slowly shift from thin and frail to lean and strong. We had been lucky with our hunting and foraging recently, and I could already see the changes to her body. Placing Cressida's reins neatly into her right hand, she reached back with her left and gently stroked my thigh. The gesture sent a jolt of excitement straight between my legs, but left quickly when she asked, "Are you all right?" We had been traveling for many hours already today, the sun beginning its dip toward the west, casting the valley in a golden glow. Floundering for some excuse to cover up my sudden emotion, I lied. "I'm fine, just a bit stiff from riding." I could almost hear her smiling when she responded a moment later.

"Let's make camp for the night, so I can take care of that for you."

Fucking Hel... she was teasing minx when she wanted to be. I was about to agree and begin searching for a place to set up camp when I spotted a mist over the horizon just ahead. Slowing Cressida to a stop with a low whistle, I squinted and studied the strange phenomena, like the ground just ahead was...

"What? What is it?" Aida said, suddenly alert. Rising away from the saddle, hand parallel to her brow, she squinted to see what had distracted me. Excitement powerful enough to take me out at the knees washed over me like a wave. I wanted to savor every second of this.

Swiftly, hands near trembling, I swung out of the saddle and reached for Aida's waist to pull her to the ground. I smiled at the confusion contorting her face, but simply ordered her to close her eyes and lead her by the hand. Cressida was content to stay behind, busying herself with sprouts of grass and purple willowherb flowers that peppered the field we stood in. The closer we got, the more confident I was that my assumption had been correct. The warm steam, now drifting in our direction, was making it difficult to keep this secret any longer.

"Open your eyes," I said, ensuring I had a front row seat to her expression when she took in our surroundings. Initially speechless with shock, after a few heartbeats, she broke into a devastating smile and said with reverence, "Gods... Tyran... It's a hot spring." I nodded with a smile and turned to gaze at the steaming thermal pools that cascaded into terraces at the base of the mountain.

The legendary Gudstårer pools were a vision of paradise, and one that I never imagined I would ever see. Unable to stand the curiosity for another moment, I walked toward the thin stone shelf that lined the pools, dropped to one knee, and cautiously dipped in a finger. The water was hot, near boiling, but not unpleasant enough to avoid. Turning back to Aida, I said tentatively, "It seems safe enough for a swim, but..." before I could finish the sentence, Aida was stripping off her clothes and moving toward the pool, as eager for a hot bath as I was. Turning away briefly to give her some privacy, I only spied the perfect roundness of her backside before she sat on the ledge and dangled her feet into the water. The sight sent spams of need through my body like a shockwave. I watched, holding my breath, as she slowly lowered her body into the pool, a hiss of pleasure slipping through her teeth.

"It's shallow enough to stand," she said with a coy smile, as if just realizing that she had stripped naked in front of me without a backward glance. She stared at me through the curling steam, water softly lapping at her collarbone. My mouth went dry at the sight. Pulling in a deep breath and willing courage into my veins, I began to undress. Her eyes never left me. Tongue delicately darting out to glide over her bottom lip, she watched as I bared myself to her and lowered into the pool. I sighed with delight. The heat of the water was sublime.

I remained motionless by the edge of the pool, waiting for her signal. She dipped her head under the water briefly before rising to her feet. With agonizing slowness, she waded toward me, the water in the pool lapping at her sweeping hips. All thought eddied from my head as she bared her naked torso and delicately rounded breasts, steaming water cascading down her form in glistening rivulets.

My mouth began to water as my cock grew firm below the water.

She was exquisite.

When she was close enough to share breath, I lifted my hands from the water and gripped her narrow waist firmly. Unabashedly, I took her in. Eyes roaming across her wet, naked body. Her small pink nipples stiffened under my gaze. Her face and cheeks, flushed from the heat, looked up at me then. "I want you, Tyran," she breathed.

My heart began to hammer like a drum as it swelled to near bursting.

"You have me," was all I said before I wrapped my hands around her delicate neck and claimed her mouth with my own. I felt her surrender beneath me as our mouths became a desperate union of sucking and clacking teeth. Her hands rose to fist in my hair, tugging gently as I lowered my mouth to suck on her neck. Her breathy moan encouraged me further as I began to trail wet kisses further south to the hollow of her throat and down her sternum. Relishing the divine taste of her skin, I dragged my tongue across each nipple. She gasped with pleasure and only fisted my hair tighter. She needed this. Needed me. Wrapping my hands around her back, I pressed my weight against her as I sucked on each breast. Her hard nipple shuddered in my mouth as her chest heaved with ragged pants. Her hands abruptly left my hair and clawed down my back, squeezing the cheeks of my backside tight in her hands; I bucked at the touch, my cock now pressing greedily against her belly. She responded by wrapping her hands around it and stroking firmly.

Gods be damned if it wasn't the most exciting moment of my life.

I had to have her. Right now.

Before I lost myself entirely in the grip of her small hand, I grabbed her by the waist and hoisted her onto the ledge of the pool, steaming water splashing across the rock.

Fuck.

With her gleaming sex bared to me, I stared for a moment, unable to comprehend the savage desire that tore through my body like wildfire. Her gorgeous face looked down at me under heavy lids as she whispered, "Do you want me?"

Fucking Hel. The question snapped something inside me. A deep growl rumbled through my chest as I gripped the inside of her thighs and dragged my tongue up her center.

Holy Gods. The taste was... soft, slick, and just a little salty.

My cock throbbed and jerked, begging for sensation. Mouth open and chest heaving, she looked at me with such heat and want, it nearly undid me. Returning my mouth to her, I gripped her thighs tighter and worked her in long, wet strokes, savoring each quiver of pleasure and every soft moan. Her hands fisted into my hair, brazenly keeping my head in a certain place, guiding me to what she needed. Using my tongue and lips, I sucked on the firm pebble of flesh at her center and watched hungrily as she writhed with pleasure.

"Tyran... Gods..." she whimpered.

I needed to be inside of her. Keeping my mouth fixated on that tight spot, her hands gripped the side of my head as she rode me. With one hand gripping her leg tight enough to bruise, I moved the other to gently insert a finger inside her tight entrance. She released a shuddering cry of ecstasy as I began to pump my finger in and out. In and out. Unable to survive without friction for any longer, I lowered a hand beneath the water and began to stroke my cock, my other hand splaying her lips wide to allow my tongue to worship her wholly.

"Come for me, Aida," I murmured against her swollen flesh. Gazing up at her torso, I found her eyes boring into mine with tenderness as she cupped the side of my face in her hands.

Enraptured, I watched her fuck my tongue, oh so gently...

Suddenly, spasms rocked through her center that sent her eyes rolling up into her head. Her back arched as she screamed through her release. My tongue continued to stroke her with long wet pulses, her fingers gripping my hair to the point of pain.

I didn't care. This was fucking bliss.

Pumping my cock hard, its tip jutting out of the water, I growled with pleasure until my spurt of release lay in clouds on the surface.

As her limp body lay splayed over the stone, breasts wobbling with each ragged breath, I slowly rose from the pool and gathered her to me, trailing soft kisses up her belly, then her chest, before coming to rest on her tender lips. We stayed there for a long time, catching our breath and inhaling each other through gentle kisses. Wrapping her arms around my neck and pressing her forehead to mine, she smiled and said, "I love you, Tyran."

The words struck my chest like lightning. Pressing her close, arms wrapped around her small shoulders, I inhaled deeply into her hair. Love didn't seem like enough. I wanted eternity. I wanted whatever lay beyond that. But for Aida? I would gladly accept whatever she wanted to give.

We left the pool, hands clasped and giggling, before getting dressed and settling in for the night. As the sun started to set, the embers from our fire swirled up into the air, glowing like fireflies against the burnt orange and magenta sky as the shadows cast by the mountains began their slow descent from lavender to cobalt. As night fell, we lay propped against a west-facing tree, content to lie still in each other's embrace.

I knew that if I died tomorrow, I would have died a happy man.

"Do you think it's possible... to stay here, in this moment, forever?" she asked, fingers lightly grazing over my chest.

My heart squeezed. The pointed silence between us was answer enough.

As I closed my eyes that night, arms wrapped around Aida, I furiously prayed it could be true.

The night air took on an unnatural stillness that pulled me from sleep.

Insects stopped chirping.

Owls halted their screeching.

The hairs on the back of my neck rose as my instincts unsheathed themselves, primed for response. Hand already gripped on the hilt of my blade, my head swiveled, eyes squinting into the dark.

Not a sound.

I reached over to grip Aida's shoulder and began to shake her. Her eyes popped open, instantly alert as she rose into a crouch beside me, reaching for her bow. The small sliver of the moon and low embers behind us provided the only light; we remained motionless, ready to fight or flee.

After a few tense minutes, Aida whispered, "If anything

happens, we run for the woods. We're too exposed on the mountain." I only nodded my head.

A heartbeat later, a light, whistling scream tore through the air, followed by a soft thump. Aida shook her head, as if trying to shake off a feeling, before slumping motionless to the ground. "Aida!" I shouted, violently shaking her and roving my hands over her body for any sign of a wound. Another quick, whistling scream sang through the night before something sharp pierced the skin of my arm.

Instantly, my head swam, and my vision blurred.

My tongue went leaden in my mouth...

I had the vague sensation of falling before being swallowed by blackness.

Chapter 35
Aida

Visions of a world ravaged by war drifted across my fluttering eyelids.

Great, undulating oceans of raging armies, unleashing Hel, and leaving massacred bodies in their wake. Lightning struck with ground-shaking booms that lit up the carnage with excruciating detail. Fire reigned down from the sky in gigantic vortices that roared with thunderous death, sucking the enemy soldiers and beasts into their towering infernos. As they blazed across the battlefield, all life turned to ash where they passed.

The sky was a choking haze of black smoke, the screams of the dying near-deafening as a pillar of flame stretching from ground to sky struck the center of the battlefield. A blast wave shook the ground to the bedrock, throwing the bodies of soldiers into the air like burnt paper. A blinding white light, like a star, began to fall from the sky. It tumbled over and over, unable to avoid its impending collision with the ground.

Awareness began to return in waves. *Was this the past? ... Or the future.*

Whose eyes had once beheld this nightmare? Was this an imagining of their fear?

...Or was it a memory?

The questions peppered my mind like hailstones, but all I could do was watch in frozen horror as the star collided with the earth, the bloodshed continuing to rage around it as if no one noticed.

The metallic scent of blood and burnt bodies assaulted my senses. I gagged and started to heave—and the vision changed.

Where the sky had been burnt with clouds of red and black, it now dazzled with clear blue. Warm beams of sunlight washed unimpeded across green, rolling hills. Opeth city lay before me... but never as I had ever known it to appear. Like a giant smudge of black coal on a bright green canvas, the city had become a smoldering ruin. The towering stone spires that once pierced the sky now lay scattered across the ground, their giant blocks crushing the fortress beneath them. The high walls had been breached, whatever was left of them charred black and crumbling.

I gasped as a tiny, rolling sensation fluttered across my abdomen. I glanced down to see a slight swell between my hips... and drifted a trembling hand down to explore the round firmness there. Fierce joy erupted through my heart. I whipped my head around to look for Tyran...

But he wasn't there.

I was alone.

Fear and panic seized my chest, sending me launching

from the dreamscape. Blinking furiously and gasping for breath, the first thing I noticed was the bright, blue light glowing from a glass tube on the ceiling. My head pounded with a teeth-shattering headache as I winced and tried to shield my eyes. It was only when I attempted to roll over onto my stomach that I realized my hands and feet had been bound with rope.

I found Tyran next, also restrained and lying beside me, his jaw clenching with fury as he took stock of our predicament. My chest swelled with relief at the sight of him, but was replaced with dread moments later when a female voice spoke low. "I would recommend not trying to escape... if you want to live," she threatened.

Whipping my head toward the sound, I beheld a young, black-haired woman crouched beside me, idly sharpening a long knife against a leather strap. Her dark skin glowed under the blue light, and her brown eyes—like warm, smoky quartz—bored into mine with a look that told me she was not to be fucked with. I said nothing as my eyes left her stare to assess our surroundings.

We appeared to be... in a cave tunnel, underground. The strange blue bulbs were fixed to the ceiling every twenty or so feet, leading down into a corridor that did not appear to end.

"Who are you? And where is my horse?" Tyran asked, now fully alert and wincing into the light. The dark-haired female only smirked at the demand, but after a moment, she replied, "My name is Sayedha. I will oversee your fate until our Sorceress Supreme decides otherwise... and the mare is someplace safe."

She leaned over us then, her voice shifting into a lower octave before continuing, "If you try to harm anyone here or make a foolish attempt to escape, I will cut you down before you can blink. Understood?"

I spared a quick glance to Tyran, whose face was in deep contemplation, before returning her gaze and nodding tersely. It appeared that we had no choice but to be led further into the belly of this cave, to whatever end.

A thought suddenly snagged my attention... *did she say, "Sorceress Supreme?"*

Spiders of ice began to creep across my stomach.

With a jolt, I realized then who this female belonged to and where she was taking us...

The Mørkbringer.

Legends passed down for generations told haunting stories about the mysterious race of people who dwelled beneath the Vazaketh. People rumored to be capable of dark power. Male hands gripped Tyran and me, righting us to our feet before cutting the ropes tied around our ankles, allowing us to walk. Six huge males, skin tones varying from tawny bronze to dark umber, had been standing behind us the entire time—silent and still as wraiths. As we began our procession further down the tunnel, Tyran turned to me and fixed me with a defiant stare. The meaning behind the look was clear: we would either leave this place together, or not at all.

CHAPTER 36
AIDA

The tunnel of blue lights seemed to descend into the very heart of the world.

We walked for more than an hour, ears popping as we traveled into the deepest and most unknown realm of Astaran. I observed no doors and no people other than me, Tyran, and our well-armed captors. Each warrior, including Sayedha, was equipped with a savage long sword sheathed across their backs and a various assortment of curved daggers strapped to their chest and thighs. Their skin-hugging armor appeared flexible, designed for speed, and painted with varying colors of white, gray, and black stripes, perfect camouflage in the mountains. Every few minutes, I would glance over my shoulder at the warrior who walked silently to my left, not believing him to be real. He stood at least a head higher than Tyran, which meant this man had to be at least seven feet tall. His long, straight black hair fell to his broad shoulders, framing his fearsome, square-jawed face. As if aware of his intimidating presence, his obsidian eyes met my stare and smirked with arrogance at the awe he saw there. Tyran said nothing as we walked, eyes fixed on the tunnel ahead and face hard as steel. I was getting plenty of backward glances of my own, of course. Sayedha had turned back to look at me more than once, her face a curious expression of... anxiety. Like she knew something I didn't. The thought only managed to make me sweat with apprehension, despite the freezing air in the tunnel.

I was almost about to ask, *"Are we there yet?"* when Sayedha raised her fist, and we all came to an abrupt halt. I could see nothing but a never-ending tunnel before us. No doors or hallways of any kind. Silently, she raised her palm in front of her and pressed an invisible wall. The light flickered and wobbled as the tunnel began to warp and bend... until it disappeared, revealing a giant steel wall in its place. It had been an illusion. Tyran and I swapped glances of disbelief as Sayedha turned a giant steel wheel and swung the door open, gesturing for us to follow. There was another brief tunnel on the other side, which ended in a waist-high railing and beyond that...

My mouth hung open with awe at the world that lay below.

It was an enormous cavern, miles high and many miles across. Millions of blue and violet lights glowed from within thousands of buildings that wrapped around a smaller mountain in the center. The homes had been cut into the mountain itself with a road that could be seen spiraling its way to the top. More buildings littered the immense valley on the cave floor far below. At the top of the mountain, perched like a crown, stood a formation of gigantic crystals as tall as castle spires. Tyran looked at me then, eyes wide with wonder, but also... hope. Sayedha, her voice resonating with pride, said, "Welcome to Overlevende, the last stronghold of the Begavet people."

Chapter 37
Aida

We were led down a seemingly never-ending staircase that zigged and zagged across the cave wall, all the way down to the floor nearly a hundred stories below. Streams of water cascaded down the cave walls, some barely a trickle and others a gushing torrent, spraying us as we passed. They all flowed down to the cave floor, where they coalesced into a huge freshwater lake. Approximately thirty stories before we reached the bottom, the stairs diverted into a long suspension bridge that soared over the buildings below, cutting a clear path directly to the mountain at the center of the cavern. Looking over the railing and down to the valley, my breath caught with surprise when I observed the veritable forest that ringed the lake. But there was no sunlight here... *how was that possible?* I turned to Tyran, who was also gazing in the same direction and shaking his head in dismay.

I knew he was thinking the same thing I was: *How did this place exist?*

How had it been kept a secret for so long?

Considering the direction we were headed, I suspected we would get answers soon enough.

Once on the other side of the bridge, our escort led us to the wide cobblestone path that spiraled up the mountain to the crystal keep at the top. If it weren't for the fact that we were miles underground, I would've thought we were in just another village. Regular people seemed to be going about their business as usual; adults bought goods from merchant carts that hugged the wall to our left, while children romped together nearby. Large alcoves had been carved out of the mountain, which contained various goods and trades; weavers selling clothes and blankets, carpenters selling furniture, metallurgists smelting and clanging over woodfire braziers, and healers displaying herbs and tonics from their apothecaries. Most of the alcoves were open to the pathway, but few had doors, and even windows higher up, suggesting that the interior space was two or more levels. A few wood-burning fires were dispersed here and there, but it appeared that most of the light came from the strange blue bulbs. They were everywhere: strung along wires across the pathway, sitting atop metal lanterns, and glowing behind every window. When we reached the top of the mountain, my chest now heaving from the climb, Tyran and I stopped dead at the sight. The cave crystals were as tall as trees and varied in color from bright white to pale blue and lavender. They jutted and crossed each other at sharp angles, with none of them perfectly vertical. In contrast to the gloom of the cavern ceiling many miles above, the crystals glowed like the moon. We followed Sayedha down another staircase, which had been carved at an angle directly below the crystal formation, and descended into the core of the mountain city. Once inside, the glowing blue was replaced with the light from hundreds of candles scattered around a large chamber. Giant bookcases covered every inch of wall space, each one stuffed to the brim with tomes and leather-bound books. I had never seen so many books in my entire life. Tyran turned to me and gave me an awe-struck look, impressed. Sayedha continued walking, and we followed until we arrived in a huge banquet hall capable of holding hundreds of people. The room was devoid of life except for the blazing hearth at the back of the hall... and the one woman who occupied one of the armchairs near it.

My heart flew as we slowed our pace and approached her. I don't know why I had been expecting some grand throne room, but I certainly hadn't anticipated this. The Sorceress Supreme appeared... relaxed. A worn leather book was spread across one leg, and a cup of tea was steaming on the table next to her.

"We found them, my Queen," said Sayedha.

The woman only nodded, closed her book, and gestured for us to sit in the armchairs across from her. Tyran and I shared a curious glance but obeyed and took a seat. For a Queen and Sorceress Supreme, she was pleasantly ordinary. Middle-aged and dark-skinned, she had no hair save for a mandala flower tattoo that encircled the crown of her head. She wore a dark lavender silk robe embroidered with whirls of blue flowers that flowed to her bare feet. Her amber eyes glowed in the firelight as she eyed us with gentle contemplation. When her gaze fell upon Tyran, a flicker of surprise alighted her features for just a moment before it vanished. She only nodded to herself, as if confirming some long-held assumption, before she directed her attention to me and said, "Welcome to Overlevende, the city of survivors. My name is Synsa. Please tell me your name, Dream Walker." Her accent was melodic and sensuous. Eyes wide, I looked over to Tyran, who was studying her, his face calm and expressionless... a poker face. Doing my best to rein in the questions swirling through my head, I responded and said, "My name is Aida. This is Tyran. We were knocked unconscious, restrained, and then dragged here against our will, and we'd very much appreciate an explanation... please." After an awkward beat of silence, she smiled wide, eyes crinkling, and gestured to Sayedha to remove the rope around our hands. She obeyed without hesitation.

"I apologize for any rude behavior you may have experienced," she said, throwing a knowing smirk at Sayedha, who smiled gently in return.

"We have much to discuss... but now is not the time. Sayedha will bring you to your chambers. Please wash and rest. We will begin tomorrow."

The relief in her offer was almost palpable, but I avoided it for a moment longer and asked, hesitantly, "So... you're not going to turn us over to The Sovereign, then?"

She stilled, blood draining from her face and eyes glazing over with contempt before she replied, "No. Never... and do not use that name here. She is only *The Fallen* and nothing more."

With that, she rose from her chair and left. Sayedha nodded to the remaining members of her escort, dismissing them, and they too left the hall. With only the three of us left, Sayedha blew out a breath, her posture relaxing by a fraction. "My great grandmother is a bit testy about...you know who, so tread carefully. Let's get you to your room." We followed her to a stairwell on the side of the great hall, which descended a few levels below to a stone corridor. No blue lights to be seen, and only candles lighting the way. Sayedha gestured to the room at the furthest end of the hall. "These are the guest chambers.

You will find everything you need there. You are the only guests, so no one else will be sharing this corridor."

As she turned to leave, Tyran asked, "Are you so easily assuming that we won't try to escape?"

I didn't let the disappointment of refusing a warm bed show on my face. But she only chuckled and replied, "Trust me. You want to hear what she has to say." Before walking up the stairwell and out of sight.

After standing in the hallway speechless for a few moments, I reached for Tyran's hand and led him to our chambers. "Just for the night," I swore, before opening the door. His knowing smirk told me he was just as exhausted and weary from our weeks in the wilderness, but repeated, "Just for the night."

Reeling in my desire to squeal with delight, we stepped into the most luxurious room I'd ever been in. From the look on Tyran's face, I knew he thought the same. The room was a small cavern with glistening stalactites that lined the back wall. Large, ornate, patterned rugs lay scattered throughout, no doubt to protect your feet from the chilled limestone floor. Hundreds of candles flickered and danced around the room, tucked into small alcoves. A shallow pool of steaming water sat on the other side of the room with a small bathroom just behind it.

And the bed...

It was a four-poster monstrosity with a canopy over ten feet high. Gauzy white curtains flowed down to the lavender silk sheets, blankets, and pillows. It was large enough for four grown men to sleep comfortably in. Somehow, I knew that Tyran and I would have no problem letting all that extra space go to waste. Exhaustion began to usurp the excitement, and I quickly shut the door and led Tyran to the shallow pool to bathe. We removed our clothes and entered the water, sighing with pleasure. An assortment of bottles lay near the pool's edge, and we both took our time soaping and scrubbing each other.

Contented and clean, I sat in his lap and watched the steam curl over the water, his hand tracing lazy circles over my shoulder.

"How did she know about me? About what I am?" I asked in a whisper.

With my head resting against his chest, I could hear his heart stutter at the question. He sighed deeply, thinking through his response before saying, "I think she is like you. She has gifts of her own...and we can only hope her intentions are benign, until we know more."

I only nodded in agreement, too tired to unpack all that just yet. Squeezing my arm in reassurance and tugging a strand of hair behind my ear, he said, "Let's go crawl into those magical-looking sheets and sleep like the dead."

Gods, yes, let's.

CHAPTER 38
AIDA

Tyran and I left the pool and collapsed into bed naked. *Gods above...* I couldn't even remember the last time I had slept in a real bed. I had just enough energy left to marvel at how soft and decadent it was before I snuggled into his bare chest. Then, he wrapped his arms around me and...

We were asleep within two minutes.

Moments later, I saw Tyran in his dreamscape, throwing blades at a target and never missing. He hit the center of the target with every throw. I left him to his devices and leaped into the void, weightless and unencumbered by my flesh. An iron chain wrapped in barbed wire caught my eye. Curious, I pulled the surprisingly heavy chain and found it was attached to the lid of an iron box. Once the lid had been pulled away, I lifted my leg over the side of the box and descended into the heavily fortified psyche of this stranger. Upon reaching the foot of the dark stairwell, a gush of emotion flooded the room.

Shit... it was a sex dream.

Often, I found myself in dreams like this and never lingered to witness this person's most private desires. But before I could turn to flee back up the stairwell, the male in the room snagged my attention.

He was almost a giant, with black hair to his shoulders... *Fucking Hel.* It was the warrior who walked beside us as we were escorted into Overlevende.

He was in bed with a woman I did not recognize. Her long blonde hair was unbound and tousled... and she was riding him. His hands gripped her back as he moaned her name... "*Maya... Gods, Maya.*"

I had officially seen too much.

Vanishing up the stairs a heartbeat later, I crawled out of the box and heaved the lid back over. Shaking my head as if to clear away my own embarrassment, I became vaguely aware of a faint chiming...

My eyes opened, once again in the land of the finite. Tyran, still asleep beside me, was breathing soft and deep. His handsome face was so peaceful that it brought a smile to mine. The candles in the room burned low, wax dripping into their own stalagmites underneath. The faint chime I had heard sounded again; this time, I counted. Seven. But without the sun, I had no idea if it was morning or evening. With all the stealth I could muster, I slipped out of Tyran's arms and silently rose from the bed, still naked. Silent as a mouse, I tiptoed across the room to investigate the dresser against the far wall, fervently praying there were extra clothes that happened to be my size. I found exactly what I needed, as if the room had been supplied to accommodate us before we even knew we would be coming. I only spent a moment pondering how odd that was before dressing myself. Marveling at its rich softness and feeling in a feminine mood, I opted for the lavender silk gown. Fastened around the waist with a brown leather cinch belt, it hugged me like a second skin and did amazing things for my breasts. I couldn't deny that I was excited for Tyran to see me in this dress. But he needed his rest. After sheathing my dagger into the scabbard around my thigh and pulling on the leather slippers I had discovered in the bottom drawer, I glided silently to the door and slipped out.

Once in the corridor, I looked toward the stairwell that led up to the dining hall and noticed a faint blue glow coming from the level directly below. Deciding in an instant that exploring this mysterious mountain city was more important than finding breakfast, I crept down the stairs. Loud clanging and muffled curses rang up from the corridor below, growing louder as I got nearer. The stairs ended, and I found myself in another giant limestone chamber, but this one... was a laboratory. Long tables divided the space into rows, each covered with a various assortment of glass beakers, smoking pots, bubbling vials, and untidy stacks of papers. The entire back wall glowed a bright blue with hundreds of glass tubes that hung over dozens of potted plants. As I walked closer, I noted that some of the tubes had writing scrawled across... dates. One of them said "Oktober 2946" ...which was almost a hundred years ago.

"Good morning!" a chipper voice shouted from behind me.

My heart nearly leaping out of my chest, I whirled around to find a young, lovely blonde woman beaming at me from under her thick square-framed glasses. Her eyes were like sparkling blue sapphires, and her smile exuded warmth by the ton.

"You must be Aida, it's wonderful to finally meet you! You're kind of the talk of the town..." she said a little sheepishly.

Remembering my manners, I grinned and reached for her hand.

"My name is Maya. I'm the chief alchemist and engineer of Overlevende," she said, shaking my hand eagerly.

I prayed my face did not betray my shock as I realized that I had seen her in that monstrous warrior's very explicit dream. *Did she know? Maybe they were together...*

Needing to change the subject away from my morbid curiosity, I asked, "What are these?" gesturing to the glass tubes of glowing blue liquid.

"Ah, yes. Our little secret down here. Our ancestors discovered vast deposits of it deep under the mountain and found a safe way to harness its power. It kept them alive and gave them the ability to build this city. It's called Soladium."

Head reeling with the information dump and feeling a little slow, I asked again, "So... what is it?" She gave me a polite giggle, as if aware of her ability to overwhelm people and replied, "It's a highly unstable mineral. The raw ore is violent and explosive when exposed to heat, fire or high-velocity impact, but when exposed to water..." she smiled proudly, gesturing to the hundreds of glass tubes that lined the wall, "It will glow for over a hundred years. In recent years, I've isolated compounds within the ore that can be used as fuel energy that we use to power machines and even weapons." She beamed. Eyes wide and mouth agape, I could only shake my head in wonder.

The sound of shuffling steps on the stairwell redirected our attention as Tyran entered the room. It appeared he had found new clothes, too, my cheeks heating as I surveyed him from top to bottom. He wore a black, long-sleeved tunic, embroidered with gold, climbing vines at the cuff of the sleeves. The regal-looking shirt hung to his hips and was fastened with a black letter belt. Sandy hair now clean and brushed, he looked like a prince. After gazing around the laboratory, his eyes found mine as he strode over to where Maya and I stood. I noticed him do a subtle double take as he took in my attire, his gray eyes roving over me like a caress. He snapped out of it to politely introduce himself to Maya, who was just as eager to meet him as she had been to meet me.

"So, this is where you ran off to?" he said. I shrugged, giving him a coy smirk.

"Was hoping I could find some food... but ended up here instead," I replied. I noted Maya's gaze floating above our heads back to the stairwell, before she said, "Gods have mercy. It's already 7:30. Let's find breakfast."

I followed her stare and found a metal sun clock above the door frame; the tiny metal sun was attached to an arm and doing a slow arc to the other side.

"Did you make that?" I asked, rapt with fascination. She nodded with a shy smile. I noted a faint blush on her cheeks as she replied, "I'm very good with my hands."

THE THREE OF US MADE OUR WAY INTO THE DINING HALL, WHERE A small table had been set up with a breakfast buffet of cooked eggs, strawberries, fresh bread, and tea. While we filled our plates, she said, "Most of our food is grown underground, hydroponically, with the help of the soladium lights. But we also have a few protected areas on the surface we use for certain crops."

While intriguing, I couldn't shake the twinge of shame at the thought that this technology was not widely used all over Astaran. Without the pressures of growing seasons, blights, and insects, this had the potential to solve the starvation crisis that plagued the villages east of the Solumine River. Plates now full, we turned to sit at a nearby table when two figures strode through the door. "Early risers, I see," said Sayedha, the barrel-chested giant stone-silent beside her. I noticed he shifted slightly on his feet when he saw Maya sitting beside us, smiling brightly at him. "Good morning, Kine. Sayedha," she said, dipping her chin and gesturing to Tyran and me, "I trust you have met the Dream Walker and her..." she trailed off, at a loss as she realized she didn't know the depth of Tyran and I's relationship. I rescued her from the slow flush of embarrassment beginning to bloom over her features and interjected, stating, "Partner." Reaching over to entwine my fingers through Tyran's, he gave me a gentle squeeze in agreement.

"We've met," smirked Sayedha as she began to load up her plate with food. Kine merely stood there menacingly and said nothing, his eyes covertly glancing toward Maya as she ate and drank her tea. Oblivious.

After finishing our meal, Sayedha announced, "I've been instructed to show you around the city before taking you to our Queen later today. She also wishes to inform you that there will be a feast in your honor tonight." Her eyes briefly met Kine's and Maya's before saying, "We have waited a long time for your arrival, Aida...and for you too, Tyran." Confused by that remark, we said nothing and only nodded. Deep inside, I secretly dreaded the answers we were soon to receive from The Sorceress Supreme.

CHAPTER 39
AIDA

Sayedha, Kine, and Maya acted as our guides as we explored the vast network of caverns that surrounded the mountain city. We learned about how they grew food, cultivated animals, and filtered water. Maya explained that there were enormous systems of pipes drilled throughout the mountain, which were used for both ventilation and water treatment. It appeared that news of our presence here had spread quickly, too. Nearly every villager we encountered gave us the same wide-eyed, beaming smile and began to grovel with offers to make this or do that. Tyran and I, unsure of what to make of it, would just politely thank them and shake our heads. On the far side of the mountain, another suspension bridge brought us through even more tunnels until we eventually arrived at something Maya called an "elevator shaft." While squeezing into the small metal box, Maya boasted that this invention had been the work of her grandfather and was powered by tiny, controlled bursts of soladium, which in turn activated a system of levers and pulleys that could move the box all the way to the surface.

I noticed that Kine never took his eyes off her mouth when she spoke.

Sayedha, always professional and assessing, did not seem to notice or care. The elevator ascended high enough to make our ears pop before it stopped abruptly, and the doors squeaked open. We were led into another brief stone tunnel before Sayedha pushed open a heavy steel door and revealed... *a forest*.

I gasped, neck craning up as I beheld a gigantic glass dome above our heads, sunlight streaming in and warming the lush, green terrarium around us. Hundreds of fruit trees and rows upon rows of crops covered one side of the dome. And on the other side, a great sprawl of open, green spaces and paved areas for training, including racks of weapons and targets.

"This is our public green space for all inhabitants of Overlevende. Our ancestors named it 'Gronnhimmel,' but we simply refer to it as 'The Dome,'" Sayedha said, affectionately. As we began to explore, a smudge of blue caught my attention just outside the glass wall. I approached warily, my fascination drawing me to it like a magnet. It appeared to be a vast lake nestled in the valley many miles below where the glass dome sat perched on the mountain. The realization hit me with the force of a hammer, making me gasp.

It was... a fjord. And beyond... was the ocean.

Utterly still, it reflected the surrounding peaks like a mirror. For a moment, I was truly speechless. It was so vast and majestic, I wanted to cry. *We found it*, I thought. My whole life, I had imagined the Furian Wood continuing forever, once on the other side of the mountains, but... it was an ocean.

Why had this fact been hidden from all of us... for all this time?

The very existence of this giant geological feature had been wiped from every map I'd ever seen. *But why?* After a quick glance at Tyran, I could tell he was just as puzzled as I was.

"That... is the Frelse Fjord. And the ocean beyond we call The Sea of Starlight." Sayedha said as she came to stand next to us.

"Long ago, many millennia before *The Fallen* ruled over Astaran, our historians documented proof of a great leviathan that once lived in these waters. Legends say the Gods placed him here as a guardian and would call upon him in times of great need."

The tiny hairs on the back of my neck began to rise when Maya cut in, "Nah, just a bunch of old ghost stories probably. The Begavet built this dome overlooking the fjord centuries ago, and no one has ever seen a giant sea creature," she said irreverently, lightly smacking Kine on the arm in jest. He tensed at the touch, standing ramrod straight. Maya did not seem to notice his recoil.

A faint tingle, like an itch, crawled across my scalp as I gazed at the fjord below. I didn't allow myself to dwell on the very real presence that thrummed with power below the surface. Yes, something lived down there... and I could sense its consciousness.

Sleeping.

AFTER FINISHING THE TOUR AND HELPING OURSELVES TO SOME RIPE

plums fresh off the tree, Sayedha walked up to me and Tyran and stated, "It's time for me to bring you to Synsa..."

The foreboding in her voice was unmistakable. But I was ready for this. I was ready to finally understand. But as the doors of the elevator shut, cutting us off from the warm sunlight, I wasn't entirely convinced it was the plummet back down to the cave that was solely to blame for the knot in my gut.

Upon returning to the mountain city, we met Synsa in the same place we had found her the night before. While still barefoot, her robe was now a deep crimson with small white flowers that dusted the hem where it glided over the floor. With a brief nod of her head, she dismissed the rest of our group. Maya's eyes met mine as she flashed a supportive smile before returning to her lab down the stairwell. As soon as we were alone, Synsa padded silently to the roaring hearth behind her and lifted her hand to raise a book from the mantle, fingers lightly pressing into the stone beneath. The motion seemed to trigger a suppression system of some kind, as the fire immediately snuffed out, not an ember remaining. The stone wall at the back of the hearth pulled apart, revealing a spiral stairwell that descended into the gloom.

"This way, please," she said, ducking through the door.

After sharing a knowing glance of apprehension, Tyran and I followed. After many tense minutes, head dizzy from our spiraling descent, we arrived in what appeared to be another library. The key difference from the bookcases in the main hall above was the seemingly ancient tomes here that had been carefully organized in neat rows from floor to ceiling. The smell of the room was thick with dust and dry rot, but was clean and surprisingly simple. Only three candles sat in metal dishes on the table in the center of the room, as far away from the tomes as possible. Synsa stopped at the end of the furthest case and carefully removed one. I noted it was not as dusty as the others, apparently having been treated with care. She brought the tome to the table and spread it open, moving the candle slightly closer before standing back. Tyran and I leaned in... and all thoughts eddied from my mind as an image became clear.

It was a woman. She was fair with long, dark hair and... brilliant, light blue eyes.

She looked just like me.

I heard Tyran's breath catch in his throat as he came to the same conclusion. She wore a deep blue robe with a sword that hung from her waist, but the most striking feature... was her helmet. It appeared to be made of gold, with great, twisting horns on either side and a long plate which ran down the plane of the nose and sides of her head. Her arms and hands were wreathed in white-hot flame, held aloft as if she were summoning the sky.

She was a terrifying vision of primordial power.

Synsa spoke then, saying, "This is Queen Mercury Drømmevandrer. She was the most powerful Dream Walker in recorded history and the leader of the Begavet people. Her mate was King Arketh." She then leaned over to carefully turn the page, revealing an illustration of the two royal figures seated together on a throne. The King was dark featured with black hair and green eyes, and just as menacing as his partner.

"*What* were they?" I asked, nervously.

Synsa sighed as she flipped to a page near the back of the tome. Tyran and I both cocked our heads as we tried to make sense of the image.

They were... *angels*.

Great black-and-white wings were attached to giant, mighty bodies—neither male nor female—as they were fornicating with humans. Great hordes of writhing bodies in the throes of passion were scattered across the land at the bottom of the painting.

She flipped to another page.

Nightmarish creatures and others with beautiful human-like features were descending from the clouds, bearing gifts and treasure, bestowing it on the humans who groveled and wept on their knees.

Shoulders tense and voice low, Tyran looked into her eyes and asked, "What is this?"

Leaving the tome and moving to the other side of the table, she seated herself and gave us a pointed look. We obeyed and sat down. After a contemplative inhale, fingers gently tapping on the table, she began.

"This is the history of the world before *The Fallen* arrived here more than a thousand years ago. The images you see here are a record of an ancient bloodline sourced from the union of both Gods and Angels... with humans."

Her words clanged through me like an echo, horror and disgust fighting for dominance. The thought of it was... grotesque. Some of the creatures in these images were truly monsters, and I knew without a doubt that not all these unions had been consensual.

After a moment, she continued saying, "The Gods of both Lyrath and Hel were... *enamored* by the humans of Astaran. The result of this interbreeding was a race of people who inherited powerful psychic gifts..." She paused, her amber eyes nearly glowing as they darted between Tyran and me.

"Foresight, the primary gift of the Seidhr. Precognition. Telekinesis. Telepathy... and dream walking."

The once-beating heart inside my ribs stilled and thudded to a stop. A shudder rippled down my spine as her words hit their mark. I was vaguely aware of Tyran looking at me and squeezing my hand under the table... but all I could do was stare at the image in disbelief. Fast as a flying arrow, a thought struck me.

"You. It was your vision I saw when I first arrived here in Overlevende. You were there when The Sov— When *The Fallen* was struck down. That makes you..."

Synsa's eyes were kind, but her features hardened at the memory. She merely nodded before replying, "Very old, indeed. Yes. As one of the more powerful Seidhrs under her command, I was valuable to Queen Mercury and the survival of our people."

Gods be damned, did I even want to know what my place was in all this?

My gut roiled and convulsed, threatening to bring up its contents. Tyran spoke, saying, "So you are a Seidhr, with the gift of foresight. And you are immortal..."

There was no mistaking the hidden question in his statement. I knew what he was asking. Synsa's eyes softened then as she nodded, her face grave as she confirmed his suspicion.

"Yes. All descendants of the Begavet, who have the gifts, are also gifted with long life. Even I have not seen my own death."

Hollowness flowed through me like a flood. My gift came bound with an inheritance of immortality. An inheritance I never would've chosen for myself.

And Tyran... No, I couldn't think of it.

I knew in the deepest parts of my soul that I'd rather join him in Hel than live without him in this wretched world.

"So, who are the Mørkebringer? Who are the people we were all told were the minions of evil for generations?" Tyran asked, his tone icy.

Synsa stilled then, slowly moving away from the table to cross her arms. A small vein pulsed underneath the delicate skin of her temple as she contemplated her response. She, of all people, knew the weight of the information she possessed and what it would mean for our future. Her continued silence was her way of giving us a choice... whether to move forward or retreat.

It had to mean something: my parents vanishing and abandoning me in the wild.

My "gift" ... and my curse.

A flicker of hope floated like an ember in the back of my mind. So many generations of people had suffered at the hands of the fallen angel who ruled over this land with an iron fist, who sacrificed young women out of her own narcissism. She had been cast out by the Gods themselves. She had betrayed them to lay waste to Astaran, and I wanted to know why.

I deserved to know.

Praying my voice was convincing enough, I said, "Tell us. Tell us all of it."

I swore I saw a corner of her lip curl briefly before she brought her hands back to the table and clasped them in front of her.

"I'd rather show you, if that's all right," she said, quietly.

I must've looked confused because her tone became instructive as she continued, "I want you to project into my mind and Tyran's at the same time, and bring us to the same dreamscape." Figuring it would be pointless to mention that I had only projected into someone's mind while awake just all of one time, with Sköll, I breathed deep and closed my eyes. With my heartbeat thrumming in my ears, I concentrated on the vibrations in the room...

The low sizzle of the candle flame.

The hum of ancient knowledge that hung over the tomes like a mist.

The roar of the blood river gushing through all our veins.

And there they were. Vibrating threads of energy; Tyran, a

glowing, golden chain, and Synsa, a vibrant, green vine, covered in razor-sharp thorns.

My astral form reached out and grabbed the threads in either hand, yanking them toward me as we tumbled into black, screaming across the void like a comet until colliding into a leafy forest floor.

Somewhere in the Furian Wood.

Lifting my head from the ground and standing upright, I noticed Tyran beside me, face serious and troubled. Synsa appeared to be wreathed in purple smoke, shadows distorting her figure. Just up ahead, two imposing figures stood near a cliff's edge, watching the vision of Armageddon taking place in the valley below.

It was King Arketh and Queen Mercury, both clad in silver armor that was streaked with blood and grime.

The Queen wore the same helmet we had seen in the illustration. Blinding white flames enveloped her in a cocoon of blistering power.

Stretching out to the horizon, war stained both the ground and skies with gore and ash.

"It's time, Mercury! Chemosh is leading the advance from the skies; we must torch her and end this!" the King shouted.

They were losing. Hel's armies were too powerful and too blood thirsty.

"We risk killing our own people by the thousands if we summon that power!" she screamed back, anguish and despair contorting her features.

"They will come if we summon them. The Gods will come and destroy her!" he said, his expression fierce with vengeance.

Her face crumpled with agony for just a moment before it slowly hardened into stone. Acceptance, I realized... She knew they did not have time.

Her posture straightened then as she rose to her full height.

Arketh kneeled, grabbing her hand and pressing it to his forehead before saying, "*May the God's forgive us...*"

A silent tear slipped down her face as she turned and walked to the cliff's edge, raised her hands to the sky and bellowed with rage. Within seconds, roaring death funneled down from the upper atmosphere in the form of mountain sized pillars of flame and slammed into the ground. Hundreds of souls in the path of the vortexes, both allies and enemies, disintegrated in an instant. The Queen's screaming turned to sobs of gut-wrenching pain as she rained fire down onto the battlefield.

Moments later, an ear-shattering boom high above the clouds sent a shockwave through the air, shaking the ground and bending the trees backward. The Queen lowered her arms as the flames began to dissipate into smoke. The Gods had come to punish the monster responsible for this carnage. But the Queen did not linger to see it. Abruptly, she turned and walked in the direction of the forest, toward Synsa. Her eyes blazed with grief; a bright, blue contrast against her filthy, tear-streaked face.

"Synsa, the time is now. Just as we discussed. You must flee with any surviving Begavet. The Gods have betrayed us. They allowed this demon to be unleashed on our world. The King and I will remain behind to ensure The Morning Star is truly gone... and if she survives the wrath of the Gods, we will bury the helmet of Brannregn somewhere it can never be found. We cannot risk its power falling into her hands. Please, Synsa, go now." She pleaded.

Synsa's memory ached with the pain of this moment, it was unbearable for her, but she only nodded silently and placed a hand over her heart. A promise.

Queen Mercury dipped her chin, eyes brimming with tears before striding back to the King. As the King and Queen unsheathed their blades and began to make their way down the cliff, the sky flashed with violent, blinding strobes. A cry of rage ripped across the battlefield as the tumbling star plummeted to the ground... her severed black wings spinning and twisting behind her.

"Go now, Synsa!" the Queen shouted before her and the King sprinted into the valley of mayhem below... She only waited a heartbeat before she whirled, shouting instructions to the commanders that stood near the cliff's edge and fled into the dark shadow of the forest.

The vision shifted and shuddered—

Violent explosions rocked the side of a mountain, triggering catastrophic slides which sent giant boulders careening down the slope like a torrent. People screamed and scattered, some crushed by debris and others funneling into cave tunnels, fiercely clinging to their children and possessions. "Run! Get inside! Flee into the mines!" Synsa screamed, arms frantically waving people through a tunnel door.

Her eyes scanned the horizon, looking for someone as the booms continued to pummel the mountain. The cave walls buckled and groaned just seconds before caving in entirely, blocking the entrance for any poor souls who remained outside. Synsa sprinted down the corridor, following the fleeing hordes before blackness consumed the memory again.

I gasped and flew out of the chair, hands braced on the bookcase behind me.

We were still in the vault, buried deep within the beating heart of the mountain city.

The city of survivors.

Gulping like a fish out of water, I tried to restore balance to my quaking frame. Tyran was still seated but gripped the sides of his head as if in pain, eyes boring into something unseen in the woodgrain of the table. My brain began to sizzle from the onslaught of questions that I needed immediate answers to. After a few steadying breaths, I looked up and found Synsa's eyes watching me warily.

"What happened to them? The King and Queen." I asked.

Sorrow crossed over her features then as she dropped her gaze to stare at her hands.

"The Morning Star had been cast out of Lyrath, her wings severed, but she still had most of her strength... The King and Queen met her on the battlefield that day and barely escaped with their lives... and the helmet of Brannregn. There was no word from them for many, many years, and we all just assumed they had vanished deep into the wilderness. But I knew they stayed away so the Begavet had a chance to survive... they did not wish to bring death upon their people again. But as Chemosh regained her strength, she continued to hunt down any gifted Begavet people that remained on Astaran. She destroyed every once great city and set fire to every library and tome that documented the lineage of the Begavet. She spread lies about the evil 'Mørkebringer' people in hopes that humans would fear us enough to turn us over to her... She tried her hardest to eradicate our species and any proof of our existence in this world. When her armies discovered our settlement on the slopes of the Vazaketh, she unleashed catapults on us all: men, women, and children. But our people had been tunneling and mining under the mountain for decades, and she was arrogant enough to suspect we could not survive there. As the centuries passed, we rebuilt our civilization underground, while the rest of Astaran fell under her shadow..."

She paused and breathed deeply through her nose, gathering her strength before continuing, "Two hundred and thirty-six years ago... *The Fallen* discovered the hiding place of

King Arketh and Queen Mercury, at their hidden stronghold in Svargad."

Tyran's head snapped up then, and we both waited with bated breath.

"...She slaughtered them. Burning them both alive in front of one another. She had somehow resisted Queen Mercury's power... and the Queen failed to penetrate her mind. She tortured them for many days trying to discover the location of the helmet... but they never surrendered. Their heads were found on spikes in front of the gates of Opeth, where they remained until time and weather turned them to dust..."

My knees shook under the crushing pressure of this knowledge.

My ancestors were the ancient spawn of Gods and Angels.

What did it all mean? Was there a purpose? Or even a choice?

I was just one person and apparently an immortal one. What could I do? Was I really going to be sucked into the delusion that a righteous few could defeat an immortal fallen angel?

Tyran's voice broke through the fog of silence that had settled on the room. "The helmet is one of the gifts from the Gods, isn't it? But it clearly was not powerful enough to destroy her. How do we learn how to kill her? If she can even *be* killed?"

Synsa's eyes floated over to mine.

"That is where Aida's powerful gift... as the last descendant of the Drømmevandrer will come into play. She alone can commune with the Gods and discover how *The Fallen* can be destroyed... through the conduit of an Obsidian Mirror."

CHAPTER 40
AIDA

"What is an Obsidian Mirror?" I asked, praying the trepidation in my voice was not too obvious. Slowly, Synsa rose from the table and glided to a bookcase behind her to remove another tome. Flipping to the right place, she angled the page toward us and pushed it across the table. The illustration showed a female in her astral form, the universe swirling beneath her skin. She walked through an archway, and on the other side... was Lyrath, the God Realm. A sprawling, glimmering citadel perched high on a mountain, picturesque with climbing roses and waterfalls.

"The Gods gave us many gifts. The helmet of Brannregn was given as a tool to defeat our enemies; its wielder would be granted God-like strength and the power to summon fire from the sky. Another gift provided only the Dream Walkers with the ability to commune with the Gods directly: The Obsidian Mirrors... But they were lost after *The Fallen* began her reign on Astaran. Either hidden or destroyed, but no one has seen one in centuries..."

A part of me wanted to heave a sigh of relief. Life could go on. Tyran and I could live here, safe, with the Begavet forever... *couldn't we?*

But the other part... a wriggling worm of vengeance, began to chew through my mind.

My role in this could not be ignored. Queen Mercury's power of both dream walking and telepathy had skipped multiple generations until it found me. *Chose* me.

It was my blood right.

Could I ignore it to live in peace?

Could I allow the people of Astaran to continue their pathetic existence of ignorance and oppression?

Could I move forward with my life knowing that the demon who dwelled behind the gates of Opeth would continue to sacrifice young girls until the end of time?

The same savage conqueror who would stop at nothing to find the remaining Begavet and exterminate them, including me and Tyran...

No.

I did not have a choice at all.

The Gods were putting their faith in me. For whatever reason. The burden of this responsibility threatened to rip me apart from the inside out. I would follow this road, but I knew I could not do it alone.

"You know where one of the mirrors is... don't you?" I asked Synsa with a pointed stare.

She only dipped her chin, giving me the space to declare my decision with finality. But Tyran interjected then, raising a hand.

"I'd like to have a moment alone with Aida. There is much we need to discuss," he said to Synsa, his tone apologetic.

Without receiving a formal dismissal, he rose from the table and offered his hand to me. Synsa's eyes softened as they roved over us both. She only inclined her head before rising to her feet saying, "I will see you both at dinner tonight. You may present your decision to me tomorrow..." Tyran nodded once, his face unreadable. Nearly fleeing from the room, Tyran gripped my hand tight as we ascended the stairs, leaving the gravity within the vault behind.

Silently, we returned to our chambers. Tyran ushered me in, eyes darting around the corridor. He locked the door and moved to sit on the bed. I only hovered close by, arms wrapped tight across my chest, mind scattered and frayed. For a long time, we said nothing. Tyran's body was rigid, hands clenched into fists over his thighs. I knew our next words to each other would define everything about who we were... as partners.

This was the largest test we may ever face.

The choice now in front of us loomed like an insurmountable mountain.

Would we face it together?

Abruptly, Tyran launched from the bed and began to pace across the room, running his hands through his hair. The low-burning candles cast their flickering shadows onto the walls of the cavern as I watched him, waiting. His pacing became more frantic before he suddenly lurched to a stop and kneeled at my feet. Pressing his forehead against my knee, I felt my heart splinter at the sound of his sobs. His tears soaking through the fabric of my dress...

"*I just found you.*", he whispered.

Tears spilled down my cheeks as he lifted his head, gray eyes swimming with despair and said again, "I just found you. And now I must go to war with a *demon* to save you. Because I won't let you do this alone, Aida. I will be whoever you need me to be, but I will not allow you to face this alone. Live or die, we do it together. Swear to me. Swear to me that we will do this together. This is not only your burden to carry. Not anymore. You have me now. All of me. Swear it…"

I couldn't find the breath in my lungs to make a sound.

Of course it was only my burden. But I was immortal, and he was not… and every single second of his presence mattered. I could not reject his offer even to save his life, knowing I would also surely die in this foolish attempt to fulfill my destiny. But we would not be separated. We would do this together and die together, *Gods willing*.

His eyes were wide as they bore into mine, pleading.

I only nodded, gently cupping his face between my hands before placing a gentle kiss on his lips. My promise.

The instant our lips met, a growl rumbled from his chest as he pulled me up against him. His hands began to roam down my spine, fingers delicately loosening the ties of the cinch belt at my waist.

"All day long, I've had to look at you in this *God's damned* dress. Now, I just want to worship you without it."

His words dripped down my legs like molten wax as he gently pushed the dress from my shoulders and shimmied it down my hips. Breasts fully peaked and aching, I pressed them against his mouth as he leaned down to remove the dress from around my ankles. He responded immediately with a low moan, tongue lashing, and sucking each nipple in turn. He stood upright then, mouth crushing into mine hard enough to bruise as his fingers began to rub my clit in slow circles. I gasped into his mouth at the contact, my hand scrambling for the button of his pants. Springing free at last, his hard cock jerked under my ministrations, eliciting sweet moans from his mouth into mine.

Suddenly, Tyran was kneeling with his face between my legs... licking and sucking me senseless. His warm hands squeezing the cheeks of my backside, pressing me into his mouth.

Holy fucking Gods. It was everything.

My body seized with sensation; stomach muscles clenched tight as he fucked me with his tongue. His eyes looked up at me as he stroked me harder. I met his stare and moaned his name, fingers gripping his soft hair.

Fuck, I wanted to come against his mouth, and I knew he would let me.

The soft sucking noise of his tender lips on my most sensitive part drove me over the edge. My release shattered through my body as spasms clenched through my core. His gentle licking never stopped, riding with me to the furthest horizon of surrendering bliss. When the pleasure was too much to stand any longer, I raised his face to look at me as he began to trail kisses up my abdomen, his warm breath leaving a trail of fire in its wake.

Gently, he began to push me back onto the bed, his powerful body mounting me with decadent tenderness. Still panting through the throes of my climax, I opened my legs and bared myself for him, fingers trailing across my slickness. His hooded gaze bore into mine as he placed his hands on either side of my face and kissed me like he was *starving*, his cock gently pushing into my entrance with slow, tantalizing thrusts. He was huge, but *fuck*, it felt so good. Moaning his name snapped the leash of restraint as he drove into me, stretching me to the point of pain. His body shook, overwhelmed with sensation just as I was. I kissed him again, softly sucking on his tongue as he moved in me over and over. The pain turned to carnal oblivion, my body squeezing and writhing independently of my fractured mind. A burning sensation on my chest distracted me for only a moment before I refocused my attention on the prince who was thrusting his tongue and his cock into me like a madman. I was mindless, whimpering, and panting. Tyran wrapped his arms around my back and hugged me to his chest as he rocked into me at a crushing pace.

We were one, and we would always be.

This was our destiny: us.

I wanted to be everything to him: his lover, his wife, whatever he wanted.

My hands pressed against his hard chest, Sköll's attack still visible in the form of tender, jagged scars. He was perfect, strong, and devoted to me.

At that moment, I truly felt that we could win. We could survive this together.

His pants became ragged as his thrusts broke their rhythm. Both trembling as our mouths collided, the kisses growing more urgent. The wet slap of our bodies became the only sound as he tensed, drawing in breath, and fucked me until I saw stars. I cried out as another shudder of release barreled between my legs, back arching off the bed. I felt him let go then, panting and barking my name as he pumped into me, spilling his seed.

He was *mine*.

Chest heaving, his heavy, limp body sagged into mine, too far gone to support his weight. My breath left in a whoosh. Noticing immediately, Tyran pulled out of me and rolled over to the side. Slick with sweat and catching his breath, he gathered me into his arms and breathed deeply against my forehead.

Gods... that was...

Perfect.

Tyran must've agreed as he squeezed me and murmured into my hair a moment later, "So glad I waited for you."

I AWOKE TO A WARMTH BETWEEN MY LEGS. STILL HAZY WITH SEX-addled fog, I cracked open an eye, stiffening at the touch. Tyran was wiping me clean with a wet cloth, his hands maneuvering my legs closed with care. Noting my sudden stillness, his eyes snapped to mine. I flushed as warmth tingled across the skin of my chest. I hadn't considered what might happen the first time. I hadn't considered the blood. I squeezed my thighs together tightly and bit my lip as I looked away from him, embarrassment threatening to swallow me whole. His warm hands only roved my bare thighs and hips in slow circles, his eyes never lingering from my face. My skin broke out into goosebumps at the contact, his breath warming the sensitive flesh of my backside.

"Don't look away from me. I only wanted you to feel clean when you awoke. You are a woman and have nothing to be ashamed of." His voice dripped with lust as his words caressed my nakedness. Somewhat shocked by his sudden boldness, I only nodded shyly. The heat in his gaze began to smolder as his lips grazed across my legs, gradually moving their way to my exposed sex, which had already started to grow wet with anticipation. My breath hitched, and my breasts began to harden at the sight of him laving my backside so sweetly. "Is it too soon? I can stop if you want..." he asked huskily. *He better fucking not.* A soft sigh was my only response as I arched my back and pressed my backside further into his grip. A rumbling moan escaped his lips as he set his mouth to me and feasted again.

Fuckkkk.

With my knees pressed together, his tongue robbed me of all sense as he sucked me from the back. A desperate, animalistic need possessed me and had me rolling onto my belly, spreading my legs wide. Tyran growled deep, his hands groping and kneading my rear as he devoured me. I couldn't take it. It was mind-blowing. I turned to look over my shoulder and nearly broke at the sight of my musky arousal dripping from his chin, his eyes almost black with savage lust. His fingers spread me wider as the sucking and biting intensified. My legs began to quake as my release approached with the speed of windswept wildfire.

"*Ah, fuck!*" I cried, as he sucked me roughly, the feeling driving me toward the edge of sanity. I came undone, moaning and screaming his name as I shattered on his tongue, panting like a wanton beast. Then his hard, warm body was mounting me from behind. His heaving chest pressed into my back as he pushed his cock into me. I took him eagerly, pushing my backside skyward to give him better access.

I wanted him to break me.

I wanted him to *own* me.

He fucked me at a punishing pace as his hands moved to wrap around my neck. He kissed and nibbled on my ear, grunting as he went, making me whimper at his closeness. His sheer male domination over me left me starstruck.

"I'll never have my fill of you." *Thrust.* "Your scent." *Thrust.*

"The softness of your skin." *Thrust.* "Your perfection. I'll never stop needing more. Wanting more," he whispered against my hair. The tightness in my belly began to build as he hauled me against him on my knees, his chest, sticky with sweat, pressed to my back. His powerful arms cradled me, one hand gripping my neck, the other slowly rubbing my slit in tantalizing circles. The ecstasy was world-ending, and I hung on for dear life as a second more powerful orgasm tore through me. Clenching and spluttering through my spasm, Tyran's pounding intensified as he rammed me like his life depended on it. With one final push, he moaned against the back of my head, his warm seed dripping down my legs as he found his climax.

Utterly spent, I collapsed forward onto the bed, my head swimming with euphoria. Tyran pulled himself out of me before reaching for my waist and carrying me away from the bed. Too dazed to struggle, I wrapped my arms around his neck as he walked us across the room and down the steps into our personal thermal spring. Hissing with pleasure at the heat of the water, I let myself float in his arms. I was too tired to open my eyes, but indulged in the absolute bliss of him washing my hair, his strong fingers massaging my scalp thoroughly. Lovingly. When he was finished, I opened my eyes to see him staring at my face. His expression was solemn. Almost pained.

"What is it?" I whispered, raising my steaming fingers to stroke his jaw, which clenched with tension. His nostrils flared briefly before he sighed deeply through the nose. He looked as if he were about to respond when his eyes did a double-take at my chest, widening with shock and confusion. Alarmed, I looked down to the skin between my breasts...

to find a symbol branded into my skin.

I gasped as I hesitantly prodded the still raw mark with trembling fingers. The brand was a fresh, deep, pink, as if the hot iron lay only inches away. The lines crossed to make an X, but with two lines that closed off each end...

My eyes darted to Tyran, who was not looking at me... but at his own chest...

Where the same symbol lay etched into the flesh of his sternum.

CHAPTER 41
RAVN

The headaches were getting worse.

In the week since The Sovereign had commanded me to tend to Helena and the two young girls in the cold dungeons underneath the palace, the searing pain pulsating through my head had only intensified. Previously, they had only occurred during my curiously pleasant dreams; now they were starting to happen at random intervals throughout the day. Every time I bathed with warm water or woke up in a bed instead of the hard, stone floor. Or every time I felt the warm sun on my face. It seemed my guilt was beginning to eat me alive. I had done all I could within my power to make the lives of the maidens more pleasant; however much of it was left. Taking advantage of the quiet hours in the night, I smuggled extra blankets, food, and fresh water to them at every opportunity. I knew what would happen if I were caught and my obvious compassion was exposed. Somehow, I didn't care.

In the service of the Anakaii, I had done many things most people would consider inhumane. Since the age of ten, we had been forced to participate in public floggings and even executions of anyone The Sovereign deemed disloyal. Our training had been ruthless, too. Frequently, our strength and resilience were tested through various combat and survival trials, aptly named "Sterk Kamps." Many cadets died during these trials either from exposure, infection, or were outright killed by their fellow cadets. My generation consisted of nearly a hundred chosen cadets who were selected to move on to the advanced Anakaii training; in the nine years since, only twenty of us remained. Growing attached to a fellow cadet was never encouraged; apart from training, eating, and bathing, we were mostly kept separate from each other. They wanted us to view one another as rivals, and only once we had sworn the blood oath could we consider ourselves "comrades."

My apparent bleeding heart for the maidens rotting away in the dark, however, seemed to be wholly separate from who I was as a cadet.

My mind often drifted to the image of Helena's soft, green eyes; now hardened with grief and hatred. While their choices had been stripped away in the same way as mine and the other cadets, the fact that someone so fair and innocent was being abused so thoroughly seemed inexcusable. The truth was: I was more of a survivor than I was a killer.

I had never intentionally taken the life of another cadet in my time here. At the age of twelve, a young boy, Shavri, had died after my blade had nicked too close to an artery. The shock of the memory still seized my chest with guilt. At the time, all I could do was watch, frozen with shock, as the blood pooled around his lifeless body. All the while knowing that the elder Anakaii were watching my reaction like eagles encircling a crippled fawn. It was fortunate that I was taller and larger-framed than most of the cadets, as this gave me an advantage not only in combat but also in the eyes of the elders; to them, I showed promise as a warrior. But in that moment, I realized that if I were to survive here, it would require full mastery of my emotions.

As I dressed for the day, head throbbing as I went, a musical rap on my door told me immediately who waited on the other side. It was difficult to contain my grin when I opened the door to see Akton standing there as irreverent as ever. Despite our reluctance to form bonds, he was the only one here that I would ever claim as my friend. He smirked roguishly as he roamed over my features before his expression tensed into a frown, "Still having those headaches, Ravn? Why don't you pop into Raziel's lab and take a tonic?" he said, sarcasm dripping from every word. No one visited Raziel unless they were on death's door. Many cadets would consider death to be more pleasant than being in his presence.

"I'll manage," I replied dryly, shutting the door and striding into the hall.

"Suit yourself, but it may give you a disadvantage during your Sterk Kamp today." I swallowed. Shit, that *was* today.

His pale, blue eyes became more concerned than before as he said, "Shit, Ravn. You *forgot*? What's got you so distracted?" I didn't dare tell him about my tasks with the maidens. While I may have considered Akton a friend, even an ally, there were limits to what you could expose about yourself here.

"I'll be fine, Akton. There's no need to fuss." I said, not believing a word of it.

His cool grin told me he had complete faith in my abilities

and wasn't concerned. Something about it did indeed lift my spirits. He waved his hand toward the hall before us and sketched into a mocking bow. "Shall we then?"

Sterk kamp days were considered a form of entertainment for the Anakaii and cadets. Even The Sovereign herself would sometimes deign to witness whatever carnage these trials forced us to commit. As we walked into the courtyard and passed the training ring in the center, I noted, with a twinge of relief, the lack of her fearsome presence. The twenty cadets who remained from my generation were already standing in loose formation near the empty ring, waiting for the Anakaii elders to arrive. After a few silent moments, ten of them walked into the courtyard, all clad in black, with their faces hidden, as always. In fact, the only Anakaii warrior's face we had ever seen was that of our Captain, Tylor. The captain approached the ring and announced to us, "The Sterk Kamp will not be taking place in the ring today." Silence settled over the cadets like a heavy cloth. I struggled to keep my composure through the pounding in my head and chest. His dark eyes found me in the crowd, and a look of... displeasure... seemed to contort his features for the briefest moment, before he heaved a weary sigh and said, "Follow me."

All twenty cadets and ten elder Anakaii warriors formed a single line and followed the captain through the palace to the southern side of the compound. The area just outside of the palace wall had once been a stone quarry when Opeth was built centuries ago; now the deep pits were mainly used for rubbish burning and... body disposal.

My stomach began to jerk with nausea at the thought of falling into one of those pits, your body breaking all the way down.

What kind of sadistic game had they planned for us now?

My palms began to moisten with the sweat of anticipation.

Whatever it was, I had to survive; there was no other choice. We arrived around the ledge of the quarry to find a single metal beam affixed to either side of the gaping pit. No one dared speak a word as we all stared numbly into the swallowing blackness, nearly a half mile to the bottom.

I became vaguely aware of Akton standing next to me and heard him whisper, "You have the feet of a dancer, Ravn. You will triumph. Don't doubt it for a second."

I knew his words were meant to give me courage, but all I could do was clench my fists and try to control my breathing. The voice of The Sovereign, like glass shrapnel wrapped in silk, drifted from the makeshift dais on the other side of the chasm; the sun rising from the east behind her and casting her in shadow.

"Today, two of our most talented cadets will prove if they have what it takes to become one of my most fearsome warriors. To be an Anakaii is to show no mercy and no fear. *Ravn. Lark.* Choose your weapons." Her orange eyes glowed like embers from the inky black of her soulless face. She found no other sport as intriguing as combat to the death.

Fuck. I whirled, breath stuttering as my eyes rested on Lark.

If I were considered one of the larger males in our generation, Lark was not only a close second but would undeniably win "most cruel" by a landslide. His black eyes met mine as his lip curled into a feral smirk. As a boy, Lark was known for breaking the necks of his opponents, taking organ shots with daggers, and even using poison on any cadets he found irksome. While a few inches shorter than me, what he lacked in height, he made up for in psychotic rage. The thudding pulse of pain in my head turned searing, but I ignored it to focus on how I would survive the next few minutes. Fanning the flames of my resolve, I breathed deep and walked to the weapons rack. Lark had already chosen his long sword and a brutal looking serrated dagger. While I was light on my feet, my heavier upper body may indeed be my downfall; with that in mind, I carefully selected a long, double-bladed sword and a light, steel hatchet, which I fixed to my waist. The sword would act as a counterweight and, Gods willing, help me keep my balance.

Before walking onto the beam, Lark turned and gave a low bow to The Sovereign. I only dipped my head, ready for this shit to be over. Feet testing the beam with trepidation, we walked out to the center, not daring to look down at the chasm that was soon to claim one of us. Or both. Instantly, my face and body slipped into the disguise I had perfected over the last nine years: a stealthy predator.

But of course, it wasn't a mask at all; I wanted this fucker dead, not me.

I knew he wouldn't hold anything back, so I wouldn't either.

"I'll see you in Hel, Ravn," Lark said with confidence.

Faster than a spitting cobra, he threw his daggers at my chest. Instinct had me blocking them by deftly spinning my sword like a windmill, feet never once shifting on the beam. He moved closer and swung his long sword, arm aloft and wobbling to one side. The weight of the sword cost him precious balance as his feet shifted slightly to compensate for the motion. I struck. Blades slicing through the air, my sword slashed across the back of his hand, and we both watched his weapon drop silently before clattering to the bottom seconds later. His eyes turned to me then, and for the first time, I saw genuine fear there.

But he was unarmed... and I was the champion. Not daring to take my eyes away from Lark, I shouted, my voice booming through the quarry, "My opponent is unarmed. Do you wish to announce your victor, Sovereign?"

Our ragged breathing was the only sound for a few tense moments, sweat dripping down my back as I commanded my body to remain perfectly balanced on the beam. Enough time had passed for me to wonder if she had maybe left out of boredom before she finally spoke.

"You are indeed the champion, Ravn...but his choice of weapons was unwise and miscalculated...We have no need for such poor decision-making amongst the Anakaii. You are to end him. Now." Her words rang with heartless finality.

My breath left in a hiss as her command struck me like a fist to the gut. Lark, face solemn, only nodded.

His eyes softened by a fraction before he said, "I guess this means... I'll be waiting for *you* in Hel then." Something inside me roared with wrath at this terrible waste.

But I had no choice. It was either him... or both of us.

I bit the inside of my cheek hard enough to draw blood as a warring conflict raged behind my eyes. Noticing this, he only nodded again...like he was giving *me* courage. A taut chain snapped. I whirled the blade fast enough to generate wind before swinging it across his neck and severing his head clean from his shoulders...

Instant death was better than falling to the floor to bleed out in the dark.

His body slumped forward briefly before following his head into the pit below.

Chest heaving, white-hot fury shuddered through my body as I slowly retreated off the beam. No one clapped or cheered. No one breathed a word as I sheathed the sword down my back and wordlessly left the quarry, without being formally dismissed.

I didn't care anymore anyway.

CHAPTER 42
RAVN

I was halfway back to the courtyard when my vision exploded into white stars as searing pain ripped through my head like a flaming sword, bringing me to my knees.

I clutched and clawed at my hair, squeezing my eyes shut as gut-purging agony tore through my skull. Bent over on the dirt and drooling through my clenched teeth, I cried out as pain I had never known threatened to boil my brain from the inside out.

Bright crimson splotches began to illuminate beneath my eyelids.

I could see... explosions.

Ear-shattering booms ripped through the palace, the impacts sending splinters of rock raining from the sky. Scattered across the ground lay the bodies of many dead Anakaii warriors, nothing left of them except shreds of torn flesh and missing limbs. We were being attacked. The palace began to groan and quake as the foundations started to sunder. The great spires above the keep swayed and jerked as they were rocked by explosions.

We would all be buried alive in minutes.

I ran to the courtyard where I beheld The Sovereign, her mighty sword *Drømmemorder,* slashing through the air as she furiously swung at the attackers.

I could only gape with disbelief. *Who in the Hel would challenge* her?

But I couldn't make out any faces amid the violent booming and spewing stone fragments.

A creeping sensation began to tingle across my scalp as the scene before me warped as if in slow motion. *Wait, was this really happening?...*

Vaguely, I was aware of my face still in the dirt and hands clutching the sides of my head.

Which could only mean that this wasn't happening right now...but would happen.

Suddenly, the vision rippled and bent into a different scene.

The sky was a blinding blue overhead as I watched a young woman entering the city astride a white mare. Her brown, flowing hair and crystal blue eyes glistened in the bright sun. A vast horde of soldiers flowed behind her as she passed unhindered through the gates of Opeth City, now black and smoldering. Her eyes softened as they fell to the tall, sandy-haired man who reached for her waist, which I noted was slightly swollen with child, and helped her to the ground. Together, they walked toward what was left of the city, before vivid green washed across the scene and carried them away...

Simultaneously, the scent of dark soil and herbs assaulted my senses. A soft, female hand tore at great clumps of roots and stems, holding them aloft and smiling brightly.

My heart slammed to a stop. I recognized that copper hair and those mesmerizing green eyes that were now turning in my direction.

Helena's face was warm and healthy, her eyes glittering like emeralds as she found me standing there. The sight of it made my chest squeeze with an emotion I couldn't describe.

Gods, she was devastating. She was the most beautiful woman I'd ever seen, and she was looking at me like she...

Tears began to spill down my face just before the vision imploded into smoke, and my eyes readjusted to the sight of the dirt floor in front of me.

"Ravn! Hey, are you all right?" a voice echoed from the corridor behind me.

I started, jumping up from the floor and nearly taking off into a run. Akton's eyes were wide with concern as he shook my shoulder and asked again. I must've looked like I'd seen a ghost because the pallor of his skin turned chalky as he roved over my features. Something like... sympathy briefly crossed over his face before he tugged me by the arm. "C'mon, we need to get you out of here."

Stunned speechless, I let him guide me through the palace until we arrived at my chambers, where he ushered me in and shut the door.

My thoughts were scrambling for purchase as I recounted my vision: Opeth destroyed, warriors infiltrating the city, and fighting with The Sovereign... Helena's gorgeous face melting me with its warmth.

How was this happening? Why was it happening?

I had read the histories of Astaran, and I knew what had

happened to those people The Sovereign referred to as the "Mørkebringer"...

Heart hammering with panic, I paced the room frantically, hardly aware of Akton watching me silently.

I knew I had two choices: tell him everything or tell him nothing.

Exposing my newfound ability to the wrong person would ensure my swift execution...or worse, turn me into a lab rat for Raziel to poke and study. Neither of us had ever had any real family or friends outside each other. As with all Anakaii cadets, we had been taken from our mothers as toddlers to live with our fathers until they turned us over to the Anakaii on our tenth birthdays, never to be seen or heard from again.

But could I risk exposure when I was likely the only person in this palace who genuinely cared for the lonely, terrified females down below?

And now... I'd had a glimpse of what the future could hold for me.

If I somehow played my cards right and developed a plan, maybe I could help those girls escape. Maybe Helena and I... Gods, I didn't even know her and, technically, I was her *captor*!

And who would I even be outside these walls? *Fucking Hel...* I didn't even know who I was inside them.

Hopelessness and anger roiled my gut and began to boil over. Without giving it a thought, I yanked the ceramic ewer from the table and threw it against the wall. The crash and clatter of the shards falling to the floor briefly pulled me from my reverie, but all I could do was stand there, paralyzed and fuming. After a moment, Akton's faint voice said softly, "This place is a real trip, huh?" I didn't move or acknowledge him. He was seeing a side of me that all cadets knew to keep hidden, no matter the circumstance... but I didn't care.

I collected myself just enough to meet his eyes before

saying, "I appreciate your presence. I always have. But I need to be alone right now, Akton."

His blue eyes warmed just a fraction as he reached over to clasp my shoulder and gave me a tight grin before silently leaving the room. Stress and exhaustion now feeling like the weight of the world across my shoulders. I slumped to the floor next to the bed.

All my training, all the horrors witnessed here since we were children...*was it all for nothing?* Did I even *want* to be an Anakaii anymore? They were brave and skilled fighters, yes... but they were also soulless killers whose allegiance to Chemosh was something they could never escape, under penalty of death. It was a cursed life to be in the life debt of The Sovereign.

But... maybe I did have a choice...

The image of Helena's mouth as she smiled at me in the vision replayed over and over in my mind, like a favorite song. Rubbing a hand down my face, I pushed out a weary sigh.

Was I really going to do this? Betray everything I had ever known... for a beautiful stranger?

As I righted myself and left the room, headed for the dungeons, the answer seemed clear enough.

CHAPTER 43
RAVN

I sprinted through the corridors until skidding to a stop just before the spiraling stairs that would bring me past Raziel's door. Heart thundering and ear cocked, I paused at the top of the stairs and took a moment to catch my breath.

As I began to silently descend the stairwell, conscious of every sound I made, a deep guttural roar echoed up from the corridor below.

In one heart-stopping second, I stopped dead. My hand slowly drifted up to unsheathe my blade, my heartbeat thundering in my ears.

What in the *Hel* was that?

It had sounded equal parts wicked and tormented. Human... and not. Immediately, my thoughts went to Helena and the other girls, as I willed my feet to continue down the stairs. Upon reaching the corridor that led to the dungeons, I noted a strange, pulsing green glow from underneath Raziel's door. Instinctually, I unsheathed my blade and walked past the door on silent feet.

The roar sounded again... but this time it was the distinct voice of a man. Pleading and in agony.

Creeping to the wall closest to the door, I leaned in to listen. Faintly, I could hear Raziel's voice... chanting in a language I did not recognize.

Hel's fucking gates... Whatever the fuck was going on in there, I had a feeling I really didn't want to know...

Holding my sword in front of me the entire time, I backed away from the door, removed the torch from its sconce, and fled into the dungeon stairwell.

I didn't know what kind of foolish hope I was holding onto when I came down here. The Helena in my vision was an entirely different person from the half-starved woman in the cage before me. She and the other two sat huddled on the ground, watching me in silence. Fixing the torch to the wall, I slumped to the ground across from the cell and held my head in my hands.

I had never been responsible for anyone's survival except my own, but a spark had ignited in me at the thought of helping them escape. But how could they ever trust me?

To them, I was only another cruel pawn for The Sovereign.

For this to work, I would need to know them better, and they would need to know me. Before I could work up the courage to speak first, Helena's voice spoke from the gloom.

"Has servicing that wicked demon become so boring then?" Her words sizzled with venom.

I couldn't blame her. Somehow, she had been captured or sold by her own family to serve as nothing more than a sacrificial lamb. I would be furiously bitter, too. Empathy coursed through me like a river. She had every right to suspect me... even hate me. I looked up to see her face still hollow and exhausted with purple shadows under her eyes.

Deep inside me, a shell began to crack open.

"How did you come to be here?" I asked, nervously.

Her features instantly contorted with anger, hands clenching into fists by her side. I was beginning to think she wasn't going to respond before she scoffed and said, "My father sold me to The Sovereign...in exchange for land rights to a mine, somewhere in the north." Her eyes, clouded with grief, met mine again. I could almost see the betrayal eating her alive. I only nodded solemnly as we continued to stare at each other, a faint dripping sound echoing from somewhere in the dark. Anguish coursed through me. I didn't even have a plan or strategy to get them out yet. I wouldn't dare give them any hope until I felt confident that we could succeed with our lives intact.

"How about you?" Helena asked, breaking my intrusive thoughts.

She wanted to know about me. I thought, confused. But my situation didn't matter... Everything about who I thought I was no longer mattered either. But I found myself wanting to share with her anyway.

"I didn't know my mother. My father brought me here to train at the age of ten. It's the only life I've ever known..." I replied, eyes trained on the ground. I hesitated... unsure whether it was wise to expose myself this way. I glanced up to see her eyes had softened slightly as she listened, and something about it gave me courage.

"I killed another cadet today...he was unarmed. He was a cruel bastard... but... I don't know. I don't know anything anymore." I finished, releasing a sigh and clenching my fists against my brow. I heard a soft shuffle and looked up again to see Helena uncoiling to her feet. Slowly, she leaned down to dip into the water bucket I had brought down to them the night before. A cup of water now clenched between her fingers, she reached through the bars and offered it to me.

She was offering their water...*to me.*

It was such a small act of kindness, but spoke volumes about who she was as a person. I didn't know anything about her save for her name and what her wretched father did to her. She could very well have a man who was torn apart by grief and waiting for some miracle that would bring her home to him.

But it didn't matter. If this were the only good deed I ever accomplished in my life, it would be worth it. To save Helena and the two young girls curled together on the filthy stone floor near her feet would be worth it.

They all deserved to be free... Sovereign *bitch* be damned.

Conviction and determination hardened my bones into steel as I slowly rose and removed the cup from her hands. As I drank, I noted the way her eyes followed the small bead of water that streamed down my neck. Something about her eyes on me filled me with boundless warmth.

She spoke then, soft as a prayer, "My mother died giving birth to me... and my father always blamed me for it. The only joy I ever found came from growing things." She shrugged slightly, her voice thick with sadness.

My heart raced with the realization that somehow, I already knew that...

"The problem is... growing things require death as well. Dead things feed the soil. The plants die and must be discarded. Death and decay are necessary for all living things to grow." She finished with a tight smile before casting her eyes down to her hands wrapped around the bars of the cell. I only nodded, stunned by her candor and wisdom. She was... lovely. Inside and out.

In that moment, I decided that she needed to have hope. She deserved to have something to look forward to. She looked up at me, lips trembling, and her eyes welled with tears. Unable to tolerate the sight, I leaned in close and whispered, "You will be able to grow things again, Helena. Do not give up hope just yet." Her breath caught, shock briefly crossing her features before she swallowed and dipped her chin, acknowledging the hidden promise in my remark. As I turned to leave, she said, "Thank you, Ravn..." I only nodded briefly before ascending the stairs, intent not to dwell on what my name on her lips did to me.

LATER THAT NIGHT, I CREPT THROUGH THE PALACE WITH FOOD FOR THE maidens in a cloth sack clutched to my chest. Despite Lark's death, the cadets had resumed their daily routine uninterrupted. The Anakaii did not believe in mourning. The night air was damp and reeked of ozone, evidence of an approaching storm. The breeze through the open windows of the corridor brought in the scent of horses, too, which was unusual for this time of night. Alarm bells now clanging through me, I slowed my pace and ducked down against the wall. Peering around the corner toward the courtyard below, my suspicions were confirmed moments later. Ten Anakaii warriors astride their horses stood together in the center of the courtyard. While dressed in their standard black garb, they also had large sacks of supplies tied to their saddles. They were prepared for a long journey. I noted that Captain Tylor was not with them, which could only mean that this was some kind of top-secret mission, with instructions from The Sovereign herself. Horses chuffing and tails swishing with impatience, the predatory gait of The Sovereign entered the courtyard moments later. Her voice, typically booming with power, was low with menace as she addressed the warriors and said, "I want her alive. She is of little use to me dead. Find her and bring her to me, and you will be rewarded. If she is in the company of any Mørkebringer, you are to show them the consequences of defying their Sovereign..."

Silently, the warriors raised their fists into the air before pounding their chests twice in perfect unison. The gates of the courtyard leading out of the city creaked open as the warriors kicked their horses into a gallop until disappearing out of sight, their hooves thundering into the dark night beyond. I didn't move an inch until The Sovereign had made her way back inside and the courtyard doors had shut behind her. Still crouched against the wall, my head spun from what I had just witnessed. They had been ordered to bring someone back, a female... and whoever this person was, she was especially important to The Sovereign.

CHAPTER 44
AIDA

It was too early for this shit.

The thought skittered across my brain just before I raised my sword to deflect a blow from Tyran. It was only nine in the morning, and I was already dripping with sweat. I lunged, attempting a low blow to the ribs, but was too slow. Tyran blocked, gripped my wrist, and started to twist it back before planting a kiss on the delicate skin of my palm. His eyes warmed as he gave me a roguish grin. Cheater.

"She'll never get it right if you go easy on her like that!" Sayedha shouted from the outside of the ring.

We had been training together up in the dome for the past three days. The feast prepared in our honor, after that fateful day in the vault with Synsa, had been essentially repeated every night since. All the important and not-so-important inhabitants of Overlevende wished to meet us and offer their services. One such swordsmith had offered to create new blades for us, which we did not decline. The swordsmith bubbled with delight, promising over and over that it would be the most exquisite blade we had ever seen. Another seamstress, with eyes that roved over Tyran in a way I did not appreciate, had offered to make us new clothes. I declined those. The idea of her hands roaming all over Tyran to get his measurements was enough to boil my blood. I had absolutely no reason to be jealous. At the same time, I'd never been in love or ever had anything to be jealous about. And it wasn't like he had become less affectionate since our first time together; in fact, it had been the opposite.

Each night, after a huge dinner and too many cups of honey mead, he would practically drag me back to our room to ravish me wholly. Exploring each other between the sheets had quickly become our favorite after-hours hobby. He seemed to prefer consuming me in almost every position I could imagine; astride his face, between my legs in our bathing pool, and this morning... I had awoken to his tongue lashing me from behind, my teeth biting into the pillow. And then there was the knee-wobbling sex...

"Kine! Get in there and don't go easy on her." Sayedha commanded. *Shit.*

Tyran tensed briefly but acquiesced and turned to bow out of the ring. I could tell the idea of me fighting Kine unnerved him, but we had all come to trust each other these past few days. Synsa had made herself scarce since showing us those tomes inside the vault, but had given explicit instructions to Sayedha to prepare us for our expedition to find the obsidian mirrors. While not inexperienced in training, I had to admit, it had been a while. Every day, Sayedha and Kine joined forces to torture our bodies into submission. Our mornings now consisted of running, lifting weights, pulling small boulders with ropes, climbing trees while being timed, and combat training. Yesterday, after breaking for lunch, Sayedha showed us the armory and barracks for the other Begavet warriors that she and Kine were responsible for training.

The inhabitants of Overlevende, many of whom were immortal, would never forget what happened to their people and had rigorously prepared every new generation for the likelihood of warfare. Living under the mountain had given them unparalleled access to various metal ores, which they mined and smelted to build impressive weapons. The warrior force was impressive too; more than 10,000 Begavet were trained and ready to defend the mountain city with their lives. Sayedha, in addition to being Synsa's descendant, was also the general of this warrior force. Kine, whom she had known since childhood, was selected as her captain and second in command. Since working closely with them, we had learned of her gift of precognition. She could anticipate the movements of any person she was close to, within a five-second interval. This made her formidable in combat and invaluable in the field. Respect for her position and abilities aside, I had to admit that I was warming up to her more each day.

Kine, on the other hand...

He approached the ring now, stone-faced. I swallowed, wiping the sweat from my hands onto my pants and praying no one noticed. *Gods*, he really was the most intimidating man I'd ever seen. I decided right then that to take him on was going to be a personal challenge, and I had no intention of fighting fair. Unsheathing his giant blade, he began to circle me. It was imperative that I remain out of his grip; my focus for this fight would be speed and agility. There was more than one way to disarm a man, however...

Gripping my dagger away from my body, I looked into Kine's eyes and said, too low for anyone but us to hear, "Does Maya know how badly you want her?"

He started, black eyes imploding with rage, and swung at me with the force of a pissed off grizzly bear. I lunged and rolled across the mat, popping up close behind him, and moved to strike his arm with my dagger. The muscles in his back and arms rippled with might as he expertly parried the blow, striking me across the shoulder. *Fuck*, that hurt. A quick glance at my arm assured me that the training armor was doing its job, but I knew the skin underneath would be black and blue within the hour. Pushing aside my rising fury, I danced around the ring, not allowing him to pin me to the ground. I rolled again, throwing my daggers as I went, one of them striking true into his calf muscle. Utterly unfazed, he ripped the blade from his leg and looked at it like he was curious how it got there, before letting it clatter to the ground. He charged and brought his sword straight down with enough force to crack open a man's skull. Still on my knees, I raised my blade to block the blow. The violent collision of our steel sent the shuddering impact through my body hard enough to clack my teeth. Before I could recover and roll away, his hands had me around the throat and pinned to the ground. While he wasn't choking me, his firm grip told me it would be a simple thing. I looked into his menacing eyes then and whispered, "I won't tell anyone. You have my word."

His grip eased by just a fraction, his features briefly... sad... before releasing my throat, rising to stand, and offering his hand to me. I gripped his giant, meaty paw and was pulled to my feet. Before letting go of my hand, he murmured, "Thanks," and stalked out of the ring.

My gaze found Tyran a moment later, and he stood as rigid as a trip wire, eyes tight with worry. I gave him a brief smile and gently tapped my temple with one finger, reminding him that I had more strength than just physical. Using my power to infiltrate someone's mind would indeed be a last resort, but it was one I was prepared to use if necessary.

We moved to target practice next.

While I had always considered myself a natural with a bow and arrow, nothing could compare to Tyran's accuracy. I noted the way the other warriors training in the dome would make their way over to loiter around the targets each time Tyran started to practice. No matter how far the target was moved, Tyran's arrow would hit the center with astounding accuracy. And it was the same with daggers, hatchets, steel stars... his aim never faltered. Crossing my arms, I scoffed with disbelief and pride. A memory of something Luke told me once flashed across my brain, and before I could think about it, I said, "You're a real Ace, aren't you?"

Tyran started and whipped his head at me, shock lining his face.

"What did you say?" his voice was... alarmed.

I began to stammer, unsure of his reaction, "I said... you're a real Ace... you know, with targets." I finished sheepishly.

He immediately put down the hatchet in his hand, stormed over to me, and tugged me by the arm and away from our puzzled audience. Dragging me a little forcefully, we came to the rail that overlooked the Frelse Fjord, hidden behind a dense wall of potted plants. He gave me an expression I couldn't describe before he asked, "Where did you hear that from?"

His intensity made me nervous, but I replied, "Uh, whenever my target practice would improve... Luke would always joke that I was 'a real Ace.'"

Tyran's eyebrows shot to his hairline, his mouth gaping with shock. Suddenly, he gripped me by the arms and said, "Show me. Show me a memory of Luke."

His eyes were fierce, but began to soften as he noted the confusion which no doubt was plain on my face. His grip on my arms loosened as he closed his eyes and waited.

Every time I did this, it felt more natural than the last. Closing my eyes and heaving open the doors to the portal within, I found Tyran's golden chain and pulled him close.

The memory was distorted by the haze of near-death I had been suffering through at the time. Tyran's glow warmed my astral form as we stood together and watched the memory project onto the glass wall in front of us...

My feral sixteen-year-old self had been caught in a poacher's snare, the wire cutting to the bone. I winced with recollection of how excruciating it had been. It took me hours to get free and somehow keep my foot, the skin around the ankle ravaged into a gaping heap of bloody tissue. I crawled my way to a hollow tree and curled up to rest. When I awoke hours later, the wound had already started to fester and burn, and the fever set in shortly after.

For three days, I remained in that hollow tree, unable to move, hunt, or find water. Just as I began to pray to the Gods and ask them to bring me to my parents upon my death... a handsome, silver-haired man began to slap my face awake. His bright emerald eyes were tight with concern as he repeatedly attempted to bring water to my lips. Tyran's breath caught, and I looked over to see tracks of tears flowing down his glowing cheeks before floating upward, suspended in space.

"*Gods be damned...* It's him," he whispered, voice thick with emotion.

I turned again to watch as the memories began to flow: Luke's hearty chuckle as he told me stories near our campfire, his grave seriousness when teaching me combat or first aid, his bright smile after a successful hunt.

It hit me then with the force of a blow.

My hand flew to my mouth in a feeble attempt to muffle the explosion of truth threatening to crush my heart.

Tyran grabbed me and turned me to face him then. His face was so beautiful as he smiled at me, tears streaming, and said, "Luke was the same man who raised me, Aida. The same man who taught me everything and made me into the man I am today. After he was banished from the estate where we lived... somehow, he found *you* and saved your life."

His hands caressed my face, tenderly stroking strands of hair behind my ears. Unable to form words, my tears streamed silently as I reached up to clutch his wrists.

"*Don't you see?* We have been brought together by forces we cannot comprehend. Every decision and path we have taken has led us to each other," he said, conviction burning in his eyes.

Suddenly, his face dropped and turned hesitant before he asked, "Where is he? What happened to him? Please... I need to know."

Grief tore at my chest like a rabid animal, and my head dropped from his hands as sobs racked my body. He stood stock-still with dread. Breathing became difficult as I sobbed into my hands before finally working up the courage to speak.

"I... it was... he was killed by another nomad. While we were sleeping." I breathed, my voice cracking around the lump in my throat.

The glass wall in front of us darkened suddenly as the

memory played out. A lone scavenger had been tracking us for days, waiting for his opportunity to steal a fresh deer kill we had hunted earlier that morning. Luke and I had been distracted by the joy of our success and went to bed that night with bellies full and our guard down. I awoke suddenly to see Luke across the campfire fighting with the scavenger and then gutting him with a dagger... but not before he had been stabbed through the ribs. I ran to him and applied pressure to the wound, sobbing and screaming as he wheezed and blubbered, before succumbing to death moments later.

Losing him had felt... total.

Before Luke, I had never allowed myself to get close to anyone. His presence in my life had resurrected my soul. It had taken many years to shove this memory down to the bottom and lock it away, and now here it was again.

Tyran lifted my chin to meet his eyes, our grief and sorrow mirrored in each other's faces. I watched his throat bob before saying, "It wasn't your fault, Aida. He would've chosen you over him in an instant. He wanted you to survive. And because of him... You survived and found me. I owe everything to him already, but the fact that he also brought us together... is something I'll never stop thanking him for every day."

I only nodded, still beyond words.

He kissed me tenderly then, his lips moving on mine with gentle need. My body responded, drawn to his flame and arching into his touch. Wrapping my arms around his neck, I melted into his embrace and surrendered to his mouth. The black, star-flecked ink of my astral form began to sizzle and drip, melding with his hazy glow. We were one body, tongues lashing and hips grinding with the heat of a thousand suns. *Gods, was it possible to love him more?* Distantly, I remembered the location of our physical bodies and reluctantly banked the growing heat between my legs. Slowly, I released Tyran's golden chain and watched it slip from my fingers before being dropped unceremoniously back into my skin. For several moments after we opened our eyes, we could only stand there, chests heaving, before a polite cough sounded from behind. Peering over Tyran's shoulder, I spied Sayedha and Kine watching us in bewilderment. Returning my gaze to Tyran's loving eyes, I only smiled before saying, "It's a long story."

CHAPTER 45
TYRAN

The weight of Aida's revelation was crushing. For the longest time, I had struggled with The General's abrupt exit from my life. And for years, I had searched for any sign of him but had never found a trace. Now, I knew why. Luke had saved Aida shortly after she had been exiled by the Villdyr children more than four years ago. It meant that if Luke had not been fired and sent away from the estate, Aida would have likely died from her wounds... alone in the wilderness. My head pounded with the enormity of it. I had searched for him for four years, and he had been dead for most of that time. Aida had said that they had traveled together for just a few months before he was killed. But within those few months, he had given her confidence, companionship, and guidance. With agonizing certainty, I knew I would never see him again or have the chance to thank him for all that he did for both of us. Before leaving the dome to make our way back underground, I had asked Aida what had happened to his body. Her eyes were so bleak and despairing as she told me that she had burned him in a great pyre, just as he had requested her to do if the time ever came. It was a burial fit for a King; not to rot in the ground but to transcend one's body and join the Gods of Lyrath.

When our group had descended back to the lower levels, a lovely, blonde woman was waiting for us just outside the elevator door.

Chipper as always, Maya beamed at us as the elevator doors slid open and said, "Good! Right on time. Follow me, I have something to show you." I noticed Kine, typically expressionless, shifted slightly when Maya's ocean-blue eyes rested on him.

Huh, maybe he had a weakness after all. After a glance toward Aida, her fleeting grin confirmed my suspicions.

Absent-mindedly pushing her glasses onto the bridge of her nose, Maya's eyes danced with fiendish delight before turning in the direction of the armory. We followed her to the lower-level weapons lab that Sayedha had given us a brief tour of the day before. It was easy to admit that the systems in place down here were more advanced than anything I'd ever seen in the Astaran Guard.

Her blonde braid swishing as she trotted ahead, Maya turned a corner after corner before stopping in front of a giant iron door with a formidable-looking locking system. After deftly keying in the code, the lock clacked and whirred as the door groaned open. Maya moved to brace her weight against the door to push it open, but Kine was there in an instant to do it for her. "Thanks, Kine!" she said brightly with a grin. He only nodded silently and turned away... to hide his blush, no doubt. The chamber behind the door held racks of what looked like various tools and weapons; the key difference was the glowing blue orbs affixed to each one.

"What you see here is a little project I've been working on for some time. It's taken years and... lots of failure to get it right. A whole wing had to be built in a defunct mineshaft so we could test them without blowing up the mountain!" Maya said with a giggle.

None of us was laughing, though. Suddenly, the room felt too small.

"So... you made weapons out of highly explosive Soladium?" Sayedha asked, hesitantly.

Maya, always the optimist, stated matter-of-factly, "These are the tools that will be used to destroy *The Fallen* and will save all our asses. So, yeah."

I didn't even try to hide my smile as I marveled at just how brilliant she really was. Sayedha and Aida mirrored the sentiment, their smiles bordering on wicked.

I knew the same thought was drifting through all our minds: *maybe this could really work.*

Maybe we had a fighting chance after all.

WE LEFT THE ARMORY AND MADE OUR WAY BACK TO THE MAIN HALL for dinner. As usual, it was a boisterous affair. Giant heaping platters of meats, cheeses, and fruits were peppered across the long tables. People chatted and loitered in groups or played chess by the hearth. Synsa was nowhere to be seen, but she had not shown her face since our first feast three nights ago.

Sensing the direction of my thoughts, Aida asked Sayedha,

"Will the Queen be joining us tonight?" Sayedha shook her head and stated, rather ominously, "She will arrive when the time is right." Aida and I shared a puzzled glance before moving to fill our plates and sit down. Since our training had started, Aida had traded the exquisitely feminine gowns for more practical attire consisting of tight-fitting pants and leather vests. As much as I loved the way the dresses flowed down her figure, I had to admit that I loved the way her backside looked in leather pants, too. Before my mouth could water at the prospect of being inside her once dinner was over, a busty female plopped down in the chair next to mine. It was the same seamstress who had offered to make us clothes the other night. Her eyes roved over my chest and neck like a caress as she purred, "I pray you've had a change of heart about my offer from the other night?" I noted with chagrin that multiple offers lay in that comment. Aida tensed next to me, but I didn't dare look to see the daggers I knew were being thrown by her eyes. The seamstress paid her no heed whatsoever, her dark eyes resting on my mouth. She surely was aware that Aida and I were a pair, and yet she continued this charade, as if she were accustomed to always getting her way no matter the situation. Not wanting to embarrass her with an affronted rejection in front of the whole crowd, I only shook my head before politely declining. "No, thank you again for your... offer. But we have all the supplies we need." Her tongue briefly darted over her bottom lip as if pondering her next move, but a moment later she dipped her chin tersely and rose to leave.

I pushed out the breath I didn't realize I had been holding back before peeking a glance at Aida. She sat rigid, staring at her plate with her fingers clenched tight around her fork. Slowly, I reached out to graze the back of her knuckles with my fingers, coaxing them to relax. She nearly jumped at the touch and began to unwind. In the next second, she had stuffed multiple bites of food into her mouth, chugged the rest of her wine, and was pulling me away from the table. If anyone noticed our sudden and urgent exit, she didn't seem to care.

When we arrived inside our chamber a few minutes later, she pounced.

We became a flurry of roving hands and flying clothes as if our lives depended on being naked. Her fingers caressed my chest and began a brazen scrape down the planes of my stomach before ripping down my pants and gripping my cock.

I moaned into her mouth as she bit my bottom lip. *Damn.*

I was instantly hard in her hand as she began to forcefully tug me toward the bed. Her mouth burned against mine with lust as I squeezed her soft breasts. Abruptly, she turned me around with my back facing the bed before pushing me down into a sitting position.

Slowly, her eyes never leaving mine, she began to remove her undergarments...

I watched her, cock twitching, as her fingers removed each button of her vest. Aching need coursed through me, but I remained still, gripping the edge of the bed.

Finally, her heavy breasts broke free, and she tortured me further by rubbing them lazily as she watched me from under heavy lids.

She was so fucking gorgeous, and I could resist no longer.

I reached out to grip her by the waist before grazing my tongue and teeth over each breast until they were red and swollen. Her back bowed against my mouth as she panted excitedly, her hands running over my scalp.

Gods, her *body*. I wanted her more than life.

But before I could scoop her up and bury myself in her, she dropped to her knees and put her wet mouth around my cock.

Oh, fuck.

My hands clenched the sheets as pleasure rolled through

me in waves. Her tongue lashed me with feverish abandon as her hands stroked me up and down. My head was spinning, breath coming in ragged gasps as she sucked me eagerly. Giving myself over to the experience, I reached up to run my fingers through her silken hair as her tongue brought me to the edge. I wanted to let go in her mouth so badly, but I resisted, wishing for my seed to fill her in a different way. My cock throbbed with near climax on her tongue, but I moved quickly and lifted her by the waist to sit astride me, my cock impaling her sweet, swollen center. She cried out as I filled her to the hilt, her hips rolling in slow, delicious thrusts. The sight of her riding me and moaning my name was a vision lovelier than Lyrath.

Fucking Hel, she was mine.

Her gorgeous face, eyes glazed and seductive, looked down at me then and smiled. I could feel my heart bursting with the love I held for her. Her moans became more concentrated as she fucked me, breasts bouncing as she angled herself to hit her most sensitive place. I gritted my teeth, trying to contain my climax for just a moment longer as my hands massaged her perfect backside. A moment later, her breath caught before her head rolled back, her cry of pleasure echoing around the cave. She continued to ride me through her climax, her inner walls milking me into blissful surrender. I finally let go and erupted into her.

Holy Gods.

I rose up to kiss her, moaning her name and dragging my tongue across her teeth as I spilled my seed into her tight heat. She was the most magnificent thing I'd ever known in this life or the next, and she was *mine*. As her breathing staggered in gasps, her small frame went suddenly limp against my chest. Gently, I pulled myself out of her and cradled her in my lap, both of us sticky with sweat. This intimacy was fucking glorious, and I knew I would never get enough. Despite all the danger on the road before us, I wanted to take the time to marvel at how wonderful it was to be with her. I didn't want to take it for granted for a second...

But our future was fraught with peril and uncertainty. I swallowed as the idea of losing her plagued me again. It had been her choice to walk down this path, and I had sworn my allegiance to walk it beside her...but to lose her would be a punishment worse than death. As I held her soft body in my arms, I pleaded with the Gods to protect her and keep her from harm. I ached with the knowledge that our time here and this moment of rest would soon pass, and I didn't want to allow anything to go unsaid when so much was at stake.

Suddenly, I realized exactly what I wanted to do before we left the mountain city and journeyed into the unknown.

I planted a kiss on her temple, and she stirred, seemingly half awake.

"Aida?"

She gave a brief "hmmm" in response.

"I want to ask you something..." She moved her head to rest against my shoulder and studied my face with a questioning grin. My heart stuttered and tripped, suddenly losing its rhythm as my fingers lightly traced the mysterious brand we now shared on our chests. But she patiently waited, too sated with pleasure to hurry me along. The sight of her beautiful face gazing openly into mine steeled my resolve, and so I asked her...

"Aida, will you marry me?"

CHAPTER 46
AIDA

It was difficult to describe the flood of emotions that ran through me the moment Tyran asked me to marry him. His eyes were silver-lined, lips still swollen from our near-feral sex.

Of course, the answer was yes. He had me, all of me...

But how long would it last? How much time would we have together before this campaign to save our world, claimed our lives?

I understood the math. *The Fallen* had ruled our world for centuries. She had more than 50,000 trained Astaran Guards and over a hundred brutal Anakaii warriors. And then there was Chemosh herself... a raging behemoth of preternatural strength.

But... maybe Tyran knew something I didn't.

Maybe he knew that even though our chances of survival were slim, being together in this moment was all that really mattered in the end. Before I could waste one more breath worrying over a future that may or may not happen, I smiled brightly and let the welling tears slip down my face.

"Yes, Tyran. I will marry you." I breathed.

He smiled down at me and pressed a soft kiss to my mouth before picking me up, laying me on the bed, and wrapping his arms around me. His warm, steady breaths on the back of my neck were the last thing I remembered before falling asleep...

In the astral form, I was never tired. This second skin seemed to be beyond the physical struggles of the flesh. Breathing deep and concentrating on the energy that surrounded me, the chasm of flickering tethers undulated and pulsed in the sky above me.

A few of them nearest to me I recognized: Sayedha's dark leather braid, Kine's barbed wire, Tyran's glowing, golden chain... and Synsa's thorny, green vine. Before I could debate whether it was considered rude to invade the consciousness of a Sorceress Supreme, I reached for the vine and tugged.

A dizzying heartbeat later, my eyes drank in the sight of a place I had only ever heard stories about: a warm, mist-veiled jungle. I stood and marveled at the vibrant, green oasis around me, toes curling into the soft moss on the floor. A staggering array of flora and fauna buzzed and chattered from every direction. Birds with hues like the rainbow darted and squawked. With my mouth hanging open with awe, tears pricked my eyes. It was so exotic and beautiful. A soft gurgling drew my attention to a small waterfall just ahead, and sitting by the edge of the pool was Synsa. She looked so still and peaceful that I almost retreated before I heard her say, "I was wondering when you would come to visit me here. Please, come sit." She turned to me, her expression welcoming, and gestured to the space next to her. I obeyed and sat cross-legged on the moss as her amber eyes roamed over my astral form intently.

"Fascinating. The ability of the Dream Walkers appears in you as the very heartbeat of the universe itself. It's incredible. I have a theory, though: it's really your simultaneous gift of telepathy that allows you access to another's mind in this way," she said, somewhat off-handedly.

What? My eyes bulged as I fought the urge to pepper her with questions, but I stayed silent to let her continue.

"Queen Mercury had the same *two* powerful gifts also. We spent many years studying the varying degrees of power in all Begavet. The Dream Walkers were always the rarest and always female, but not all of them could physically project themselves into someone else's consciousness. Until you, only Mercury had been able to do it."

My heart skipped a beat at this revelation before I asked, "... and what about the ability to manipulate someone's thoughts? Is that special too?"

Her eyes returned to the pool before us. Sighing deeply through her nose, she replied, "No... All people are susceptible to suggestion. The unconscious mind is very vulnerable. It is only by the most fateful stroke of luck that you have not abused your power. It would indeed be a very terrifying thing. Kingdoms would fall at your feet. Maybe even entire *worlds*..."

The weight of her words chilled me to my core. This power was not mine by choice. Not only did I not want it, but the consequences of it were too large to comprehend.

Suddenly, a thought struck me.

"Why couldn't Mercury use her power against Chemosh on the battlefield that day... or later when they were discovered at Svargad?" I asked, immediately regretting my casual tone as she winced slightly at the memory.

"*The Fallen* had prepared for Queen Mercury's gifts before she arrived on Astaran. Somehow, she learned of a way to close off her mind to intrusion... If it was a chemical, it worked in opposition to how synthesized Soladium affects the body," she replied solemnly.

I was stunned. *Had I heard her right?*

"Wait, do you mean that you can *ingest* Soladium? For what purpose?" I stammered.

"Not the physical ore, no. Our ancestors and their alchemists learned of a way to purify it into a stable compound, and human trials indicated that it could render a person into a weak, paralyzed state, their mind becoming a blank slate. Vulnerable to outside influence," she replied.

The hair rose along my forearms.

She had the gift of foresight... *what did she know?*

Unable to contain my curiosity any longer, I said, "When I first arrived in Overlevende, I saw part of your memories from the war with *The Fallen*... but I saw something else too. Something that hasn't happened yet..."

I faced her then, the question hanging over the water like a fog, but she kept her eyes trained on the pool and whispered, "My visions are not concrete. They are subject to decisions not yet made. Each path laid before us is never a straight line. Some overlap, some tumble into darkness, but most twist and bend beyond the horizon, too far to see."

Suddenly, the colors of the pool before us began to ripple and wobble as an image took shape. I shielded my eyes from an iridescent glare that reflected brightly from a suit of... *armor.*

Armor that *I* was wearing. Into battle.

The dark plates covered my body like a second skin, the light bouncing off and distorting into rainbows, like an oily sheen on the water. They looked like... scales.

And on my head... the helmet of Brannregn glowed with an otherworldly, white fire.

My face was contorted with blood lust as I bellowed with wrath, a giant, ferocious-looking scimitar sword in the air above my head. Chaos flowed around me like a river as a mighty fighting force charged from behind...

The image warped and faded into something else before my mind could implode from shock.

It was Tyran, his eyes burning with fury, arms outstretched in front of him. He gritted his teeth in effort, the cords of his neck bulging as he began to levitate three giant, stone boulders...

with his mind... before hurtling them into a grouping of the enemy; their bodies exploding into red mist as they were crushed.

Holy Gods...

The image shifted again and showed Tyran and me walking into a crumbling stone ruin. Now just a shell of its former glory, the forest in the advanced stages of reclaiming its bones.

Instantly, I knew it was the stone fortress of Svargad, the hidden Kingdom of King Arketh and Queen Mercury.

My mind was reeling as the image vanished and the calm mirror of the pool returned.

I could not form words. It was too much. All of it was too much.

I was destined to wield the fire-bringing helmet gifted by the Gods... and lead warriors into battle. Tyran was... *Gods*, did he even know about his power yet?

Was it something not yet activated in his blood?

Synsa turned to me then, her eyes glowing with knowledge and... pity. She looked at me with understanding. Like she knew that the excruciating pressure of all our fates now rested on my shoulders. She reached for my hand and held it tight before looking into my eyes and saying, "Aida, you are not alone in this. We have trained for centuries for this moment to come. To stand beside you and destroy the conqueror of Astaran. Slavery, sacrifice of the innocent, genocide... it ends with *us*. Find the obsidian mirrors and commune with the Gods. They loved us enough once to give us an advantage, and I have hope that they are placing their bets on us winning now."

My mouth was dry as my clammy hands clutched my chest on instinct. I caught my breath as another question struck me. Glancing down to ensure it could still be seen on my astral form, the glowing shape of the tipped-over hourglass shone bright gold in the center of my chest. Synsa's eyes warmed as she beheld the symbol. "What is it?" I breathed nervously. Synsa's face turned serious for a moment before her amber eyes lifted to mine.

"A long, long time ago, before humans took their rightful place as the custodians of this world...we were animals. Driven by our primary needs only. Survival. Sex. War... The Gods we worshipped were heathen Gods. Beings who only came to Astaran to play...and destroy. We were their slaves and toys, bound to their will and high on their glory. A few took pity on us and chose a select few to teach language, physics, art... And one of those languages was called "The Lyrathian codex." She lifted a finger as she gestured to my mark. The one that had seared itself into my flesh after my first union with Tyran.

"This is a symbol from that same codex. I can't tell you why you have it... Alas, the will of the Gods is typically a mystery to even me. But I can tell you what I *think* I know about it."

My heartbeat thrummed through my ears as I waited.

"It's called the Dagaz. It's a symbol of... opposing forces. Light and dark. Day and night. End and beginning. It's a reminder..." her eyes snapped to mine with predatory focus. "To never give up hope. To never stop. The sun will rise each day, and the darkness will come each night. An endless cycle of death and rebirth. A never-ending metamorphosis. Just as our opportunities to change our fate... are infinite."

CHAPTER 47
KINE

She knew.
    Somehow, the Dream Walker knew about my feelings toward Maya. The girl—now woman—I had loved since I was a boy.

As unnerving as it was to have a dream walker poking around in my head, something about it was also a relief. Not that it mattered. Maya was out of my league in too many ways to count. She'd always been the smartest, kindest, and most outgoing female.

I, on the other hand, was always the bulky, awkward, and quiet brute.

Maya, Sayedha, and I had known each other most of our lives, since being the same age placed us in the same school classes. She had always been ten steps ahead, with lightning-quick wit. And she was funny, and so... *effortlessly* beautiful.

I still remember the first time I ever saw her, at our school up in the dome. It was our first day of grade school classes; in Overlevende, those started the autumn after your seventh birthday. Before that age, it was typical for parents to rear their children at home or bring them along to study their trade.

Shy and timid by nature, I had arrived at the dome full of anxiety, even though most of the children were already familiar to me. I had spotted Sayedha almost immediately across the room, her tight black curls bouncing as she chatted with another girl.

But I just stood there, frozen. Until a sweet voice, like a tinkling bell, said from behind me, "Hello. Is this your first day, too?"

I turned to see Maya, eyes the color of the blue sea and golden hair braided to one side of her neck. She gave me a toothy grin before stretching out her hand.

For me, it was love at first sight.

She giggled as I struggled to contain my blush and stammered my name in response. Sayedha rescued me a moment later when she skipped over and introduced herself. Maya's eyes widened before she said, "I know who you are. You're the Queen's... er... granddaughter?"

Sayedha grinned and shot me a knowing glance before replying, "Great, granddaughter, yes... So, I see you've met Kine here. He doesn't talk much, but he's one Hel of a bodyguard."

It was true. Sayedha and I often found ourselves amid gaggles of older children, usually playing sports like soccer and having to defend each other when things got heated. Just the week before, a boy larger than Sayedha had pinned her to the ground as they fought over who had the rights to the next game. I had tackled him before he could land a blow and squished his face in the dirt. Maya's eyes danced as she peered up at me, taking stock of the obvious physical differences from those of a normal seven-year-old.

"So, what do you wish to study here?" Sayedha asked.

Maya practically glowed with excitement as she replied, "Science. I want to be an engineer like my grandfather. What about you two?"

Sayedha smirked and stated confidently, "I'll be studying war and combat. I wish to be the general of Overlevende's fighting force one day, and he will be my second in command." She finished, jerking her thumb in my direction.

And that was that.

Over the next fifteen years, Sayedha, Maya, and I were nearly inseparable. We explored abandoned mine shafts and tunnels, swam in the pool below the falls, and snuck up to the dome late at night to gaze at the stars.

Maya had only grown more beautiful with each passing day. Her lips became fuller, her eyes became more cat-like, her hair was more voluminous, her stature grew more feminine, her backside got rounder, and her breasts...

We were all fourteen the first time I noticed Maya's fuller breasts while swimming in the pool at the bottom of the cavern. It had been like a seismic shift in my brain... which traveled straight down to my cock. Before anyone could notice the growing inside my pants, I had jumped into the water to hide it. As much as I had loved and admired Maya before... in that moment, I realized I now wanted her in other ways too.

But it was never to be.

Boy after boy made their move to talk or flirt with her, despite my looming presence somewhere nearby. Mostly, she refused, content to remain in our group, until the day came when she said yes. We were all seventeen, and I would never forget how the boy had beamed when she had accepted his offer to go on a date, just the two of them. The three of us had been taking a break from our studies up in the dome when the gangly, freckled male approached. My heart thundered, hands clenching into fists as he spoke with her. Her eyes were always kind toward everyone, but when she spoke with him, I noticed something different... an attraction. When he had finally left and the risk of me crushing his skull had dissipated, Maya's eyes had turned to mine. She was blushing, a little embarrassed, but she had also seemed... disappointed.

But of course, I wanted to believe that. I was the only person who wanted her more than anything.

But I said nothing. Through every heartbreak and every lover, I said nothing to her about how I felt. It had become apparent that if I ever told her the devastating depth of my love for her, our friendship would be forever changed.

So, I decided that having her in my life as a friend, despite the agony of watching her be with other men, was more important than how I felt about her. I would be anything or do anything for both Maya and Sayedha, even if that meant I would never know the touch of a lover.

A few brave females had expressed interest over the years, but I had never given them the time of day. My heart, my body... it all belonged to Maya, if she wanted it.

Some days, however, her full-grown womanhood was too much to take...

Now that we had adult responsibilities, I could not see her every day. But the three of us would try our best to schedule lunch a few times a week, for old times' sake. When she would breeze in, golden hair braided into a crown above her head and hips swishing, it always felt like my first breath of air in days. And that night... my dreams would be filled with the soft touch of her mouth and her hands. More often than I cared to admit,

I found myself launching from sleep, drenched in sweat and furiously pumping my cock at the thought of her.

It was that action that I found myself attending to this very moment.

The dream of her heavy breasts bouncing as she rode me, still pulsed through my body with lingering need as I gripped my cock under the bedsheets and jerked wildly. It was during moments like these that I was grateful that I no longer slept in the barracks. Closing my eyes to relish these last moments before my climax, I reached into my mental archives of Maya and withdrew one of my favorite fantasies...

She was naked and lay bare on a bed before me, her mouth gently sucking on the fingers of her right hand, while her left hand rubbed her gleaming, pink pussy enticingly. Her heavy-lidded gaze stroked me like a caress as her pink breasts peaked under my stare.

Gods, what wouldn't I give for this to be real? It became too much then. I grunted with pleasure as my release soaked into the blanket.

As my breathing began to regulate, desire banking, I sat up in bed. It had to be nearly dawn, but there was no way to know until the sun clock chimed from the hall. I rose from the bed and moved to drink a glass of water when I heard a light tap on the door. I groaned. It was probably Sayedha waking us all up before dawn for another torturous training exercise.

I walked to the door, pulled it open, and stopped dead.

It was Maya.

Her hair had been unbound from her braid and lay in soft waves across her shoulders. She was clutching herself tight around the middle, and... she was in her nightgown. Nearly swallowing my tongue at the sight, I started when I noticed her wary expression.

"Hey... Can I come in?" she whispered, nervously tugging a stray hair behind her ear.

Still numb with shock, I only nodded and opened the door wider for her. My room had little to offer in terms of seating space, but I did have a single chair and a small desk. Before I could offer her a seat, however, she sat on the edge of my bed, the sheets still mussed.

Inhaling deep, I fought to push down my dismay. Maya was here... in my room. Sitting on my fucking bed. Which was still wet from my...

"I'm sorry to come here like this," she blurted, her eyes wet with unshed tears.

Fucking Hel, I had never seen Maya cry. Not once.

Suddenly alarmed, I dragged the chair over and sat in front of her before asking, "What is it, Maya? What's wrong?" She bit her lip, scattering my thoughts, before raising her glassy eyes to mine.

"I've heard rumors of a secret mission taking place. With Aida and Tyran. I have no doubt that the Queen will be sending you and Sayedha with them. So... I'm going, too." she stated defiantly.

No. Fuck no.

Though Sayedha and I had suspected something like this was coming, we hadn't had an official briefing about it with the Queen. But none of that mattered. We knew it would be dangerous, and there was zero chance I would allow her to accompany us. Her sapphire eyes were pleading as they ripped me to shreds. I only shook my head and stared her down.

She started to stammer with panic, "Please, Kine. I can't stay here, knowing the two of you will be in danger... and may never come back. All my science is safe here. I've already trained my replacement. I would be an asset. I've trained in combat just like you both have. I'm more familiar with the weapons... I can help if something goes wrong... I can--"

I cut her off abruptly by pressing my fingers to her lips, barely aware I was doing it. Her eyes widened at the contact, and I retreated instantly, tucking my tingling fingers under my thigh. Embarrassment flooded through me like a torrent as I realized it was the first time I had ever touched her, outside of a bashful elbow to the ribs.

"Kine..." her voice was low and tense. I snapped my head up to meet her gaze and found her eyes soft. Hungry...

My chest seized in a vice. No, it was just my imagination. I glanced down at my feet, confident it had been a mistake.

Tentatively, her trembling hand reached out and caressed the top of my knee. The touch sent a jolt of electricity through my body, pebbling my skin.

"Look at me, Kine," she said firmly.

I obeyed and found her lip wobbling and chest heaving. Slowly, she rose from the bed and started walking toward me.

Was I still asleep? Surely, this was just another dream.

As if in tune with my thoughts, she gently removed the robe from her shoulders and let it drop to the floor. I nearly jumped with the shock of desire that struck me like a hammer. Her blue, silk nightgown left fucking *nothing* to the imagination. The garment clung to every dip and curve of her perfect frame... and her peaked breasts. A soft buzzing filled my head as all thought left me. Her bare feet padded across the floor until she stood between my legs. With aching slowness, she brought her fingers to graze across my bare chest. My hands clenched the chair tight enough to splinter wood as my breathing became more ragged.

How could this be happening?

She had been so upset... what if she was only doing this out of sadness? No, it wasn't right. I moved then, gripping her small wrists and slowly shaking my head. She only held my stare, lips parted, her tongue darting over them.

Fuck, how many times had I fantasized about her giving me that look?

"Are you trying to tell me that you don't want this?" she said in a slightly mocking tone.

Gods be fucked, I wanted it more than breath in my lungs, but I couldn't survive her regret if it wasn't what she really wanted. It would destroy me.

Desire and honor warred inside me with violence... but she only moved closer, her breath warming the skin of my neck.

"I want you, Kine. I've wanted you for a very long time," she whispered into my ear.

The words dropped into my chest like a stone. And all I could think was, *"this can't be real..."*

She was brilliant, gorgeous, and full of light. I was just a hulking, beastly shadow compared to her.

But Gods... I *wanted* to believe it.

"I can't lose you and Sayedha... but not just because you're my closest friends. It's because... I love you, Kine. I think I've loved you for most of my life... I just never had the courage to say it, but I do now."

Her eyes pinned me to the floor as she pulled down her nightgown to stand before me in nothing but her lace underwear. White hot need raged through my body like a firestorm, my cock hardening under her gaze. Unable to help myself, I dropped my eyes to her fucking *perfect* breasts; my mouth watering at the prospect of finally being able to taste them. Gently, she lifted her legs to straddle me on the chair, the soft skin of her breasts pressing against my chest. Instinct had my arms reaching around her back to bring her closer. It was something I had imagined doing countless times.

Gods, her skin was like velvet.

Maya's body trembled as she writhed against the hard length beneath my pants. She looked into my eyes, lips parted in invitation, before she whispered, "Do you love me, too?"

Everything I had ever wanted had just taken place in the matter of a few minutes.

My head swam with a kaleidoscope of emotion: doubt, insecurity, desire, and... hope; all fighting for dominion.

But I wasn't a fucking idiot. She had come to me and made her move.

And she wanted *me*. She... *loved* me. I wouldn't let this chance pass me by. I was smarter than that. Her fingers found the tender skin of my neck as she began to toy with my hair. My eyes fluttered at the touch, hands gripping tighter around her waist.

It was now or never.

Raising my hands up to grip her delicate neck, I stared at her mouth and said, "Maya... I have loved you since the first moment I saw you, and I will love you till the day I die."

Her lips briefly curled into a smile before her mouth was on mine. There were no words to describe it. She was sweeter and more tender than I had ever imagined. She kissed me passionately; her wet, eager tongue tasting my mouth. I surrendered to her, our kiss igniting into a blazing inferno.

All this time. All these years.

My body shook with the power of it. Maya was in *my* arms and kissing *me*. She was finally mine... and I would never let her go.

CHAPTER 48
AIDA

When I awoke the next morning, Tyran's heavy arm still draped across my waist, I had the distinct feeling that the world had shifted under our feet.

Synsa's visions told of a future I could've never imagined. At the same time, each vision was subject to its own infinite variations of change, fully dependent on every decision we made. It meant that I could wake up today, call off this whole mission, and hide here forever; everyone I cared about kept safe...

And that frightening vision of my future self, clad in iridescent armor and roaring with blood lust, would vanish into smoke...

But what a *waste* that would be.

The Gods had knowledge about the location of the helmet, but they also knew how Chemosh was able to deflect the Dream Walker's power. This knowledge could indeed change the tide of this conflict. Perhaps some epic battle could be avoided entirely if I could only learn how to penetrate her mind.

No, I would not hide when the salvation of this world rested on my ability. I would not cower and allow her reign to go unchecked... and I would not be alone.

Suddenly, deep in my belly, I felt a slight twinge. The sensation was odd, less like a cramp and more like something... being knitted together.

Before I could let myself wonder what it was, Tyran's groggy form began to stir before pressing a soft kiss to my ear.

"Good morning," I said, rolling over to face him.

His eyes were barely cracked open as he gave me a sleepy grin in response. His hand lazily stroking my shoulder as we looked at each other fondly. He had asked me to marry him. My throat squeezed with the stress I was withholding as I gave him a pained smile. In truth, I wanted nothing more than to selfishly continue down the safer road with him by my side. He became more alert as he noticed my expression shift.

"I want to wait to get married. I want all of this to be behind us first," I said softly.

His face turned understanding then, and he only nodded before abruptly moving to reach for the knitted wool blanket at our feet. Drawing up the cream-colored blanket, his brow furrowed as he yanked off two threads. Gently, he grabbed my left hand and tied the thread around my ring finger to make a small band. I lifted my hand to inspect the makeshift ring and smiled brightly before sitting up and wordlessly tying the other thread around his finger. He sighed deeply as he stared at our fingers, and when he looked up, his eyes were welling up with tears. I moved to sit next to him and clasped his solid, warm hands between my own.

"This is all I need. You and me." I stated.

One tear streamed silently down his cheek as he nodded and raised my hand to press his lips to the newest symbol of our bond.

WE DRESSED AND MADE OUR WAY TO THE MAIN HALL FOR BREAKFAST. Upon arriving at the top of the stairwell, I nearly choked at who I saw seated there, in remarkably close proximity. Maya was practically in Kine's lap, nuzzling his neck. Before they could notice our presence, Sayedha entered the hall, her quick stride stuttering to a stop as she noticed them too. Maya nearly jumped out of his embrace and tried to act normal, both going crimson with embarrassment. Unsure what was about to go down... Tyran and I waited against the wall.

Slowly, Sayedha walked up to the table before stopping and crossing her arms; ever the superior, looking for an explanation. Sensing an interrogation was about to commence, Maya and Kine put down their utensils and looked up at her with apprehension on their faces. Sayedha stared them down for a heart-stopping moment before her lips curled over her teeth in a warm smile. Then... she began to laugh.

"It's about fucking time!" she chuckled.

The whole room released a collective sigh of relief, which was our signal for Tyran and me to fill our plates. As we sat down next to Sayedha, my eyes briefly met Kine's.

Gods... he was *smiling*. While still a hulking behemoth, his expression was now softer than I ever thought possible. It was so infectious that I couldn't help but smile back. Maya, of course, was beaming warmly at all of us, her hand absent-mindedly rubbing Kine's back, as if she couldn't keep her hands off him. Sayedha's voice broke through the happy glow a moment later when she said, "We are to meet The Queen here shortly. She wants to see all of us in her chambers as soon as we are done."

We finished our breakfast in silence before clearing our plates and following Sayedha to the stairwell on the opposite side of the main hall. Like most areas of this inner sanctum, the only light provided was through innumerable candles in sconces and in small alcoves. The stairwell to Synsa's chambers brought us to another stone corridor. Unlike the guest corridor, however, this one was filled with paintings, tapestries, and various exotic sculptures. Bizarre-looking stuffed cats, spotted skin rugs, and garish tribal masks; all completely foreign to anything I'd ever seen on Astaran.

Where did she get all these things? Where did it come from?

We followed the corridor until we arrived at her door, and Sayedha knocked softly.

"Come in," Synsa said in a muffled voice. As we filed into the chamber, I was immediately struck by the size of the room. The cavern was sprawling, at least five times larger than ours in the guest corridor. Giant natural cave formations dripped from the ceiling and pierced through the floor. Each wall that encircled us had been gouged to create countless alcoves, all filled with flickering candles, making the room appear like a holy temple. Dozens of exotic potted plants with deep green leaves and brightly colored flowers adorned the space, and in the center was a gentle waterfall that trickled into a natural pool.

It was Synsa's oasis from her dreamscape, or at least as close as she could get while living under a mountain.

Synsa did not acknowledge our presence as she waved a glowing, blue torch over each plant and watered them affectionately. When she was finished, she turned to our group and smiled warmly, waving her arm in the direction of the private dining area nearest to the falls. The five of us seated ourselves around the table, which was covered in various maps and charts of Astaran. Some of the maps appeared ancient, creased, and brown with age. Kine and Sayedha were already examining them in detail and murmuring to each other about preferable routes. Synsa glided over then and seated herself across from us before saying, "These maps are the last of their kind. They show locations The Fallen was eager for humans to forget—among them the former kingdom of Queen Mercury and King Arketh: Svargad. As she spoke, her finger drifted to a six-pointed star nestled in a bend of the Solumine, hundreds of miles to the south.

Holy shit. Traveling that far would take weeks.

"In a month's time, on the eve of Litha, the sun will be in its strongest position. When this happens, the wards put in place by the alchemists long ago will seal the chamber where the mirrors are stored, somewhere inside the ruin. If you do not reach the chamber before this happens, you will not have another chance until next summer." She finished, giving me a pointed stare.

I swallowed. That meant another *twelve* maidens would be butchered needlessly.

We had no time to lose.

An errant thought formed into a question on my lips, "If you knew how this all worked, why didn't you send an expedition to bring the mirrors back here a long time ago?"

Synsa's gaze fixed me seriously as she replied, "We did. The problem was, the vault where the mirrors were said to be stored required a blood payment. None of the Begavet we sent were able to unlock the vault..."

I knew where she was going with this.

"It requires the blood of a Dream Walker." I finished for her.

She only nodded gravely before turning to address Kine, Sayedha and Maya.

"The three of you will accompany them, in addition to three other warriors and a falcon emissary of your choosing," she stated.

Kine visibly bristled, but Maya only put a hand on his arm and nodded. Empathy washed through me as I realized that Tyran and I were in the same boat that they were: partners who had finally aligned with their mates, only to be thrust into a dangerous and unknown future.

Synsa sighed wearily as she looked each of us in the eye before saying, "*The Fallen* is not to be underestimated. Her spies are everywhere. Travel with stealth and look after each other. You leave at first light."

As we stood up to leave Synsa's chambers, she quietly asked Tyran and me to stay behind, making a silent demand to Sayedha to clear the room with a jerk of her chin. We lingered behind as they filed out, curious. When it was only the three of us left, Synsa said, "There's something you need to see, Aida," before she stepped away from the table toward the gentle waterfall at the back of the cavern. Tyran's eyes met mine with silent support as we followed her. When we joined her to stand at the rim of the pool, she left us again to move closer to one of the large stalactites that hung from the ceiling next to the falls. With a gentle graze of her fingers, she located a square shaped depression on the surface of the calcified rock and pressed down. Suddenly, the stone beneath us began to shudder and quake as the water in the pool started to thrash, splashing our feet as it sloshed from side to side. Tyran gripped my arm to steady me as we both watched in fascination as giant stone objects began to rise from their hiding place at the bottom of the pool. When they had finally unsheathed themselves from their watery vault, my eyes blew wide as the realization struck me—they were statues.

Three stone figures stood close together on a single round pedestal, their backs turned to each other. A soft ringing filled my ears as I studied them, rivulets of water cascading down their forms. Synsa left the stalactite that was obviously a ruse to hide the mechanism within and came to stand beside us.

"These statues are the only remaining effigies of the Gods still in existence. Long before The Fallen had come to Astaran, Mercury commissioned our priests to sculpt the figures of the three Gods she believed to be the most influential in the God realm...

The Goddess of War and Justice.

The Goddess of Love and Peace

...and the God of Kaos.

They had stood in a great pantheon inside of Opeth for centuries before they were moved here in secret when it became clear that the Kingdoms of Astaran would not survive Chemosh's vengeance."

My eyes never left the statues as she spoke, my heart keeping an odd rhythm as unease slithered down my spine. Slowly, I walked around the rim of the pool as I studied them. Though time had begun to soften any fine details, it was clear that two were female and one was male. One of the females wore hardly any clothes; her tall, lithe form exuded power and dominance as she raised a hand to the sky as if summoning a storm. Her face was etched in cruel lines as she looked outward with a glare, her hair floating around her head in a chaotic halo. I noted curiously that almost every inch of her skin was marked—not with scars, but with strange symbols. The Goddess of War, if I had to guess.

The other female was the exact opposite. Her long robe hung to her feet, a thick, hooded scarf wrapped around her head, a long braid hanging across one shoulder. Her face, while still intimidating, was markedly softer, her uptilted eyes stoic with contemplation. The Goddess of Love and Peace, surely...

"What happened to this one?" Tyran asked as he stared up at the third male figure.

Following his gaze, my eyes roved over the statue's lean, muscular build. His long robe was open, exposing his chest, his hands curled with the palms facing upward as if he had been holding something. But his head was missing.

"Damaged on purpose or during transit, I'm not certain," Synsa replied, her eyes tight with concern. "But what I do know is that Mercury was always the most afraid of him. She claimed that the God of Kaos was the most cunning of them all."

My scalp tingled as her words settled like stones in my gut. The idea that the Goddess of War was somehow less intimidating than the God of Kaos unnerved me, and it served as just another reminder of how insignificant I felt in this whole scheme.

How could I possibly speak to any of them?

As she returned the mechanism that would bring the statues back down, Tyran and I watched in silence as the figures descended into the dark pool. I pretended not to be disturbed by what I had seen, but Tyran knew better, his eyes strained as he noted my blank stare. Synsa approached us again, her eyes calm but serious as she said, "Mercury was always more than a Queen. And always more than a Begavet. To us, she was our last line of defense against the Lyrathians, who had questionable intentions... but to the Gods, she was a threat. As you will be. Do not shy from your power, Aida. You bare your teeth with *pride*."

CHAPTER 49
AIDA

Before Sayedha and Kine had departed Synsa's chambers to brief the warriors who would accompany us, Sayedha had told us where to find the horses, and instructed me to choose one for our journey. For the first time since we had arrived more than two weeks ago, we left the mountain city and followed the spiraling path down to the valley on the floor of the cavern. Soladium lampposts were erected every few yards, casting their blue glow on the grass and trees nearby. Up ahead, the thundering roar of the great falls grew louder as we approached a fenced-in meadow. Tyran's eyes lit up when they found Cressida, lazily grazing near a few other horses. When he whistled low to her, she perked up her ears and trotted over to us. We spent a moment greeting her before my eyes drifted to the other horses in the field and rested on a solid black gelding. He was the same size as Cressida, his shiny coat glimmering under the blue light. Alerted to our presence by the horse chatter, a young man emerged from the nearby stables and walked over to greet us.

"What can you tell me about the black male over there?" I asked.

He smirked proudly before he replied, "His name is Vilje and he's about as willful as they come, but sturdy and even tempered enough." I found that description fitting, so I requested the groom to have him ready for departure by morning. After some coaxing with a few carrots, Vilje allowed me to stroke and brush him. He was magnificent and appeared to be somewhat enamored by Cressida too, nickering softly as he nuzzled her neck. Tyran shot me with a look of warm amusement as we watched them. I returned it with a soft chuckle. If we weren't careful during Cressida's heat, we'd have young foals to rear before long...

The thought zapped me, a sharp reminder of the tension I could feel coiled in my abdomen—and of the cycle that, curiously, had not yet arrived. I didn't dare lift my hand to prod my belly, however; that potential reality was too intense to even consider. And I didn't want Tyran to become more anxious about my well-being more than he already was. Especially considering we were on the eve of this journey to find the mirrors and already contemplating every lethal hazard we might encounter...

Surely it was too soon to know such a thing anyway, wasn't it?

How long had it been since Tyran and I first had sex? Two weeks?

I'd lost count of how many times since then too...

Cold sweat broke across my palms as I bit my lip. That couldn't be possible. *Right?*

Tyran, noticing my subtle anxiety, tenderly stroked my wrist. "Are you all right?" he murmured.

I shook the haze of panic and readjusted my features. I didn't want this far-fetched possibility to weigh on his mind. No, this would be my burden to ponder, until I knew for certain.

I nodded with a tight smile, taking his hand in mine as we turned and left the meadow.

Upon leaving the cavern floor and returning to the city, our next stop was the swordsmith. The alcove where he operated was hotter than Hel, the walls stained black with soot. The air was somehow clean though, thanks to the efficient ventilation system Maya had told us about. The swordsmith was in the middle of pounding a steel bar into submission, sparks flying as he went. Upon noticing our arrival, he beamed and removed his leather gloves to shake our hands before gesturing to us to follow. He took us to a room where all his finished pieces were displayed on the wall: long swords, scythes, daggers, throwing stars and others I did not recognize. Reaching behind his small work desk, he brought out two long shapes wrapped in velvet and unwrapped them both with care. His dark eyes sizzled with anticipation and pride as he presented them to us, head slightly bowed.

All thoughts evaporated from my head as I beheld the two blades.

One was an intimidating long sword obviously meant for Tyran; its hilt glistening with gilded, gold climbing roses, just like the dagger Luke had made for him.

And the other...

I felt the blood drain from my face as I gazed at the gleaming scimitar sword.

The same exact one from Synsa's vision.

The silver sword was longer than my forearm, the curved edge gleaming with countless folds of steel. My hands flexed without my consent; I had never owned a blade this fine. The weapon almost pulsed with power, calling to me. As my eyes roved down the blade, they pricked as I admired the intricate swirls of stars and planets carved with meticulous attention onto the hilt...

If the sense of foreboding, now making me nauseous, had not been so powerful, I would've marveled more at its beautiful craftsmanship. Clasping my hands together to avoid anyone noticing they had started to tremble; I could only nod appreciatively and left it to Tyran to express our gratitude. My words had left me.

We left the alcove, new blades in tow and began our climb back to the inner sanctum. Before we reached the giant crystals at the top, Tyran tugged me over to the railing.

"You going to tell me what all that was about in there?" he asked in an accusatory tone.

So, he had noticed. Figures.

Blowing out a breath, I replied, "Synsa showed me a vision... of me... holding *this* sword." I said, gesturing to the blade at my waist. Tyran's eye widened at that, but he stayed silent.

He needed to know... surely, it was important for him to know what I had seen. But a nagging voice told me not to reveal everything... as if it were aware of how his decisions would play into the equation.

Choosing my words carefully, I said, "I saw you in one of the visions. You were uh... moving objects... with your mind." Tyran's brows shot to his scalp before furrowing in disbelief. I nearly choked on the other words I wanted to spill...

In another vision... I was with child... and you were nowhere to be seen...

A lump formed in my throat as I swallowed this truth. Only a slight thread of hope kept me stable, Synsa's words:

"Each path laid before us is never a straight line. Some overlap, some tumble into darkness, but most twist and bend beyond the horizon, too far to see."

We stood there silently for a moment more before he gripped me gently by the shoulders and pinned me with a serious stare.

"I need you to promise me that we are together in this. Where you go, I go."

Lifting my hands to rest on his heart and thinking there was no way I could guarantee it, I replied, "I promise."

Chapter 50
Kine

Sayedha had given me specific instructions to choose three of the best trackers from our fighting force. Immediately, I knew who I would select. All three were unmarried, childless, and eager for their first real mission.

After leaving Maya at her lab, where I had lingered longer than intended as she kissed me breathless, I made way my down to the barracks. The men here now were all off-duty and milled about doing various hobbies: playing chess, cards, reading or tinkering with various equipment. I assumed anyone not here was either home with their wives or making strides to find one in one of the many taverns throughout the city.

"Micah! Will! Kaleb!" I shouted across the room.

All three of them dropped whatever had been in their hands and nearly jumped out of their skin at the sound of my voice before rushing over to line up in front of me.

"We have been tasked to join Tyran and the Dream Walker on a mission to Svargad. If there is any reason you do not wish to join this mission, please state so now." I said gravely.

All their eyes widened with shock, but they stayed silent.

"Good. And Will, you are to bring your falcon and act as emissary. Go prepare and ready your horses, we leave at dawn. You're dismissed." I concluded firmly. The three of them nodded and filed from the room, gently shoving each other excitedly.

Upon leaving the barracks, I was nearly sprinting at the prospect of seeing Maya before skidding to a stop when I noticed the couple embracing each other on the path just ahead.

It was Sayedha and her partner, Ivy.

They stood across the pathway in front of Ivy's bakery, the smell of fresh bread cloaking the air in front of the shop. Not wanting to interrupt, I moved to stand behind a food stall, pretending to browse through the produce. I could tell from their conversation that Sayedha had just told Ivy about our mission. Ivy's petite frame was hunched as she gripped herself around the middle. They had been together about five years and in that time, I had never seen Sayedha happier. Ivy's head hung low with sadness before Sayedha gripped her by the chin and spoke seriously into her eyes. Ivy nodded, tears welling and slipping down her cheek. Sayedha brushed them away with a thumb before pressing a gentle kiss to her mouth and wrapping her in an embrace.

Fuck... I hated goodbyes. I knew they would have one last night together before we departed in the morning, but it made my heart ache knowing how long they had to endure being separated... if we all survived.

The panic and anger I had shoved down earlier that day when the Queen had ordered Maya to join this expedition began to rise back to the surface. A war was raging inside me. On one hand, I didn't want to be separated from Maya for more than a second, but on the other, I didn't want her to be in danger. As I watched Sayedha and Ivy part ways, I decided that I needed to try harder to convince Maya to stay behind.

The rest of the day was a flurry of activity in preparation for our journey. Horses needed to be shoed, weapons needed to be cleaned and organized, food needed to be packed. I spent most of the afternoon making various demands to an assortment of necessary personnel. Suddenly, the sun clock chimed nine as I made my way to the dining hall to find it mostly empty, dinner long past. A few trays had been left behind for the stragglers, so I heaped enough food for two people onto a plate and made my way down to Maya's lab.

When I arrived, it was empty.

Heart plummeting for a moment, I shook it off as I realized how busy she had been today too. She was probably just as tired as I was and needed time to prepare her things before morning. Walking much slower now, I headed for my chambers. When I arrived at my door, plate of food still in one hand, I fumbled with the key for a moment before turning it in the lock and pushing it open. My heart lurched into my throat as my body froze at what I saw there.

Maya, a wicked grin on her beautiful face, her head propped up by her hand, was lying naked in my bed. She giggled as she took in my stunned expression and helped me along by whispering, "Close the door, Kine."

Frozen no longer, I quickly shut and locked the door before snagging on a thought.

"How did you get in here?" I asked as I made my way to set down the food on the desk. Her eyes followed me across the room, her grin turning positively feline before replying, "Brilliant engineer, remember?"

Oh, right. Unsure of what to do in this situation, I stood there awkwardly, eyes darting to her naked form under the sheet. She only stared back; her full lips parted in invitation. Shaking off the fog of desire beginning to cloud my blood, I remembered my earlier anger and leaned on it like a crutch.

Clearing my throat first, I said, "Maya... we need to talk." A shadow passed over her eyes, and in an instant, her body turned defensive, hands clutching the sheets over her chest.

What? Ah, fuck. I was so bad at this.

"No... not about us. I mean... we need to talk about this mission. Listen, Maya. You can't go. I can't stand the thought of you getting hurt. Please." I stammered, trying and failing to establish authority in my tone.

Her eyes softened as her body slowly relaxed. She stared for just a moment longer before she said softly, "Come over here."

My mouth dried up, cock instantly hard. I obeyed, walking to the edge of the bed.

Slowly, her eyes never leaving mine, she pulled the sheet away from her body and laid bare beneath me. I couldn't help the moaning sigh that slipped from my lips as my eyes consumed her fucking perfect body.

Gods... My cock ached to be touched but I resisted, breaths turning ragged.

"Will I be your first lover?" she asked boldly, voice low.

I couldn't believe this was happening. Maya was giving herself to me. As much as I had dreamt about this moment, I hated to admit that I didn't know where to begin. I nodded my head, suddenly feeling very much like an amateur. She only smiled warmly and said, "I'll go easy on you. I promise."

Her face suddenly became the vision of lust as she rose up onto her knees and began to unbutton my pants.

Fucking shit.

Quickly, I pulled my shirt over my head and unhooked the scabbard at my belt, letting it clatter to the floor. My cock sprang free, and I noted her surprise as she marveled at its length and girth. While I had not done extensive study on the subject, I had seen enough naked men in the barracks to know that I was slightly more endowed than the average male. When her hands began stroking me, it took everything I had not to explode right then.

Her sapphire eyes glowed in the candlelight as she took me into her mouth.

Lyrath damn me. My fantasies had nothing on this.

My core muscles tightened at the touch of her warm, wet tongue. I was starting to shake with the urge to touch her, so I reached out to stroke her soft golden hair away from her face.

Fuck, she was tasting *me*. Swallowing *me*.

My balls ached with the anticipation of every stroke.

I wanted to burst my release into her mouth but didn't know how she'd feel about it. Before I lost my head entirely, I pulled myself from her lips and pushed her back onto the bed. She pulled my face to hers and kissed me savagely, her tongue and teeth colliding with mine.

Fuck, I wanted to taste every inch of her. Needed to. Had wanted it for so long.

My lips began to roam across her face and jaw before drifting to her neck and sucking the soft skin there. My need for her was hot and consuming, she was like a live wire over my skin. I longed to be joined with her but also wanted this moment to drag out for as long as I could, my muscles quivering with restraint. She was so soft and small. I didn't want to hurt her.

Shifting my body to hover over hers, my teeth and tongue grazed down her chest until arriving at her Gods-sent breasts. She gasped excitedly, running her hands through the strands of my hair as I sucked each breast in turn. They were fucking delicious. I found myself thinking that I could do this all day and never get enough. Something about it was not only erotic but comforting in some primal way.

I continued to explore her body with my mouth, licking and sucking down the planes of her stomach, over her soft hips and finally, her soaking wet pussy.

My chest rumbled with a growl at her throaty moan as she bucked her hips up, eager for me to devour her. I had never wanted anything more.

I got comfortable and pushed her velvet-soft thighs apart before I ravaged her like a decadent meal. Her swollen clit throbbed across my tongue as I looked up to see her writhing and moaning with pleasure. *She was finally mine.* I would do this for her day and night if she wanted.

Dragging my tongue flat in a long stroke sent shivers and spasms through her body, and it fucking excited me. So, I did it again and again. She whimpered, her hands gripping my hair tight as her hips rolled against my mouth.

"Kine..." she pleaded. Fuck, I loved the way my name sounded on her lips. I licked her harder, mouth dripping as my cock pressed uncomfortably against the mattress.

"Kine!" she moaned, head rolling back and stomach muscles clenching tight.

"Fuck!" she screamed. She was losing control, hips bucking wildly. With a final drag of my tongue, her body shuddered, back arching off the bed as she roared through her release. My lips and tongue working her though the upper echelons of pleasure. I lapped up her release as I watched her body contort and jerk, mesmerized.

It was the most amazing thing I had ever seen.

I needed to be inside her. Slowly, I raised my body to hover over hers, my cock gliding against the moist lips of her center. She looked at me, eyes wide and desperate.

"Please make love to me, Kine. Please," she begged against my mouth.

I didn't need to be told twice.

My cock nudged her entrance as I slowly pushed my way in, watching her gasp through every inch.

Holy fuck... it was...

She was suddenly biting my bottom lip, and I plowed into her, filling her to the hilt.

I began to shake with the overwhelming sensation that rolled through my body like a warm wave. She was gasping and moaning under me, hips beckoning me to move. My restraint popped and frayed as I began to fuck her wildly, her inner walls hugging me tight. Her mouth continued to suck on my mine as I pounded her, her whimpers making my head swim as my hands gripped around her soft neck.

Fuck, I couldn't handle how amazing this felt. I knew I was close. Her soft hands roamed across my back and squeezed my backside as I slammed into her, our skin slapping together. I gazed into her beautiful face, and when she smiled and said, "I love you," my cock erupted.

Fucking Gods! I rocked into her hips and moaned with ecstasy as my release pumped into her warm heat. It was absolute fucking *bliss*. It was the best thing to ever happen to me.

She was the best thing to ever happen to me.

I buried my face against her neck and breathed deep, my mind and body effectively in tatters.

As the haze of profound euphoria began to dissipate, I looked down at her smiling face and kissed her gently on the nose.

"I can't believe I waited this long... for *that*," she said happily.

I couldn't agree more, but I was beyond words. I only nodded and kissed her soft mouth before removing my slick cock from her body and pulling her into my arms. We lay there, sated and content for a long time. Just as I was on the edge of sleep, I heard her whisper, "I'm still going... and you can't stop me."

CHAPTER 51
AIDA

Sleep deserted us that night, our morning departure for the lost ruins of Svargad looming like an ancient promise of dread. It was the slaughterhouse of my ancestors, and the last known location of the obsidian mirrors. Above all, this mission was my sole responsibility as Mercury's heir.

Thump, thump, thump. The steady beat of Tyran's heart was not enough to lull me into rest.

I laid there, ear to his chest, all night. Sleep had forsaken him in fits and spurts as well, it seemed, his fingers idly tracing small circles across my shoulders throughout the night.

We said nothing. Even as I ghosted my fingers across the Dagaz brand in the center of his chest. Across the raised, pink scars left there by SkÖll's murderous claws. Even when I laid a gentle kiss to the skin there. He only squeezed me tighter. We both knew that, come morning, our lives would be heaved into chaos yet again.

My mind raced and fumbled through all that had changed in the last month.

Tyran and I had always been connected somehow, but now our bond had been fused. Our fates were intertwined. The warm blood of our hearts, now pumped in the same rhythm.

The fate of this world, this kingdom... the weight of it settled against my ribs, threatening to crush me from the inside out. I closed my eyes at the sting of tears as I thought back to the moment when Tyran had asked me what Synsa had said about our twin Dagaz symbols...

I had just told him about Synsa's vision as we stood near the rail, overlooking the twinkling blue lights of the city below. Chest tight with trepidation, I had repeated her translation.

"It's a reminder... To never give up hope. To never stop. The sun will rise each day, and the darkness will come each night. An endless cycle of death and rebirth. A never-ending metamorphosis. Just as our opportunities to change our fate... are infinite."

When the initial stunned expression had left his features, he only smiled warmly. Ever the optimist. He had cupped my face gently, angling my mouth to his. The kiss had been gentle and sweet but rang with searing promise.

"The Gods have marked us for each other. Together, we are unbreakable." He had whispered across my lips, the heat of him drilling deep into my core.

Unbreakable.

Was such a thing possible? With him at my side, I fervently believed it could be. As my hand now rested across the solid lines of his stomach, I glanced down to the thread tied around my ring finger. Suddenly, the weight of the future seemed to dissipate by just a fraction.

The Gods have marked us for each other... They were betting on us. Luke was betting on us. As sure as Tyran's warm skin beneath my palm, I knew it to be true. With that final pulse of hope, I found sleep in his arms.

SIX CHIMES RANG OUT FROM THE SUN CLOCK DOWN THE HALL. IT WAS finally time to go.

The mountain city still slept as Tyran and I somberly gathered our supplies and made our way down to the horses.

Without the chatter of its inhabitants, the vast cavern hummed with the soft roar of the falls at the bottom. About halfway to the valley floor, we spotted Sayedha walking out of a residential alcove before turning around to passionately kiss a petite, brunette woman.

My heart throbbed. Sayedha was leaving someone behind, too.

The woman sobbed quietly as she embraced Sayedha, whispering in her ear. As we approached, they both dipped their heads toward us solemnly, but we only returned the gesture briefly and continued down the path. To give them some privacy. Tyran slid his fingers through mine and gripped tight. The movement spoke silent volumes: the consequences of our decisions were now shifting into place.

We arrived at the valley floor to see Kine and Maya in the process of saddling their horses. Maya, way too energetic for this time of day, skipped over to us before wrapping me in a great bear hug. Finding her energy to be irresistible, I clutched her back.

"I want to thank you..." she said, pulling away to look into my eyes.

"If it weren't for you and Tyran... I might have lived in ignorance forever." Her eyes briefly slid to Kine, who was shifting on his feet with poorly suppressed joy, which made her smile brighter.

"Seeing the two of you together... It showed me that life is too short to live in fear. To not take chances. To let your desires go unheard..." Her tone turned serious then as she gripped me by the shoulders.

"For centuries, the people of this city have lived in fear of the world outside of these mountains. But no more. It ends with us," she finished firmly, her blue eyes hardening to steel.

I swallowed and nodded, heartened by her conviction. *Yes, it does.*

Cressida and Vilje, saddled and ready to go, stood patiently as we strapped on our supplies. Three other warriors joined us shortly after. Kine introduced them as Micah, Will, and Kaleb. One of them, Will, had a hooded falcon in a wicker cage which was sturdily fixed to the horse's rump. For our travel to be swift, we had elected not to bring a wagon and only what could be carried on our horses. With that, we were ready to go.

Just then, a robed figure emerged from the other side of the stables. Synsa approached us, her bare feet barely a whisper through the soft grass.

When she arrived to stand before us, her eyes drifted to each of our faces, her features contemplative. When her eyes rested on mine, she spoke and said, "This is a defining moment for the future of not only the Begavet, but for all the oppressed peoples of Astaran. We have been hunted, tortured, and enslaved by a tyrant for centuries. It ends now. With all of you. May the Gods protect you all."

Struck speechless by the gravity of her words, we all bowed

our heads before guiding the horses up the steel pathway that hugged the wall of the cavern. As we climbed up in elevation, the path zigging and zagging higher, I gazed at the wondrous blue city where my life had been forever changed. We had only been in the mountain city for a few weeks, but it felt like months considering all that had taken place. As we approached the long tunnel that would lead us out of the cavern, I took one last look at Overlevende and wondered if I would ever see this place again.

The steady clopping of horse hooves remained the only sound for miles as we moved through the tunnel. I knew the hearts of our companions were heavy with trepidation; some of them had never left the cloaking fortress of the mountain city. After what seemed like an eternity, we finally reached the giant steel door that led out of the mountain. Kine and Sayedha worked in tandem to turn the great steel wheel at the center until the locks boomed open, the sound echoing off the stone. Creaking and groaning, the door swung open. Blinded by the brilliant daylight, everyone, including the horses, winced as our eyes struggled to adjust. After a moment, we all proceeded through the door and into the crisp mountain air. The pathway leading from the tunnel was almost invisible to the untrained eye, cleverly cloaked with rocks and boulders to hide the giant door tucked into a shadowed crag of the mountain. Cautiously, we descended past the rocky slopes until we reached the valley at the base of the mountain.

Spring was in full force with the buzzing and droning symphony of life busying itself with the great swaths of wildflowers that covered the valley floor. We all stopped to marvel at its beauty as the breeze rippled through the flowers. I glanced over to Maya to see her eyes well up with tears at the sight. Kine walked next to her and wrapped an arm around her shoulder briefly before turning to us and saying, "Mount up. We ride south until dusk."

Shortly after we began our descent away from the valley, we entered the emerald shadow of the Furian Wood. For my entire life, the vast forest had been my haven and shelter; now it filled me with dread. The sudden pressure of the tangled canopy above our heads gave me a sense of confinement that I didn't anticipate, especially considering we had just spent days in an underground cave. A quick glance at Tyran's expression as he rode beside me confirmed that he was equally apprehensive about what lay before us in this ancient forest.

"I've never seen so many trees..." Maya mused, eyes bright with wonder.

"Well, get used to them. The forest continues south without end until the Cliffs of Höd, and the ends of the world..." Tyran replied.

A shiver crept down my spine at the reference; the cliffs of Höd were rumored to be the demarcation line between Astaran and whatever abyss lay beyond. Some legends said that the cliffs dropped off into open space, others said it was a vast ocean from which no ships returned, while others claimed it was the beginning of a barren wasteland with no end. No one alive knew the truth. Long ago, even before Chemosh had conquered our world, a giant wall had been erected that stretched for thousands of miles, keeping whatever lay beyond a secret for eons...

Maya's awed gaze turned sober then. I shot Tyran a sharp glance, he only smirked with a shrug, clearly not above scaring the daylights out of anyone.

"Enough chit-chat back there. We have ground to cover!" Sayedha barked from the front of our group as she kicked her mare into a quick trot. Right. With the towering peaks of the

Vazaketh growing smaller behind us, we rode deeper into the wilderness.

Every mile bringing us closer to the ruins of Svargad.

Chapter 52
Tyran

We rode hard for twelve straight days.

Each day when dusk fell, our cadre would slip into the practiced rhythm of setting up camp. Aida and Sayedha would wander off to set snares or find water at any number of small streams and ponds available, thanks to the spring melt. The three young men who accompanied us would attend to the horses before starting their watch rotation: one always stationed in camouflage, just out of sight, until switching with another to sleep. Maya, a surprisingly good cook, would get to work scraping, chopping, and peeling whatever food was on hand. Which left me and Kine to collect firewood and erect our tents. After eating supper, which typically consisted of rabbits, squirrels, and a few quails who had flown too close, our fireside conversations would be brief before collapsing with exhaustion. And nearly every night, the howling of a distant wolf pack would send a ripple of unease through the camp. Aida's body would tense next to mine, no doubt remembering that the former commander of Hel's armies was now their Alpha.

As we traveled further south, the familiar foliage of girthy, sprawling oaks began to shift to mighty, towering pines. While fewer rabbits were being snared, we got lucky when a few panicked deer bounded across our path, one of them quickly falling under my arrow. As the supply of low-hanging oak branches began to dwindle, Kine and I resorted to felling smaller pines with our axes for firewood.

On our twelfth night in the wilderness, we arrived at a small clearing before stiffly dismounting from our horses and falling into our usual routine. All except Kine, who was studying one of the maps we obtained from Synsa. After dropping an armful of firewood, I walked over to join him. With the evening dwindling toward dusk, he angled the chart toward the light to show me our current location. According to the map, the ruins of Svargad were somewhere near the Solumine, roughly another fifty miles southeast. At this pace, we would reach the ruins by sundown tomorrow. With that knowledge shared with the group, a somber hum of silence settled over the camp. As darkness fell, everyone had returned from their various chores, except Aida. Before I could begin to fret, Sayedha emerged from the dark wall of the forest and jerked her thumb over her shoulder before saying, "She's that way, about two hundred yards. Near the stream." With just enough light left in the sky to see my feet, I entered the woods to search for her. After a short hike, a soft gurgling sounded from nearby. I followed the sound to find Aida sitting on the bank of a small creek, the water gently running over her bare feet. She was cast into shadow, with her head bowed and her arms wrapped around her knees.

She appeared to be... praying. My heart lurched at the sight of her. Just a few short months ago, she was adrift and alone out here. Now, she had me. But not even I could remove the chains of fate that had bound her to the path we now found ourselves on. I knew it had to be a terrible burden, and I was honored to share it with her, even though I would have sold my own soul to provide her with a life of peace instead.

Without lifting her head, she said, "If you're trying to catch me unawares, you failed about thirty paces ago." Slowly, she turned her head and gave me a smirk.

I could tell she was trying to hide her obvious pain. She didn't want me to worry about her, but it was too late for that. Fireflies began to flicker to life around us as I walked over to sit beside her. Silently, I removed my boots and placed my feet in the water next to hers. It was almost as rejuvenating as a bath. In addition to the soft sigh of the wind in the trees, crickets chirped, frogs sang, and owls hooted. We sat there together, wordlessly enjoying the sounds of the creatures beginning their evening shift, until the violet light faded to black.

Suddenly, she broke the silence, her voice thick with sadness. "Gods, Tyran... what if I *fail?*" Her body curled inward as she began to quake with silent sobs. Her agony hit me like an arrow to the gut. She was still so *young*. Often, I found myself forgetting just how young she was. Aida had always carried herself like someone who had lived many lives before this one. An old soul. And part of that was true; Aida's life had forced her to grow up at breakneck speed, her childhood eviscerated just as mine had been.

I reached for her then, wrapping my arms around her entire body to rock her gently as she wept. When she began to collect herself, she looked up at me, her eyes like black pools in the night, and whispered, "What if they get hurt? What if they die? For me? What if something happens to you? How am I going to do this if you're not with me?"

I could feel my heart splintering into fragments with her every word. I didn't have a convenient answer. I only shook my head and rested my hands on either side of her face before choosing my words carefully.

"Keep moving, Aida. Never stop moving, and you will survive."

Glistening tears streamed down her cheeks, running down the length of my palm. It was Luke's mantra for her, as it had been for me as well. I wouldn't make promises I knew I couldn't keep. So, I said the one thing I knew would always be true, even beyond death.

"I love you, Aida. Our souls will always be together. Where you go, I go. Never forget."

She nodded fiercely before pulling me down into a heart-shattering kiss. With the salt of her tears on my tongue, I kissed her back, trying my best to consume her despair. She moaned deeply when I crushed her neck to my mouth and sucked, grazing my tongue and teeth down to the velvet-soft skin along her collarbone. A hum of need began to pulse between my legs, and before I knew it, we had stood up and I was pressing her back against the nearest tree. Our lust for each other turned ravenous as clothes began to peel away. It had been almost two weeks since we had last made love, and that was just too fucking long. Her soft body warmed me as the evening chill nipped at my bare skin. Her kisses became desperate as she rubbed her hands over my back and chest. I wanted to remove all the pain and sadness from her mind.

I needed to remind her that she was alive.

Gripping her hips in my hands, I pinned them to the tree before nudging her legs apart and kneeling at her feet.

"You are *mine*. Nothing can take you from me, *little shadow*." I said softly, my lips brushing the soft skin of her belly, surprisingly firm. Maybe I was imagining it... But I thought it was slightly swollen too. The brief snag of thought dissipated as I returned to the task at hand. Aida convulsed with need as I slowly pressed wet kisses to her stomach and hips, my fingers kneading her thighs and backside as I went. She gasped and writhed with each touch, bringing a hand to squeeze her breast as she looked down at me. My eyes never leaving hers, I moved my hands to spread the skin of her gorgeous pussy apart and kissed it tenderly. Once. Twice.

She whimpered as I dragged my tongue flat down her center before pushing it inside her. She needed this, and I needed her. I would do anything for her. I met her gaze, cursing against her skin at the sight. *She was so fucking beautiful.*

Her eyes hazed over with lust as she gripped me by the hair and fucked my mouth, hips rocking eagerly.

Yes, baby. Don't stop.

I continued to devour her, determined to drive away every dark shadow from every corner of her soul. The rhythm of her thrusts began to stutter before she went taut as a bowstring, her release exploding on my tongue. I sucked her delicately and watched her cry out until she begged me to stop. A heartbeat later, I was standing with her thighs in my hands, her body suspended off the ground and pressed against the tree. Her mouth crashed into mine as my cock slid home, the taste of her still coating tongue.

Being inside her was incomparable perfection. So far gone with need, I fucked her greedily, unable to get close enough. With her arms wrapped around my neck, she moaned my name against my tongue and bit my lip. The brief pain sent a jolt straight to my cock, and I began to thrust faster. "Fuck me,

Tyran... I'm yours... always," she whispered against the heated skin of my neck, pulling a growl from my throat.

Unable to stop myself, I latched onto her neck with my teeth before my cock erupted, spurting my seed deep into her body. *Gods be damned*, it was glorious. She whimpered softly as my body began to relax and I released my teeth from her neck, purple-tinted scrapes now marking her skin there. Carefully, I pulled myself from her before gently setting her feet back on the ground, noting the glistening rivulets dripping down her thighs. She flashed me a lazy grin and pressed a brief kiss over my heart, making mine skip a beat. Even in the dark, I could see the flush of her skin, and the slight sheen of sweat across her collarbone.

My mind emptied as I looked at her... I couldn't believe how lucky I was...

"For a moment there... I thought you were going to eat me." She breathed, her fingers trailing playfully across the skin of my chest. I chuckled, a little self-consciously, and stole another kiss.

"I can't help how delicious you are to me," I murmured against her mouth.

She laughed breathily, pushing a strand behind her ear before walking around me to rinse herself in the shallow creek. When we were both presentable once more, she entwined her fingers through mine.

We walked unhurriedly through the dark toward the distant glow of the campfire.

CHAPTER 53
AIDA

With our arrival at the ruins imminent, no one appeared to have slept very soundly, considering we were all awake before dawn. The tension was drawn tight enough to crack the air as we wordlessly snuffed out the fire and packed away our supplies. Eagerness and trepidation made my hands tremble as I fastened my pack to Vilje's brawny flank. Eyes swiveling through the pale, bluish light of the morning, I covertly stole glances toward my companions. My friends. With a sudden and sickening realization, the thought struck me: *I had never had them before.* Not real ones. Luke had been the first one I had ever dared to trust. The only one I had ever considered to be a real friend. Until Tyran. And Sayedha, Maya, and even Kine. Any alliances I had made within the Villdyr had always been just that. We were allies against the roving packs of slavers who wished to hunt us down and rip away our innocence. But never friends. Life had only been about survival, not bonding.

And now...

I could lose them all. Or die right beside them. I would take the latter in a heartbeat. I fought the lump threatening to grow in my throat as I blinked away the warmth behind my eyes.

No. I would be brave for them. I would not cower or tremble. Whatever the Gods had prepared for me to endure, I would face it. Or die trying.

Vilje flinched slightly with a frustrated chuff as I tightened his straps, readjusting his footing. I hadn't realized how forceful I was being. "*Sorry*." I winced, mentally.

Tyran and Cressida approached out of the corner of my vision. A small gasp left my lips as I appraised Tyran's form, his long strides closing the gap to me through the mist. He was dressed for battle. Our time in Overlevende had made him stronger, leaner, and somehow, more confident. He had always been swift, ruthless, and deadly with a blade. But now... he carried himself like a warrior. His black armor seemed to absorb the light, with only his impressive assembly of daggers glinting across his waist and chest in a grayish glow. Fresh from the creek where we had fucked like rabbits last night, his skin and hair dripped as he smiled at me, a little smug. My breath hitched, all my prior tension ebbing away as he reached for me and planted a warm kiss on my forehead. I relished in his scent as it washed over me. Steady and strong. His cool gaze found mine, the strength of him almost dizzying.

"Are you ready?" he murmured across the skin of my brow. The question was simple, but the note of ringing depth to it was unmistakable. I could only breathe him in deep, turning the key to my resolve and locking it up tight. "Yes. I am." I stated.

As the sun began to break over the trees, we mounted our horses and returned to the forest, heading east. Only stopping once at midday to water the horses and stretch our legs, we pressed on without delay.

The sun had arced its way west and sat at the five o'clock position when we spotted the first signs...

Seemingly out of place and alone in the woods sat a gigantic, white stone boulder. It was obvious that it had been carved by human hands, due to its mostly cube shape and the faint decorative etchings now barely discernible. One half had been chewed and gouged as if it had been ripped from its source. An explosion. *Gods...* how violent it must've been to fling a chunk of stone this size deep into the forest.

Now on high alert, our pace slowed to a crawl, everyone swiveling their heads to scan the surrounding woods. Just ahead of us, Kine, Maya, and Sayedha all had their weapons drawn. I shifted uneasily when I noticed that Maya had strapped a black crossbow to her back, the quiver glowing blue with soladium-tipped arrows.

Back in Overlevende, one of the places they had shown us had been an abandoned quarry in a deep subterranean offset, far away from the main tunnels. They explained that it had been one of the first soladium mines built by their ancestors. The terraced stone leading down into the blackness showed evidence of great calamity. A pulley system had snapped, and raw ore had rained down through the quarry, leaving giant craters with every impact. The loss of life had been so great, they waited another decade to begin mining again, this time with more advanced and safer technology.

Tyran, eyes fixed on the trail ahead, had already knocked an arrow into his bow as well. The forest shifted into eerie silence as we followed a nearly disintegrated stone path. Birds stopped chattering, crickets stopped singing, and even the wind had stilled, as if holding its breath. The heat had been intense all day, the sun unrelenting as it beat down through the trees. But now, the sky had gone gray with overcast clouds, sending the forest into soundless shadow, and a shiver down my spine.

We were close...

Just ahead, bright light penetrated through a break in the tree line. A collective gasp sounded through the group as we cleared the line of trees and beheld what awaited on the other side: we had arrived at the ruins of Svargad.

The forest in front of us had been cleared in a giant circle many miles in diameter. Crumbling stone buildings radiated outward from the enormous, terraced pyramid of white stone that stood at the center. I could almost picture how this once vibrant kingdom had shone like a beacon. Centuries of growth and decay had now rendered the stone with streaks of black and brown; the roots of trees and climbing vines long since breaking through. Encircling the city was evidence of a once-towering wall, which had been reduced to rubble when the city had been conquered. Even in the exhale of extinction, the city was staggering.

This is where it happened. Where the once mighty rulers of the Begavet people had hidden for nearly two hundred years until Chemosh had gathered enough strength to annihilate them.

Perched on the flat roof of the mighty pyramid at the heart of the city, a steel, dome-shaped skeleton indicated there had once been a glass cupola which would've allowed the sun's rays to illuminate whatever chamber lay below. That's where we needed to go. I could feel it.

"Will. Kaleb. You'll remain here to patrol the perimeter until we return. If anything happens, send up the falcon and get a message to Synsa without delay." Sayedha ordered from the front. With one last glance to Tyran, who nodded supportively with a tight-lipped smile, we nudged our horses into a walk and crossed the threshold leading to the center of the city.

Even though the forgotten fortress was now littered with countless small caves and alcoves, no wildlife could be seen nesting anywhere amongst the stone. The emptiness enveloped the ruins like a fog, as if the animals could sense whatever horror had taken place here long ago. This kingdom was once the beating heart of Astaran, with the thriving civilization of the Begavet people acting as its lifeblood.

For centuries, the forest had reclaimed dominion over the stone, and only a husk of its former glory remained. The stone path led us to the ascending staircase that climbed high up to a darkened archway. The entrance into the pyramid. As we dismounted, I could hear Kine giving instructions to Micah to remain with the horses and be ready to send a signal to the others if anything should go wrong. After a final weapons check, we began our climb.

Suddenly grateful to Sayedha for the intensity of our training while in Overlevende, I counted ninety-nine steps before we reached the archway. If there had once been a door here, there surely wasn't one now, so we carefully proceeded inside. Tyran's tall frame hovered behind me like a shadow as we walked through the stone corridor, which led us to the inner chamber. I stilled, drinking it all in... The once magnificent throne room of Queen Mercury and King Arketh. Through the exposed cupola above, gray light filtered down to reveal clues of the monarchs' last moments. Great, granite obelisks lay scattered and crumbling. The stone dais had been crushed. Along the walls, barely visible through the climbing vines, were carvings of celestial beings depicted in various states of play and pleasure. Among them lounged nightmarish creatures—reclining lazily while human women poured wine into their gaping maws. Others, flawlessly beautiful; their wings spread wide as they embraced a human lover. These were the same historical accounts Synsa had shown us in the tomes. While disgust naturally roiled within me, the images seemed more haunting and garish in this place; they were *terrifying*. I pulled my eyes from the walls and froze at the image in front of my feet.

In the center of the floor, a huge, black stain marred the marble. A scorch mark. My breath caught as I realized what it was: this was the very place where the King and Queen had met their end. Where Chemosh had burned them alive in front of each other...

Acting with the same mind, we all stopped in the center of the room and bowed our heads in a moment of silence for our ancestors. And for all they had sacrificed.

The titter of a bird flying over the roof broke our solemn reverie before Sayedha said, "Let's find the mirrors and get the fuck out of here..."

After briefly nodding in agreement, we began to spread throughout the chamber. Tyran and I slowly made our way toward the back of the room, behind the broken dais. As we scanned the vaulted wall at the far end of the chamber, I noticed the hidden mural barely visible behind the green veins of plant life that had spread across it. Using my dagger, I began to saw at the vines before yanking them out of the way. When I stood back to appraise the image, my breath went still at the sight...

It was a female in her astral body. And she was walking through an arched gateway, the dark void of the universe beyond depicted as a great spiral carving in the center of it. The hair stood up on my arms as I shivered, the room suddenly going cold. *This was it...*

Out of my peripheral vision, a small depression could be seen on the ground directly in front of the wall. Crouching low, I brushed the mud and debris away from the shallow bowl. Once clear, I discovered a solitary symbol etched into the stone. I recognized the symbol from the image Synsa had shown us of Queen Mercury wearing the helmet of Brannregn. The symbol had been repeated along the perimeter of the page in such uniformity, I assumed it was an illustrator's flourish. At first glance, it appeared to be the first number in our numerical system, but that had been my mistake.

My breath shuddered through my teeth as I realized what it really was: the sleep thorn.

The symbol of the Dream Walkers.

Tyran, noticing my frozen expression, silently gestured to the others to join us near the wall, the search now over. The silent pressure of expectation was palpable as I drew a dagger from my waist and quickly sliced it across my palm. Bright crimson bloomed from the cut before streaming down my hand and dropping silently into the bowl. Suddenly, the ground began to quake, the sound of grinding stone nearly deafening as it erupted from all around us. Tyran reached for me, keeping me upright as the vaulted wall before us groaned apart. With an echoing boom, the stone doors finished opening, revealing a darkened chamber just beyond. Thinking quickly, Maya removed a glass tube from her pack, gave it a gentle shake, and handed it to me. My hands trembled as I reached for the blue, glowing torch and held it in front of me. Tyran fixed me in his gaze, his expression grave as I moved toward the chamber.

Inhaling deeply and steeling my nerve, I walked inside.

The room was shaped like a dome, but not exceptionally large; the ceiling was only about twenty feet from the floor. As blue torchlight washed over the walls, I saw that every square inch of them had been etched with the sleep thorn symbol. Sweeping the light down across the floor, I had to squint to ascertain what I was looking at. It was a perfectly circular, stone depression, the encircling wall slightly raised just a few inches off the ground—a pool. Confirming my suspicion a heartbeat later, I spotted the rusted drain in the center.

But no mirrors. Leaving my companions in the doorway, I circled the room and shone the torch over every surface but found no evidence of another door or chamber. *How was this possible?* I thought in a panic.

I was supposedly the only Dream Walker left on Astaran... So, *who could've taken the mirrors? And for what purpose...?*

I stood there frozen, nearly hyperventilating as my mind reeled and sifted through every impossible scenario. It didn't make any sense. The silence of my companions ensured that they were all thinking the same thing. Hesitantly, Tyran approached and reached for my hand.

"Come on, Aida. We will make camp for the night and figure this out. Let's get out of here," he said, voice low and calm. Before hysteria could grip me in an iron fist, I turned heel and stalked from the chamber, back into the fresh air, and down the steps. No one spoke as we mounted our horses and trotted back to the tree line, a little faster than when we had entered.

With the sun now finishing its descent beyond the horizon, we were losing light quickly. Skirting around the ruins, we continued east for a half mile before arriving at the Solumine River. With spring in full force, the river flowed strong and swift. Needing to collect my thoughts while the others started the fire and erected the tents, I made my way down to the soft, muddy bank on the river's edge.

Breathing deep, I let the rushing roar of the river drown out the screaming in my head.

What were we to do now?

Without the mirrors, we had no way to find the helmet of Brannregn.

Without the mirrors, I could not commune with the Gods and learn how to defeat Chemosh.

We were vulnerable, and we were losing this fight. It was my one chance to use my power as a tool for good, and it had been the redeeming hope of the Begavet people for centuries.

And now... it was gone.

To distract myself from the breakdown threatening to rip me in two, I kneeled in the mud and splashed water onto my face and into my mouth. Clarity barely restored, it quickly shifted to sadness. I had failed them. So many people for so long, all their hope resting on me, and I failed them.

Gods... I missed Luke. Tears stung my eyes at the lump in my throat as I took a moment to not only yearn for him, but for my parents as well. I had been so young when they disappeared. A part of my heart longed to hope that they could still be alive, and maybe even looking for me...

But the part of me that knew loss, heartbreak, and desperation knew better.

Slowly, I backed away from the river and strode for the camp, ready to get this dreaded discussion over with. Cast in silhouette, the fire crackling bright from the other side, I saw Maya and Kine speaking softly to each other. Unable to avoid the encounter as I approached, I smiled weakly at Maya as she removed the crossbow and soladium arrows from her back. Kine, naturally, was in the process of strapping on more weapons since he had elected to take the first watch of the night. Maya, ever a beam of sunshine, grabbed me in a firm embrace. I inhaled deeply as I was enveloped in her unique scent, like freesia and smoke.

Pulling away to fix me in her gaze, she said, "This is just the beginning, Aida. We will figure it out. Together." *Gods, how did she do that?* I was starting to believe she was incapable of losing her spirit. Kine, typically expressionless, even gave me a tight-lipped smile in support. Maya was a miracle worker indeed. I nodded to them both and continued toward the others sitting around the fire. Tyran's eyes watched me warily as I dropped to the ground next to Sayedha and began to drink from my canteen. I knew if I met his gaze, it would be my undoing, and I needed to hold it together for just a little longer.

After a few minutes, Kine and Maya joined us and took their seats across from us. Briefly clearing her throat before speaking, Sayedha broke the silence.

"So... the mirrors are missing. It would seem the only choice we really have is to return to Overlevende and seek out clues from the tomes in the vault. No other place in Astaran has as much information on the subject as we do. We will send out the falcon tonight with a message for Synsa, informing her of our discovery... and imminent return," she stated wearily. We all nodded in silent agreement, disappointment hanging over us like a dark cloud.

With that, everyone scattered to their respective tents, leaving only Tyran and me sitting near the fire. With the events of the day no longer distracting my body, my stomach began to grumble. Feeling the heat of his stare on my face, my eyes finally met his from across the flames. The warmth and love on his face stole the breath from my lungs and brought my crippling sorrow crashing to the surface. I averted my gaze, tears streaming onto the dirt. In an instant, he was there and tugging me against his chest. I surrendered, drinking in his comfort and pressing my ear to his heartbeat. We remained that way for a long time, his warm hands stroking my hair, calming me like a child. The love and peace I had with him was like nothing I had ever known. Before Tyran, the only soft touch I had ever treasured had been from my parents, and while Luke's presence had been its own comfort, it was never in a physical way.

Slowly, my breathing steadied as the weight of exhaustion began to press against my eyes. I became vaguely aware of my body sagging against him before he maneuvered his arms under my legs and lifted me from the ground. A moment later, he was laying me down on the bedroll under our tent and covering my body with a wool blanket. As I drifted to sleep, his hands gently rubbing down my arms, I could hear the faint screech of a falcon flying into the sky.

Chapter 54
Aida

My eyes flew open at the sound of quick footfalls approaching our tent. My head snapped up at the same time as Tyran's.

Instantly alert, we sprang to our feet and peered out of the tent to see Kine sprinting toward the camp like a juggernaut as he shouted, "FIRE! FIRE IS COMING! RUN NOW!"

Tyran and I scrambled from the tent and looked east toward the river; a shuddering gasp broke through my lips as we beheld an enormous, roaring wall of flame fueled by the breeze... and blowing right toward us.

Chaos erupted.

Tyran and I abandoned everything except our weapons and water and ran toward the horses. Out of the corner of my eye, I saw Kine ripping Maya from the tent and dragging her toward their mounts. Sayedha and the three other Begavet warriors had taken off into a sprint and were nearly to their horses already, a few paces west of the camp. As we approached Cressida and Vilje, I glanced behind us to see the fire already torching our tents and moving with terrifying speed. It seemed to be encircling us, coming from both east and west, and moving fast to close the gap to the south.

Before I could ponder how in Hel a fire of this magnitude had spread so quickly, we reached the horses and launched into the saddles before kicking them into a hard gallop. The rest of the group was already mounted and trotting impatiently, the flames licking their way toward them from the west. By the time we had reached the others, the only viable path appeared to be toward the north, where the fire had not yet spread.

"Let's GO!" Sayedha bellowed as we galloped in formation through the narrow gap just ahead. Tyran and I, being at the rear of the group, were the last to clear the blaze.

Illuminated by the glow of the inferno behind us, I could just make out Micah, Will, and Kaleb a few yards in front of us. We galloped at breakneck speed for about a hundred paces before the unthinkable happened.

In one heart-stopping second, three black arrows soared out of the darkness—fired from the direction of the river—and struck the chests of our three young companions in perfect unison.

I screamed, shock and fear ripping through my throat like fire.

The impact had thrown them from their horses, who balked and stomped with panic around their motionless riders. Cressida and Vilje, having no time to slow their speed, reared up on their back legs, shrieking with fright.

Sayedha, Kine, and Maya, hearing my scream, turned around and began to gallop in our direction just as another barrage of arrows tore across the trees, missing us by just inches.

"Fuck! They're coming from the east!" Kine shouted, releasing his own arrows blindly into the dark. I spared a moment to glance at the three men sprawled across the forest floor, whose hearts had just been beating only moments ago, and sent up a prayer for their souls. I had no doubt they had been killed on impact; the arrows were perfectly aimed for their hearts.

Maya galloped over and stared down at them, eyes wide with terror. Her eyes met mine then... and I saw that the happy, loving woman I knew was nowhere to be seen. Without taking a breath, she unsheathed a soladium arrow, nocked it into the crossbow, and shouted, "GET DOWN!" before launching it skyward. For two heartbeats, we tracked the blue orb as it arced across the sky—then all Hel broke loose.

The arrow exploded on impact with the force of a bomb, generating a tsunami of fire that washed through the rows of trees closest to the river, the billowing smoke coalescing into a mushroom cloud that rose higher, singeing the leaves of the canopy above. Cast as silhouettes in the bright light of the inferno behind them, we could finally lay eyes on our attackers: seven Anakaii warriors sprinted toward us while three others flailed on the ground, their bodies consumed by flames as they shrieked in agony.

The remaining seven careened down the hill, shooting arrows as they ran; two of them penetrated Vilje's flank and Maya's mount in the same moment. The world spiraled and crashed around me as Vilje bucked and flailed, throwing me to the ground and knocking the breath from my lungs.

"AIDA!" Tyran shouted as he jumped into a crouch beside

me and continued to release arrow after arrow. From the ground, I watched as Sayedha leaped from her horse and charged toward the warriors, one breaking formation to take her on as the other six barreled toward us. Gasping for air like a fish, I pushed myself to my feet. Before I could consider the decision a second longer, I yanked the arrow from Vilje's flank and slapped him hard against the rump. Needing no encouragement to flee, he bolted into the dark woods toward the west. Tyran, sensing my intention in an instant, did the same to Cressida. Whatever fate awaited us here, at least the horses might survive it—or, Gods willing, we would find them nearby.

Kine and Tyran launched more arrows, successfully bringing down two more Anakaii, but the remaining four were closing in fast, their serrated swords drawn. I heard Maya grunting as she struggled under the weight of her dead horse, her leg crushed beneath it. I rushed over and used my feet to lift the body just enough for her to pull her leg out. An instant later, the four warriors were upon us and crossing blades with Tyran and Kine.

"Can you walk?" I demanded. She only nodded grimly and attempted to stand. Finding that acceptable, I turned from her and launched my dagger into the ribs of one of the warriors taking on Tyran, feeling somewhat out of my body as I watched him drop like a stone. The other warrior did not even spare him a glance; his attack never faltering.

At least the odds were considerably more acceptable. Three against three.

My heart skipped a beat as I realized I couldn't see where Sayedha had gone or if the warrior she was fighting was still alive. I shouted her name, projecting my voice toward the smoldering blaze crawling toward us from the east, where I had last seen her. There was no response.

The three remaining black-clad warriors fighting with Kine and Tyran moved with the grace of striking serpents. While Kine parried with skill, his girth was no match for the speed of the fighters who ducked and lunged for his lower half.

As I raised my sword to assist Kine, a bone-chilling scream erupted from Tyran. I whipped my head around to find him on his knees, blood streaming in thick rivulets down his leg from a vicious gash across his thigh.

In less than a second, the warrior was raising his sword for the final blow, to sever Tyran's head. My voice broke with a furious roar as I charged, impaling him through the torso, soaking my hands with the copper scent of his blood. His eyes widened briefly before collapsing to the ground, body sliding off my sword with a sickening thud.

Behind me, Maya was limping toward Kine, sword drawn. In the half-second it took for Kine to glance at her over his shoulder, it cost him dearly. Working in unison, the two remaining warriors tackled Kine and had their swords at his throat in an instant.

"Move another inch and they *both fucking die!*" the Anakaii bellowed, chest heaving. Kine struggled and made to get to his feet before the warrior struck him with a dagger through his shoulder, his roar of agony shaking the forest.

"NO! KINE!" Maya screamed, her sword still angled in front of her. But I knew she was in no position to take them on with her leg practically dragging in the dirt behind her. I looked at Tyran, whose face was beginning to pale from blood loss, but his body trembled with wrath. He clutched a dagger tightly, waiting for his moment.

We could still make it. There was one last card to play. Mine.

I closed my eyes as if contemplating my surrender and dug deep, sliding into my astral form. Like casting a net, I reached for the two minds of the warriors in front of me. In the periphery, I could see Tyran's golden chain, Kine's barbed wire, and Maya's glittering, blue chord...but the other two remained out of reach, as if behind a glass wall.

And I could not detect Sayedha's energy anywhere...

I panted through my teeth as panic and fury gouged at my heart. *How the fuck was that possible?* With his blade still inches from Kine's jugular, the Anakaii pointed to me and Maya before saying, "You... and you. Are coming with us."

A growl ripped through Kine as he struggled in their grip, the sword at his throat slicing deep enough to send blood streaming down his chest.

"Like fucking Hel, they are!" Tyran shouted before launching his last blade. It struck true, right through the center of the warrior's hand, his bellow of pain ripping through the air. In the split second after the sword had dropped from Kine's throat, he rolled onto his back and kicked the Anakaii with devastating force. But the second warrior elected for a different strategy and sprinted toward Maya—I lunged, bringing my sword in front of her just before he landed a blow that was intended to cut her hand clean off.

Kine, now on his feet, yanked the dagger from his shoulder and charged toward us. We could do this. We could make it out of here. Just as hope began to swell in my chest, the warrior Kine had kicked back into the dirt, had sprung to his feet, drew back an arrow, and fired it into Tyran's right arm. The world began to tilt as he stalked over to him and readied to impale him through the stomach. "NO!" I screamed, the distraction costing me precious time. The second warrior had me then. Gripping me by the throat, he shoved my face into the dirt and began to tie my hands and feet, bearing his full weight against my neck until stars began to pop across my vision. I watched helplessly as Kine charged at the warrior still standing over

Tyran before a dagger launched from the hand of the Anakaii on top of me and pierced him through the back, sending his gigantic frame buckling to the ground.

"KINE!" Maya roared, her voice breaking with a sob.

Gods... I was going to watch them all die. Right here.

This couldn't be it. This couldn't be how it ended for us. This couldn't be what the Gods intended.

Before I could calculate my odds of survival, I screamed, "Stop! I'll go with you! Please, don't kill them!" The warrior standing over Tyran paused for the briefest moment before glancing toward the other, who was finishing my restraints.

"Please, I'll go willingly. Just don't kill them." I pleaded, my breath shallow from the Anakaii's weight on my back. Tyran moaned and writhed, the side of his face scraping against the dirt as his despairing eyes met mine.

"No!" he ground out and made to move upright.

With brutal speed, the warrior slammed the hilt of his sword against Tyran's temple, and I watched in terror as his body fell limp to the ground.

Sobs rocked through me as I screamed his name.

Kine was on his hands and knees, blood streaming from both his shoulder and his back, the dagger lodged just south of his ribs, near his vital organs. With an injury like that... his survival would totally depend on the will of the Gods.

He gave Maya one last look, grief blazing behind his eyes, before he, too, was struck over the head.

Maya and I wailed with despair at the sight of them. The warrior who had restrained me lifted his body from mine and lunged for Maya, pressing a dagger to her throat.

"If either of you makes one more fucking sound. I will cut off *both* their heads and leave the bodies here to rot," he hissed.

Wisely, she went still, allowing him to tie a rope around her wrists and ankles. As numbing defeat stroked me with cold fingers, I could only lie there, staring at Tyran's lifeless face on the ground across from me.

How could this be happening?

Unceremoniously, we were hoisted to our feet before being thrown over their shoulders like sacks of grain and carried toward the smoldering trees near the river. With the fuel in this section of the forest now spent, the fire had shifted away to the south. As Tyran's and Kine's bodies faded into darkness, I glanced over to see Maya, head dangling and eyes wide with terror. An instant later, a pang of dread coiled around my stomach when I noticed the quiver of soladium-tipped arrows now gripped in the warrior's hand.

After a brief descent down a ravine, they waded across a shallower stretch of the river before arriving at their horses on the other side. After dropping us face down over the rumps of the horses, they further secured our bonds and tied us to the saddles. Wordlessly, the Anakaii moved to collect the remaining eight horses, now riderless. The thought made my head throb with savage delight.

But as they kicked their horses into motion, my momentary bloodlust shifted into despair.

Three Begavet warriors were dead, Tyran and Kine were gravely injured and left stranded in the wilderness without food, water, or shelter... and Sayedha had seemingly vanished.

As for me and Maya... well, I knew exactly where we were going.

CHAPTER 55
SAYEDHA

The moment the soladium arrow ignited the forest, the bright flash had illuminated the tree line to reveal the Anakaii warriors. Some burning and dead within seconds, and others charging toward my dearest friends. Arrows from Tyran and Kine took down another two as I charged toward the enemy, roaring with rage. As soon as both Aida and Maya's horses had been shot, I knew they wouldn't have been able to flee in time, and I wanted to give them a chance to increase their odds. My goal was simple: to use myself as bait to draw away as many as I could.

A hulking warrior in head-to-toe black spotted my charge and peeled away from the group to challenge me. My chest heaving and lungs burning, I bolted south, and he followed, just as I had anticipated. While these warriors were lethally skilled, I had the real advantage.

Being able to sense the intentions of your enemy seconds before they acted easily made me his worst nightmare.

I broke through the trees and leaped onto the pitch-dark riverbank, the warrior nearly flying from the brush just a few yards behind. The moon, in the phase of Máni, barely cast enough light to see the white froth of the raging torrent to my left. A tingling sensation alerted me to his movements behind me, and in an instant, I knew he was drawing his dagger. But not before I could draw mine.

In less than a second, I skidded to a halt, spun on my heel into a crouch, and let my daggers fly. One missed his ear by an inch, the other struck true through his neck… but he didn't even flinch. My eyes widened with realization just a second before he barreled into me with the force of a ten-ton hammer; he was high on moondust.

My breath left my lungs in a whoosh as his body slammed into mine and we tumbled together into the raging rapids of the Solumine. The water was near freezing as it seized my lungs like a reticulated snake. Gasping and flailing, my body was completely at the mercy of the river.

The churning roar of the water was deafening as I struggled to keep my head above the water.

Just ahead, I could barely make out a few giant rocks that I could attempt to climb onto. But the flow of the river ripped me around them before my fingers could find purchase.

Fuck, I could drown. I had always been a good swimmer, but only in the placid pool under the falls in Overlevende. This was an alternate universe compared to that. Suddenly, a vortex pulled my body under before slamming me against the river bottom.

A deep crack echoed through my skull... before my vision went black.

Chapter 56
Ravn

The day after I had seen the Anakaii leave the palace under the cloak of darkness, each thing that happened became more unusual than the last.

As I made my way from my chambers to stand in formation for the day, my heart lurched into my throat when I turned the corner to see The Sovereign's elongated frame lazily perched on the sill of the stone window that lined the corridor. She was waiting for me...

Noting my stunned silence, she smirked before dropping to the ground with the grace of a stalking cat. I only bowed meekly, allowing her to complete her predatory assessment of my demeanor. A few tense moments passed before she finally spoke.

"I take it that the maidens are being well cared for. We wouldn't want the holy ones to be displeased," she sneered.

While surprised to hear her mocking tone regarding the Gods, I kept my face expressionless and only nodded. Her blazing eyes dilated as her lip curled into a wicked grin.

"Soon... it won't matter anyway. Soon, I'll take back what was stolen from me."

I suppressed the shudder that rippled through my body in response to her ominous tone. Her face dropped suddenly as she withdrew from my space and rose to her full height, her head just a few inches from the ceiling. She gazed down at me and breathed deep as if what she was about to say displeased her.

"You can tell those females that their Offering Day has been postponed until next month. I'll be... busy with other things until then," she finished before stalking away, malice rolling off her in waves.

I could only stand there, my mind reeling with equal parts joy and dread. This gave me so much more time to plan their escape...

But on the other hand, never in my lifetime or even the lifetime of my forefathers had an Offering Day been postponed. The Sovereign had preached for centuries that it was vital to the success of Astran's growing seasons and harvests. But of course, this had been a well-crafted lie; blights and famines were as constant on Astaran as stars in the sky. Not realizing I had locked my knees and stopped breathing as she spoke, I shook my head to clear it before continuing toward formation. I was eager for the day to be over, so I could deliver the news to Helena.

Over the next week, an odd flurry of activity began in one of the abandoned subterranean tunnels on the opposite corridor from the dungeons. A stone wall had been knocked down, and various masons carried tools and supplies into the new chamber at all hours of the day. Raziel's wraith-like presence stood watch over the project day and night, guarding whatever secret lay within. His black eyes were glowing with fiendish knowledge every time I was forced to pass him on my way to the dungeons. The night I had told Helena about The Offering Day being postponed, she stood there, staring, her face pale with disbelief. I still didn't know if I believed it myself. Soon after, I started smuggling various kinds of supplies, and even a few weapons, which they could hide under the loose stones of the cell floor. For their escape to be successful, it would have to be a last-minute decision... when The Sovereign, Raziel, and the Anakaii were all looking the other way; I would need a sophisticated diversion.

I had been doing my research on the schematics of the tunnel system beneath the palace and had even paid a visit to the entrance to the catacombs, the sewer tunnels leading to the river running just beneath. It was a section of the palace that held such ancient darkness, I didn't dare linger. The tunnels of the catacombs seemed to be older than Astaran itself, the ceiling so low I had to duck my head as I weaved through each bone-filled chamber. Royalty, nobility, and even some treasured pets had all been entombed here like some sick collection. Everyone on Astaran knew that the only way to be one with the Gods was through cremation. With no body remaining to tether you to this plane, your soul could be free. Suddenly, I realized that maybe all these people buried here had not been revered at all...maybe this form of burial had been their punishment.

Just before I retreated to the fresh air above ground, my torch light shone onto a chamber door. It was the only door I had seen down here, with all other chambers open to the connecting tunnel. The door was made of solid iron and bore a single symbol etched across it; the symbol appeared to be a wheel of some kind with eight identical beams that radiated from its center, with each beam splitting into a three-pronged fork. Encircling the wheel were various ancient symbols which I did not recognize from any texts provided by the Anakaii.

Suddenly, a rough scraping sounded from the other side of the door... like a body being dragged. In the same moment, a sickly, green light pulsed from under the door frame before an otherworldly growl rumbled from inside the chamber, making my stomach roil with fear.

Fucking Gods... what was in there?

Before I could find out the hard way, I turned heel and nearly sprinted back toward the stairwell. Something—not human—was protecting whatever lay inside that room. I flew up the stairs and back into the eastern corridor, glancing over my shoulder every few feet until I turned the corner and collided headfirst into Akton.

"Damn, Ravn! What's got you so spooked?" he asked me, irritably readjusting the collar of his training leathers. I only stood there, hands on my hips, vacillating. He only watched me with an expectant expression. I still had not told him anything about my vision or the maidens in the dungeon, but somehow it felt wrong not to.

But what would he think of me? A traitor? A deserter? Some weak, lovesick boy who fell for the first woman who had ever spoken with him?

Would he feel betrayed when I told him I planned to leave this place and never look back? But... I knew it didn't really matter. He was my only friend and family. He needed to know about what I had seen and the dangers of staying in this palace. I owed him the truth.

"Follow me," I said, and turned toward the direction of the dungeons.

The sun was long past the horizon when we reached the stairwell to the dungeon. Wordlessly, I motioned to him to be silent and peered around the corner to ensure the coast was clear. Raziel was gone, and the newly built chamber had been sealed with a door. He followed me down the corridor until we arrived in front of Helena's cell. At the sight of the stranger, the young girls huddled closer together on the floor. Helena's green gaze was calculating as she roved over Akton's features before turning to me with a questioning look.

Fuck, I was really doing this. There was no going back now.

I pulled air into my lungs and clenched my hands into fists at my sides before lifting my chin and turning to Akton. "I'm going to help them escape." There, I said it. Akton's brows flew to his scalp, his mouth agape with shock... but said nothing.

"I had a vision... or, rather, I've been having them. I don't really know. They started the day I killed Lark." Helena's eyes flew wide at that. She inched closer to the bars, her gaze penetrating my very soul, and said, "*You*... you saw the future? Saw what has yet to happen?" I nodded and turned to Akton. His face was pale as he began to shake his head in disbelief. I knew I had to salvage this quickly.

"Listen... there is going to be an attack on the palace. I've seen it. A female will lead them into the city... I don't know who she is. But... many Anakaii will die." Akton took a single step back, head shaking as his expression began to harden. Fuck. He made another quick glance at Helena before fixing me with a disappointed stare. I had to admit, the sight of it hurt badly.

"You're a fool, Ravn. Every one of us will die... because you're a fool," he whispered. With one last glance at the females in their cage, he slowly turned and made his way up the stairwell. Shit—what had I done? Taking only a second to hate myself, I ran up the stairs and quickly found him in the middle of the southern corridor. I gripped him by the shoulder and winced when he batted me away like an insect.

"Akton... *please*. I need you to listen." I pleaded.

"No! *You* want me to look the other way while you get yourself drawn and quartered! This won't end well, Ravn... no one is stupid enough to challenge her!" he hissed, baring his teeth. Maybe he was right... But I knew what I saw. Before I could draw breath to argue, a shuffling sounded from the courtyard below. Even though it was past ten in the evening, the gates were being opened. Akton, sensing my distraction, looked toward the direction of my gaze: two Anakaii on horseback trotted through the gates—eight riderless horses towed behind them. I could feel Akton's body tense beside mine. To kill one Anakaii was nearly impossible... but to kill eight? The two riders dismounted and began to unfasten the... women... who were strapped across the horse's rumps. As the warriors began to lead the restrained females inside the palace, I noted that one was blonde, average build, and may have even been pretty, if it weren't for the scorching rage contorting her face around the gag in her mouth.

And the other was a slight framed brunette...

The air in my chest suddenly evaporated as I backed away from the ledge until I hit the far wall, dragging a hand through my hair in disbelief. Akton turned to me, face grim and eyes wide with concern. "What is it? Who is that?" he asked.

My voice trembled with poorly suppressed panic as I replied, "It's her."

Chapter 57
Tyran

I was relatively certain I was in the process of dying.

Pain was everywhere.

It consumed me with scorching fire and white, hot lightning. I coughed, spewing dirt and rustling the leaves that had settled around my head. A grating screech followed by a snapping beak sounded somewhere near where I lay on the forest floor. Fucking vultures. Squabbling over who would get to claim my corpse first.

Before I could summon strength into my limbs enough to shove them away, an ear-shattering cry descended from above on heavy wings. The scavengers bolted skyward, wings beating the air into a fierce wind. With the woods silent around me once more, I cracked open an eye.

A gigantic golden eagle had landed not six inches away, its yellow-eyed gaze fixed on me, head slightly tilted in curiosity. The massive raptor made no move to snap its razor-sharp beak or peck at my flesh; it only stood there... as if guarding me.

Yeah, I had to be dying then.

My consciousness slipped away again like sand through fingers...

"Oi... look at these lads. Someone did a number on these two, eh?"

I groaned as a boot nudged my leg, sending streaks of pain rippling through my body.

"Fuck! He's alive! Gods... check that one there." Footsteps shuffled through the leaves about ten paces before another deeper voice replied, "He's fucked up. Breathing... but it's shallow. Looks like the blade missed his kidney by less than an inch, or he would've been dead already..."

My stuttering heart began to leap... Kine was alive, but barely.

"Let's take 'em to Shira for healin.' They're both good-sized men. We could fetch a handsome sum at Kalboros," said the man closest to me.

Their words barely registered as weakness and exhaustion threatened to pull me under again... but then something clicked.

No... No, we had to find Aida... and Maya.

Alarm gave me the adrenaline I needed; my arms shook as I tried to lift from the ground... to run... I had no clue where.

"Whoa, whoa, big fella. You're in no shape to go anywhere. A boot pressed against my ribs and pushed me onto my back with minimal effort. The muscle of my right arm, where the Anakaii arrow was still lodged deep, erupted with blood-curdling agony. I cried out, throat raw and aching, before going limp. Above me, the canopy swayed on a gentle breeze before my view was obstructed by the haggard faces of two nearly toothless men, both grinning down at me like fiends. More fucking scavengers.

The one with the accent was completely bald and was apparently missing an eye, considering he wore a threadbare eye patch over his right socket. The other was considerably taller but just as thin as his companion, his copper hair and beard streaked with silver. The two of them worked in tandem to lift my legs and arms, grunting and baring their teeth with effort, before heaving my body into a small wagon. I barked a curse at the impact, hissing through my teeth. As they moved toward Kine's body, I heard the bald one say, "We need to remove this blade before trying to move 'em. Chance he'll bleed out... but for sure he will if the blade nicks something."

I turned my head toward them and made a pathetic effort to sit up. "Don't fucking touch him!" I spat. They barely spared me a glance. I held my breath as the bearded one kneeled beside Kine and yanked the blade from his back. While unceremonious, it had been done with precision. A small rivulet of blood streamed from the wound but did not gush... which was a good sign.

It took them even more effort to lift Kine's giant form into the wagon next to me. Not wanting to take their chances, they restrained our wrists and ankles before climbing into the wagon and slapping the reins on the rump of a half-starved mule. As the wagon wobbled into motion, I turned over to look at Kine. His long black hair was crusted with blood and dirt as it hung across his face. Hope swelled in my chest as I saw his eyelids flutter weakly.

"We're going to be all right. Just... hang on, Kine," I whispered, desperate to believe it myself. Suddenly, I realized I had no idea if Sayedha was even alive or lay injured somewhere nearby. I grunted with effort to prop myself up on an elbow and scanned the forest. I saw nothing but dead Anakaii and blackened trees, trunks still smoldering with inner fire. My stomach roiled from the pain that blazed through my arm and leg with every jostle of the wagon.

I rolled onto my back and gazed at the sky, unseeing. It took everything I had left not to scream at the top of my lungs.

The person I loved most in the world had been ripped away.

Our friends had been murdered in cold blood.

I had no clue whether Sayedha had been killed or taken prisoner.

And we were now in the possession of two desperate nomads who sought to sell our flesh to the darkest pit in all Astaran: The Kalboros mine.

CHAPTER 58
AIDA

Our Anakaii captors rode through the night. It wasn't until midday the next day that we finally took a break for water. Maya and I were still draped across the horses' rumps like deer kill, our hands and feet bound with more rope tied around our waists to prevent us from rolling away. The constant jostling of the horse's swishing gait had sent my neck into fused agony hours ago, and the only way I had gotten any relief was to hang limp as a fish. When we finally stopped, I lifted my head a fraction and noticed we had already made it to the outer ring of villages that radiated away from Opeth.

At this pace, we would enter the city by tonight.

The Anakaii had said nothing to us or each other the entire

trip, and I wondered if they were even capable of grieving for their dead companions. The warriors untied the restraints around our waists, letting us crash into the dirt, groaning, too stiff and sore to stand. After taking a moment to stretch my limbs, I began to army crawl toward Maya.

"Get up and relieve yourselves. We leave again in one hour," one of them said before throwing down a sack in front of us. I didn't acknowledge him. When I reached her, I struggled to sit upright before using my bound hands to help ease her into a seated position. The dust from the road had caked her face, the muddy tracks of her tears flowing through the grime. It made my heart ache to see her like this, considering the only life she'd ever known had been within the safety of the mountain city. She looked over to me then, and I was surprised to see her grinning slightly. In response to my puzzled look of concern, she said, "You know... this is exactly what I pictured the rest of Astaran would look like?"

She was joking... Her heart was broken, but she wasn't going to let it destroy her, not yet. I couldn't help but flash her a small grin in return as I rifled through the sack that had been tossed at our feet. It contained one canteen of water, four cords of dried venison, and one apple. As Maya and I divided the meager meal and began to eat, I noted that the soladium-tipped arrows had been taken by the warrior who had led the horses away to drink at a nearby pond. The other stood motionless, eyes never leaving us. Upon leaving the shadow of the Furian Wood a short while ago, we were now exposed to the hot sun as it beat down on the crop fields surrounding the village. I looked up to the warrior and asked with mock meekness, "Would it be too much to ask for a little privacy... You know, to tend to our lady bits?" The Anakaii didn't so much as shift his weight, continuing his stare. After a tense moment, he simply turned his head to look straight across the field, instead of directly at us. Fine.

Maya and I managed to pull down our pants enough to pee in the dirt, but needed each other's help to pull them back up. Once that awkward business was finished, we took pleasure in standing upright and rolling our necks and shoulders. The muscles in my neck and back are clenching tight with every movement, sending bolts of ache into my backside and down my legs. For the next few minutes, we stretched as much as we could until the other Anakaii returned and informed us that our time was up. Once again, we were lifted and dropped onto the backs of the horses, waist restraints cinched tight, before continuing our journey toward Opeth... and whatever horror awaited us there.

As the sun began to fall behind the western horizon, golden light washed over the stone of the city walls. Since our stop earlier that day, hundreds of villagers had looked at us wide-eyed on the road, but none had made any effort to help us. Such was the fear of the Anakaii. It was inherently understood by all that if an Anakaii warrior had taken you prisoner, your next stop was to The Sovereign.

My blood boiled at the thought; she was no Sovereign at all.

Only a fucking traitor and exile.

The gates of the city groaned wide as we approached a massive stone archway. I noticed two wooden spikes that lined either side of the path, long since weathered and beginning to crumble. The truth struck me like a slap; those were the spikes where the King and Queen's heads had been impaled after Chemosh's siege on Svargad. It had once been a symbol of her dominion over this world. The gates shut behind us with an echoing boom as we made our way to the central palace. We passed countless buildings and multiple squares filled with vendors and merchants going about their evening routines. While not joyous by any means, the people of Opeth seemed pleasantly distracted by their wares enough to ignore us. Or maybe this society had been oppressed for so long that the best distraction they had was survival. Unless it affected them personally, they were happy to look away. In the centuries that Chemosh had reigned, she had not only turned us into her unwilling slaves, but she had managed to turn us against each other, too.

Now fully dark, we passed under another iron gate before stopping in a wide courtyard with three levels of corridors that lined the perimeter around three sides. Above the gate we had just entered, a high stone bridge was manned with sentries. A stunned silence settled around the space as the eight riderless horses were brought in behind us.

A moment later, we were being removed from the horses and freed from the restraints around our ankles before being forced through the wooden doors that would take us into the palace.

At the end of the dark, vaulted hall, which was devoid of any furniture or decorations, stood another Anakaii warrior in front of a pair of enormous onyx doors. This one, however, did not have his face covered by a black mask like the others. He was an older man, his face and body beginning to soften with age, but his expression remained hard as steel. His black eyes roved over both of us with disdain, pupils flaring with incredulity.

"Do you mean to tell me that these two females killed *eight* Anakaii?" he whispered, voice low with restrained rage.

"They were not alone. We left their companions to die from their wounds in the wilderness," replied the warrior behind me. The elder man, whom I assumed was in a position of authority, looked into my eyes before he stepped into my space. I stiffened and lifted my chin, pouring every ounce of defiance into a stare of my own. His voice, like churning gravel, whispered, "It ends here, girl. All hope and all chances to flee have left you. She will take such pleasure in breaking you apart... and I'll find my own joy watching you scream..."

My blood ran cold as fear began to coil in my gut. Suddenly, Maya spoke beside me, her voice trembling with wrath, "If you touch a fucking hair on her head, and I will gut *you* first, before we turn this place into ash!" His eyes briefly flicked from mine to hers before backing up a step, a smirk curling over his lip. "Oh... I doubt that," he grinned deviously.

"They were carrying these... lit up the forest with the fire of a hundred suns, killing three Anakaii in the process." The warrior behind Maya said as he pulled the quiver of soladium arrows from his pack and handed them to the elder man. His eyes glowed with awe as he fingered the blue orb just below the arrowhead. "Incredible... I'm sure Raziel will be intrigued," he mused, black eyes glowing with mischief.

Our chests began to heave with panic as we realized that we had just given over the most valuable secret of the Begavet people... *to the enemy*. The elder warrior smirked at us triumphantly. I knew he was savoring the fear he saw there...

Wordlessly, he gestured to the men who had restrained us as he pushed open the onyx doors and led us all into a glittering throne room. The space sparkled with the refracted torchlight held in sconces above the huge, gilded mirrors that encircled the rotunda, as well as from the glowing, crystal chandelier above. Its opulence had been designed with one purpose: to overwhelm and intimidate. A defiant voice inside me chuckled, unimpressed. A peacock without its feathers was just another soft-bodied bird... and could be plucked and roasted. The room was empty, though the iridescent opal throne was vacant. Abruptly, the warriors behind us pushed us down to the floor, which sent my knees barking at the affront. I turned my head to the side to meet Maya's gaze and found nothing but defiance shining there. I nodded to her, breathing in her courage like it was my last breath, before my ears perked at the soft, padded footsteps that entered the room through the door behind us. The sound briefly disarmed me with its grace and simplicity. My eyes remained fixed on the floor as the figure slowed and circled in front of us. Steeling my nerves, I slowly lifted my eyes to find a giant staring down at me.

I struggled to suppress the quake of fear that roiled my insides at the sheer enormity of her presence, her towering frame looming like a golden, armor-plated pillar of rock. The long coils of her hair, black as pitch, swayed as she slowly shook her head at me, her feline face bright with... amusement.

"Finally," she purred with satisfaction.

My heart skipped a beat.

Suddenly, she crouched low and pinned me under the gaze of her blazing orange eyes, studying me like an insect.

"I have seen your eyes. They once belonged to your ancestor. I'll admit that she was a more worthy adversary compared to some—sacrilegious heritage notwithstanding."

Mercury...

"It was immensely helpful indeed that I was able to withstand her... gift. And it's a skill I have since shared with my Anakaii... as you no doubt have learned," she said, baring her teeth in a triumphant grin.

I squared my shoulders and bit the inside of my cheek to hide the tremors rocking through me.

"What do you want with us, demon? You already control this world. You already have dominion over our people. Why don't you stop toying and tell us!" Maya spat, her voice sharp as a razor.

I held my breath but kept my face guarded. Maya was brave... but reckless.

The giantess cocked her head toward Maya, bristling with irritation; a predator sizing up her prey. Without a word, she rose to her full height before striding toward the opal dais, her golden train whispering over the floor. She lounged back into the throne, her posture lazy... as if awaiting entertainment.

"RAZIEL!" she shouted without warning, her deep voice booming through the chamber and shaking the glass of the chandelier.

A moment later, a rough scraping could be heard from the corridor outside the chamber in addition to another pair of feet. The steps grew closer before a cloaked figure stood and looked down at me and Maya.

He was... the ugliest villain I'd ever seen. His black beard quivered as he smiled down at us, baring his dark, decaying teeth with black eyes that sparkled with wicked intent.

"Ah... the Dream Walker is yours at last, I see," he crooned, lifting his gaze to her and bowing low.

Her hands, resting on the arms of the dais, didn't move an inch before a single finger pointed to Maya.

"That one... needs to be shown some manners expected of this court."

Fuck, Fuck, Fuck. No, please.

"You want me, not her. Let her go, and I will do whatever you want," I said firmly.

I was ignored entirely... Raziel only smirked briefly before snapping his fingers twice. The scraping sounds grew louder as a rumbling growl echoed around the walls of the chamber. The hairs on the back of my neck stood up straight as my bowels began to loosen in response.

What the fuck...

Maya and I glanced at each other wide-eyed before turning

our heads toward the chamber door behind us—and all thought in my mind shattered as knee-wobbling fear gripped me. Maya whimpered beside me, her breath hitching with the instinct to flee. Even our two Anakaii captors slowly retreated toward the far wall, leaving us kneeling and exposed on the floor.

I had few words to describe what began to emerge through that door: it looked like a man, yet I had no doubt it was no longer truly alive.

Its skin hung in tatters over its bones, with some chunks of the chest and torso missing completely. Its face was barely more than an eyeless skull, teeth exposed as if it had just emerged from the grave. But the most horrifying feature was the sickly, green glow that pulsed from behind its eyes and inside its chest; I knew in my gut that some sadistic form of sorcery had reanimated this creature.

"Don't you recognize him?" Chemosh drawled from her perch on the dais.

I whipped my head toward her, eyes bulging with shock. She leaned forward, lips curling into a sneer, "He's the one who told me you were even alive. All this time, I thought you were dead... and what a *waste* that would be. But then a few members of the Guard went missing while hunting for an escaped prisoner..."

My chest locked up. I couldn't breathe.

"Their bodies were later found burned in a gorge, with little remaining... except for a few bones. And that was all Raziel needed."

Holy Gods...

"This one spoke of a young woman who threatened to break into their minds—and I knew it had to be you. The one I needed." She finished, eyes simmering with hatred. A quick flick of her fingers sent the creature hobbling toward us, one foot dragging behind it. Maya and I both squirmed and tried to roll across the floor, but it snatched Maya by the ankles with preternatural speed and began to drag her from the room; her shrieks of terror threatening to shatter the mirrors in the chamber.

"*NO! MAYA! NO!*" I screamed, reaching for her hand. But the Anakaii had me pinned, holding me back. I bucked and thrashed, but had no leverage to move, their fingers squeezing tight enough to break bone. Maya continued to scream as the creature dragged her out of sight and into the corridor until I could only hear her faintly from a distance. Boiling wrath began to bubble up my throat as I panted and tried to free myself from their grip.

"WHERE ARE YOU TAKING HER? WHY ARE YOU DOING THIS? *WHAT MAKES ME SO FUCKING IMPORTANT?* TELL ME!" I roared.

Chemosh leaped from the dais and was on me in an instant, her giant hand clenched tight around my throat. Her eyes were like a raging inferno of supernatural power as she bared her teeth and squeezed my throat tight enough to make me see sparks at the corners of my vision.

"You—are going to obey me. You—will help me finish what I set out to do more than a thousand fucking years ago. With your power, I will finally have my vengeance," she seethed.

My eyes bulged as I struggled for air, body jerking with panic. In the next heartbeat, Raziel ripped my hair back and poured a glass vial of glowing blue liquid down my throat.

No.

No. Please...

It seared my throat like fire, and I coughed and spluttered before Chemosh released her grip and dropped me to the floor.

Suddenly, my body went taut, back arching off the ground. I bellowed in agony as fire rippled through my veins...

But in its wake... a soft, warm complacency took its place.

Time stopped.

All worry and stress floated away on a gentle breeze as my body relaxed into placid calm. A tiny voice locked far away tried to call out... but she was too far to hear.

"Rise," said a commanding voice nearby. I obeyed. The two figures before me were foreign, strange... but neither my mind nor body was responding to external stimuli.

I only wished to obey.

The two figures seemed pleased enough and made their way from the room.

So, I followed.

Chapter 59
Aida

I was only vaguely aware of being led away from the glittering room of gold and down numerous stone corridors and stairwells. I had no sense of time or place, only eager to serve the figures who walked ahead of me. At last, we arrived at a locked door. The sickly, bearded one fumbled with a large iron key before successfully turning the lock and opening the door to—a spa?

Warm, moist air wafted up from the shallow, circular pool that sat directly in the center of the room. The ceiling twinkled like a billion stars as the flickering candlelight reflected off the black mirrors.

That far away voice somewhere deep screamed again, but her pleas were too muffled to discern.

Dozens of the mirrors had been fixed to the domed ceiling directly over the pool; some were circular while others were misshapen shards, but all coalesced perfectly to cover every inch.

"Remove your clothes and step in." ordered the tall one, who was not quite male or female. I obeyed. The water was pleasant and perfectly room temperature. The tall one stood beside the pool, and her eyes, like glowing embers, roamed over me in approval.

"What a good girl you've become, Aida. Aren't you curious as to how I obtained these mirrors without your blood? Or maybe none of that matters to you anymore—but I still think you should know..." she purred

"I used your mother's blood instead."

The distant voice inside went quiet.

"Didn't you know about your mother's gift? You see, Raziel spent decades using scrying bones to locate the last female descendant of Queen Mercury—just as the alchemist before him tried, and so on. They were never successful. Your inherited ability remained locked away for nearly eight hundred years. By that time, I had almost given up the chase."

She circled the pool, hands clasped behind her back.

"And then, thirteen years ago, we tried again... and found not one but *two* female Drømmevandrer."

Her pacing stilled as she turned to face me again... distantly, a keening wail threatened to break out of its cage.

"Of course, you were just a child. Your gift had not yet developed, so I couldn't know for certain if you had the same abilities as Queen Mercury. You see, she was special. Not only did she have the dream walking gift, but she could also communicate telepathically. Her gift allowed her to physically enter anyone's consciousness, against their will. And with the help of the obsidian mirrors and some deep concentration...

she could commune directly with the Gods of Lyrath. And often did."

A memory, buried deep, flashed briefly: the pool... behind the crushed dais... in Svargad.

That far away voice within was cursing and beating against its cage.

The tall one heaved a weary sigh.

"It's a shame that my alchemists had not yet discovered the blue mineral. Or all of this could've ended with her... So, centuries flew by and all I had to go on was that annoying prophecy Mercury had shared with me... just before I set her mate on fire." She smirked.

"She said that a young, female Dream Walker would inherit her unique combination of gifts... and destroy me."

She paused, looking around the room as if lost.

"Where was I going with this? Ah, yes. Your mother and father. You see, somehow they knew I was coming, and they had just enough time to hide you away in the woods. But with your mother, I still had a fifty-fifty chance of finding the right dream walker so... I rolled the dice and brought her to Svargad. And while her blood could access the vault... she unfortunately was incapable of direct communion with the Gods. Her mind liquified as a result. Pity." She clicked her tongue in mock sympathy.

The distant female curled in on herself... silent and shaking.

"So, I brought the mirrors back here and waited another thirteen years for *you* to resurface. Raziel could never pinpoint your exact location in the vastness of the Furian Wood, and you never stayed anywhere long enough to be captured anyway."

She leaned in suddenly, face contorted with malice.

"And even though it cost me *eight* Anakaii warriors, I

would've sacrificed a thousand more to find you-the same way I sacrificed every female given up for The Offering, another failed strategy in the hope that you would fall into my lap. Now...lie down."

The voice inside my head grew louder. It pleaded, begged, and screamed. But I obeyed and laid down in the pool, floating on the tepid water, eyes unseeing as I gazed at the reflection of my body in the mirrors above me.

She crouched low beside the pool and angled her body over the water to whisper in my ear.

"Now... we are going to test this theory first. I can't have you waltzing into Lyrath and acting on your own volition, now, can I? I need to be certain your power is firmly in my grasp. So, I want you to find someone by the name of Captain Mavers. You see, I've grown bored with his spineless acts of compassion. You're going to give him the command to conduct a raid on any village of his choosing... and burn it to the ground."

My eyes stung with unshed tears—or at least the illusion of them—before I closed my eyes and did what she wanted.

My astral form glided past the cage where the female stood, hands gripping the bars of her cell, her blue eyes glassy with hopelessness. I ignored her and the feeling the sight of her gave me.

I cast my net into the shimmering infinity of vibrating strings and located the captain moments later. I gathered his braided, steel cord in my hand and pulled myself into the very core of his person...

He was dreaming about a young man he had lost. Someone he had cared for and wished he could find. The young man was tall with dark blonde hair that hung to his shoulders, his gray-blue eyes were piercing and yet glowed with humor in this memory. The sight of him began to stir something inside me...

I could feel my heart splintering, each breath becoming more excruciating... but I didn't understand why.

Suddenly remembering my purpose here, I tore my eyes away from the handsome young man and whispered the command the tall one had asked me to deliver. Confused by the ache in my heart, I quickly retreated into my physical form.

"It is done." said a voice that sounded like mine.

The black-haired giant smiled brightly for a moment before turning her head toward the bearded male with the black eyes.

"How long will this compliance last, Raziel?" she asked smugly.

"She will receive another dose in a few hours, Sovereign," he replied.

She turned to me again and rose to sit on the ledge of the pool, her eyes glowing with satisfaction, like I was a prized horse who would win her the gold. Her fingers clenched the lip of the pool, as if about to explode out of her skin with triumph.

"It's time, Aida... time to see if your gift is as powerful as your ancient Queen. Here is your next command..."

She reached out her hand and gripped my jaw, turning my face toward her to gaze into my eyes.

"You are to travel to the God realm of Lyrath and find Raseri, the Goddess of War. You are to *demand* that she unleash the armies of Lyrath upon the other Gods... in *every* realm. Once they are dead, The Morning Star will inherit all the power of the God realm and be restored to her full might."

The woman in the cage gaped in horror, her eyes bleak as tears streamed down her face. She began to scream, but there was no sound...

I obeyed and closed my eyes.

A heavy weight lay over me. The same one that had laid over me my whole life.

Cloaking. Suffocating. Blinding.

The reality I had grown accustomed to suddenly felt so... cumbersome.

And then, like ripping away the warm swaddle from an infant, I was exposed.

Exposed to the dawn. Naked to the light. Bared to the stars.

The heavy weight of my dulled human senses melted away like never before...

A numbing heartbeat later, my astral form was sitting on a dock, legs dangling. Dipping my toe into the warm water, I traced lazy circles which rippled with the reflection of the universe that exploded with life in the sky above me.

The same super novae and nebulas that churned above me, also glowed inside my skin.

At that moment, I finally understood what the astral form really was...

A gateway.

A conduit for the universe itself.

Suddenly, the dock began to wobble and thrash. Ripples shuddered across the lake as the shaking violence distorted the perfect mirror on the surface. I stumbled on my hands and knees, trying to stay upright and reaching out for anything to keep me steady. With my hands planted beneath me on the dock, I gaped in dismay, eyes widening as I tried to process the sight before me—it was like watching the arc of the sun arc across the sky but speeding up by a factor of a hundred as the horizon flipped on its head. I stared, dumbstruck, as the star-flecked oblivion in the sky rolled in a semi-circle before being replaced by an entirely *new* landscape...

And the dock I had been sitting on... was now a bridge.

I scrambled to my feet, jaw hanging with astonishment as I beheld a bridge composed of prismatic energy. Every color and hue in existence gleamed and refracted within the crystal structure. I peered over the side and went breathless as the sight, eyes going round with shock...

In every *direction*, above and below, giant, swirling vortexes yawned with thrumming power.

Wormholes. They had to be.

Portals... to other realms.

And they all led here.

And when I looked ahead, across the bridge, I gasped when I beheld Lyrath.

My senses were *alive*. Like I was really *seeing* for the very first time. Never had I seen colors so bright. Or smelled anything so intoxicating. Or heard every frequency that seemed to sizzle across the air. Never in my wildest imaginings, could I have envisioned the complete perfection of the God realm as I was witnessing it now.

Its sky was a swirling sunset of orange, lavender, and magenta; complete with fluffy, ethereal clouds. But unlike Astaran, great planets and moons... dozens of them, hovered just beyond its vast domed atmosphere. The citadel at its heart reached into the sky like a glimmering beacon. The white, domed structures were polished and gleaming. And interwoven throughout the metropolis were great, cascading waterfalls, infinity pools, parapets, and terraces. Blooming flowers and climbing vines spilled from every balcony, giving the city a steep contrast of organic beauty. It was larger than any city I had ever seen and seemed to throb with life. Millions of lights twinkled from windows and down cobbled stoned streets. Faintly, I could hear music, the notes swelling and melodic. Unconsciously, I stepped forward as if in a trance, drawn by its serene magnetism. No painting or even my own memory could ever do it justice.

Suddenly, a figure began to take shape on the other side of

the bridge. It wobbled and shifted like a mirage until it stopped just a few yards away.

It... she... was a woman.

Her long silver hair flowed around her head, weightless. She wore armor across her neck and chest composed of thousands of opaque crystal plates and a flowing lavender skirt down to her toes. Every inch of her russet skin, from her bare feet to her face, was covered in intricate tattoos and strange symbols. She was *bizarre*. And breathtakingly beautiful.

Her eyes, white like the snowy peaks of the Vazaketh, gazed into mine.

She studied me for a moment as her expression began to soften as she said,

"Hello, Dream Walker. We have been waiting for you."

ACKNOWLEDGMENTS

WOW.

Thank you, thank you, thank you!! My gratitude is overflowing.

This story grabbed me by the throat one evening in August 2024 upon waking up from an afternoon cat nap (kid you not). I began the plot outline that same day and had it finished in a week. For five straight weeks it literally consumed my life until the first draft was finished. I woke up early and stayed up late; determined to get the words on the page that were desperate to be free. After a long year of editing and a lot of and back-and-forth about going trad, I decided to self-publish this book in December of 2025.

I want to thank my husband, my family, my closest friends, my beta reader's, and my editor's for supporting me and backing me up 100% the entire way. Never once did anyone say "girl, this is a crazy idea", (even though you were probably thinking it) and I appreciate that!

Shout out to my homie J and my fellow indie author friends who have been so patient with my overstimulating nature and have answered oodles of my questions regarding indie publishing. Could not have done this without y'all's help. Seriously.

And, most importantly, I want to thank YOU, the reader, for giving this story a chance to become something I have only dreamed of. If you loved this book and are feral for the next installment, please, *pretty please* leave a review on Amazon, Goodreads, Instagram, Tik Tok etc. And come find me on socials @dakodamazziiauthor for all the updates, artwork drops, and sneak peeks for what's coming next.

If you really, *really* loved this book and want to help spread the word, please scan the QR code to sign up as a future ARC reader and join my street team! Big things are coming and I want you in my cuddle puddle!

www.ingramcontent.com/pod-product-compliance
Lightning Source LLC
LaVergne TN
LVHW091659070526
838199LV00050B/2206